# THE INJUSTICE

## Carol Kravetz

## DEDICATION

*I had my first book published in 2017, and my dad, Randal, never knew because dementia had stripped him of his ability to lead a normal life. When he passed away in October 2019, I had 4 books released and he never knew about any of them. If his mind had not been robbed by this hateful disease, I know he would have been proud of me. I know he is now.*
*My mum, Norah, was diagnosed with dementia in February 2019. She did get to read 3 of my books – and even liked them!! – before her beautiful, loving mind was taken from her. She was proud of me then, she would be proud of me still, no matter what. She is still here and I thank God for her every single day.*
*Thank you for being my parents. I love you both, always.*

# CONTENTS

# CHAPTER ONE

A lone figure trudged slowly over the sand. His head was down, his hands thrust deep into the pockets of his thick fleece jacket. The wind was moaning dolefully, ruffling his thick blond hair and kicking the surf into choppy whitecaps. Seaweed and driftwood washed up on the shore by the tumultuous ocean, provided a refuge for miniature crabs, sand hoppers, wagtails and other tiny marine creatures and enabled them to forage for snippets of food.

It was the middle of November and it shouldn't be this frigid but 2020 had been an unusual year, full of sickness and fright, hate and worry and a lot of violence. The Covid-19 pandemic still gripped the world and showed no signs of abating. Globally, over two million people had already died from it. Covid didn't discriminate between age or gender, color or creed. It had shattered families, defied doctors and scientists and stripped people of basic human needs like being able to hug a loved one, or sitting with a relative as they drew their last breath. The unfairness of the pandemic knew no bounds and had changed the face of the world in so many ways, perhaps forever.

By late spring, people in the United States were emotionally exhausted by the deadly virus and the imposed restrictions of not being able to get out and work or socialize. Despite the danger, the limitations forced upon the country eventually brought on waves of frustration and unrest. It might have gone a completely different direction if it had not been for the killing of an innocent black man by rogue cops in Minnesota. The act triggered mass gatherings and protests up and down the country and spawned the Black Lives Matter movement that was soon supported in other countries around the world. It also triggered a rise in cases of the virus, as more and more people ventured out in defiance to march and protest against police brutality.

The rallies were usually peaceful. Sometimes they were not. The Coronavirus didn't care. If there was a gathering of two people or a hundred, it was right there, ready to spread its deadly arms around whoever it could catch. Physicians' pleas to wear a face mask in public places, or maintain social distancing to help contain the spread of the virus, was often ignored. Even when restaurants and bars started opening again after a long three or four months of lockdown, some people chose to continue to ignore the rules. Then they wondered why daily numbers of people infected by Covid were on the rise again.

The effect on the economy had been horrendous. Jobs were lost, companies folded, schools were closed, and their employees being forced to stay at home unable to earn money to support their family prompted an increase in domestic violence.

To make matters worse, 2020 was an election year in the United States and the current president stopped at nothing during his campaigns around the country to get his rabid supporters to the rallies. Despite the numbers who defied the odds and attended, they weren't encouraged to wear face masks in public. Again, the number of cases continued to rise. After a bizarre, fraught election the world was provided with scenes and speeches that only served to show the defeated president was nothing more than a petulant, sore loser.

2020 had been one hell of a year. And it wasn't over.

The overhead wail of a seagull caught the man's attention and he looked skyward. He tracked the bird against the deep gray sky, watching it glide on the strong currents, seemingly effortlessly as it swooped further and further away until it was no more than a tiny white dot in his vision. When he could see it no more, he turned the collar of his coat up and shoved his hands deeper into his pockets. He wished he could be as free as that bird, able to take flight and go wherever the wind took him; take him far away from the sights he had seen a mere half an hour ago. Sights that had sickened him despite having seen similar atrocities countless times in his life.

Detective Paul Cameron had been subjected to many a horror throughout his career. Despite being a highly respected officer of the law, only those closest to him knew his history, knew he had been a victim of domestic abuse when he'd been a child. He'd been born to an alcoholic mother who, ironically, had done her best to stay off the booze the whole time she'd been pregnant. But as soon as he'd come into the world, she made up for lost time until she couldn't get out of bed without first chugging back whatever cheap booze she was able to afford.

Drug abuse soon followed and, when Paul was old enough to understand what was going on, he knew his mother was taking any outlet she could to numb the pain of living with an abusive, violent husband, Paul's father. His older sister bore the brunt of her father's abuse too, sexually, physically and emotionally. She ran away when she was sixteen, leaving her thirteen year old brother at their father's mercy. Paul's father thought it was perfectly all right to punch, kick and slap Paul whenever he wanted, which was all the time. Like his mother, Paul's father was an alcoholic and his abuse inevitably got worse when he was drunk. Paul soon learnt to stay away from home as much as possible and sought refuge with kindly, understanding neighbors whenever he could.

He had never been able to understand why his mother, a woman who was an intimate part of his life every single day, had never once stood up to the horror that was the man she had married. Never once had she tried to protect her children from his violence. Never once had she tried to compensate for their father's violence with her own love. When Paul was sixteen, she took her own life by overdosing on heroin. The pain was over for her and he almost envied her freedom. He wouldn't have wanted that kind of freedom but he knew he was now the only target for his deplorable father. He had to do something and, as soon as his mother's pathetically sparse funeral was over, he ran away. He had a lot of friends he could turn to and New York City's massive borough of Brooklyn had a lot of hiding places to ensure his old man never found him. He knew the monster would kill him if he did.

When he'd stepped into the crime scene earlier, slipping the mandatory facemask over his face and pulling on a pair of gloves, it had almost been like going back in time. There was a strong feeling of déjà vu as he took everything in with a slow, sweeping glance. The girl, barely nine years old, cowering in the corner, her underwear around her ankles, her top torn. The boy, a couple of years younger, sitting in the middle of the filthy living room, crying hysterically, his mouth red with blood dripping from his broken nose. Both children had turned away from the female police officer who had tried to offer comfort, both had stared blankly into space, refusing to look at the bruised and broken heap that was their mother, whose face had been smashed to a pulp. That she looked like that and was still alive was a miracle in itself.

Paul shuddered at the sight of the female officer gently wrapping the little girl in a blanket, trying to cover her exposed, underdeveloped private area. The little girl didn't resist as she reverted her gaze to her mother, her teeth chattering, betraying her shock. A thin trail of blood had dripped down her leg from her inner thighs, a clear indication she had been sexually abused. Paul recalled similar sights from his own childhood and he hurriedly tamped them down. He needed to focus on what was happening here and now.

He didn't know for sure but he could imagine the turn of events. The abuser, perhaps the father, or boyfriend of the mother, had molested the woman, who had probably refused his advances. After beating the crap out of her, he turned his rage towards the little girl. The little boy had tried to protect either his mother, or his sister, or both, and had earned a busted nose for his bravery. Of the man, there was no sign. Cowardly enough to molest a little girl, he was, predictably, also cowardly enough to take off before law enforcement could get him.

The report had come through from an anonymous caller, but that was okay. Before the day was over, both children and the mother would have been medically examined and placed in the care of Child Protection Services and a social worker. Paul hadn't had time to check if this was the first report concerning this sorry family, but, although they were now getting what was desperately needed, he could only hope they wouldn't get lost in the system. With a little luck they might even make it all the way to a safe, comfortable life.

Feeling an uncontrollable desire to get out of the house as quickly as possible, Paul left the uniformed officers to go over the crime scene. He turned to his partner, Detective David Andrews, and told him he needed a bit of time to himself.

As Dave scribbled something on his notebook, he cast a sideways glance above his mask at his friend. He could see the troubled look behind Paul's deep blue eyes and understood immediately what was going on. He was one of the few who knew the story of Paul's past and he also knew just how much Paul hated scenes like these. He would do his job and whatever was necessary to catch the abuser, but he was always uncomfortable and had to avoid hanging around too long. Dave knew this particular event was too close to home for Paul and, snapping his notebook shut, he laid a calming hand on his friend's arm. He wasn't going to get into the logistics of bodily contact being *verboten* because of the virus. All he wanted to do was show his support.

"No problem, pal," Dave said softly. "We came in your car, you go on, do what you need to do, I'll get a ride back to the precinct with one of the guys here."

Paul nodded slowly, his face softening just for a moment to show his appreciation. He left immediately and drove to this beach where, for a while, he'd watched the surf crashing on the shore from the comfort of his car. It had a therapeutic effect on him but he wanted fresh air and had gotten out to start his lonely walk.

The wind was brutal and he was grateful for his thick coat as he wandered along, kicking up the sand and seaweed with his sneakers. He knew he should start making his way back soon, but he wasn't quite ready. Glancing skywards again, trying to locate the gull but not seeing it, he begrudgingly turned around and walked slowly towards the car.

Halfway there, his cell phone beeped, indicating he had a text message. He knew who it was from even before he opened it and he smiled, his heart warming. It was from Krista, his wife, his love, his reason for being and he read the text quickly.

*U ok?? Wanted you to know I'm thinking of you. Love you, baby. xoxo*

That was all she'd written, but it was enough, and his heart soared higher than any seagull ever could with love for the woman he'd been smitten with from the very moment he'd set eyes on her. He knew Dave would have told her what had happened, which was fine, and he knew she would have been upset for him. He quickly texted her back.

*Doing ok, sweet-face. Will be home soon. Want me to bring anything back?*

Her return text came through after a couple of minutes: *Cathy and Dave joining us, they're bringing Chinese. Have ordered kung pao chicken for you. See you in a little while xo*

Paul texted her a kiss emoji and, pocketing his phone, hurried to his car. He was clear on the other side of the city and would be hitting rush hour so he wanted to start home as quickly as he could. Especially if there was going to be Chinese food. The chance to kiss his wife wasn't such a bad thing either.

# CHAPTER TWO

After Paul left the crime scene the day before, Dave had remained on site for a while to knock on some neighbors' doors to see if anyone had heard or seen anything. He managed to get a few witness reports, but at least they had been able to give an accurate description of the man who lived in the apartment with his partner and two children. A couple of neighbors had even been able to provide a name.

It was fast approaching lunch time and, although the weather had warmed up a few degrees, now there was a low-pressure system working slowly up the eastern coast of the United States. Rain and wind were the main features of the system, flooding the streets of Bathville, Massachusetts in no time. The rain lashed against the windows of the precinct, the wind blew garbage and debris all around and the storm raged all morning. For once, it was just as the weathermen had predicted.

As the window panes in the office rattled from the force of the howling wind, Dave lifted a few sheets of paper off the printer and read through them carefully. He was sure they would find the abuser in no time, especially now they had a name and a photo of him to go by. He glanced at the clock. It was twelve thirty and there was still no sign of Krista or Cathy so he could only assume they were detained in court.

"Want to go for a quick bite?" he asked Paul.

"Sure. Do you mind going to that bar on the Gardiner Expressway that does a great job of maintaining social distancing?"

"Was going to be my suggestion too, pal," Dave obliged. He shrugged his jacket on, checked his pockets for his face mask and pulled it on so he could walk the three flights of stairs down to the lobby. It was mandatory to wear face coverings anywhere in the police station and it had stirred up endless cop-humor jokes. Wearing a mask in a police station didn't exactly separate the cops from the robbers. It was sort of like going into a bank too, where you had to wear a mask just to do a transaction.

The short drive to the bar was passed in relative silence. They were each going over in their minds what they'd discovered that morning about the abuser, and with the BOLO – the Be on the Look Out - out already, hopefully it wouldn't be too long before they got a hit.

The usually busy bar was quiet, a sign of how bad the bars and restaurants had been effected by the coronavirus. It used to be standing room only. The food was cheap but incredible, the bar offers on beer always decent. Today, they could attribute the poor attendance to the horrendous weather but, really, it was largely due to the virus.

Paul and Dave slid into a booth, facing one another and keeping their masks on. A waitress they'd never seen before came over almost immediately, the clear shield protecting her face but not hiding her perky smile.

"Hello, boys," she said cheerily. "What brings you in on a horrible day like this?"

"Lunch," Paul said.

"And a beer," Dave added.

"I'll bring the menus on over. Our specials today are a bacon double cheeseburger with chili fries, or chargrilled chicken alfredo with garlic bread. Buds okay or do you want something on tap?"

"Bud's fine with me," Paul said, and Dave nodded it would do him too.

"You doing okay?" Dave asked carefully. He didn't want to bring up the memories of the crime scene from the day before but all morning they'd been talking to people on the phone and there'd been no getting away from it.

Paul shrugged, a brief cloud appearing over his eyes. "Yeah, no worries. Hopefully we'll catch the sonofabitch soon and we can throw his sorry ass in jail. Once his fellow inmates get wind of what he did, he'll learn the meaning of the word 'abuse'." He looked up briefly at the waitress when she brought their beers and, after they each ordered the burger special, he took his mask off to take a sip of the beer.

Through the window, Dave watched a woman clad in a short skirt and short jacket battle with an umbrella that kept getting blown inside out as she teetered along the street in too-high heels. Definitely dressed inappropriately for the weather. He looked back at Paul. "He'll get everything he deserves, that's for sure."

The waitress came over with silverware wrapped in thick napkins and packages of ketchup, mayonnaise, mustard, and salt and pepper. She lingered for a moment longer than was necessary, hoping either one of these incredibly handsome men would ask her for something and give her a chance to flirt with them. They didn't and she turned away, her perky smile faltering just a bit.

Paul took another sip of his beer. Dave hadn't touched his yet and still had his mask on. "Dave, can I ask you something?" Paul said softly, suddenly looking uncomfortable.

Dave's eyes widened in mild surprise. "Sure." He wasn't used to being asked if it was okay for Paul to ask him a question. Their relationship was wide open and as comfortable as an old pair of slippers.

"Don't fly off the handle, okay? I know you don't like talking about this but it's all just curiosity on my side, I promise."

"Okay, go for it."

The two men had been partners and friends for nearly eight years. They were closer than brothers and had always been able to talk openly and honestly with one another, about anything. However, Paul recognized that what he wanted to ask was a bit off their usual strain of conversations and knew he should tread carefully. He took a quick swallow of beer, almost regretting wanting to bring the subject up at all. But now he had no choice but to carry on.

"Okay...here goes...what was it like growing up rich?"

The mild surprise turned instantly to irritation. As many people who knew of Paul's abusive upbringing, far less knew of Dave's privileged upbringing. He had been born and raised in Las Vegas, Nevada, the only son to parents who owned three successful hotels and were living life as multi-multi-millionaires. Dave stood to inherit a fortune when his parents passed away, but despite having the luxury of a comfortable retirement to look forward to, Dave really couldn't care less if he never saw a penny of the money.

The only similarity between Dave and Paul's childhoods were they had each been born to parents who didn't know how to show love to their child. Dave may have had anything he wanted, when he wanted, but he had never had the one thing he craved the most: his parents' love. Despite their coldness towards him, he had at least grown up knowing love. It was thanks to his nannies or house staff who had all been happy to take him under their wing and shower him with the love every little boy, or girl, craves. They sang happy birthday to him, they kissed his cuts and scratches, they congratulated him on his good grades, encouraged him on his sporting prowess, commiserated on failures without making him feel useless. He was taught manners and was told how proud of him they all were and, in many ways, he lacked nothing. Except his parents' love.

But being asked such a question triggered the deep feelings of loss and abandonment he always felt when his parents came into the conversation, which was rare. His eye narrowed. "Why the hell would you ask about that?" he snapped. Despite having been honest about his upbringing on the very first day they had met, he knew Paul recognized it as a taboo subject and had appreciated him not bringing it up any more than was necessary over the years.

Paul could handle his partner's short fuse. He knew he

was out of order and, in truth, he still didn't know why he had asked, but now that he had, it warranted an answer. "I'm sorry, pal, don't get mad, I just wanted to know what it's like getting everything you ever wanted. Birthday and Christmas presents, graduation gifts, your first car bought for you, ski trips to Colorado or Switzerland, spring break to Florida or the Bahamas. You know I never had anything given to me so...I was just wondering what it was like to get stuff like that."

Dave tamped down a sneer. He hated talking about his parents money as much as he hated talking about his parents. But he also knew the events at the crime scene yesterday had stirred deep, painful memories inside Paul and he knew Paul wasn't asking to be facetious. He recognized the curiosity for what it was. "Okay," he said slowly, "I'll be honest with you. I was given a lot but I had people in my life who taught me not to take anything for granted. I had no siblings to squabble with over toys or treats but I was still taught to share, to give freely and it wasn't always okay to get something just because I asked for it. I was taught to work for it too, especially my first car, I had to help the staff in the hotel, and do odd jobs. I was literally taught the value of a dollar and I hope it's paid off. But...okay, yes, fair enough, it was nice not having to worry about money."

As Paul listened to the words he felt guilty at having asked Dave to explain. He already knew Dave was one of the most generous people he'd ever met and he also knew it had been wrong to assume Dave had been given everything when he was growing up. Paul was faintly amused – or perhaps impressed – that Dave had had to work for his first car, same as millions of less privileged kids. "I guess that answers my question. Sorry I brought it up, I know you don't like talking about your childhood any more than I like talking about mine."

Dave took a long swallow of his beer. His temper had dissipated and now was the time to change the subject. "Cathy and I are starting to look at houses," he said.

"Really? That's great, any particular neighborhood in mind? No, let me guess, somewhere near the ocean, right?"

"Right. You know my wife well. Don't know how she thinks we can do it on our cops' salary but we might get lucky."

Paul's wicked sense of humor was legendary and he couldn't resist saying what he did next. "You could always ask mommy and daddy for a hand-out, you know."

Dave's eyes dripped ice for a moment until he caught the twinkle in Paul's eye and he allowed himself a soft chuckle. "Never going to happen. I'm living on the premise that they'll need me before I need them. Getting paid so well when we were in Northern Ireland last year, and having our rent paid while we were there, helped us bump up our bank account enough for a decent deposit."

Paul nodded sagely. He wasn't going to mention Dave's parents again. It wasn't fair but he understood the remark about the extra pay and benefits while in Northern Ireland. He and Krista had earned the same. "What is it with Cathy and the ocean anyway?" he asked to change the subject.

"Who knows? But if it makes her happy, then I'm happy." Dave looked down at his bottle of beer. Technically he shouldn't be drinking alcohol because he was driving and was also on duty. He figured what the Powers That Be didn't know wouldn't hurt them. "Did Cathy, or Krista for that matter, because I'm sure Cathy would have said to Krista, ever tell you about the phone call to my parents after we got back from Northern Ireland?"

Paul drew back, frowning as he tried to recall. "That was a year ago. But no, I'm pretty sure neither of them mentioned it."

"Didn't think so. Cathy said when I was lying in the coma in the hospital in Belfast that she felt guilty she didn't call my parents to let them know their son and heir was lying at death's door. I told her I was glad she didn't. Then, after a lot of discussion, she thought I should phone them anyway, so I did." Dave shrugged dismissively before he continued. "Turns out they were about as interested in the fact I nearly died as they would have been if their car had gotten a flat tire. So, surprise, surprise, I ended the conversation as quickly as I could."

Paul listened intently, searching for hurt in his friend's eyes but seeing nothing other than disgust. "Jesus...Dave... what did we ever do to get such lousy parents?"

"Nothing. I would rather ask what did we ever do to get the amazing wives we did?"

"Now that's something to be thankful for." Paul looked up as the waitress brought their food and tipped her a wink. "Thank you, Celeste."

"Y-You know my name?" she asked breathlessly, nearly tipping his plate of fries over him, stopping just in time.

"That's what it says on your name tag," he said, popping a fry in his mouth and nodding towards her ample chest.

"Oh. Right." She had seen him put the fry in his mouth with his left hand, therefore seeing his wedding ring, and her heart plummeted. She had been watching him from behind the bar and couldn't deny how incredibly good looking he was. Seeing the wedding ring and then hearing him say her name flustered her and she stepped back, holding her hands up in an attempt to regain her composure. "If there's anything else you need, just holler."

Dave watched her walk hastily away and broke into a grin. "She has the hots for you, my friend."

Paul shrugged his indifference and opened a ketchup packet. They ate in silence for a while and, as luck would have it, were nearly finished when Dave's cell phone went off. He answered in a hurry when he saw the caller was their superior, Captain Bob Hamilton.

"Andrews?"

"Yes, cap."

"Just got word from the hospital. The woman who was beaten yesterday by her husband, Vinnie Mason, passed away twenty minutes ago. Massive brain hemorrhage brought about by severe trauma. Almost certainly caused by severe kicks to the head."

"Ah, shit, Bob, we were really hoping she would have

made it. Those poor kids."

"Yeah, they're with Child Protection as you know, hopefully they'll be able to fast track a foster placement for them."

Dave looked down at the few fries still left on his plate. He pushed it away, his appetite gone. "So this is now a homicide investigation."

"Yes. The BOLO is still out on Mason and will remain so until we find the sonofabitch."

"Thanks, cap. I'll pass the news on to Paul, he's with me right now."

Paul watched Dave close the phone call and knew by the look on his partner's face what he was about to hear. "Homicide now?"

"Yeah. Mrs Mason passed away just a short while ago."

Paul nodded, his expression carefully blank. "The kids still with CPS?"

"Yeah." Dave looked miserably out the window again. There was no sign of the woman who had been battling the elements in her short skirt and high heels. Hopefully she was somewhere warm and dry now. He was about to reach for his wallet to pay for their meal when his phone rang again and he saw it was the captain calling him back. "Yes, captain?"

"Just got a hit on the BOLO. Came through just after I hung up. Vinnie Mason has been spotted at a warehouse on Ocean Industrial Park, Building 17, which belongs to a printing and packaging firm. He's holding several people hostage at gun point and he's making demands about getting out of there alive and on his terms."

Dave nestled the phone between his shoulder and ear and hastily threw thirty dollars on the table. He motioned to Paul to get going and heard the rest of the situation as they hurried to their car. "Got it, Cap, he's armed and dangerous. We're five minutes out and we'll let the units already there know we were at the scene yesterday."

Paul drove and when they arrived at the warehouse they saw the area immediately surrounding the warehouse had been cordoned off by several police units. Paul parked as close as he could get and, after putting on bullet proof vests, they both swept a glance around the scene. They took in the waiting ambulances, fire trucks, news reporters and a small gathering of curious gawkers. Ducking under the police tape, they were pointed towards the lead officer, Lieutenant Jayden Greene who was facing the warehouse, a megaphone in his right hand and a cell phone in the other.

Paul and Dave introduced themselves and after showing their badge, asked for a rundown of the situation.

"Mason has been in there about half an hour," Greene said. He was a tall, muscular black man, mid-forties and despite the waterproofs he was wearing over his suit and bulletproof vest, he looked like he was soaked to the skin. Reaching inside the car he was standing beside he took out a towel to wipe the rainwater off his face. "Sonofabitchin' rain," he muttered, giving his glistening skin another going over with the already damp towel. "Detective Andrews? You were lead detective at the perp's home yesterday, right?"

Dave nodded. "Yeah. Too bad we got there too late. Missed Mason by about three minutes, so we were told. Is there a SWAT team on the way?"

"Not yet, we're hoping we can get this situation diffused and Mason off to County before he even knows what hits him." Greene jerked his head in the direction of one of the squad cars. A police officer was leaning over a young man who was sitting in the front passenger seat, the officer appeared to be writing down whatever it was the young man was saying. "That poor bastard there, he was inside with Mason for about two minutes but managed to get away. He's the one who called 911. From what I can gather Mason is as high as a kite and armed with what sounds like a semi-automatic. What the kid was able to describe, it sounds like a Heckler & Koch MR series, but we'll find out for sure when we apprehend him. No idea where he got his hands on one of those babies but hopefully he's no clue how to use it and ends up shooting his own dick off."

Paul looked in the direction of the warehouse. There was no sign of life through the gaping doors or anywhere behind the multiple windows in the front of the sprawling building. There didn't appear to be a second floor, which was good. He wondered how far inside the building Mason and his hostages were located. "Have you made contact with him yet?"

"Nope. He ignored the megaphone. We're assuming he has a cell phone and I gave him my number to call so we could talk properly. That was five minutes ago. Nothing. We're still waiting on the phone company to come back to us with his number so we can call him instead, but we're shooting blind on that one too because we don't know which phone company he's with."

"Any ideas, Dave?" Paul asked.

"What's at the back of the building?" Dave wanted to know.

"Two entrances and a loading dock. The rolling gate for the loading dock is locked but the entrance doors are unlocked."

Paul and Dave looked at each other, a plan formulating in their minds. "You thinking what I'm thinking?" Dave asked Paul.

"Yeah. In through the back, come at him from both sides and bring him to Lieutenant Greene here, with or without his dick."

Dave looked up at the angry gray sky. He wasn't sure if it was his imagination or not but the rain seemed to have eased just a little bit. The wind had definitely died down. "Okay, Lieutenant, have everyone on standby. We're going round the back. If we're not at that front door in ten minutes, send the boys in."

Checking to make sure their firearms were fully loaded, they took off at a run around the right side of the building and came to the back doors within seconds. They couldn't see much of anything on the inside, except rows of crates and boxes stacked three or four high against the walls. A walkway between the crates gave them a way to get further inside.

Dave carefully opened the door he was closest to, praying it wouldn't make a noise that would alert Mason to their presence. Luckily, it opened without a sound and they slid inside, their senses on high alert. They paused for a few seconds, their heads cocked as they listened for signs of life. The unmistakable sound of a slap, followed by a female crying caught their attention to their left.

They checked their surroundings, looking for the best way to approach Mason without being seen. Dave looked upwards, to the top of the crates and boxes and, tapping Paul's shoulder to get his attention, pointed to the crates and gestured he was going to climb to the top and get the lay of the land.

Paul clasped his hands together to give Dave a foothold and stepped back to watch as his friend stealthily climbed silently upward. Keeping as flat as possible, Dave crawled to the crate at the front of the stack and peered over the edge to see what was happening.

Mason was in the middle of the warehouse, staggering and lurching as he pointed his weapon at three men and two women who were sitting propped up against other boxes. One of the women was crying, perhaps she was the one who had gotten slapped, the rest were cowering away from the gun, their fright etched clearly on their face.

Dave could see Mason was high, possibly drunk, maybe starting to come down, which meant that with or without the gun, he was dangerous. The gun certainly looked real and was as Greene had described it, but there was no way to tell from his vantage point if it was loaded or not. Dave was going to assume it was fully loaded.

The crates were stacked on trestles and there were wide gaps between them to enable the crew to stack and unstack them with forklift trucks. Dave took a careful look at the layout and saw there was a way to approach Mason both from the front and rear, hopefully without being seen. They would need to stay hidden from the hostages, too, so none of them would react and give them away.

Dave crawled back to where Paul was waiting and landed noiselessly on the concrete. He filled Paul in, told him there was a pretty good chance as long as they didn't make a sound or were spotted, and described the floor plan of how the crates were stacked. Dave whispered he would go around the right side of the warehouse and approach Mason from the front. Paul was to go to the left, find the first lane and zigzag his way toward the front. Paul had less distance to travel but Dave knew he would wait until he had Dave in his sights before they made their move towards Mason.

Checking their weapons, and setting their cell phones to silent, they parted company. Hopefully they would have Mason disarmed and apprehended within a matter of minutes. As simple and doable as their plan was, all it would take was one wrong move and it would all go pear-shaped. All it actually took was the crying, hysterical female to catch sight of Paul for all hell to break loose.

# CHAPTER THREE

Through her tears and misery, Jonella Wilkes thought at first she was seeing things. She had been staring down the barrel of a gun for what felt like an eternity, she had been slapped and pushed around, called names and demeaned and she wasn't sure the tall blond guy edging out of the aisle directly behind the gunman was an actual person or a mirage.

Jonella was an overweight but very pretty black woman in her early twenties and she had been working for this firm for just over a year. She had been one of the lucky ones to keep her job throughout the pandemic and she had never taken for granted how kind and considerate her employer had been in doing what he could to keep his business going. She had never been as frightened in her whole life as she was now, knowing that she, or her co-workers cowering beside her, could die at any moment.

She had caught Paul's movement out of the corner of her eye and turned her head so she could see better. She saw he had a gun but, with his bulletproof vest covering his winter fleece jacket, there was something authoritative about him and she knew he was their salvation.

Paul was peering around the corner of a stack of cardboard boxes, trying to be quiet and unseen, while at the same time trying to get a fix on what was happening; and to see if Dave had moved into position yet. He figured Dave would be close and just as he was about to go behind cover again, he realized the black woman was staring right at him. He raised his finger to his mouth to indicate not to say a word, but the woman was too overwrought to understand the need for secrecy. She slightly shook her head, her eyes widening and, despite his drug and alcohol addled brain, Mason caught the stare and reacted to it by turning round to see what she was staring at.

Paul immediately grasped what was about to happen and, crouching low, he released the safety on his Glock and stepped into the open, just as Dave appeared behind Mason. Both Paul and Dave saw Mason raise his weapon towards Paul and hoping to stop any shooting, Dave hurried closer.

"Freeze! Police!" Dave yelled.

With a snarl of rage, Mason turned towards Dave, swinging his gun around to take aim. Dave waited a nanosecond for Mason to freeze and when he didn't, fired a shot directly into Mason's left leg. Instead of stopping, Mason assumed a shooting stance and would have fired had Dave not pumped three more rounds into him, one in the chest, one in his right leg and one in his right shoulder. The bullet in the chest ripped a hole in his heart and the force of the one in the shoulder threw his arm backwards, his finger still on the trigger. As he convulsed and went down, a spray of bullets got three of the hostages, including Jonella, killing all three instantly.

Mason was dead within two seconds of hitting the concrete. He landed on his back, his eyes open and staring upward at the empty darkness. Dave holstered his gun and ran towards Mason to get the gun off him and when it was safely out of range, he turned to Paul to see if he could assist with the hostages. He froze for a second when he saw Paul was lying on the ground and even from where he was standing, Dave could see a pool of blood oozing out under Paul's left shoulder. The bullet, or bullets, must have entered through his upper arm or shoulder, which weren't protected by the bulletproof vest. The force of the bullets going into his body had been strong enough to knock him off his feet and daze him. At least, as the best case scenario, that was what Dave hoped had happened.

Dave was torn between going to his partner and tending to the shell-shocked hostages who were still alive but heading towards hysterics at seeing their colleagues dead beside them.

Dave's first instinct was to go to Paul but he was saved having to choose when he heard a commotion behind him. Pivoting on his heel, he saw Greene and three uniformed officers barreling towards him, guns at the ready.

"Call the medics!" Dave yelled and pointed towards the hostages. Holstering his gun, he ran towards Paul and kneeled beside him. "Paul! Paul! Come on, Cam, quit laying around, I need your help here." Dave swiftly looked him over. The blood pooling underneath him indicated a bullet had gone right through him. That was the good news. The longer it stayed in him, the more chance of infection. The bad news was, if it had nicked a vein or an artery, it would make the clotting process harder to achieve. The even worse news was that if it had damaged any nerves or tendons, or had entered his chest cavity, Paul would be in serious trouble. To ascertain the damage, Dave pulled open Paul's jacket and reflexively grimaced at the amount of blood soaking through his light blue sweater. The entry wound was just to the right of his left shoulder and did, indeed, seem to be near his chest cavity. At least there was no sign of labored breathing so maybe, just maybe, it looked worse than it was.

Paul was slowly coming to and he felt like he'd been kicked in the head and chest by a rampant elephant. Not that he'd ever been kicked by any type of elephant but he imagined, if he had, it would feel like this. He couldn't understand why Dave's voice sounded like it was coming from so far away and realized he had minor hearing loss. He had been in close proximity to a car bomb just over a year ago, a bomb that could have killed him had he not been standing where he was at the time. But he'd still been close enough that the loud bang had resulted in temporary noise induced hearing loss. It had made everything sound as if it was coming to him from under water or through a wind tunnel and, although not painful, had been unpleasant.

"Wh-what happened?" he said, grimacing further when he felt Dave's hand press tightly just above his chest. His whole left arm was tingling right down to his fingertips, as if he'd lain on it and the feeling was just now coming back.

Hearing his friend's voice was music to Dave's ears. Paul had opened his eyes and, although he seemed dazed, he didn't look like he was going into shock. "Hold still pal, let me look at you." Shrugging out of his own jacket, Dave bundled it up into a make-shift pillow and put it gently under Paul's head. He knew he'd have to give Greene a brief rundown on what had happened and to help secure the scene. After ascertaining Paul was going to be all right for a few moments, he trotted back to where Greene was standing a few feet away from the surviving hostages, barking orders into a cell phone.

"Just get the medics here...and the coroner. We also have an officer down, I repeat, an officer down. I want them here ten minutes ago. Get on it now, officer, or it's your balls on a platter." He ended the call with a growl of contempt and looked expectantly at Dave.

"Who shot him?" he asked tersely, nodding towards Mason.

"I did."

"And did you shoot your partner too?"

"What? No! I got Mason first in the leg to try and stop him charging either me or Paul, and then, when he kept coming, I had to fire again. He kept a hold of his gun when he went down and kept firing. One of the bullets got Paul."

"And you're quite sure about that?"

Dave bit his tongue to stop an angry retort. The questioning was out of line. "Find the bullet that went through Paul and you'll find it didn't come from my gun. I knew what I was firing at and I've never missed my target. Never."

Greene stared Dave down for a few seconds then blinked in submission. "The medics are three minutes out. I'll get your report when you get your partner seen to. Does he have a mask for the ambulance ride?"

"Yes, it will be in his coat pocket." Not needing to be told he was dismissed, Dave went back to Paul. Still no sign of labored breathing, or shock. "Hey buddy, how you holding up?"

Paul shook his head. "Weird. Am I still bleeding?"

"No, I think I got it stopped when I applied pressure. But you're going to need to be checked out at the hospital. It's an in and out so they'll want to check for nerve damage. You know the protocol for a GSW."

Paul nodded. He felt more than a little light-headed but strong enough to sit up and, against Dave's protests, used Dave's arm to pull himself up to a sitting position. The world started spinning alarmingly but he fought it and eventually it slowed down to a gentle swaying motion. Which, although disconcerting enough, wasn't as bad as a full-blown spin. "Don't let Krista know just yet."

"You sure about that? She'll be mighty pissed if she doesn't hear as soon as possible."

"I'll handle her. I want to wait to get the all clear from the doctor before I tell her." He looked over Dave's shoulder in the direction of the crime scene. Someone, perhaps one of the officers, had placed a blanket over a prone figure on the ground. Paul hadn't seen him fall but assumed it was Mason. He was lying apart from the three dead hostages, who had been huddled together. "Christ!" he hissed. "Four dead bodies?"

Dave glanced back and nodded. The officers were tending to the hostages who were still alive and, just as he turned back to Paul, he saw three teams of paramedics rushing in. They were pushing gurneys laden with medical bags and dressing packs and one of the team came towards them.

Paul didn't want to go to the hospital but the lead medic insisted. He had lost a lot of blood and he'd need to be tested for nerve damage, especially since he'd complained of having some tingling in his middle two fingers. Also, much to his chagrin, as soon as he stood up, on his own amidst protests, the world resumed its manic spinning and he dropped like a stone, unconscious.

Dave clicked his tongue in irritation, especially when he saw the amount of blood that had been covered by Paul's upper body when he'd been lying. The medics wound a pressure bandage from front to back and, because he hadn't regained consciousness, hoisted him on to the stretcher. Dave hated that Paul was in worse shape than he had first thought but he kept his cool and let the medics do their job.

"Which hospital you taking him to?" he asked.

"Bathville Memorial, it's closer. We'll radio ahead and have a trauma team ready. I wouldn't be surprised if they take him directly into surgery."

"Okay, I'll phone his wife and I'll see you down there." Remembering just in the nick of time to retrieve Paul's car keys out of his jacket pocket, Dave got Greene's card from him with the promise he would call as soon as he could. He lifted his jacket off the floor and, with one last check to make sure the hostages were being looked after, he ran out to the car. He called up Krista's number on the Bluetooth and was surprised when Cathy answered. "Hey baby, wasn't sure if you were done with court yet or not. Is Krista there?"

"She's gone to grab a bite. We just got out a little while ago. And what, pray tell, is my husband phoning my best friend for?"

He could hear the teasing in her soft Northern Irish voice and, despite everything going on, he smiled. "Got a bit of bad news, sweetie. And I'm being serious, okay? Paul and I got a call in response to the BOLO on Vinnie Mason. There was a hostage situation and I'm afraid Paul got shot."

Cathy frowned, but, although the news was bad, she couldn't understand why Dave sounded so relaxed. "Oh no... how bad is it?"

"Not sure. He took a bullet to the shoulder and it was an in and out, but he's lost a bit of blood and there's concern for nerve damage. He's being taken to Memorial right now and I'm following the ambulance there. Was hoping to have Krista and you meet me there too?"

"Sure, no problem. And is he really okay otherwise? You know Krista will want to know every minute detail."

"He was alert and talking, but he passed out when he stood up. Probably the blood loss. I didn't get a chance to give him a more thorough going over because the medics arrived but they seemed satisfied there was no head injury or anything else." Dave paused as a memory from just over a year ago came into his mind. He was the one who had been shot then, he was the one who'd had a brain injury, he was the one who'd been in a coma...but that was then and this was now, he could reflect on the past at another time. He needed to concentrate on his driving and worry about Paul.

Surprised at the long moment of silence, Cathy checked to make sure the phone was still connected. "Dave? You there?"

"Sorry, love...miles away. Anyway, I'm about half way to the hospital, can you be here soon?"

"We're at the precinct, so yeah, Krista should be back any moment. I'll tell Captain Hamilton real quick and we'll see you there. Text me where you are when you're at the hospital." Cathy tapped the screen to end the call and tossed her main of curly hair over her shoulder. She blew out a long breath and was about to go knock on Captain Hamilton's door when she saw Krista had returned.

"Who's at the hospital?" she asked cheerily and then rolled her eyes. "*There's* my phone, I thought I had it on me." She took it out of Cathy's hand and then tilted her head to one side. There was something going on and she searched her friend's eyes for a long moment. "Okay, who's at the hospital?" she asked again. Then realization spread slowly over her face. "Oh no...is it Paul?" She set the bag of food on her desk, her eyes not leaving Cathy's. "Tell me, what's happened?"

Cathy urged her to sit down first. "Dave called your phone while you were gone and I answered it. I'm sorry, Kris, Paul's been shot, they're on the way to Memorial now and I think -"

"*What*? What do you mean, Paul's been shot? Is he...?"

Cathy placed a comforting hand on her friend's arm. "He's okay, Dave assured me he's okay, I promise you. Let me tell Captain Hamilton real quickly and then I'll take you to the hospital, okay?" When Krista seemed to be taking too long to process the news, Cathy squeezed her arm to get her attention. "Okay, love?"

Krista nodded slowly, her bottom lip quivering but then, as she nearly always did in a crisis, she pulled herself together and stood up. "Yes...okay...okay...let's get going."

# CHAPTER FOUR

The prognosis for Paul was great. The tingling he'd experienced in his fingers had vanished before he'd reached the hospital, so no explanation could be given as to why it had happened. There was nothing to indicate the damage had spread to his chest, no referred pain down his arm or into his neck, no weakness, no obvious nerve damage and an almost full range of motion. A couple of courses of physical therapy would restore complete range in no time. He was discharged home with a broad spectrum antibiotic to ward off infection, moderate painkillers and a sling to wear morning till bedtime for a few days. He was instructed to make an appointment with his family doctor to get the sutures removed and a re-check for infection. He was also given some arm and shoulder exercises to do at home until he started the physical therapy, which was set to begin in a couple of days.

He remained in good spirits, took the gentle bantering from Dave that he had 'fainted like a girl' when the medics had got to him and accepted Krista fussing over him in the way only she knew how to do. Cathy had driven Krista to the hospital and Cathy was able to bring Dave home, while Krista brought Paul home. He was glad he wasn't forced into an overnight stay and happily allowed the porter to wheel him to the exit for Krista to pick him up.

In retrospect, it would almost appear as if the call-out to Mason's family home the day before was the precursor to a period of bad luck, not just for Paul but for all of them. There were minor irritations, like Krista getting a flat tire on her way to a dental appointment and finding the spare was also flat. Usually so careful, she couldn't understand how the spare could be flat when she hadn't had a flat tire with this car before.

Dave stumbled over an uneven pavement outside a coffee shop and twisted his ankle. Nothing was broken, but it was painful to walk on for a few days and, used to being active, he hobbled around the office and home with an angry, impatient scowl on his face.

Cathy nearly had a heart attack when she went to the grocery store to stock up on a few items and, when she got to the check out, realized her purse wasn't in the front of the cart. She was about to check with security or the store manager to see if a purse had been handed in. She looked up just as a young woman pushing a cart laden with already packed groceries and a toddler in the front coming towards her, holding her purse out in front of her, smiling broadly.

Cathy had spoken with the woman in the bakery section, about the merits of red velvet cupcakes and pumpkin spiced muffins the store was famous for, but how she had wound up with her bag was a mystery.

"I'm so sorry," the woman started sincerely, "it's Kimmie's new trick – hiding mommy's purse when she's not looking. Kimmie must have seen your purse and lifted it into my cart when we were talking. I am so sorry. I can assure you I didn't look inside or take anything from your wallet but please feel free to check."

Cathy had instinctively trusted the woman. She looked too frantic and apologetic not to be telling the truth and she assured her everything was fine. What Cathy didn't tell her was she was relieved she wouldn't have to report stolen bank cards, a cell phone, and, most importantly, her off duty revolver. If the child had gotten her hands on the latter....well, it didn't bear thinking about.

Paul recovered from the gunshot wound quickly but, to his annoyance, was forced to work a full week at his desk. With everyone on high alert because of the coronavirus, the health and wellbeing of the workforce was of the utmost importance and Captain Hamilton was hyper-vigilant in maintaining the safety of his detectives.

Cathy and Dave's realtor finally gave them the green light to view a few houses but after looking at just a couple, they realized they'd have to up the ante as far as their price point was concerned. Which meant they had to clamp down on their spending and ramp up their savings.

The week before Thanksgiving, Krista got a nasty stomach flu. Paul phoned her doctor to describe her symptoms and even though she had a temperature, she had no persistent dry cough. Her lack of sense of smell and taste was attributed to her constant nausea and, because she also had body aches and pains, she was assured her symptoms were more indicative of a standard flu rather than Covid. She couldn't keep anything down for three days, not even water. Lime-flavored popsicles were her only salvation but, more often than not, even they went the way of the great white toilet bowl.

All Paul could do for her was hold her hair back for her while she threw up and rub her back when it ached from the constant throwing up. He phoned her doctor for advice again on the third day and was told to keep pushing fluids on her when he could. The longer Krista could keep them down, the sooner she would start to feel better.

The flu zapped her of her energy and she spent her days flitting between the bathroom and her bed. Cathy checked in on her as often as she could, always wearing her mask so as not to spread anything even worse to her. Sometimes Cathy just sat with her in her room, quietly reading her Kindle and always making sure Krista had tissues, fluffed up pillows, warm blankets and fresh, cool water laced with orange slices.

Although Krista slept most of the time, she was vaguely aware of everyone's attempts to make her feel better. She could feel her strength slowly returning and was able to convey her gratitude to them all for looking after her.

On the fifth day, after telling Paul she was sure he would be able to leave her alone now so he could get to work, she, like all of them, was unaware a stranger had arrived in Bathville.

He limped into the city in an old beat-up Ford Focus that had once been a fiery red but was now a faded pink heap with over 200,000 miles on the odometer. It was anybody's guess how much longer it was going to last.

The man driving it had been planning this trip for some time. He had fled his one room apartment with the clothes on his back, a crumpled suit, a single change of clothes, two ounces of stolen coke and two bottles of Jack Daniels. His money situation was dire, with just over eleven hundred dollars to his name and no chance of any other income other than the pittance that was his social security. His credit cards had all been maxed out and subsequently cancelled when he hadn't attempted to make any payments, and because of the deathly low cash situation he was forced to book into the cheapest motel he had been able to find online.

The Blue Moon motel, set in the sleaziest area Bathville had to offer, had seventeen rooms to rent out by the hour, day, week or month. At thirty five dollars a night, he knew he wasn't going to be sleeping in luxury but at least he'd have somewhere to lay his head at night. Most importantly, because he'd be paying by cash, no one would be able to trace him. Any gas or food he'd needed on his drive to Bathville had also been paid for by cash. Staying under the radar was essential.

He had done his homework finding the person he wanted to see and, after checking into the motel and securing a room for the next week, entered an address into his cell phone. It was the only thing he had of any value, and he'd had the foresight to turn the GPS off to avoid being tracked. The address was about fifteen minutes away and, using Google Maps, drove to it so he could lie in wait for the person he was looking for.

Patience wasn't one of his biggest attributes but he had a lot at stake here and would be happy to wait as long as was needed. Three hours later his patience paid off. From his vantage point, he could see two figures leave the building he had been staking-out and seconds later, both got into a black Camaro. He slumped low in his car, waiting for his target to drive by. He then straightened up, coaxed the Focus into action and started following the black Camaro. Ten minutes later, he saw the Camaro signal a right turn into the parking lot of an apartment complex and he pulled over to see which apartment they would go into.

Only one man got out and said something to the driver but, although he couldn't hear what had been said, he didn't care. He had identified the person he wanted and now he could do what he needed to do.

He waited in the car five minutes and then, smoothing down his greying dark hair, he got out and walked slowly to the apartment he'd seen his target enter. As he moved forward, he looked around the parking lot first and saw a pristine white Ford Mustang parked in the space designated to the apartment he was about to enter.

*Christ, if he drives a Mustang....* He thought, his stomach flipping in excitement. Clearing his throat, he toyed putting on a mask, as was mandatory in public places, but then thought better of it. He felt it was essential to be recognized as quickly as possible. Reaching out, he rang the doorbell and stepped back. Seconds later, the door opened and he tried not to show his surprise at the person standing in front of him. Whoever she was, she was absolutely stunning and he knew he was staring but he couldn't help it. Her long, glossy dark hair and killer, toned body aside, her emerald green eyes were mesmerizing.

She was looking at him inquisitively and, pulling himself together, he forced a friendly smile on his face. "Good afternoon, I'm sorry to bother you but is this the home of Paul Cameron?"

Krista was carefully scrutinizing the stranger in front of her. There was something about him that was vaguely familiar but she couldn't put her finger on it. He was tall and slim, his eyes blue, his dark hair dusted with white but it was his smile she was trying to place. She didn't open the door any wider and when the stranger stepped closer and tried to look past her shoulder, she eased it closed to lessen the gap and prevent him from seeing inside.

"Who would like to know?" she asked coolly.

He caught a hint of an accent and his heart flipped over in pleasure. *Good looks* and *an accent? God....*He smiled again. "I'm Kenneth Cameron," he said smoothly, "Paul's father." He carefully tamped down his pleasure at her sharp intake of breath at his announcement. "At your service."

# CHAPTER FIVE

As soon as he'd arrived home minutes earlier, Paul had gone upstairs to change. He was nearly finished when he heard the doorbell but there was no need to hurry, Krista was down there and would answer it. Moments later, as he descended the stairs, he heard Krista's sharp intake of breath. He had a clear view of her standing at the door and he paused for a second to read her body language. The front door was solid wood but even if there had been glass in it, from his angle he wouldn't have been able to see who was standing outside.

Krista had heard him coming down the stairs but she couldn't take her eyes off the person on her doorstep and she waited until Paul was standing directly behind her. She glanced at him and saw he was looking at the caller, his head tilted slightly and she knew, apart from the initial suspicion when looking at someone for the first time, he was thinking he recognized the stranger but didn't know where from.

Ken Cameron saw his son appear behind the woman and he fixed a friendly, welcoming smile on his face. "Paul!" he greeted. "Is it really you?"

It was the oddly familiar voice that caused Paul to frown in suspicion and then, all of a sudden, the penny dropped. He hadn't seen this man in well over fifteen years and yet his stomach immediately lurched up to his mouth. "Get gone, old man," he said softly. "You're not welcome here."

Ken grasped his hands in front of him as if he was about to pray. "Is that any way to greet your father?" he said in pseudo indignation. "And here I am, so happy to have found you after all this time." He looked his son up and down, hiding his surprise at how much he had filled out. He had sprouted up several inches in his late teens, too, and Ken instinctively knew the days were long gone when he could intimidate him physically.

Krista stepped to the side to let Paul come closer. She wisely kept her mouth shut and chose to follow her husband's lead. She could feel the irritation and anger emanating off him.

"How did you find me?" he asked tersely.

Ken grinned. "Google," he said cheerfully. "How else? Isn't that what everyone uses nowadays to find things? You know, like a car, a pair of shoes…a long lost son? I typed in your name and there you were, recipient of a medal of honor for catching a bad guy a couple of years back."

Paul curled his lip into a sneer. "Good for you, you found me, now get going. Turn around, get in whatever vehicle you came in and slither back to the rock you crawled out from under." He reached over Krista's shoulder to close the door and the last thing he saw of his father was the look of surprise that he was about to be shut out and there wasn't anything he could do to stop it. He slammed the door and immediately pulled the safety chain into place. He was breathing heavily and shaking in anger and he glared at the door for a long moment, listening for any sign of his father either approaching again or retreating down the path. He didn't think he could be held responsible for his actions if his father tried to gain entrance again.

Hearing nothing, he went to the kitchen window where he could see the path and only let his breathing return to normal when he saw there was no one there anymore. He couldn't see towards the street but it didn't matter, there was no one there. He lowered his head and allowed his shoulders to slump in relief. His father had been there barely thirty seconds and that was all the time it had taken to awaken a tidal wave of hatred and animosity.

Krista came to stand beside him. "Sorry, baby," she murmured.

He gave some semblance of a smile. "Not your fault," he replied.

"No, but I can still be sorry." She rubbed his shoulder and then slid her arm around his waist. "You okay? You want to sit down?"

He couldn't fail to hear the concern in her voice and he pulled her closer to him. "I'm okay. Just can't quite believe he was actually there. But the main question is *why* was he there? Why, after close to sixteen years did he suddenly show up?"

"He must want something," she stated without hesitation.

His eyes narrowed, knowing she was right. "Too bad. He came knocking on the wrong door." He kissed the top of her head. "Enough about him, tell me how *you* are doing. Feeling better?"

"Mmm, so-so. I still don't feel I've got much energy but I did manage to keep lunch down so I think I'm on the mend."

"Hope so. Captain Hamilton said to me just as I was leaving you are not to hurry back until you feel completely, one hundred per cent again. You know how he is with the health and safety aspect and keeping everyone as risk free as possible from catching Covid."

"But I didn't have Covid."

"No, but your immune system is compromised for now. Take advantage of his orders, sweet-face. Day after tomorrow you could be knee deep in a case you didn't see coming."

"You're right." She nodded, acquiescing. "And now, I need to sit down."

While Paul and Krista were talking in the kitchen, Ken Cameron was sitting in his car seething. *How dare that punk speak to me like that!* He fumed. *How dare he think he can dismiss his own father as if I'm a nothing!* He was so angry, he didn't trust himself to drive just yet and he sat calming himself down, replaying over and over the brief interlude with his son. Inevitably, his thoughts turned to Krista and he couldn't deny she had to be one of the most attractive women he had ever seen. Of course, she hadn't said her name but he had seen both her and Paul's wedding rings to he could only assume they were married.

He knew he wanted to get to know her better. He certainly knew he had a lot of work to do to try to get back into Paul's good graces and he wondered if he could use her as a pawn to bring Paul over to his side. He desperately needed to get some money and, although he thought he was safe enough from the people in New York, who knew how long it would last?

He started to formulate a plan and, convinced it was one he could put in motion sooner rather than later, he coaxed the car to start and pulled out into the early evening traffic.

# CHAPTER SIX

Thanksgiving was a subdued affair this year. A traditionally family-oriented holiday, citizens were advised to remain apart as much as possible to help stop the virus spreading. Gatherings within different households were discouraged but not forbidden which meant the advice was largely ignored.

Dave and Cathy were part of Paul and Krista's social bubble and, with the added benefit of being work colleagues, they spent Thanksgiving together as if it was just a regular day. They were mostly in each other's company anyway so they felt as if they were in the same household and wouldn't need to abide by any restrictions. Even so, they were careful, wearing their masks whether they were in the precinct, visiting one another or in one of their cars. They got random temperature readings through the course of their work and at the start of lockdown in March, their desks and work environment had been moved six feet apart to maintain proper social distancing. For all intents and purposes, they were compliant with the rules and remaining virus free.

Thanksgiving took place in the Camerons' abode. Krista had bounced back from her flu and, although still tiring easily, had Cathy's help to make an outstanding dinner. They were settled in the living room with full bellies and glasses of wine in hand, bantering about whether to watch the one and only football game televised this year, or yet another re-run of *Miracle on 34th Street*.

This was Krista and Cathy's fourth year in the States and they had yet to adopt their husbands' love of football. They compromised by watching the first quarter of the game, switch to the movie, then go back to watch what was left of the football after the movie finished.

Half-way through the final segment of the movie, the ringing of the doorbell prompted Krista, who was nearest the door, to jump up and answer it. She flung the door open, only to gasp in displeasure at the sight of her father-in-law standing there. He was smiling in as friendly a way as possible and trying to look past her into the apartment.

"You're not supposed to be here," she said coldly. "I advise you'd better leave before Paul sees you."

Ken sized her up again, mentally licking his lips at the sight of her. She was wearing a long, deep mauve sweater and black skinny jeans, her hair was brushed back from her face in a long, glossy sheath and her incredible eyes, hostile as they were, stirred something inside him. "I really wish I could have the chance to talk to my son," he said in an as non-confrontational way as possible. "And since it's Thanksgiving…" He trailed off deliberately, hoping she would pick up on his meaning.

She didn't. "He made it clear he doesn't want you here. If you'll excuse me, I have guests."

As she started to close the door, he shoved his foot in the opening to stop her. "I don't think you understand, I have a right to see my son."

Krista wasn't getting impatient; she was becoming irritated but she was saved further interaction when she heard a shout of rage behind her. A second later, Paul was holding his father by the throat, a move that Ken hadn't even seen coming.

"What are you doing here?" Paul demanded.

"L-let go…of…me," Ken choked. His son's fingers were like steel and, although his windpipe wasn't being pressed, he didn't want to push his luck. He threw his hands up in a gesture of submission and tried to back away. "Please…let go."

Paul recognized the submission and instantly, if more than a little reluctantly, eased the grip. He heard movement behind him and knew that either Dave or Cathy had come to see what the commotion was about. That was good, if he needed their help to remove his father from the premises, he knew they would provide it.

Krista stepped backwards and looked at Dave. He saw she had one eyebrow raised, her head tilted, as if asking him to take her place and he nodded briefly. As soon as he stood beside Paul, she retreated to stand beside Cathy. Neither of them spoke, they didn't have to, this was how they worked when one of them confronted a suspect. They did what they were trained to do, which was listen, observe and provide backup if needed.

Ken glowered at the tall, dark stranger who had suddenly appeared beside his son. He vaguely recognized him from the first day he had come here as the person who had dropped Paul off.

"What do you want me to do?" Dave asked Paul.

"Stop me from killing him." Paul kept his glare on his father. "Why did you come back?"

"To see you," Ken said quickly, seizing what he hoped was an opportunity. "Hopefully to talk to you. I want to let you know how much I've changed and how much I want you back in my life. I've done the same with Maria and she and I are on very friendly terms now."

Paul flinched at the mention of his sister's name. "Where is she now?"

"Still in Brooklyn, and she's getting married, too. Frankie Benetti, you remember him?"

"Of course I do. His mom and dad were better parents to me than you and mom ever could be."

Ken slid a guilty glance in Dave's direction. Dave was stone-faced and passive so Ken had no idea if he knew anything about Paul's upbringing. "Which is why I want to make amends," he said frantically. "Please, son. Give me a chance."

"You dying or something?" Paul asked.

Startled at the question, Ken shook his head. "Not that I know of."

"Then why do you want to make amends after all this time? You want something?" Ken's hesitation to answer gave Paul what he was looking for and he laughed bitterly. "Thought so. Just leave, old man. Turn around, walk away and don't ever come back. If you show your face around here one more time, I'll have you arrested."

This wasn't going at all the way Ken had intended and he held his hands up in desperation. "But Paul...please...for the love of God, it's Thanksgiving. A time for family. A time to reach out and -"

"Leave," Paul said. "Now. I won't say it again."

Ken knew his son wasn't joking and, unable to hold back a sneer of contempt, he backed away a few steps and then turned on his heel and walked away. This time, Paul watched him get into a beat up Focus and quickly memorized the license plate.

He closed the front door and turned to Dave. "That was...pleasant." After a long pause punctuated by a smirk, he added. "Not."

Dave knew of the first visit a couple of days before and he threw his friend a look of support. "Hopefully he get the message this time. I saw the plates too, I'll run them when I'm back in the station tomorrow."

They turned to go back to the living room but Paul veered off to the kitchen first to get him and Dave a beer each from the fridge. When he got to the living room, they were all waiting for him. He sat down on the sofa where he'd been sitting when his father had come knocking. "I'm fine, guys, I promise," he said, twisting the cap on the bottle. "Are we going to watch the rest of the movie or can we switch back to the game?"

"It's half time," Dave informed him. "You want to talk about what just happened? Figure out what to do if he shows his face here again?"

"If he does, I'll arrest him on the spot."

"What do you think he's after?"

Paul rocked his head back and forth, weighing the possibilities. "Money, I'm guessing. If he read anything about me online he probably assumes I earn a lot of money." He gave a short, sharp chuckle. "If only, eh?" He took a long sip of his beer and reached for his cell phone. He scrolled through his contacts and pressed the call button. Seconds later, his face lit up. "Hey, Mama Rosa. How you doing?"

Dave glanced at Krista and shared a warm grin with her. Rosa Benetti was the woman who had always taken Paul in when he needed shelter and solace or even just a loving hug. He hadn't seen her in a while but had kept in touch over the years since he'd left Brooklyn.

"Who is this?" Rosa said, her gruff suspicious voice contradicting a heart of pure gold and a sweet, caring nature.

"Ah, Mama, it's me, Paul." He heard her soft sigh of pleasure and he chuckled. "You doing okay?"

"Pauly! At last, you call me on Thanksgiving! It's been a long time."

"I know, I know, and I'm sorry. Been busy."

"Last time we spoke, you were getting ready to go on a trip. Then I no hear from you. Santo and I, we begin to think you dead."

"Very much alive. It's good to hear your voice. Santo doing okay?" He could hear commotion in the background and conjured up an image of Rosa's family gathered round the dining table. He hoped the numbers were greatly reduced this year.

"Santo's doing fine, fixing himself a turkey sandwich last time I looked. Got only some of the family here too. Trying to be good."

"I'll not keep you, I just called to ask you something. Have you seen my sister Maria recently?"

"No, not since...long time."

Paul set his lips in a thin line. "I heard through the grapevine she was getting married to Frankie, so I thought you would be seeing more of her."

There was a long silence, broken only by a muffled sob. "My poor Frankie...he no here no more. He's been gone five months now."

"*What*? What do you mean 'gone'?"

"Oh Paul, my poor boy, my Frankie... this 'Rona got him, not long after the city realized something had to be done before shutting everything down."

Paul's eyes clouded over. "That's awful, Rosa, I am so very sorry, he was a good guy. Why didn't you call me? I would have come down."

The muffled sob continued and then, "I know, you're my boy too and I should have. But you couldn't get down, Brooklyn was in lockdown then, no one in or out. It's okay, I know you were with me in spirit."

"Soon as this whole thing clears up, I'll be down, I promise."

"Only if you bring me that beautiful bride of yours so I can meet her."

"She will love that. Much love to you and Santo and the rest of the family, Mama. I'll be in touch soon, I promise." He ended the call and, while he digested the news that a man who had been like a brother to him in his youth had passed away, he realized he had caught his father out in a blatant lie. He relayed the sad news and got the expected sympathy from Krista and his friends but it didn't take them long to figure out what he already had.

Ken Cameron had point blank lied. Which made it all the more reason to steer clear of him.

# CHAPTER SEVEN

A desperate man often makes stupid mistakes when he's trying to save his own hide. Ken Cameron was no exception. He simply wasn't going to take no for an answer. Twice more between Thanksgiving and the first week of December he forced his presence on Paul. The second time he made the mistake of showing up, he turned nasty and tried to make a lunge towards Krista. He had been filled with cheap booze and false bravado when he realized Paul wasn't home and thought he could intimidate her. He didn't know she was trained in self-defense and she easily sidestepped him but what he also didn't know was, although Paul wasn't there, his dark-haired friend was.

Krista relaxed as soon as Dave appeared by her side. "Look who's here," she said smoothly. "And he just tried to molest an officer of the law. Tell me why I shouldn't arrest him right now?"

Ken inwardly groaned. *Christ...another police officer.* "You two got a thing going behind my son's back?" he said with a sneer.

Dave didn't speak, he simply moved to the front door and grabbed Ken by the throat, pretty much the same way Paul had on Thanksgiving. "You heard the lady. You are five seconds away from getting arrested. Leave. Now."

Ken's throat was held in a vice-like grip and the thunderous look in this dark haired guy's face told him he meant business. He would have had to be completely stupid not to realize this asshole was a cop too. "Or what?" he managed to gasp. "It's against the law now to visit family?" Feeling the grip tighten just a fraction, he put his arms on Dave's forearms and tried to push backwards to free himself. "Okay, okay," he said, "I get it. I'm leaving."

Dave released his grasp and stepped back out of Ken's reach. "Show your face one more time, you'll be arrested. Got that?" He didn't give Ken a chance to answer, he slammed the door in his face and turned to Krista with a bemused expression. "What is wrong with that guy?"

She rolled her eyes in derision. "I'll tell Paul to look into getting a restraining order. Something tells me this isn't the last we'll see of him."

"Mightn't be a bad idea. You ready to get going?"

"Sure, thanks for picking me up. Paul got a call from Jim asking if he could relieve him at the warehouse for an hour and Cathy didn't answer the phone."

"So you were stuck with me," he teased. "It's all right, I don't mind being third choice. Cathy's phone was dead this morning, she forgot to plug it in but she said she would charge it at the station." He opened the door again, checked first there was no sign of Ken, and gestured to the outside. "Shall we?"

Although Dave was calm and his usual pleasant, witty self on the drive to the station, inside he was seething. He knew Krista was right. They hadn't seen the last of Paul's father and he wanted to put a stop to any future visits. He dropped Krista off, but he didn't get out of the car, he told her he had an errand to run and would see her inside in about half an hour. Because he looked so relaxed and cheerful, she had no reason to think he had other plans. He even promised he would bring Dunkin' Donuts coffee and donuts back with him.

He remembered Paul telling him that Ken had said he was staying at the Blue Moon motel. He knew where it was and knew it was in a disreputable area of the city. It didn't matter, it wouldn't be the first time he had gone to a fleabag motel to get the bad guy. The only drawback he might have was if Ken hadn't returned yet but when he pulled into the parking lot, maneuvered around the potholes and overgrown weeds, he saw the faded red Ford Focus with the New York plates and pulled in beside it.

Knowing he was going into this unprovoked this time, Dave had to be careful in case Ken tried to turn this to his advantage and claim harassment or police brutality. Lord knows he didn't want to have Bathville Police Department added to the growing list of police departments in the country that had been charged with wrongful arrests and unnecessary force against innocent people. He decided he would take the friendly, inquisitive approach first then let it play out depending on what Ken said or did. With that in mind, he put on his face mask, knocked sharply on the door and waited.

It took only moments for Ken to open the door and thanks to the mask, it took him a few seconds to recognize who was standing there. He took a couple of unsteady steps backwards, his hand flying to his bruised throat. He could still hear a clicking sound every time he swallowed.

"What do you want?" he asked in pseudo bravado.

"A chance to talk," Dave answered affably. He gestured inside. "May I…?"

Curling his lip into a sneer, Ken reluctantly nodded. "Suit yourself."

It was standard protocol for Dave to introduce himself as a police officer but he wasn't here on legitimate police business so he entered the room and, after a quick look around, tried not to wrinkle his nose in disgust. The smell in the room was rancid, probably from the empty pizza boxes and fast food wrappers strewn around the floor and table. There was faint evidence of a white powder beside a rolled up one dollar bill on the bedside table. He couldn't help wondering why the cleaning staff hadn't been doing their job. To ensure his privacy, he started to put the "Do Not Disturb" sign on the door just as Ken was closing it and he saw the sign already hanging on the outside handle. Which was probably why the cleaning crew hadn't been in, he mused.

It would also explain the dirty sheets, the unmade bed, the towels in a bundle on the floor. Ken obviously liked living in squalor and must have requested no room service. That would have been okay for a couple of days but even a dive such as this had Health and Safety rules to abide by and if the work didn't meet a certain standard, it would be closed down. Or maybe the cleaning crew weren't allowed into an occupied room while Covid was still running rife, it was hard to say.

Dave waited for Ken to come closer to him and he smiled warmly. "I'm going to come right out and explain why I'm here, Mr Cameron. I know all about the life you gave Paul and his sister when they were growing up. Paul told me all about it the very first day we met, which was over eight years ago."

Ken went straight on the defensive and he folded his arms across his chest. "Did you ever think that punk is lying?" he asked.

"I know he's not." Dave carefully studied Paul's father for a long moment. If his memory served, he had been in his early thirties when Paul was born, which made him in his mid-sixties now. He was tall and had dark brown hair that was showing no signs of thinning and just a little bit of graying. His eyes were a more muted shade of blue than Paul's but his mouth and nose were the same shape. He must have been handsome in his youth but years of alcohol and drugs abuse had taken their toll. His skin was rough and heavily lined, aging him by fifteen years and, aside from a slight middle-aged paunch, he was scrawny and undernourished looking.

Ken ignored Dave's response. "So what anyway? Whatever he got, he deserved. They both did, the little bastards."

Dave lowered his gaze for a moment so Ken wouldn't see the anger bubbling within. He needed to keep his cool. "If you think raping your own daughter is something she deserved, man, you're way off base. And as for beating up on a poor, defenseless child…only a sad, sick psychopath thinks it's okay to do that."

Ken felt his own temper simmer. He knew he was physically no match for this man standing before him, but he could defend himself with words. "You've got it all wrong, asshole. What those kids got, they deserved it all right. Paul took himself off when I needed him most, just fled and never once tried to contact me. It's been sixteen years since I've seen him so why wouldn't I want to make amends? Especially after all this time."

"Nobody deserves getting raped or abused. Certainly not your own children. A bottle of booze and a hit of blow, or pot, or H, that was what you wanted more than your son or your daughter. You don't deserve to be a father and if I'd been there, I would have sliced your balls off when you slept and fed them to the dogs."

The image that remark conjured up incensed Ken and, without thinking, he clenched his hand into a fist and took a swing at Dave's face. Luckily Dave saw it coming and easily ducked away from it and, staying down, he head-rammed Ken into the nearest wall. Winded, Ken struggled to get his breath back, and his discomfort was exacerbated when he felt the vice-like grip on his throat again.

"Stop!" he croaked, feeling his lungs deflate further. "P-Please!"

The panic in Ken's voice, and bloodshot eyes was obvious but Dave couldn't tamp down his rising fury. Every time Paul had mentioned his abusive childhood, Dave had always felt the urge to find Paul's father and kill him, if only to avenge what his best friend had gone through. He fought hard to retain some semblance of calm but he couldn't guarantee it would last.

"I'm going to say this to you one last time, Ken. You come anywhere near Paul, or his wife, ever again, I will find you. And I will kill you." He pressed his full weight in against Ken and tightened the grip just a little bit more. He knew he wasn't blocking Ken's air supply but he also knew a couple of millimeters right or left and he would be. "If you're not out of Bathville by this time tomorrow, I will come for you. I'm not saying this as an idle threat either, take this as a promise. I will come for you and I will kill you. And if I don't kill you, Paul will. Understand?"

Ken's eyes were locked with Dave's and he knew this man was telling the truth. This was not an idle attempt at intimidation.₋ He closed his eyes in submission, wanting more than anything to get a decent amount of air into his tortured lungs. "I, I... Y-Yes...I understand." Miraculously, he felt the iron grip on his throat relax and he gulped in huge breaths, wavery dark lines clouding his vision. He knew the man was still standing within inches of him and as his lungs filled, his head cleared. "Who the fuck are you anyway to be threatening me?"

"Doesn't matter who I am. And I told you, it wasn't a threat. Now, be a good little boy and repeat back to me what I told you to do. If I haven't made myself clear, I'll go through it again."

"You dumb fuck," Ken rasped, feeling his stomach churn. "I heard you loud and clear. Gone by this time tomorrow or else you'll kill me."

Grinning ominously, Dave playfully slapped Ken's cheek. "Good boy."

"Piss on you, pal, you can't come in and intimidate me like that. I'll call the police and get you arrested."

"You do that, *pal*, and I'll be sure to tell them you're in possession of drugs. Been using too by the look of it. It's your choice." Dave strode over to the door and then, with a malicious grin, he turned and said, "You have a nice day, Mr Cameron."

Outraged, Ken lunged forward with a hate-filled glare. "Who sent you anyway? My pathetic, deadbeat son?"

That was the breaking point for Dave's self-control and with a roar, he lunged toward Ken and floored him with a single punch. He looked down at him, wishing he had knocked him unconscious. "No one sent me. Paul's not a deadbeat, he's a zillion times the man you could ever dream of being. Go back to Brooklyn, your type of scum is not welcome in this city."

And with that, figuring he had done Paul proud, he turned on his heel and strode purposefully away.

Dave had been so intent on getting his point across, he hadn't taken into consideration one tiny factor. The walls in this motel were paper thin and the words he had intended for Ken's ears only had been overheard very clearly by the occupant in the room to Ken's left. A twenty-three-year-old woman, Gabriella Rossini, who was staying indefinitely in the hotel to get away from her vicious, abusive husband, had heard the sounds of a scuffle. She had also heard every last word one man had said to the other, the threat that one would kill the other sticking in her mind.

Frightened, she had crouched beneath the window, afraid to move, afraid to breathe. After the shouting stopped and a shadow passed by her window, she opened the curtains a crack to see a dark haired man walk purposefully away from the motel and get into a black Camaro. She took in his thick, dark winter jacket, blue jeans and what looked like white and blue striped Nike trainers. Even with the mask covering half his face, he seemed angry as he settled into his car, but he drove away without so much as a backwards glance.

Feeling uncertain about what to do, she closed the curtains, scribbled down the license plate of the Camaro and as much detail of the conversation she'd heard. She couldn't ignore the fact a murder threat was a murder threat and she wanted to be of help in case that dark haired man ever came back and carried out the threat. She was a severely abused woman but she was also a law abiding citizen and she would help the police if she could. Shaking, she then crawled into the bed the maid had just made up an hour earlier, pulled the covers over her head and let the silence wash over her.

Dave returned to the station, feeling immensely light-hearted. It felt good to have had the chance to defend his best friend and he was sure Ken wouldn't be so stupid as to ignore what was clearly not an idle threat. It had also felt good giving Ken a taste of his own medicine. Although one sucker punch and one warning was nothing compared to the years of continuous abuse Paul and his sister had had to endure, at least it had been something.

Dave walked into the office a short while later, four cups of Dunkin' Donuts coffee and a box of a dozen assorted donuts in hand and laid them on his desk with a broad grin. Paul had only gotten in about five minutes before and he looked suspiciously at his friend.

"Why so chipper, Big D?" he asked, accepting the coffee Dave handed to him with a murmured thanks.

"Just thinking about a couple of houses Cathy and I are going to see later. They both sound awesome, so hopefully we'll get lucky." He looked expectantly over at his wife as she picked a honey-glazed donut from the box and, within no time, she was talking animatedly about the layout of the houses, the location and the pictures they'd seen online.

Paul had heard from Krista that Ken had been to their home earlier and, as he sipped his coffee and listened to Cathy, he slipped Dave surreptitious glances every once in a while. Paul couldn't be a hundred per cent sure where Dave had been the last hour but he could make a fairly good guess. Because it was probably one of those situations that was better left undiscussed, he chose to do just that.

# CHAPTER EIGHT

The Massachusetts weather had been as much of a talking point as the Coronavirus and the fiasco that had been the Presidential election in November 2020. Temperatures fluctuated from the mid-seventies down to the low thirties, to bounce back up to the high sixties before levelling off in the mid-fifties as November bowed down to December. The day Dave visited Paul's father had been one of the coolest so far but the day after, the temperature shot back up again.

Ken Cameron sat miserably in his hotel room, flicking the air conditioner on, then turning it off and putting on the heat, never finding a comfortable setting. He had been in this Godforsaken town for almost two weeks now and had gotten absolutely nowhere with his son. His meagre reserve of money was fast depleting and he still had no means to top it up. With no fixed address, no one would hire an out of towner in this dreadful employment climate but he would start looking around tomorrow.

It wasn't his fault he had picked up a woman at the bar he'd gone to the evening before. He had promised himself one beer but she had been there, not a bad looking woman in a life-had-been-hard kind of way. She eyed him up unashamedly from the other end of the bar as soon as he'd come in. When he moved over to her, she said all the right things and put her hands on him in all the right places and he talked her into coming back to his room. She had stayed the night and when he'd woke up in the morning, he found she had drank what was left of his booze stash, had taken a healthy snort of coke and had stiffed him for a hundred bucks.

What way was that to repay him having given her what

had undoubtedly been the ride of her life? And then, to add insult to injury, he found out she had charged a hefty breakfast bill to his room. She had seemed so nice too. Just went to show you shouldn't always judge a book by its cover. Then, to make a bad situation even worse, that maniac friend of Paul's had dropped by and made his intentions perfectly clear. Ken was still on the fence as to whether to heed the warning or not.

Maybe moving on wouldn't be such a bad thing. He was tired of eating fast-food burgers, he was fed up drinking the cheapest wine he could find, he was sick to death having to walk to get food or alcohol, just to conserve gas. He was down to his last couple of hundred dollars too, but it didn't occur to him then, nor would it, that if he hadn't been put in touch with a supplier who sold him two full ounces of coke, he would have much more money.

The last thing Ken Cameron wanted was to go into withdrawal and after snorting up a line of coke, he laid back on the filthy bed and felt himself relax. When he was relaxed, he could think straight. Only problem was, any time he came up with solutions, by the time the coke wore off he would forget whatever bright ideas he'd had.

But this was serious. He needed money. Fast. He had a feeling the Romano family in Brooklyn would soon be able to figure out where he was, especially if they did a little digging around and found out he had family in Massachusetts. He knew the rich and powerful Romanos employed people to find their enemies and the fact he owed them thirty-five thousand dollars unquestionably made him an enemy. Some might say thirty-five thousand was a mere drop in the ocean to a wealthy family like the Romanos but it wasn't going to convince them to let him get away with it just because it was chicken feed.

Ken knew he had to strike soon so he came up with a simple plan as the coke swirled around his senses, not realizing it was clouding his judgement. He would go to his son's apartment in the morning, wait for him to leave for work and then, hopefully, somehow gain access to the apartment. A swift in and out job, get what he could that looked to be of value, maybe even hit pay dirt and find cash or bank cards. Maybe even find the car keys to that beauty of a Mustang! The car alone might take care of a third of the debt.

The evening wore on, giving him ample time to work on the plan and then, having the foresight to set the alarm to get up at five in the morning, he snuggled in under the covers and drifted off to sleep.

At six o'clock the following morning, Ken Cameron was parked about fifty yards from the entrance to the parking lot at Paul's apartment complex. It was still dark and cold but, careful to conserve gas. Ken was forced to keep the car engine off. He had a coffee cup he'd filled at the lobby of the motel before he'd left and it was still warm enough to enjoy. He wrapped his hands around it and tried not to think of the chill seeping into his bones.

He had no idea what time Paul left for work. He had no idea if Paul was even going into work today but he figured if there was no movement by eight o'clock, he'd have to come back tomorrow.

At just after six thirty, he heard the sound of a car slowing down and he glanced over his shoulder toward the road. He recognized the black Camaro he'd seen the last time he'd waited outside Paul's apartment and involuntarily shuddered. He knew the dark haired guy who drove that car was dangerous and he didn't want to be seen and maybe beaten up again. He slunk down further in the front seat, making sure he could still see what was happening.

Ten minutes later, he saw the Camaro pull out onto the road again, two shadowy figures inside. He assumed one of them was Paul. His next problem was whether his wife was still inside. He had no idea what kind of schedule she was on; as a police officer, he knew they worked odd hours so she could have left ages ago. Or maybe hadn't made it home yet if she'd pulled an all-nighter.

Crunching up the empty coffee cup and throwing it

carelessly in the passenger footwell, he made a hasty decision and got out of the car. Squaring his shoulders against the cold, he zipped up his jacket and strode quickly and purposefully towards Paul's apartment.

He couldn't see any lights from within, which he took as a good sign, and he figured a good, swift kick would open the door for him. To make sure the apartment was empty, he rang the doorbell and stepped back.

Krista opened the door to him and they looked at each other in shock. She had been expecting Cathy, he'd been expecting no one. The smile on her face disappeared in a flash and she held her hand up in a back off gesture.

"Leave right now, Mr Cameron," she said authoritatively. "If you fail to obey the direct order of a police officer, I will place you under arrest."

He ignored her words and, instead, barreled into the hallway, his hand grabbing for Krista's throat and, kicking the door closed behind him, pushed her against the nearest wall.

"You don't get to tell me what to do, little lady," he snarled into her face. He had seen fright in her clear, green eyes, but only for a second and he wasn't accustomed to anyone he was trying to intimidate be so unfazed. Still, it wasn't enough to make him release his grip.

Recoiling from the fetid breath of stale coffee and booze, Krista lifted her knee and connected squarely with Ken's crotch. As his mouth let out a *whooft* of air, both hands flew to his groin and he backed away. Krista's bag was on the hall table and, beside it, lay her handcuffs, but as she lunged towards them across a distance of about seven feet, he caught her wrist and pulled her cruelly back. He thought he'd used enough force to pull her shoulder out of its joint but she spun round instead, a murderous look on her face and both arms moving freely and painlessly.

As soon as he saw the look, he knew he had to do something radical, and quickly, or else he'd be on the ground and cuffed in no time. He was well aware that police officers today, both male and female, were highly trained in self-defense. He was also aware that sometimes they furthered their training by taking up martial arts or kick boxing or some other combatant sport.

Ignoring the fire in his balls, he sprang forward and pushed her face first against the wall again. Then he pressed against her, holding her head still so she couldn't do a reverse head butt. He felt her struggle against him and if it hadn't been for the fact that she had got him in the groin, he would have been instantly aroused. Instead, he kept a hold of her head and slammed it against the wall, then, snaking an arm around her throat, he forced her to the floor and got on top of her. He sat on her upper legs so she couldn't kick at him and pinned her shoulders down.

Krista was seeing stars and, although she still had her wits about her, she couldn't get either her arms or legs free to get him off her. It was rare that she let an attacker get the better of her like this but on those occasions, she had backup in the form of Cathy, or any other available officer.

As she tried to figure out the best way to protect herself she realized Cathy should have been here by now. She had texted fifteen minutes ago to say she was on her way. So where was she? With an inward groan, Krista knew she was on her own as she looked up into her father-in-law's hate-filled eyes. The return glare told her she'd have to do something quick to get herself free.

She tensed her body and then, despite Ken's weight, she arched her back with enough force it toppled him off her. He fell sideways, giving her ample time to roll away from him and bounce to her feet. Unfortunately she had landed further away from her bag, handcuffs and gun than she had intended and Ken was between her and them.

Ken roared his agitation at her agility and, as before, lunged for her. This time she caught his arm and pushed him backwards, at the same time hooking her foot around his ankle and pulling him to the floor. He kept a hold of her arm and pulled her down with him, and that was when he saw a red curtain drop in front of his vision.

He caught a hold of her head again and hammered it repeatedly against the floor. When it was obvious she'd lost consciousness, he took his anger out on her face, punching it until blood spluttered from her mouth. He stood up, breathing hard, but he wasn't finished with her yet. He kicked her in the sides, the arms, the legs, her back and, finally deciding she'd had enough, he planted one last, vicious kick to her abdomen.

He looked down at her in disgust, his face dripping with sweat and then, smirking in satisfaction, the red curtain lifted and he realized he could now do what he'd come here to do: find money or items of value.

The first thing he took were Krista's engagement, wedding and eternity rings. He wrenched them off her finger and even a brief glance at the precious items told him he had a pretty penny right there. He pocketed them carefully. Five minutes later, he fled the apartment with other items of jewelry, including expensive looking men's and lady's watches and a copy of a two week old bank statement that had shown a balance of well over twenty thousand dollars.

When he stepped out into the street to go to his car, he slowed his pace so as not to draw attention to himself. He didn't see Cathy's blue Ford Focus pull into the apartment complex. Cathy didn't see him either, which was too bad, because if she had, she would have recognized him from his visit on Thanksgiving night. She parked the car and, bracing herself against the biting wind, strolled up to the front door of Paul and Krista's apartment.

She would normally have her key at the ready by now but just as she was about to give the customary one ring of the bell first, she noticed the door was ajar. Unless Krista had been in the kitchen and had seen Cathy pull up, there was no reason why the front door should be open on such a cold day. For one thing, it was too cold to leave the door ajar and the strong breeze could have opened the door further, letting more cold air in. For another, Krista might not have been in the kitchen to see Cathy arrive.

Gut instinct told her something was very wrong and, thumbing the snap on her holster at her waist, she took her gun out and slowly opened the door. There were no lights on anywhere downstairs and it was still dark enough outside to warrant them to be on. The lights on in the parking lot enabled her to see inside a few feet and when she saw Krista lying in the entryway to the living room, she re-holstered her gun and, with a strangled cry, ran to her motionless friend.

One look at Krista's bruised and battered body told Cathy she needed medical treatment fast.

# CHAPTER NINE

Remaining as calm as possible, Cathy immediately dialed 911 on her cell phone. In the few seconds it took for the call to connect, she gingerly felt at Krista's neck for a carotid pulse and was relieved to find there was one, weak but steady. She informed the operator of the situation, gave the address, included the fact Krista was a detective in the 7th precinct, and hung up.

Knowing help was on the way, and because she had already established Krista was breathing, Cathy unholstered her gun again and moved cautiously from room to room checking for an intruder. Upstairs, there were four rooms in the form of two bedrooms and two bathrooms. She checked them all in case the attacker was lying in wait, or simply waiting for the chance to get away without being seen. She quickly established that no one was there but she couldn't fail to see the complete state of disarray in both bedrooms. In the spare bedroom there was a filing cabinet in which Cathy knew Paul and Krista kept their important paperwork. If she looked in it, she would find the titles to their cars, birth certificates, passports, bank statements and anything else that needed to be stored securely.

She noticed the top drawer was slightly open. Knowing Paul and Krista were sticklers for keeping the filing cabinet neat and locked, she pulled a Nitrile glove from her back pocket, opened the drawer and saw the disorder inside. She had no idea what, if anything, had been taken and made a mental note to tell Paul about it.

In Paul and Krista's bedroom, she noticed the dresser drawers had been opened and ransacked. She knew which drawer Krista kept her jewelry in and, sure enough, she wasn't surprised to find most of the jewelry missing.

Feeling her temper simmer, she bounded back down the stairs to give Krista her full attention. Kneeling down, she placed a gentle hand on Krista's arm. "Hey, Kris, you with me, chum?" She grimaced at the lacerations and bruising on her friend's face but when she leaned closer, she could hear Krista seemed to be having trouble breathing.

Fearing a punctured lung, possibly from a broken rib, Cathy knew she shouldn't move her. She was lying half on her side and, retrieving a couple of cushions from the living room, Cathy propped them against her back to give her some support.

Knowing there wasn't anything she could do for her, Cathy sat on the second stair and was about to phone Paul when she heard the wail of sirens and moments later, saw flashing red and white lights outside. She ran to the door and opened it to escort the medics inside. She had already donned her mask and saw they were wearing one too.

As soon as they tried to move her, Krista moaned in pain, her eyes fluttering open. She pulled back when she saw two strangers in front of her but when Cathy came into her line of vision and she visibly relaxed.

"C-Ca-ath…" she said, only to start coughing. Her face pinched in agony and she held her hand out to Cathy for her to come to her.

Giving the medics plenty of room, Cathy fell to her knees beside her friend and gently pushed the hair back from her eyes. "It's okay, chum, you're in safe hands. Can you tell me who did this to you?"

Krista's chest was on fire as she tried to pull in a deep breath. Fuzzy images were beginning to sharpen, but although she understood Cathy's question she couldn't get enough clarity to give her an answer. "A-A man," she managed to say.

"No worries, we'll let the medics make you comfortable then I can ask you questions later."

Krista felt the medic's hands working over her, ascertaining what, if anything was broken. She had no idea what injuries she had, she had no clue her face was battered and bruised, all she knew was she was hurting all over. And then, out of nowhere, her eyes shot open again and she looked up into Cathy's kind, worried face. "Ken," she said weakly, "it was Ken. Paul's father."

Recoiling in shock, Cathy carefully tamped her rage down and she smiled her encouragement. "Good girl, now we know who we're looking for." She looked at one of the medics. "What's going on with her?" she asked.

"We need to get her to the hospital. I can't tell for sure if she has broken ribs and or a punctured lung but I don't like the sound of her breathing and they need to check her for internal bleeding." He gently lifted Krista's top up a little. "See these?" he said, a scowl etched on his face as he pointed to very obvious boot marks on her abdomen. "Whoever did this meant to hurt her as much as he could." He caught the eye of his partner. "Memorial's the closest, let's get going."

"I'll follow you there," Cathy said, "I've got a siren and a flasher on my car so don't worry about losing me in traffic."

As the ambulance drove away at top speed, lights flashing, siren screaming, Cathy jumped in her car and started to follow. Bathville Memorial hospital was a fifteen minute drive in light traffic but at this time of the morning it could be longer. The morning commuters, despite hurrying to get to work, knew to pull over to allow the emergency vehicle free passage. Nevertheless, it still took over twenty minutes to get to the hospital.

On the way, Cathy called Paul but it went straight to voicemail. She tried Dave next and his phone went to voicemail too. She deliberated who to try next and decided she would try the captain. He mercifully answered on the first ring.

"Cathy, where are you and Krista? You missed roll call."

Cathy's shock was starting to hit home and, for a moment, as she weaved in and out of cars and buses, all she could see was Krista's poor face and the boot marks on her abdomen. She swallowed her fear and anger and tried to stop her voice from quivering. "Captain, I'm trying to get a hold of Paul but he's not picking up. Is he at his desk?"

Surprised she hadn't given him an excuse for her tardiness, he nonetheless recognized the strain in her voice. "No, he's not here, I got him and Dave on their way in to go to a homicide on Concord Street. What's going on?"

"I'm on my way to the hospital. Krista has been beaten up pretty badly and I want to let Paul know."

Captain Hamilton felt the familiar twist in his stomach that he got every time he heard one of his officers had been injured. "How bad?"

"Bad. I'm following the ambulance to the Memorial and we're nearly there. How can I get a hold of Paul? Or Dave?"

"I don't know why they're not answering their phones, I got Dave on his no problem to send them to Concord. Jim and Mark are at their desks, I'll send them to take over from Paul and Dave and I'll tell them to tell Paul to ring you immediately. Did you want me to meet you at the hospital too?"

"I don't like the idea of us having to be in the hospital at all because of Covid, I'm hoping Krista will be looked at quickly, then sent home. There are some items missing from Krista and Paul's home but I don't want to turn it into a crime scene - not unless Paul tells me to. Krista was able to identify the attacker and we still need Paul to figure out what's been taken."

"I understand. Keep me informed won't you?"

"I will, you know I will. Just get me Paul, please. Talk later." Cathy disconnected the call and signaled to turn into the entrance to the hospital. She parked as close as she could get to the ambulance bay and ran into Emergency.

She flashed her badge at reception and asked which triage bay the ambulance had taken their patient to. Maddeningly, but necessarily, the receptionist only smiled, nodded and asked if she knew if the patient had any medical insurance. Pulling up a note on her phone, where she had stored her, Dave's, Paul's and Krista's medical information, she gave it over to the woman. Paperwork completed, the receptionist pointed down the hall. Following the woman's terse "room three" instruction, Cathy rushed through to the examination area and saw Krista, who had just been triaged, being moved into the first empty bay. Two doctors and a nurse, all in surgical scrubs and full PPE, moved over her body, asking questions, taking her blood pressure, checking reflexes and determining if her pupils were reacting.

Cathy stood silently at the bottom of the gurney, but kept out of their way. She was listening to the questions, she could hear Krista's answers, so at least it proved she was coherent. But her voice was weak, and she seemed in tremendous pain, no matter how gentle the medical team tried to be.

One of the doctors took the stethoscope from around his neck and listened to Krista's chest again. "Okay, Krista, we're taking you down for a CT, I want to see what's going on inside. I don't think your lung has collapsed but we need to rule it out. I'll get a couple of images of your orbital socket as well, I don't like that swelling on your cheek. Okay?"

Krista knew Cathy was standing at the foot of the bed and she sought her eyes. Her own eyes filled with tears when she saw how worried Cathy looked. "Okay, doctor. Can my friend come with me?"

The doctor gave Cathy a perfunctory glance and smiled down at his patient. "Sure she can, she might be able to fill me in better on what happened to you."

While waiting for the CT to be performed, Cathy confessed she didn't know much of how it had happened. In her capacity as a police officer, she was able to relate that the scene of the attack had been secured but there was no need to make it a formal crime scene. She knew who the attacker was and Krista's husband would be able to ascertain what was missing. She asked if there was a chance Krista could be moved to a more solitary location, to lessen her chances of being exposed to the virus and the doctor agreed to a private room.

He put a rush on getting the results of the CT and about twenty minutes later, his tablet beeped indicating he had a message. He had been checking Krista's vitals again when the message came through and he quickly scanned the reports from the radiology department.

Cathy was sitting to Krista's right, gently stroking her hand and, thanks to some IV pain medications she was drifting in and out of a sedated doze. Cathy hated having to wake her properly so she could hear the results but she knew she had to so pressed more firmly on her hand to bring her round.

The doctor read the reports one more time. They had been thorough, taking images of her brain, skull, face, chest and abdomen, as he instructed. Knowing Krista and Cathy were waiting expectantly, he turned towards them. "Okay, mostly good news. No subdural hematomas, no brain swelling, no fractures in your face or skull. No loose, broken or missing teeth so the bleeding in your mouth no doubt came from your gums taking the force of your facial beatings. No punctured or collapsed lungs. A broken rib is causing the difficulty in your breathing. Two more ribs are badly bruised but all organs are intact and showing no signs of bleeding."

Cathy felt her spirits soar. She had been expecting the worst news and what she'd just heard was certainly encouraging. "What's the prognosis doctor?"

"Rest, no heavy lifting, ice packs for the swelling, painkillers as needed and no strenuous exercise. You'll probably feel more discomfort from the ribs than from anywhere else." The doctor paused and looked over Krista's face again. "I was concerned about your left cheekbone; I had a feeling I was going to have to send you to plastics but the CT confirms it's just swollen and an ice pack will help reduce the swelling." He slipped his tablet into the front pocket of his scrubs. "You're a very lucky young lady, I was very concerned when you first came into the ER. Those bruises on your face are nasty but I am hopeful everything will heal and you'll be as good as new."

"Thank God, I was worried my modeling days were over."

The doctor looked surprised until he realized she was

only joking. "You can still give Kate Moss a run for her money. You rest up there for a little while and I'll send a nurse in to clean up your face for you, and get you moved to a private room. Despite the radiology reports all being good, you're here for twenty-four hours observation, forty-eight if I'm not happy with your progress."

Krista was fighting the mild sedation but when she heard she was being kept in, she woke right up. "Oh no, please don't make me stay here. I'm sure I'm going to be fine."

The doctor gave her a calm smile. "All great to hear, but what if you're home and you get up in the middle of the night to use the bathroom and you trip and fall? Any unexpected movement and that rib could punch a hole in your lung before you know it. Plus, although the CT brain was clear, I want to keep an eye on that too."

Krista suppressed a scowl. "But there's no Covid at home."

"There's no Covid in this wing of the hospital either. Sorry, Krista, I must insist we keep you here. You really were very lucky, some of those lacerations looked deep but you don't even need stitches. Some steristrips and you'll be as good as new."

Krista knew she was fighting a losing battle and conceded with a tired roll of her eyes. "If you say so. I have to trust your judgement."

The doctor excused himself and Cathy encouraged Krista to give in to the medication. "I'll go to your place and get an overnight bag packed for you."

Feeling as if she was floating on water, she nodded absently. "Did I tell you it was Ken who did this to me?" she asked suddenly.

"You did. I checked your apartment and I'm sorry, it seems like he's taken some jewelry. He was also in your filing cabinet but I don't know if he took anything."

Krista shook her head in derision. "What a bastard." She noticed then something was missing and she held up her left hand, shouting in anger. "Oh Jesus, he's taken my wedding rings!"

Appalled, Cathy grabbed a hold of Krista's hand and laced her fingers through hers. "Don't worry, we'll get them back. When Paul gets here, after he's seen you settled, I'll take him home and get him to go over your belongings, see if anything other than jewelry was taken. Right now, just rest. Stop fighting the meds. Let yourself go to sleep."

Miserable, Krista settled back on the pillow and looked like she was drifting off but then said, "I'm so sorry for this, Cathy."

"What? Why? No need for you to be sorry. I'm just glad you're as well as can be expected."

"Is my face a mess?"

Cathy couldn't suppress a smile. "Never thought I would say these words about you, but yes, your face is a mess. Your left eye is nearly swollen closed but your right eye is at least half open. Which means I can't make faces at you when you're awake because you can still see me."

Despite the seriousness of it all, and despite the pain caused by her injured ribs, Krista couldn't stop a ripple of laughter at Cathy's words. "Don't make me laugh," she pleaded.

Cathy leaned over and planted a kiss through her mask on Krista's forehead. "Wouldn't dream of it, chum." She smoothed Krista's hair and waited for her to settle again. "Hey, before you go to sleep, you going to tell Paul you know who attacked you?"

But before Krista could answer, there was a noise behind Cathy and she turned towards the doorway. There stood Paul and Dave, both of them staring in shock and anger when they saw how badly Krista had been beaten up. That she was awake and seemingly having a conversation was a miracle in itself but they knew from experience she would be on heavy painkillers and wouldn't let something like this slow her down much.

Putting his horror aside for the moment, Paul rushed to

his wife's side to see the damage up close. His throat clicked when he swallowed and with a tentative hand, he reached over and pushed back a stray lock of hair from her face. He was so afraid of hurting her, he had been so gentle she hadn't felt him and she looked up at him as best as the swelling would let her.

"It's okay, baby," she said softly, "the doctor assured me I can still give Kate Moss a run for her money."

He collapsed into the chair beside her and took her hand in his. "Oh wow, Krista, what the hell happened?"

Krista's eyes locked with Cathy's. He was going to hit the roof when she told him and she wanted him distracted first. Cathy understood the unspoken message conveyed to her and she stepped in before Krista had to answer his question.

"I feel so awful about this, Paul," she started. "I was running late in picking Krista up and halfway to your place, the fuel indicator light came on so I stopped to fill up. Unfortunately, there was a problem with my bank card -" She shot Dave a swift glance, "it's been sorted now, it was actually a problem with their machine but it took a while to get it sorted. Anyway, I also got caught behind a bus and...well, I didn't get to your place until nearly seven thirty. I came up the path, and saw your door was ajar and when I opened it...that's when I saw Krista lying in the hall."

"You were attacked in our home?" Paul hadn't expected that but before Krista could reply, Cathy took over again.

"Paul, I'm going to need you to come home with me, your home I mean. There's some jewelry missing and I noticed your filing cabinet was opened. I'll need you to give me a report of what is missing so I can do a formal statement in case your insurance company asks for one."

Paul was holding Krista's left hand, and at the mention of missing jewelry he realized some other, more important jewelry was missing also. He straightened out her fingers. "Jesus sonofabitch!"

Dave came closer to see what had gotten Paul even more upset and it took him mere seconds to see what was missing.

"That sucks, Kris, I'm so sorry."

A heavy silence descended on the room. Paul had already figured it out, Dave was about two steps behind him and, his eyes darkening, Paul held Cathy in his intense gaze.

"Let me see if I have this all straight: she was beat up in our home, the door was open, jewelry and perhaps other stuff, maybe the title to my car, maybe something else, were stolen. Care to tell me who did this to her?"

Krista looked worriedly up at Cathy. They all knew the answer now but Paul needed confirmation and when he got it, he was going to go ballistic. He was already half way there.

# CHAPTER TEN

"Are you going to answer me?" Paul persisted coolly after a lengthy silence.

Cathy kept her eyes on Krista and when Krista gave the slightest of nods, indicating it was okay to tell him what he had obviously guessed, Cathy cleared her throat and said, "It was your father, Paul. Your father did this to her."

"Sonofabitch!" he hissed. Getting the confirmation didn't make it any easier and he abruptly stood up. They had come to the hospital in Dave's car, his was still at his apartment. "I'm going to kill him. I swear to God, I'll choke him with my bare hands."

As he started to get up to leave, Dave stepped in front of him. "Hold on, Paul, don't go to him when you're this angry. Go home with Cathy, look over your stuff to see what he's taken, then go and arrest him. I'll stay here with Krista, take some pictures of her in case they're needed in court and I'll also have a BOLO statewide and into Connecticut, Rhode Island, New York, New Jersey and Pennsylvania put out on his car. I've still got his make, model and license plate."

"Are you kidding me, Dave? You want me to *wait*?" Paul gestured towards Krista. "Look at her, man, just look at her. Look what he did to her. Tell me you wouldn't want to get him immediately if that was Cathy lying there."

"You know I'd be doing the same," Dave acquiesced calmly. "At least give Cathy the chance to take you home and see what he's stolen. After that, you can do whatever you want but hopefully with less anger and hopefully without setting yourself up for a fall."

Paul stared moodily at his friend, wanting to push him

to one side but Krista's soft plea to listen to Dave won through to his level-headedness. He stepped back towards her again and softened his expression. "I love you, sweet-face," he murmured. "I hate what he's done to you but you're in safe hands here. See you later, my love. You ready, Cathy?"

Cathy grabbed her bag and gave Krista a quick kiss. "I'll see you later too, chum, with your overnight bag. If you think of anything you need besides the usual, have Dave text or call me."

"Thanks, Cath."

Cathy gave Dave a quick kiss and told him she would text when she was on her way back. She knew Paul would be less than talkative on the way to his apartment and she was right. Hardly a word was spoken between them as she let him work it out inside his head, but a quiet fury emanated off him and she figured that was okay too.

When they got to his apartment, the first thing he looked at was the filing cabinet. He was not surprised to find the title to his car was missing, as well as the one for Krista's car. Their passports were still there, as well as birth and marriage certificates – not that they would have been of any use to his father, but at least they hadn't been destroyed. He was about to close the drawer when his eye fell on the hanging file named "Bank Statements". He had tidied the file up himself less than a month ago and, although he hadn't touched it since, he knew he had left it neat and orderly.

He lifted the complete file out and flicked through it quickly. The only thing missing was the most recent statement. He immediately pulled up his bank's app on his phone and punched in his account number and password. All the money was still there and he pressed the tab that would lock his account until he unlocked it again. Not even the bank itself could override him.

A perfunctory check of his and Krista's jewelry told him what was missing and, while Cathy finished packing Krista's overnight bag, he hastily wrote down what had been taken.

Cathy was adding toiletries to a vanity bag when he caught her attention.

"Thanks for looking after her for me, little dude."

She nodded slowly. "She's my friend, you know I will do my best for her." She studied him carefully. "You're going to go now, aren't you?"

"Yes." He threw his hands up helplessly. "Don't try to stop me, Cathy, please. Don't offer to come with me either, I don't need a witness. Much as I want to, I'm not going to kill him but I might have to hurt him pretty badly."

Cathy pressed her mouth into a hard line, but she nodded her head in acknowledgement. "And I understand that, I really do. But why don't you send a couple of uniforms instead to the motel to pick him up? I'll phone the motel and warn them not to go into his room until we've got there and gotten back all your stuff."

"And do what with him at the precinct? Question him and hear more of his lies? Wait until everyone has turned a blind eye before I can pulverize him?"

"You'll get your chance." She thought of another possibility. "So what are you going to do if you go there and find out he's already gone?"

"He's trying to clear out my bank account, he'll be trying to get my car sold, he has to come back here for that. He'll probably want to try and sell the jewelry. He's been here a couple of weeks, he's probably already sourced the seedier citizens of Bathville's fair city and he'll be waiting until dark to seek them out. If he's not at the motel, and if nothing comes up on the BOLO Dave said he was issuing, I can wait for him to come here." Paul paused for a moment before adding softly, "He took our watches, Cathy."

"Your watches?" She looked like she didn't understand and then her eyes closed in acknowledgement. "Your watches. The ones the boys in Belfast gave us all?"

"The very ones. They're of no use to anyone else with the inscriptions on them but I guess that can be an easy fix if he wants to try and pawn them. He's taken some of her other jewelry as you know but I can't get over him taking Krista's wedding rings, which he took right off her finger."

Cathy closed her eyes and nodded. "I know, he's beyond despicable." She emitted a short, mirthless laugh. "For a second there, I was going to apologize for saying that about your father. Glad I stopped myself." She levelled her cool stare on him. "I want you to get him, don't think for one moment I want that man to go free, I just don't want you to do anything stupid."

"I will do whatever I think is appropriate."

She studied his face for a long moment and then she nodded. "Just do me one favor, Paul."

"Be careful?"

"That too. Wear a mask."

He closed his eyes briefly in acknowledgement and then, giving her a kiss on the cheek, he grabbed his keys from his bedside table. It looked like Ken had done a thorough job in ransacking the place so how he had missed the keys sitting on top of the table was hard to imagine. He bounded down the stairs and seconds later, Cathy heard the front door slam.

She took out her cell phone and sent Dave a text. *He's just left to go get him. I've got everything I need for Kris, will be there soon. Xo*

A minute later, a reply came back. *Ten four. She's sleeping right now. Bring coffee.*

She sent back a thumbs-up emoji and, checking to make sure she had everything she thought Krista might need, including her Kindle, cell phone and charger, she left.

As Paul drove to the motel, he tried to clear his head. He concentrated on his driving, but images of Krista and her injuries kept clouding his vision. How he made it to the motel without running anyone over or rear ending anyone at a traffic light, he would never know.

When he pulled into the parking lot, he immediately saw Ken's beat up Ford Focus. *Stupid bastard hadn't had the sense to hightail it to another location the minute he left the apartment,* he thought. Remembering the one favor Cathy had asked of him, he reached into his pocket and took out his mask. He put it on, pinched at the bridge of his nose to keep it in place and then got out of his car. He hesitated for a second, his hand hovering over the gun tucked safely inside his jacket and then, on impulse, he reached in and took the gun out. He looked at it for a moment before placing it under the driver's seat of his car. The last thing he wanted was to be in such a blind rage that he would actually use the weapon on his father. Not that he cared if it caused harm, he just didn't want the paperwork that would ensue because he had fired his gun at an unarmed civilian.

Besides, he didn't want to go into this mission as a cop. He was simply a man seeking retribution for the his wife. And maybe his own wretched childhood too.

He remembered Dave telling him Ken was in room eleven. He went up to the door, put his ear to it and listened for a few seconds to ascertain what might be going on inside. All he heard was a Dairy Queen commercial for a new burger meal.

He deliberated for a moment what to do. Kick the door in or knock and wait? He decided on the former and within a second, the door flew open and he stood in the threshold for a long moment to observe what was going on.

Ken had been sitting on the bed with his back to the door. He was on his cell phone, holding in his hand what Paul instantly recognized as his bank statement, while yelling at whoever was on the other end of the call. "What do you mean I locked the account? I did no such thing, I want to speak to your man - " Which was as far as he got when he felt the icy blast behind him and saw the shadow appear on the floor. He whirled round in anger that swiftly turned to fright as soon as he saw his son standing there. He pressed the disconnect button on the phone and stumbled to his feet, his face registering his shock.

Paul deliberately didn't move. He wanted Ken to see the

thunder in his eyes and know he was in serious trouble. He looked quickly around the room. The table that had served as Ken's dining table for his burger and pizza meals had been cleared of wrappers and pizza boxes. In their place, Ken had carefully laid out the watches, bracelets, necklaces and earrings he had stolen. In a separate pile were Krista's engagement, wedding and eternity rings. Beside the rings were a couple of one ounce bags of presumably cocaine. He could also see the car titles.

Seeing everything he needed to see, including the fact it looked like Ken had started to pack his belongings into a beat-up hold-all laying at the foot of the bed, Paul stepped towards his father. Ken was desperately trying to retain his composure and gain control but all of a sudden, Paul hit him with a vicious right hook and the next thing Ken knew he was staring dazedly up at the water-stained ceiling.

The first punch was strangely cathartic for Paul. He waited patiently for Ken to get to his feet and then floored him again. His left hook was as vicious as his right hook.

Ken staggered to his feet again, this time wiping blood from his lip. "Back off, loser," he snarled. "You'd better have a good reason for being here or else I'm going to call the cops."

"You know why I'm here. And as for calling the cops? Go ahead. I could arrest you myself but I'd rather watch someone else put the bracelets on you and take you away. I'll be sure to have them arrest you for being in the possession of drugs, for breaking and entering, grand theft, and, oh yes, for beating up my wife."

"The bitch deserved it," Ken said.

Paul grabbed his father by the front of his filthy t-shirt and flung him roughly against the wall. "She deserved it, did she?" He wasn't looking for an answer and he slammed Ken's head against the wall with just enough force to hurt him but not enough to knock him unconscious.

"Yes, she deserved it. The bitch kicked me - "

"She kicked you? Where? In the balls?"

"Yes, if you must know. Well, technically she kneed me but she's still a bitch."

Paul couldn't hold back a grin of satisfaction. "Good for her for getting you. Too bad she didn't push them up into your throat. I would have paid to see that. You're going to pay for what you did to her, I'm going to hurt you in the way you hurt her only I'm going to do it better. And if you come looking for more, I will kill you."

"K-Kill me?" As dazed as he was, Ken was still holding on to his lucidity and he knew Paul meant every hard hitting word. "Paul wait, son, please wait. You've got to help me. Please. I'm sorry for what I did to you and your wife and look..." He pointed in the direction of the possessions laid out just so on the table. "There's all your stuff, you can take it back but please, you've got to help me. There are men after me, I owe them thirty-five thou and I'm pretty sure they've tracked me all the way to here. If I don't give them what they're looking for, *they'll* kill me for sure."

"Fine! I'll hold the door open for them."

"You don't mean that. I know you don't. I know I did wrong, I know I shouldn't have hurt your lovely wife like that, but I'm desperate and when she made it perfectly clear I wasn't welcome in your life, I saw red. I saw the opportunity to save my own skin slipping through my fingers and I panicked. I guess I just panicked. I'm sorry I hurt her, I'm a thousand times sorry but I couldn't help myself this morning."

Paul didn't doubt for one second his father was, for once, telling the truth about the men who were coming after him. The fear and terror in his voice and eyes were too genuine. The only thing was, he didn't care. He slammed his father's head against the wall again. "I don't give a flying shit who's after you, old man, I reckon you deserve their wrath and more. You lied to me from the very moment you first came to me, about yourself, about Maria, about everything else and I really don't care what happens to you. You're nothing but a low-life, a no good, lying coward."

"I'm your father," Ken gasped desperately.

"You would rather snort a line of coke and drink a bottle of booze a day than be a father. You're nothing to me. A worthless nothing. And after what you did to Krista? You deserve to die." Krista's beautiful, battered face danced in front of him then and his fury erupted. His frustration and his shock eclipsed his rationale and he laid into his father with as much venom as he possessed. The fact Ken didn't retaliate in any way didn't stop him. Every punch, every kick, every mark he bestowed upon his father were all for Krista and maybe this wasn't his preferred way of doing things, but he didn't care about that either. This was for her.

He only stopped when his eyes were blinded by the droplets of sweat from his exertion and he let Ken slither to the floor with a thump. Ken had been beaten almost to a pulp but he was still conscious, and even though he didn't know if Paul was finished with him or not, he was stupid enough to think it was okay to taunt him.

Ken tried to open his eyes but his cheeks were already swelling. He peered up at the shadowy outline and licked the blood off his front teeth. Incredibly, he started to laugh. "M-Make you feel like a man doing that?" he goaded. "I-Is that what you do to that whore of a wife before you try to slide your miserable dick into her?"

Paul's eyes glinted dangerously again. "You are one sick fuck, old man." Leaning down, he pulled Ken roughly to his feet again and pulled him close. "Give me a reason why I shouldn't kill you right here and right now," he said right into his father's face. "Give me a reason why I should let you live."

Ken couldn't come up with a reason quick enough and, although Paul wasn't expecting an answer, he dropped Ken like a sack of worms and kicked him squarely in the balls. He hoped Ken still hadn't recovered from Krista getting him in the same area. Ken grunted one last time and then let his body flop loosely against the carpet.

Paul could see his father's chest moving in and out as he

breathed so at least he knew he was still alive. He also knew he really had done a number on him and he searched his heart for regret. There wasn't any and he kicked Ken in the thigh to get his attention again. "Listen up, you miserable slime, this is the last time you and I will ever see one another. I hope you die and the sooner the better. Good bye."

And with that, he turned on his heel, gathered up his belongings, including the bank statement that had floated to the floor beside the bed, and walked out without looking back.

If he had thought to check he had gotten everything, if he had taken a few seconds to give Ken one last, hate-filled glare, he would have seen that sometime during the fight, his handcuffs had been ripped from the belt loop at the back of his jeans. They were now lying on the floor to Ken's left and partly under the bottom of the bed quilt.

Unknown to him, Gabriella Rossini was next door and had heard practically everything. A lot of the angry conversation, every sound of flesh hitting flesh, every thud of a body being flung against the wall or being thrown to the ground and every grunt of pain. She had heard the threats that someone was going to be killed and when a silence that was somehow worse than the violent acts she had witnessed ensued, she took up her covert position at the window behind the curtain again. She was half-expecting to see the dark-haired man she had seen the previous morning so she was surprised to see a blond man this time leave from next door.

She saw him get into a white Ford Mustang, not the black Camaro as she had seen yesterday. Grabbing a pen and notepad, she hastily jotted down the make, model and license plate. She also added the time, eleven forty-three in the morning.

It never crossed her mind to go and check on the occupant in room eleven but it did cross her mind to go and tell the manager of what had just happened. However, she quickly talked herself out of it. The manager scared her, he kept making suggestive remarks towards her and was always leering down the top of her blouse.

Besides, she was busy, she had to meet her estranged husband at one o'clock for lunch, and she was running late. She knew from past experience that if she kept her husband waiting, there would be hell to pay. No matter how much he kept promising he wasn't going to beat her again, no matter how much he told her he loved her, no matter how much he said he was going to change, he was going to get help, she knew she couldn't trust him.

When she left her room approximately forty five minutes later, she was so focused on being on time she didn't notice the green van pulling into the parking lot. She didn't see it stopping outside the room on the other side of number eleven. She certainly didn't notice the two black men get out of the van, look all around them and then go into her neighbor's room.

She didn't notice anything. She was too busy being on time.

# CHAPTER ELEVEN

When Paul made it back to the hospital, his anger had dissipated but the adrenalin was still coursing through his veins. Finally, after years of abuse, he had gotten his pound of flesh and he knew it was something to be grateful for. He knew his father would never bother him again which in turn meant his father would never hurt Krista again. Now he could look at Krista and feel he had done her proud. Another thing to be grateful for.

When he quietly entered her room, she was sleeping. Cathy was finishing emptying the overnight bag she had packed earlier. Dave was thumbing through his phone but looked up when he saw Paul.

"Okay, partner?" he asked carefully.

Paul met his eyes and nodded briefly. He came over to Krista's side and looked lovingly down at her. He closed his eyes as it all finally started to sink in and he sat down heavily on the chair beside her. Cathy could see his face more clearly than Dave could and she reached over the bed to take his hand. She noticed the bloody scuff marks and abrasions on his knuckles but there were no other signs of a physical combat.

"You going to tell us what happened?" she prompted gently.

Not taking his eyes off Krista's face, he hesitated for just a moment then said, "I didn't kill him. I wanted to, and Lord knows I could have, but I didn't kill him. Roughed him up pretty badly though, don't think he'll be pulling any chicks for the next few weeks but that's not my concern. I think I'm doing the female race a huge favor. All I know is, every punch I landed on him felt good." He reached into his pocket and took out three rings, which he slid gently on Krista's ring finger in the order he knew she wore them. He laid a very soft kiss on top of them. "Got these back too," he stated unnecessarily. "And the rest, including our watches and the car titles. I'll keep the lock on my bank account until tomorrow, just in case he's somehow managed to memorize the account number or had it written down elsewhere."

Dave and Cathy exchanged knowing glances. They knew Paul was telling them the truth and not just what they wanted to hear. "You need some cash to hold you over?" Dave asked.

Paul checked his wallet. "I've got close to fifty bucks, I think I'll be okay but I'll let you know. Thanks for the offer."

"You want something brought back for lunch?" Cathy asked. "Dave and I were just talking about getting something when you arrived."

"No, I think I'm good, thanks."

"There's a Subway around the corner," Dave said, "I'll bring you back something for later if you like. Don't know if Krista will be in the mood for anything but the nurse said they'll bring her something when she's had a rest."

Paul nodded absently. He had barely taken his eyes off Krista and his expression was that of someone who was trying to comprehend something that couldn't be comprehended. "Just look what he did to her," he said softly. "Look at those bruises. She's so beautiful and yet...look at her."

Cathy did as he asked and, her expression softening, shook her head. "They will heal," she said solemnly. "The doctor was very optimistic she will be left with no scars."

Paul shuddered and he gently stroked Krista's arm. He didn't want to wake her and he seemed at a loss for what to do. "At least I know he'll never be able to hurt her ever again."

Dave and Cathy exchanged a brief, quizzical glance. "Uh...how can you be so sure about that?" he asked carefully.

Paul didn't answer for a long, tense moment. "Because what I did to him, he won't be in any fit state to come anywhere near anyone I love ever again." Suddenly realizing what Dave had asked him, and how he answered, he looked briefly at his friend. He knew just by looking at him what Dave was thinking. "I said I didn't kill him. Leave it at that."

Dave studied Paul's body language, searching for a hint of a lie or something that would explain the darkness emanating off him. He couldn't see anything and, not wanting to push it, he put an easy smile on his face. "You got it, partner." He stood up. "You want to go get lunch, my love?" he asked Cathy, holding his hand out to her.

"Sure," she said, gathering up her bag. She looked down at Krista and smiled sadly. "I'll be back soon, chum," she whispered. She gave Paul a smile. "We'll phone Captain Hamilton, give him an update. He might want to come down later but I'll try to convince him otherwise. The fewer people in a hospital nowadays, the better."

Paul waited for the quiet click of the door after his friends left and immediately let out a long, low mewl of pent-up despair and anger. He couldn't take his eyes off Krista and he was having a hard time trying to picture her face returning to its former beauty. There was hardly an inch that didn't have a bruise or a cut or a contusion somewhere on it, the swelling under her eyes distorting her entire visage. He did know, of course, that time would heal her, that soon the last bruise would fade away and her beauty would be restored. But he knew emotionally she would never forget this brutal beating. And for that, his heart broke for her.

He knew she was sleeping peacefully; she had moved hardly at all the whole time he'd been beside her and he hoped that if she was dreaming, she was dreaming sweet things. He laid his head down beside her, as close as he could get and willed his roller coaster emotions to calm down. He didn't want to waste time thinking about his father, or what he'd done to him. That episode was going to be placed firmly inside a box, inside his head and marked "Trash". With a capital T.

Slowly he felt himself relax and, holding Krista's hand

loosely in his own, he managed to drift off into a doze.

It was Dave giving him a gentle shake that woke him with a start and he looked up at his friend in bewilderment, wondering where he was and how long had he been out. He glanced at his watch and saw roughly two hours had passed and he rubbed his hands over his face, stifling a yawn. He looked at Krista and saw she was turned towards him, the semblance of a mischievous smile on her face.

"Welcome back, sleepyhead," she said softly. "I told Dave not to wake you but he insisted."

She sounded so *normal* and he grinned widely. He threw Dave a pseudo dirty look. "Thanks for that, partner." He yawned again and patted his stomach. "I'm starving."

Krista pointed at a tray on her bed table. "I've eaten. I would have shared but I didn't want to disturb you."

"How did I miss that? You were very quiet."

"You were out of it, love. I saved some orange Jell-o for you."

He grimaced. "Thanks but no thanks. Of course, you know that if it had been lime I would have fought you for it."

Dave reached down to a bag at his feet and pulled out a foot long sandwich still in its Subway wrapper. He threw it over to his friend. "Italian cold cuts, just the way you like it. You're welcome."

Paul nodded and tore the wrapping off. He took a big bite while glancing around the room and frowned as something occurred to him. "Where's Cathy?" he asked with his mouth half full.

"When she phoned the captain earlier, he asked her to come in for a little while. Something about an unsigned report that couldn't wait. She should be back soon. You can use my car if you need to get home in a hurry. Otherwise I can take you home later."

"No need, Dave, Cathy dropped me off at home, then I left to go to the motel and returned here in my own car."

"Cathy said she wanted to see me again before she went

home," Krista stated. "And I want to see her too."

"You know she'll be here soon." Paul smiled into her eyes. "How you feeling, sweetie?"

"As high as a kite, if you must know," she said with a gentle chuckle. She obviously wasn't going to let herself laugh too hard. "Don't feel much except some discomfort when I breathe or laugh. I'm trying not to do either." She reached over to her husband and settled her hand on his arm. "I see I got my rings back. Thank you. And Dave assured me you didn't kill him. Thank you for that too. How are *you* feeling?"

He chewed some more on his sandwich, his brow furrowed. "Getting there, it just all seems a bit surreal. It's only four in the afternoon and it feels like an age since I left the apartment this morning. But tomorrow's another day and I'm ready to put this one behind me."

"Copy that," Krista stated. She sounded sleepy but in otherwise good spirits.

"I could murder a beer right now," Paul said as he worked on his sandwich some more. "Maybe two or three."

Dave cocked an eyebrow. "You'll be home alone tonight, want to see if we can find a bar open somewhere and have a drink? Or five?"

Paul looked guiltily at Krista. "Doesn't seem fair, me going out to enjoy myself while you're lying here."

"Do what you want, Paul, I think you've earned yourself the right to get as pickled as you want to. I'll be lying here, hopefully still high, feeling no pain, and flirting with the sexy intern who was in here earlier."

Paul allowed himself a grin. "Great! It's decided then, he can keep you entertained while I'm not here."

And so it was settled. When Cathy returned, she gave her approval for the guys to go out and have a bit of fun. It was long overdue and she knew Dave would be able to look after Paul if he decided to really let his hair down.

Paul felt like letting off steam and once they settled into a sparsely-populated bar closer to his home than to Dave's, he downed three beers in half an hour. He was drinking fast, very fast and, although he didn't need to ask, Dave knew his friend was trying to cope with the events of the day. Knowing Paul would probably be a sorry sight by the end of the evening, Dave paced himself with one beer and then switched to soda.

After an hour-and-a-half of idle chit chat, Paul, who was on his seventh beer, turned away from the football game playing on six different large-screen TVs around the bar area and stared moodily at his bottle of beer.

"I hate him, Dave," he suddenly announced. "I hate him so much it actually scares me that I'm capable of hatred to that level."

"What do you want instead, partner? To sit there and profess undying love for the sonofabitch for what he did to you and your sister, and now your wife?"

"No, it only makes me hate him more." In despair, Paul buried his face in his hands. "Why couldn't I kill him this morning?" he lamented in a voice that sounded perilously close to tears. "Why couldn't I have ended his miserable, sorry life there and then? He would have deserved it, I would even have been prepared to do time for the murder."

"And how much good do you think you would be for Krista if you were in the joint?"

Paul shrugged. "None, I suppose." He swigged back a large swallow of beer and barely stifled a burp. He knew how much he'd already had to drink but he wasn't feeling so much as a glimmer of a buzz. Not yet anyway. He lapsed into silence for a long moment but Dave knew what was going through his mind; it was obvious in his eyes. He was trying to forget the images of Krista lying in her hospital bed,  her face reduced to a mess and her body broken and battered.

When he started talking again, he embarked on a long spiel, all about her, telling Dave things he already knew and a lot of things he didn't. He paused intermittently to order more beer and even though some of the things he said were of an intimate nature, he knew Dave wouldn't mind. That was Dave, his friend and confidante, someone who could keep a secret and take it to the grave with him. He was the only person in the world Paul could speak openly and honestly to, and get an open and honest opinion from. Paul could tell Dave things he couldn't even bring himself to tell Krista and it was an aspect of their friendship he cherished deeply.

When he finished talking, it was fast approaching nine o'clock. Although the night was still young, Dave wondered if he should maybe plant the seed about getting home into Paul's head. With roughly ten or eleven beers down his throat, Dave knew it was going to be a long night and, when Paul got up to go to the men's room, he phoned Cathy.

"Hey baby," he said softly.

"Hey you," she returned. "Everything okay?"

"Although he would argue the point, Paul's three sheets to the wind. He decided he wanted to drown his sorrows so that's what he did. And then some."

"Oh dear, I don't pity him his hangover in the morning."

"Exactly. I might have to stay with him tonight, is that okay?"

"Of course it is, just do what you have to do."

"Will you miss me?"

She chuckled. "Only if I know you'll be missing me."

"You know I will." Dave looked across the bar and saw Paul lurch slightly as he came out of the restroom. "He's on his way back. I'll phone you in the morning."

"Hope you get some sleep. Good night, love."

Dave tapped his phone to end the call and looked up expectantly as Paul slid ungracefully into the booth. "You ready to call it a night, Paul?" he asked cheerily.

Paul looked at his three-quarters full bottle of beer and shook his head. "Only just getting started, Big D. I've got a mighty thirst tonight and this beer's going down awfully well."

As a result, they stayed until after eleven o'clock. Paul commanded most of the conversation, rambling on about how much he loved Krista, how much he hated his father, how much she meant to him and how he couldn't live without her. And on and on his lamentations and glowing praise went, and often he didn't make any sense so that if a stranger had been listening, he wouldn't have known what this very handsome but very drunk blond guy was talking about. But Dave followed every word. Luckily for Paul.

To Dave's surprise, when the time finally came to leave, Paul was able to walk out of the bar all by himself. He lurched and swayed only a little, corrected himself every time and walked out proud and erect and seemingly sober as a judge. Until the frigid night air hit him. It went straight to his head and he would have keeled over on the way to the car if Dave hadn't been there to steady him.

The journey home was eventful in the respect that Dave just about managed to stop the car in time for Paul to fumble for the handle to the passenger door, stagger away a few feet and proceed to empty the contents of his stomach.

Dave waited patiently in the warmth of the car and, when it seemed Paul had finished, he got out and went around to the other side. He saw Paul leaning over, his hands on his knees, swaying slightly. The expression on his face said he wasn't sure if his stomach had settled or not. He groaned and spat some more, waiting to see what was going to happen. Now would have been the right time to announce he was fine and could they go home please but instead he leaned over further and threw up some more.

Luckily there were few passersby to witness this sorry event. Any car that drove by barely even slowed down to gawk. In the darkness, nobody knew Paul was drunk, he could have just been getting rid of a bad taco or something.

Dave waited some more and then, when all was quiet for several minutes, he approached his friend. "You finished?" he asked gently.

Paul squinted at him and wiped his streaming eyes. "I think...I'm going... to *die*." He slurred. "Kill me now...please."

Dave hooked his arm around Paul's shoulders and

steered him in the direction of the car. "No chance, you're going to have to suffer gracefully. Let's get you home, we're nearly there."

Paul didn't protest and once he got to his apartment, he reeled up the path and somehow, miraculously, managed to get his key in the lock first time and staggered up the stairs. Dave heard the bathroom door close and, with a wry shake of his head, went to the kitchen, grabbed the biggest glass he could find and filled it with cold water straight from the tap. He knew where Krista kept a bottle of Tylenol and he carried it and the glass of water up to Paul's bedroom and left them on the bedside table.

There was no sound from the bathroom and after fifteen minutes, Dave knocked softly on the door and entered. Paul was lying flat out on the tiled floor, dead to the world. A quick peek down the toilet told Dave it was clean. With a resolute sigh, he pulled Paul up, slung him over his shoulder and carried him to his bed.

After undressing him down to his underwear, Paul stirred. "Whassup, Big D?" he slurred.

Dave reeled from the stench of alcohol and averted his face slightly to avoid being assaulted again. "Glass of water to your right, basin on the floor beside you, Tylenol beside the water." But Paul was already sound asleep and with an amused shake of his head, Dave went to the spare bedroom to get some sleep.

He kept the bedroom door open to listen for Paul in case he got up in the middle of the night and needed to be rescued from the bathroom floor again. He didn't know it of course, but he would be spending the next night with Paul again, just not in his apartment.

# CHAPTER TWELVE

Dave got up around six thirty and immediately texted Cathy. He knew she'd be up, possibly even on her way to the precinct, but when she replied seconds later, it wasn't via text but by phoning him from their bedroom.

"Morning, love," she purred. "How lies the land?"

"He will be one sorry bastard when he gets up. I've never seen him down so many beers in one night and still be able to stand on his own two feet. He was sick though, a lot, but I didn't hear anything through the night so I'm hoping he's okay. Unless he's died from alcohol poisoning or something, which wouldn't surprise me."

"Don't let him come to the hospital if he's still under the influence. It's not fair to Krista and you know she'll only worry about him. Get him to sleep it off. She's not going anywhere until at least tomorrow so he'll have plenty of time to sober up."

"Yeah, good idea. Did you sleep okay?"

"So-so, it was strange without you. My feet were cold."

"A-ha! Now I know why you married me."

"Busted." She chuckled softly and the sound made his insides melt. He felt a sudden rush of yearning for her. "I'm going into work for a bit this morning, then I'll go to the hospital. I'll phone Krista about eight o'clock to see how she is and if she needs anything. Shall I tell the captain not to expect either of you in until later?"

"Yeah, tell him what happened but if he wants to phone me, he can. Okay, baby. I'll keep you posted about Paul. In the meantime, I'm going to do a bit of laundry, wash my clothes and what he was wearing yesterday. I'll have to borrow a pair of jeans and a shirt from him but that's okay. I'll see you later. Love you."

"Love you too."

They blew kisses down the phone and when he hung up, he climbed out of bed and used the guest bathroom to shower. He dressed hurriedly, gathered up his dirty clothes and went to check on Paul, who was still sound asleep.

He picked up the discarded clothes, bundled them in the towel he'd dried himself with after his shower and went to the complex's laundry room, three doors away. While the washer was doing its thing, he made some scrambled eggs, toast and coffee for himself and settled down to watch what was happening around the world on the news.

It was nearly eleven thirty when he heard movement from upstairs and, moments later, Paul arrived in the living room. He had put on lounge pants and an old t-shirt but he was unshowered and unshaven. He was also pale, bleary-eyed and not quite with the program yet. He slouched down on the sofa and suppressed a shiver.

"Morning," Dave greeted cheerfully.

"Yeah. Whatever." Paul smacked his lips together and grimaced. "Christ, my mouth tastes like the insides of an elephant's ass. Just what did I *do* last night?"

"You got drunk, you threw up, you made your bed on the bathroom floor so I moved you to your bedroom and made sure you were nice and comfy before I left you to sleep it off."

Paul felt his stomach somersault and he willed it to settle. "Did I drink much?"

"Last count, about eleven beers."

"Eleven? Jesus, four's usually my limit."

"Did your laundry for you too." Dave nodded to the easy chair where he'd folded everything nice and neat when they came out of the dryer an hour or so before. He gestured to his body. "And yes, these are your jeans and t-shirt, you'll get them back whenever."

Paul waved him off dismissively. "Whatever." He looked

like he was going to fall into a doze but he suddenly sat up straight and started looking round for something. "Oh no, Krista, I need to call her."

"Cathy phoned about fifteen minutes ago, Krista's going for an x-ray of her cheek again. Apparently, the attending physician from plastics just wanted to see for himself if there was anything broken inside. She had a comfortable night but she's still in pain and she told Cathy to tell you she loves you and hopes you're not too hungover. Cathy also said when she's back from radiology, she'll phone."

Paul slumped back against the sofa, his eyes troubled. "Poor Kris. I should be with her."

"In your condition?" Dave chuckled. "You smell like a brewery, partner. Want some coffee and toast or something?"

At the mere mention of food, Paul felt his stomach somersault again and he shook his head, only to clutch it in agony. "I am never, ever, *ever* getting drunk ever again. Ever."

Dave suppressed a smile. "Sure, whatever you say. Why don't you go back up to bed? An extra couple of hours might do you the world of good. I'll wake you around one thirty and we'll take it from there."

Paul didn't need much coaxing and he shuffled out of the living room. Suddenly remembering he had a duty to report to his superior officer, he turned back to Dave. "You spoke to Bob?"

"Yup, Captain Hamilton says don't come anywhere near the station until you are alcohol free. I think he's taking pity on you because of Krista. He actually did sound very understanding."

Paul gave a timid nod and went upstairs, stopping in the kitchen to down a huge glass of water. Mercifully, it felt like it was going to stay down. He filled the glass again and took it upstairs, not having noticed Dave had left a glass for him when he'd put him into bed the night before.

By two thirty that afternoon, Paul was shaved, showered, dressed and eating toast smothered in strawberry jam. He looked less strained, certainly more sober, but he was very tired. When he finished eating, he phoned Krista.

"Hey, sweet-face," he greeted.

In her hospital bed, Krista visibly brightened as she answered. "Paul! Are you okay? Do you want me to whisper?"

He grinned broadly at the sound of her voice and her slight teasing. "No, I'm good. I took a couple of Tylenol earlier and I've just had some toast."

Cathy stood up, indicating she was going to leave for a while and give Krista a chance to talk to Paul. Krista nodded her thanks. "I'm sorry you're hungover but I hope whatever you did last night helped you put yesterday to rest."

"Yes, well, I'm over what I did to him, but I'm still trying to get a handle on what he did to you."

"I understand but I don't want this to be all consuming for you." She snuggled down under the covers a bit more, trying to get comfortable and not aggravate her abdominal injuries. "They took another x-ray of my cheek. They're satisfied now there's no underlying problems and the swelling will go down in time."

Paul had a vague recollection of Dave telling him something about the x-rays earlier that morning and he kicked himself for not asking before calling her if there had been any update. "That's great, baby. How's the pain level?"

"On a scale of one to ten, about a twenty seven. But that's when the painkillers wear off. I really do think they're pleased enough with me and they should be letting me home tomorrow."

"Amen to that."

"Will I see you later?"

"Of course, I miss you like crazy. Even when I was recovering from my...um... celebrations, I missed you. Dave and I will have supper and then we'll come right down."

"Sounds like a plan. I'll send Cathy over so she can see Dave and eat with you both, then she and Dave can go on home to give them a break from baby-sitting the Camerons."

He smiled, even though she couldn't see him. "Okay, my love. Do you need anything brought to you?"

"No thank you, just you. Cathy's been great, doing what she can for me."

"I bet she has. See you later."

"Love you." She hung up and immediately texted Cathy the coast was clear to come back and when Cathy returned moments later, she looked expectantly at her friend.

"How is he?"

"Sounds sober and in good enough form. He's lying low until after dinner, then he's coming to see me. I would really like it for you to go eat with him and Dave and then you and Dave can go on home."

Cathy mulled over the idea but couldn't seem to come to a decision. "But I don't like the idea of leaving you."

"I know, chum, but really, I'm fine. You know how much I've been dozing on and off today because the painkillers are making me sleepy. I think I would benefit from a proper nap before he gets here."

Cathy mulled it over some more and then, reluctantly, nodded. "Okay, love, but only if you promise if you need me anytime, you'll phone me to come down."

"You know I will." Krista carefully pushed herself up again. She could only stay in one position for so long before she started hurting. "Get going now, if you want."

Cathy gathered up her belongings and leaned over to give Krista a gentle kiss on her forehead. "Love you chum, hope you get some good sleep. Call me after Paul has been to see you."

"I will."

When Cathy made it to Paul's apartment a short while later, Dave grabbed her at the door and held her in a tight hug. "*There* you are," he murmured into her ear, smelling her coconut shampoo as he closed his eyes and breathed her in. "Feel like I haven't seen you in ages."

"It's been a while," she agreed, melting in against his

solid frame. "Where's the alco?"

"He fell asleep, in the living room."

She turned towards the kitchen and was pleased to see there was a pot of coffee brewing. It smelled fresh and she poured them each a cup. "Krista still looks pretty awful but she's in good spirits. It was good news about the x-ray, she was worried she was going to be told she might need surgery on her cheekbone."

Wanting to keep the bodily contact with her, Dave reached across the table and clasped her hand. He listened intently as she filled him in on how her day at the hospital had gone and how Krista was doing. They were still quietly conversing when Paul appeared in the doorway a short while later and beamed a welcoming smile at Cathy.

"Hey little dude," he greeted and indulged in a jaw-breaking yawn. "You been here long?" He slid in beside Dave and helped himself to Dave's coffee that Cathy had topped up only moments before.

"About an hour. Your lovely wife practically threw me out, claimed she needed some sleep or some flimsy excuse like that."

He chuckled. "Yeah, I can just hear her say that. I can't wait to see her."

It was fast approaching five o'clock and Cathy hadn't had much to eat today. "Want me to make something or do we want to order in?"

Paul waited for a negative reaction from his stomach but when there wasn't one, he figured it would be safe to eat whatever he wanted. "Don't want you going to any bother, Cath, we can order in. Whatever you want, my treat."

"You planning on paying with pixie dust, partner?" Dave teased. "You cleaned out your wallet last night and you haven't gotten any cash out today. Plus, you still have the block on your account."

Paul rolled his eyes in derision. He pulled his cell phone out of his pocket, tapped on the app for his bank and unblocked his account. "I can pay over the phone when I make the order, no problem."

They were discussing what to order when there was a knock on the door and, because she was closest to it, Cathy answered it. She was surprised to see two uniformed police officers standing there, both of whom she recognized, even behind their masks. "Officer Williams, Officer Hernandez, what can I do for you?"

"Detective Andrews," Williams said, obviously just as surprised to see her as she was to see him. He was a tall, skinny, black guy, in his late thirties and from what Cathy could recall, his wife had just recently had a baby. But she refrained from asking about the baby until she knew why he and his partner were here.

"Detective Andrews," Hernandez greeted in his Boston accent. He was Latino and around his mid-twenties but he was as tall as his partner and double his weight. "Is Detective Cameron in?"

"Paul or Krista?"

"Paul."

"Sure, he's through here, come on in."

Dave and Paul looked up with the exact same expression of bewilderment when Williams and Hernandez entered the kitchen. The uniforms both stood awkwardly side by side, reluctant to talk, knowing they were about to drop a bombshell.

Cathy pushed past them, coming to a halt beside Dave. "Can I get you guys anything? Coffee or something?"

Williams shook his head. "No thanks, ma'am. We're… uh…we're here on official business."

Tension was mounting by the second and Paul narrowed his eyes as he looked from one officer to the other, trying to second guess what was going on. "Oh? And what might that be?"

Williams stole a glance at Hernandez, who nodded for him to go ahead. Pulling himself up to his full height of six foot five, Williams' face grew serious. "Detective Paul Cameron, we are arresting you on the suspicion of murder. If you could please stand so I can read you your rights."

The silence that followed was heavy and, at first, Paul thought Dave, or someone at the station, had set him up for a prank. This had to be a joke or a mistake, but even as Paul looked at Dave to see if he was behind this, his heart sank. Dave looked as genuinely stunned as Cathy did and Paul suddenly knew this was no joke, cruel or not, this was as real as it could get.

"On what charge did you say?" Dave asked quickly. "Suspicion of murder?"

Hernandez had the good grace to look like he couldn't believe his partner's words as he nodded in response to Dave's question. Williams was trying to retain his composure so he could Mirandize Paul but he was obviously uncomfortable doing it.

Taking in a deep breath, Williams tried again. "Paul Cameron, we are arresting you for the murder of Kenneth Cameron, formerly of Brooklyn, New York. You have the right to remain silent...."

And as Paul listened to the Miranda rights he had quoted on countless occasions, and could probably quote backwards if asked, he finally realized this was a genuine charge.

He was being arrested for the murder of his own father. He just didn't know how that could be.

# CHAPTER THIRTEEN

Paul had stood during the Miranda reading, he had listened dutifully and carefully, letting the officer do his job. But when Hernandez tried to turn him to put handcuffs on him, he took a step back, his palms raised in a back-off gesture.

"Wait, just wait a minute, you know there has to be a mistake here. I didn't kill my father. Last time I saw him, he was very much alive."

Dave stepped between Paul and Hernandez, his arms raised to keep the two men apart. "Officer Williams, Officer Hernandez, you know Paul's speaking the truth here. There has to be a mistake."

"No mistake," Officer Williams said, "we have an eye witness who said she saw Detective Cameron leave the scene at just before noon yesterday. The autopsy is still pending but the coroner has given the preliminary time of death to be recorded between eleven a.m. and two p.m. yesterday." Williams sounded as if he didn't believe a word of what he himself was saying but he was acting on instruction and had to perform his duties. He carried on relating what he knew. "The same eye witness gave a positive ID of you leaving your father's motel room after what sounded to her like a major fight. She also heard more than a few threats. She saw you get into a white Ford Mustang and she wrote down the license plate. It matches yours, Paul. Your father's body was discovered mid-morning today by the motel manager who was calling for Mr Cameron to settle his bill. It only wasn't discovered yesterday because the 'do not disturb' sign was on the door."

"So it's too early to state what the cause of death was?" Dave interrupted. If Williams stated the preliminary examination at the crime scene was a fatal gunshot wound, at least that would be easily proved it hadn't come from Paul's gun. However, what Williams said next chilled Dave to the bone.

"The coroner doesn't need a full examination or autopsy, it was obvious at the scene Mr Cameron had a broken neck. They will find the true cause of death only upon autopsy."

Williams shot Paul an apologetic glance. "But the most telling evidence was, your father was found with his hands in handcuffs. They were dusted at the scene and your fingerprints were all over them."

If Paul had been pale before, he was now ashen-faced and he sank blindly back onto his chair. "Dear God, I didn't even know I'd lost the cuffs."

Dave flicked him a glance to not say another word. "Yes, okay boys, it's very telling evidence. But it still doesn't prove Paul killed him."

Cathy hadn't said a word but had been listening quietly, trying to piece everything together and figure it all out. She couldn't find a solution but she also knew Williams and Hernandez had a job to do and she could feel the tension mounting. "Okay, let's take a second here. Paul is officially under arrest, you've done what you came here to do, guys. *But*, you know and I know, and we all know, he is innocent of the charges he's being arrested for."

"But we don't know that for sure," Hernandez said and immediately regretted his words. He couldn't meet Cathy's eyes as she glared at him.

"We'll pretend we didn't hear that," she said icily. "You guys go on back to the station and Dave and I will bring Paul down later."

Williams and Hernandez exchanged another look, one of uncertainty. "Er...you know we can't allow that, Detective Andrews."

She waved impatiently around the room. "We're all police officers here, we know the seriousness of this situation and we're not going to do anything to prevent Paul coming in for questioning. We're just asking for a bit of time so we can figure out what the hell has happened for him to have these charges brought against him."

It took nearly ten minutes of arguing and cajoling but finally Williams and Hernandez accepted they were on the losing team. After Cathy repeatedly swore that she would have Paul at the station by no later than eight o'clock that night, they reluctantly left. There were all kinds of rules being broken, but a blind man could have seen Paul had been completely floored by the charges.

When Dave closed the door behind them, he went back to the kitchen and stared at Paul and Cathy. For a few moments, none of them spoke; none of them knew what to say. Dave was absolutely furious but he needed to keep his temper in check for now. Paul needed him, not his anger.

"Well, there's nothing like an arrest to kill an appetite," Paul said shakily.

"This is ludicrous," Cathy declared, "there has to be a mistake, which means we have to find it and fix it."

Paul ran his fingers through his hair, trying to get his muddled thoughts into some sort of order that made sense. "I don't even know where to start. I think I'd like to go down to the station now, get this over and done with."

"You're not going anywhere," Dave announced.

"What choice do I have?"

"I'm not taking you anywhere until I can figure out a way to clear you of these bogus charges."

The look on Paul's face told Cathy he didn't want any favors or preferential treatment and she made a swift decision. "If you won't take him, Dave, then I will."

Dave whirled round to face her. "What did you just say?" he yelled.

"You heard me. If Paul doesn't answer to these murder charges, he'll be in even more trouble. One of us *has* to take him in so if you won't, it falls on me to do it."

"I can't arrest my own partner, Cathy, and neither can you."

"Neither of us has to, he's already under arrest. But he still has to go to the station." She turned to Paul and gave him a look of such love and sympathy, his heart broke for her. He knew she wasn't relishing what she had to do. "You ready, Paulie?" she asked softly.

He looked sadly at Dave, then back to her. "Sure, just let me get a pair of shoes and my jacket."

"Don't do this, Cathy," Dave seethed, "don't bring him in on these trumped up charges."

She stared stonily back at him. "I don't have any other choice. Instead of looking to incriminate me because I'm taking your partner in for questioning, why don't you try and get a hold of a lawyer for him? Something tells me no matter what we try to do for him, he's going to need one."

Paul re-entered the room holding his jacket and nodded at Dave. "She might be right. That lawyer you had at your trial with Guido Andretti a couple of years ago, I heard he's now doing criminal defense law. Ted Reynolds, was that his name?"

Dave couldn't take his eyes off Cathy and his bitterness and disappointment in her were evident in the deep blue of his eyes. "I'll look him up," he said tersely, and then, with one last look of disgust at her, he grabbed his cell phone and went into the living room to start making calls.

Paul followed Cathy to her car but before she could start the engine, he put his hand on hers to stop her. "You're doing the right thing, little dude. Don't let Dave bully you into thinking you're wrong."

She chuckled at his remark. "He's never been able to bully me before. Don't worry about how he's acting towards me, I've had worse from him. He's just defending you and I can't blame him for that."

"Maybe, but I don't want this to cause a rift between you."

"It won't. I know he's angry, and in shock, and more

than a little scared, too. He'll calm down soon enough." She glanced at the clock on the dashboard and saw it was fast approaching six o'clock. "I promised I would have you at the station by no later than eight so we'd better get moving, we have a lot to do in the meantime."

Paul looked at her quizzically, furrowing his brow. "Like what?"

"You'll find out. Trust me." Cathy's first stop totally surprised him. She pulled into the hospital, stopping directly outside the main entrance. "You wanted to see Krista, so go on and see her. It's up to you to tell her what you've been charged with but you've only got fifteen minutes so make the most of it. I'll wait right here for you and if security asks me to move, I'll flash them my badge."

"You're not coming in with me?"

"Not this time. Fifteen minutes, Paul, make them count."

He tipped her a wink and got out of the car. He hurried up to Krista's room, pulling on his mask just before he entered. He knew she would be able to tell he was smiling by looking at his eyes but Krista was sleeping and the smile disappeared as he sat down beside her. He couldn't help examining her bruises again, feeling his insides churn and his temper start to bubble. He had to remind himself there was nothing he could do for her, bruises had to heal on their own.

Remembering he only had fifteen minutes, he picked up her hand and stroked it gently. "Krista?" he asked reluctantly. "Sweetheart, can you hear me?"

She had only been dozing and at the sound of her name, she woke up with a start. "Paul, hi," she said sleepily, a smile spreading slowly across her face.

"Hi to you too, baby. How are you?"

"Fine, just don't make me laugh." She looked into his eyes and her smile faltered. "You look tired, you okay?"

"Still just a big hungover. I'm fine, only myself to blame." He continued stroking her hand, grateful he could touch her. "Sorry I haven't made it in to see you before this."

"It's okay, you're here now." Her eyes hadn't left his and she suddenly frowned. "What is it you're hiding from me?"

"Huh?" He had forgotten she could read him like a book but he didn't want to have to tell her the truth. Not just yet. He wanted to crawl into bed beside her, snuggle down and hold her gently in his arms while she fell asleep. He needed bodily contact with her but he knew he wasn't going to get more than holding her hand. He tried to smile again but he couldn't quite make it. He cleared his throat. "I'm not hiding anything."

"Yes you are. There's something wrong, something more than just a hangover."

He knew he was trapped, there was no way he would be able to talk his way out of this one. If he tried to laugh it off, she would know. If he flat out lied, she would still know. On the other hand, telling her what had happened would upset her deeply and he didn't want to do that to her. But she was staring at him expectantly - and he was also mindful of the fifteen minutes he had with her, now reduced to ten minutes.

He brought her hand up to his covered mouth and kissed it. "Krista, I love you so much, you know that, right?"

There was a strange light in his eyes that she caught immediately and she pulled back slightly so she could get a better look at him. "Of course I know, just as you know I love you."

"I do." He wanted time to freeze right at this moment, make it stay where it was for a long time so he could continue to hold her hand and look into her startling green eyes. "You are so beautiful, even now with your injuries you are still the most beautiful woman I know. And... and...well...you know I wouldn't hurt you or worry you unnecessarily for the world. You know I would sooner hurt myself than cause you harm and yet I'm about to do just that. The worst of it is, I didn't know this was going to happen, and as soon as I tell you, I'm going to have to leave you. I won't be able to stay around and comfort you."

His voice had started to break and she was alarmed to

see tears in his eyes. Tears that started her own. "Paul, you're scaring me here. What's wrong?"

"I'm sorry, Krista, so very sorry. Cathy's waiting for me out in the parking lot. She wanted me to come talk to you so you would hear it from me and not from anyone else. It's just, you see, well, it's like this. I've been charged with my father's murder."

Shocked silence followed after his softly spoken words and she searched his eyes for some hint of a joke. Something, anything other than the truth she could see in his eyes. A low moan escaped from her throat and she tightened her hold on his hand. "That's not funny," she said bluntly. "What's really wrong?"

It was a futile question and she knew it but she would take anything from him other than what he had just said.

"That's really it, baby. Apparently there was an eye witness when I was at the motel yesterday, cheerfully beating up my father. The eye witness got my license plate, which is how they found me. But the worst is..." His voice faltered again and he swallowed audibly. "The worst is, sometime during my fight, my handcuffs must have come off my belt because when they found his body, they were on his wrists."

Krista's eyes widened in horror. She had arrested, and gotten convictions for, many a guilty person on far less evidence. Her coping mechanism, one of the strongest points she had, kicked in and she pulled back the cover. "Okay, I'm getting out of this hospital bed and coming with you to the station. You're not going through this without me."

He stopped her before she could even swing her legs over the side of the bed. "You're going nowhere, Kris, I mean it. I appreciate your gesture but I really don't think I could cope if I'm in a cell worrying about you and how you're feeling. Please baby, please, just stay here."

She tried to push past him but he wouldn't let her and, her injuries getting the better of her, she sank back against the pillow. "This is awful," she said angrily, "I can't even support my own husband when he's been wrongfully arrested. I'm totally useless!"

"Hey, hey," he chastised softly. "You're supporting me by staying right here, okay? Cathy's bringing me to the station and we'll take it from there. If they let me out tonight, I'll drop by again and tell you there's been some awful mistake."

"Are they at least working on getting you a lawyer?"

"Yeah, Dave said he would."

She digested this horrid pile of information and took in a shaky breath. "Oh my, this is for real, isn't it?"

He nodded miserably. "I'm afraid so."

She couldn't help it, she started to sob, but she was worried, and scared and terribly upset. But it hurt her damaged ribs to sob and she battled to calm down and just about managed to stop crying and return her breathing to a more normal, less painful pace.

He knew he had to leave and she knew it too but it didn't stop them from holding on to each other as if their lives' depended on it. Very reluctantly, he stood up and, tearing his mask off, he gave her lips a slow, loving kiss. "I love you, sweetface, I just do," he murmured as he gently wiped away her tears. "I will see you soon."

She nodded, her eyes brimming as she watched him go towards the door and when he turned back for one last look, she blew him a kiss. When she heard the last of his footsteps echo away along the corridor, she started to cry again and this time, she ignored her abdominal pain. The pain in her heart was far worse.

# CHAPTER FOURTEEN

Cathy was waiting for him exactly where she'd dropped him off and when she saw him coming towards her, she leaned over and opened the door for him. She could tell by looking at him he was upset and she squeezed his hand briefly. "You were exactly fifteen minutes," she congratulated him. "How did she take it?"

"You knew I was going to tell her?"

"I wasn't sure, but I can tell by looking at you that you did."

He looked moodily out the window as he waited for Cathy to start the engine and move on. "Yeah, I told her and it was probably the worst thing I've ever had to say to her, especially when I knew I couldn't stay and comfort her. She was upset, naturally, and wanted to leave to come with me."

Cathy clicked her tongue in sympathy. "I'll come see her after we finish at the station. If, in all likelihood you're allowed home tonight, you can come see her yourself and I'll leave you two to have your quiet time. I'll see her tomorrow." She put the car in gear and at the hospital exit, she turned left, not right as he had expected if they were going to the station.

"Where are we going?" he asked.

"My favorite place, where else?"

Which meant they were going to the beach. "Why?"

"So we can talk...*really* talk, strictly off the record." A short time later, when she pulled into a parking lot overlooking the ocean, she turned the engine off and looked over the inky expanse of angry water. It was fully dark, overcast, freezing cold and a wind was picking up; there was just enough light to see the beach. "You want to stay in the car or do you want to go for a walk?"

He considered for a moment. "Let's just stay here, at least there's heat in the car."

"As you wish." She half-turned towards him. They were parked close to an overhead light and she could see his face clearly. "Okay, Paul, before we do the off the record stuff, I'm going to ask you one question in my capacity as an officer of the law *on* the record."

He nodded expectantly, already knowing the question before she asked it. "Sure, ask away."

"Did you kill your father?"

He sighed, almost as if in relief, glad someone had asked it so he could answer truthfully. Then he gave a short, sharp laugh. "No, Detective Andrews, I did not."

"Then that's good enough for me. Anything between us now is *off* the record. I know I will believe everything you tell me and, with your permission, I can use your words on your behalf when, or if, this goes to trial."

"But you're not the one I have to convince, Cathy. The evidence Williams and Hernandez told us about might just be enough to put me behind bars for a very long time. Massachusetts doesn't molly coddle murderers. You know that."

"We will find what we have to, to make the charges go away. You will have the full support of the whole 7th precinct behind you. Captain Hamilton will move heaven and earth to keep you out of jail. You certainly know Dave and I will and Krista too when she gets back on her feet."

He turned towards her so he could see her better and the first thing he noticed was the determination on her face. He had heard it in her voice, too, and he knew she meant every word. He took her hand and folded it inside his. "Thank you for everything you're trying to do for me Cathy, not just by being on my side but by giving me those few minutes with Krista. I appreciate that more than you'll ever know."

"I'm not doing it for your thanks, Paul, I'm just trying to figure out some stuff so I know I can go into this knowing everything there is to know."

Paul tilted his head quizzically. "Stuff like what?"

"Well, for starters, just how awful was it growing up with a monster like that?"

"If I tell you, that would give me a motive."

"It won't take much for them to find out what I've just asked. You know they're going to be digging deep into your past. I asked because my stepfather was no angel, my childhood certainly not one to write home about after he came into it, but to have someone like *your* father? I can't even begin to imagine. With the terrible fathers we each had, I might be able to identify better with you than Dave or Krista could and therefore will be able to help you more simply by understanding."

He stared out at the restless, rolling waves, watching the surf kicking up with the steadily rising wind. He seemed pensive and she waited patiently for him to start talking. "Over the years since we've known each other, I've always been forthcoming about my childhood. I don't need to go into detail because I've told you in some form or another just how evil that man is...*was*. But I believe the question was, 'just how awful was it growing up with a monster like that?'. The short answer is, it was awful in ways you couldn't imagine. I knew from a young age there was something...different...about my family. Anytime I wanted to escape his abuse, the household I always went to was a home full of love and nurture and happiness. Loving parents, close siblings, no alcoholism, no drugs, just a steady, safe environment. That's how I knew how awful my own childhood was."

As she listened to him, her gaze softened. "This reminds me of when I told you about my family the first time. We were in different circumstances maybe but I'm getting the same feeling I got when I told you - a feeling that means I'm about to share a deep secret with a very dear, close friend. Does that make any sense?"

He nodded wordlessly and settled his gaze on the ocean

again. It had been nearly two years since Cathy had told him about her malicious, cruel stepfather. The different circumstances she had referred to had certainly been different in the effect of trying to stay alive after being kidnapped and chained in a cave near Burlington, Vermont. The story of her upbringing had been horrific, her need to tell it great, his need to comfort her greater. And he had comforted her all right, with a deep, passionate kiss that had led to another, and then another, until they couldn't stop their rising passion and had very nearly made love. The very second before he took her, they had come to their senses and halted themselves before it went any further.

But their easy going friendship had changed dramatically after that near disaster. For a long time afterwards, although they had each tried to pretend otherwise, they were uncomfortable in one another's company. They didn't like being left alone together and had only really become close and completely relaxed with one another again when they had been keeping vigil at Dave's bedside when he'd been in the coma.

It was amazing how a crisis brought people together again but Paul had often wondered that if Dave hadn't been so close to death, if life had gone on as normal, would he and Cathy have regained their friendship again naturally, through time? Or would they have continued to go through the motions of being close friends when in truth they were drifting further and further apart?

"I often think about that time," Paul said suddenly, breaking the easy silence that had descended upon them. "That one time with you that I will never, ever forget. When I can't sleep at night, when I'm killing time during a stakeout, when I'm standing in line at the grocery store, I think about that time with you. Do you?"

Cathy knew only too well what he was referring to and she felt her heart quicken in her chest. "I don't allow myself to think about it too often," she confessed softly.

"Why not?"

"Because I'd rather keep it in a special place inside my memories. When I *do* think about it, it's often with great sadness. How much we could have lost had we completed the act."

He knew what she meant and he understood why she would feel like that. "Does Dave ever mention it to you?"

"Not once. I tried to talk to him about it not that long ago, after we came back from Belfast. He just kissed me, hugged me and told me to keep it all in the past because that's where it belongs. He was so indifferent about it, sometimes I have to wonder why. He's the one who was effected the most by it after all, he's the one who wanted to end everything between him and me and you and your partnership. It was pretty scary for a while, not knowing if he was ever going to be able to forgive us."

"He's nothing if not a fair man, Cathy. He knew it would never have been repeated, he also knew it wouldn't have happened if we hadn't been forced into that situation, it just took him a while to realize that. Krista doesn't talk about it either, and not because she doesn't want to, but more because she feels it's a waste of time and energy to talk about something that was just one of those unexplainable events."

"That sounds just like Krista." She gave him a very sad smile. "It was still very nice though. As wrong as it was, the kiss, the feel of your hands on me, the way you made my whole body tingle even though we were both starving to death, it was pretty amazing."

He squeezed her hand tighter and the atmosphere between them shifted slightly. Neither of them seemed to know how to interpret these new vibes and, in the end, he reached up and gently traced the outline of her lips. "It was pretty amazing," he agreed. "And at least we know we won't repeat it anytime soon. If ever."

The atmosphere shifted back to something near normal and she smiled again. "You did well to take the focus of you and your arrest there, Paulie," she scolded gently.

"I did, didn't I?" he teased proudly. He returned her smile but then he grew serious again. He wanted to be entirely honest with her in the hope they would both be able to put this to rest completely. "You know, you're a very special lady and for that, you will always hold a very special place in my heart. I know that if I wasn't involved with Krista, or you with Dave, you and I would be together. You would be the woman I would want to spend the rest of my life with because you are awful easy to love."

Cathy shivered slightly at his words but she knew what he meant. Their lives had been constantly intertwined for closing in on five years. They had shared a lot in that time, both professionally and privately and it was hard sometimes for her to remember Paul was just a friend and not an extension of her own being. They loved one another deeply and loyally and not in any other way.

"You're very special to me too, Paul. I would be lost without you in my life." And she would be, of that she had no doubt. But now there was a shadow hanging over them. Paul was in big trouble, arrested for a murder he didn't commit and, if he was convicted, he would be exiled from her life after all. Cathy didn't want that to happen, this was Paul, her special friend, the same Paul who teased her with one breath and said something kind with the next, who loved to introduce to strangers Krista as his wife and her as his girlfriend, just to get a shocked reaction. He could brighten up a gloomy day in the office, he held her hand and sympathized with her when she and Dave had had a particularly harsh argument. And he could make her laugh with a few carefully chosen words when she was feeling low. She would miss him for all that and a whole lot more. Not to mention Krista would be devastated and Dave would be destroyed. At that moment, she made a solemn, silent vow that she would do everything she could to get the charges against him dropped.

Cathy's thoughts were interrupted by the crackling of her police radio and seconds later, Dave's voice came over the airwaves. She wondered why he was using an open band instead of her cell phone, or Paul's, but then she remembered she had turned hers off and Paul might not even have his with him.

"Paul, Cathy, either one of you two out there?"

"He said your name first," Cathy stated, "go ahead and talk to him."

Paul picked up the mike. "Yo, Dave."

"Paul, where the hell are you?"

"In Cathy's car."

"I know that, you answered the radio. But *where* are you? You know what? Never mind, when will you be down here?"

"Here as in at the station? By eight o'clock, just as we promised. What have you got for me?"

"Your lawyer is on his way. Would be nice if you could be here when he arrives."

"Ted Reynolds?"

"The one and only. He's anxious to get talking to you, so is Captain Hamilton. He wants to know how you've gotten yourself into this mess."

"You know the answer to that one as well as I do, Dave." Paul shot a glance at Cathy. She was staring out the window but he knew she was listening to every word. "Hey, Cathy's here too, you still mad at her for nothing or do you want to talk to her?"

"I know she can hear me. I'll see her when she gets here. In fact, I'll see you both when you get here. Over and out."

Paul replaced the mike on its holder and patted her knee. "He sure knows how to be a jerk."

Cathy clicked her tongue in wry amusement. "I'm not going to disagree with you. I don't care about his tantrums right now, it's you I'm concerned about. I'm very scared for you and if this is the way *I'm* feeling, God alone knows how you're feeling. As I was listening to you talking to him I couldn't help thinking how can you seem so calm?"

"You think I'm calm? Actually, I'm nowhere near it, I'm scared out of my mind. I even told Krista as much, although

I wish now I hadn't." He held his quivering right hand out in front of him to show her he was shaking. "That's not got anything to do with the alcohol I consumed either, that's pure fear making that mother shake."

"Are you upset that your father's dead?"

"How could I be upset? I never made it a secret about the way I feel about that man and, although I'm not exactly overjoyed he's dead, I know I'm relieved, *greatly* relieved. I really can rest assured now knowing he's never going to get his filthy paws on Krista ever again. No matter what's going to come of this charge against me, if I'm going to be locked away, I'll rest easier knowing she'll never be subjected to violence like that from him ever again."

Cathy ran her fingers through her hair in frustration. "This is absolutely insane, Paul, I can't believe we're sitting here calmly discussing a murder charge brought against you."

"Most of my life has been insane in one way or another. Man, some of the things I could tell you would piss off the pope. Like the time my father held my sister under a freezing cold shower, in our freezing cold apartment, on a freezing cold night during a freezing cold winter. The poor girl came down with double pneumonia after that particular episode. Then there was the time..." Paul's tongue seemed to have been magically loosened, or maybe he had just decided to relate a few choice childhood tales. But whatever it was, he simply started talking, telling Cathy stories that saddened and sickened her. He repeated them as easily as if he had been reading from a storybook, and he certainly wasn't going to allow her to shed any tears for him. Anytime her tears threatened, he shook his head and put a finger to her lips to shush her.

On and on he talked and neither of them noticed they had gone past the eight o'clock deadline. Cathy was so engrossed in what she was hearing she wouldn't even remember switching off her radio, she just wanted to listen. She knew she couldn't do anything to erase these very real events from his past for him, she even knew that talking about them wasn't necessarily going to make him feel better. This wasn't a confession, it was just him trying to ease his burden, but it was enough that she was there to listen and when he seemed to be all talked out, with a gentle smile of love and understanding, she pulled him towards her and held him close for a long moment.

"Now you know why I can't get upset over my father's death," he murmured. "I hope he's already burning in hell."

"That's pretty much a given, love."

"You were very sweet for listening, Cath, thank you." He pulled back so he could look into her eyes. "I told you a couple of things there Krista doesn't even know about. Dave does though, he knows just about everything. And he listened when I told him and didn't try to pass judgement either, just the same as you. Between the two of you, I've managed to lay to rest some pretty painful memories. And with friends like you, I think I'm the luckiest guy on earth."

"That's the way we feel too, about you and Krista."

He reached out and buffed her cheek. "Then all four of us are lucky." He turned to face the ocean again and as he did so, he caught the time on the dashboard clock. "Jesus Christ, it's eight forty! We were supposed to be at the station forty minutes ago! We're *both* in shit now."

Reality was now upon them and with a soft sigh, Cathy started the car. While waiting for it to warm up, she leaned over and hugged him close. "You ready for this?" she asked hoarsely.

"As I'll ever be."

As she pulled away moments later, she knew this was it. There was no turning back now.

# CHAPTER FIFTEEN

Dave watched grimly as Cathy led Paul into the interview room. They were over an hour late and he was angry they had kept everyone waiting. Ted Reynolds had been pretty decent about it, as had Captain Hamilton. But Dave knew his superior would be looking for an explanation.

Dave curled his lip in contempt when he saw Cathy holding her handcuffs in her left hand. He didn't know if she'd used them on Paul and had escorted him in from the parking lot like that or if she was just holding them for effect.

"What took you so long?" he snapped.

"Cathy and I got to talking is all," Paul said as he sat down on one side of the interview table. He had been in this one numerous times since working at the 7th precinct and he knew the viewing room on the other side of the two-way mirror was large enough for four or five people. "She's very easy to talk to, as you well know, she had me spilling my guts in no time. And if you're still pissed with her because she's agreeing to the arrest, I want you to go home and calm down. I'm with her all the way on this one."

Cathy eyed Dave coolly. She wasn't intimidated by his anger and she shrugged indifferently. "Leave it, Paul," she said softly, "he'll want to be here and it's only fair he should be." She looked in the direction of the two-way mirror. "Who all's going to be here?"

Dave swallowed his displeasure at having to speak to her. This was official police business now and he would have to treat it as such. "Ted and Captain Hamilton are there, along with a Union rep and someone from Internal Affairs. Ted insisted on you having the appropriate representation while the questioning takes place."

"Who's doing the questioning?" Paul asked.

"I wanted to," Dave said, "but Ted said no, as your partner it wouldn't be appropriate. Conflict of interest. He wants someone less biased. Only problem is, everyone here is going to be biased so we asked for volunteers who could remain impartial. Detective Turner and Detective Chipman put forth their names and they're on their way in now."

Paul hid his surprise at hearing two of his closest friends would be conducting the interview. He wondered if the captain had been instrumental in getting him two experienced officers he could be comfortable with, rather than speak to someone he didn't know or who didn't know him as well. "At least I know Jim and Mark can do an interview that will disclose everything that needs to be disclosed."

"Captain Hamilton and I will be on the other side," Dave stated. "Your IAB and Union rep will be in here with you with, of course, Ted." He turned to include Cathy in this. "You can be wherever you want, it's up to you."

She didn't detect any softening towards her at that remark, but then again, she didn't detect any animosity either. "I think I'd like to be with you and the captain."

"Suit yourself." Dave glanced up when the door was opened and in walked Jim Turner and Mark Chipman. "Hey, guys, thanks for coming down."

Jim and Mark didn't have to say anything, their wish to support their friend and get justice back on track was evident in the way they were looking at Paul. In a less serious situation, they would have started the ribbing immediately upon arrival but they knew everything from this point forward had to be done by the book. They each looked bemused, unable to comprehend their friend and colleague, a man they had worked alongside for several years, whom they trusted with their own lives, had been arrested for murder.

Paul gave them an encouraging smile. "It's okay, guys, really. You have a job to do and my lawyer is already here, as are

IAB and a Union rep."

Jim and Mark were even tempered and as close to each other as Paul and Dave were, both as partners and friends. Jim was the older of the two, by about five years and he was usually the one who did most of the talking. This time, however, he seemed too upset and only gave monosyllabic responses as he struggled to get his head around this surreal event.

The door opened again and in came Captain Hamilton and Ted Reynolds. In the three years since Paul had seen Reynolds, he hadn't changed much, other than a more modern hairstyle and a more expensive suit.

"Paul, good to see you again," he said, "I'd shake your hand but we know I can't. I can say I'm sorry I'm here under these circumstances.

"Good to see you too, Ted, thanks for agreeing to take my case. Have you had the chance to look over the charges?"

"I have and I'm sorry to say that after reading the witness' report, there really is a lot of incriminating evidence against you."

Paul nodded glumly. "So I've gathered."

Captain Hamilton, as the superior officer, commanded their attention and he came and stood directly opposite Paul. He gestured for him to remain sitting. "I want to believe you're innocent Paul. I really do, which is why I'm going to ask you one question. Then I'll hand the questioning over to Detectives Turner and Chipman, with your rep, IAB and Ted here. This is on the record so make your answers count. You've never lied to me before but that doesn't mean I won't know if you're lying to me now, so for your own good, tell me the truth. Did you kill your father?"

"I've already answered that one to Cathy."

"I'm not asking her, I'm asking you. Just tell me the truth."

"I'll tell the truth, with all of you in this room and on the other side of the mirror as my witnesses, I did *not* kill my father."

Captain Hamilton nodded at the mirror, which was the cue for the official reps to come in. Then he, Dave and Cathy retreated to the room on the other side and made themselves comfortable to watch the proceedings. While waiting for Mark to set up and test the camera and recording equipment, Cathy sent Krista a quick text to let her know the interview was underway and she would contact her again when it was over.

Jim Turner, as was usual when he and Mark Chipman conducted an interview, made the formal announcement the interview had started at nine thirty pm on Tuesday December 8th 2020. He recited the names of those present, remembering to include the new protocol stating everyone was wearing a mask and practicing social distancing, asked Paul if he understood the seriousness of the charges against him and turned to Mark to take over. They had already been briefed by Dave, via a lengthy conference call, on the facts and circumstances so they would know what to ask him. Paul knew their style and wasn't concerned they were going to ask him misleading questions to try and trip him up.

"Paul, you have stated you did not kill your father."

"Correct."

"But you were at the Blue Moon motel on the day in question, namely Monday December seventh, 2020?"

"Yes."

"At what time were you there?"

"I'm not sure exactly, around eleven fifteen, maybe eleven thirty in the morning, give or take."

"And what did you go to the motel for?"

"To see my father, to seek retribution for what he did to my wife."

Mark knew what he was referring to and turned to Jim, indicating it was time for him to take over the questioning. "What do you mean by 'to seek retribution'?"

Paul glanced at Ted, checking it would be okay to answer. Ted nodded it was. "He had beaten my wife up pretty badly, she's currently still in hospital recovering from injuries he inflicted on her. He had also stolen personal items from our home, including our car titles and jewelry. I couldn't let him get away with it."

"Did you go to the motel intending to harm your father?"

Again, Paul looked at Ted for guidance. Ted shook his head and spoke for the first time. "Rephrase the question please, Detective Turner."

"Okay. Did you know what was going to happen when you got to the motel?"

"Of course not. I didn't even know if he would still be there. He might have checked out or fled town. My partner, Detective Dave Andrews, had a BOLO out on him and his car."

Jim looked down at the notes he had scribbled when he'd been on the phone with Dave. He asked the next question in a way it wouldn't harm Paul's case. "Is it safe to assume you did beat your father up?"

"Yes. I beat him up and then left. But he was very much alive when I left him. He was breathing and moving."

"Did you handcuff your father?"

"I did not."

"So can you explain your police issue handcuffs being found on your father's body?"

"I can't, other than I knew I would have had them on me as I always do, before I even thought about going to the motel. During the struggle with him, they must have been ripped from the loop on my jeans."

"Will you be able to produce the jeans to see if there was a ripped belt loop on them?"

"If there is someone with me, we can go through my closet."

In the other room, Dave leaned over towards Captain Hamilton. "I can tell you right now he'll be able to. I did his laundry this morning and the jeans he was wearing had a torn belt loop."

"Good to know. Make sure they're produced as evidence."

It was Mark's turn again to take over the questioning. "Were you able to recover the items your father stole from your apartment?"

"Yes. He had also taken my wife's wedding rings - right off her finger as she lay unconscious after him beating her up - and I was able to recover them, too."

"How long were you with your father?"

"I'm not sure to the minute but it would have been about ten to fifteen minutes."

"Did he give you any explanation as to why he stole your personal items?"

"He said he was in trouble with some family from somewhere. He didn't say where the family was from but I assumed Brooklyn, where he's from. He was under the impression they had found out he'd been hiding out here in Bathville and were coming after him."

"Did he explain what kind of trouble?"

"That he owed them money. Around thirty five thousand dollars but he didn't say what for."

Attorney Ted Reynolds' face retained a bland, professional demeanor but his mind recognized the first opening for a defense. Paul had just introduced a potential suspect and provided a motive. Cathy, Dave and Captain Hamilton also sat up a little straighter in their seats. Paul had omitted to mention this to either one of them, purely by accident they were sure. His senses had been foggy most of the day because of the booze he'd consumed and everything after that had happened too quickly for him to be able to pull it all together.

Reynolds cleared his throat and addressed the Union rep and the IA officer. "I think we can end the questioning at this point. Detective Cameron has stated his father was alive when he left him and has also, unprompted, thrown in reasonable doubt as to being the only suspect. There seems to be at least one other potential suspect, if not an entire family of them, and in light of that I think we should have the charges against Detective Cameron dropped."

Seymour Wendell, a proud black man and a thirty year veteran in the Bathville Police Department Internal Affairs, mulled over everything he'd just heard. He knew Paul well, and liked him too, but he had no choice but to deny the request. "Unfortunately, Mr Reynolds, we can't agree to that. Detective Cameron has been arrested, for murder. We don't have the authority to drop any charges. Until we get further evidence proving Detective Cameron's innocence, he will have to remain under arrest."

Paul looked steadily at Jim and Mark. He was reading their body language and every twitch of their face or jerk of a muscle told him they were ready to end this farce and release him. Wendell's words, although they stung, were nonetheless words they couldn't ignore.

"Do we need to continue with the line of questioning? Don't we have enough?" Jim asked.

Wendell considered for a moment. "It's getting late. We have enough. Paul is to be arraigned tomorrow morning, hopefully the judge will see sense and drop the charges."

Mark Chipman leaned over to the recorder. "Interview terminated at nine fifty seven pm." He switched it and the camera off and leaned back in his chair. "Man, this sucks. Paul, you know we're on your side on this one."

"Of course, Chips. Thank you both for making this as painless for me as possible."

"We'll have the transcript for this interview ready for your arraignment tomorrow, in case your lawyer needs it," Jim said. He gave Paul a soft look of support and, feeling himself becoming upset, he hurriedly followed Mark out.

Ted Reynolds waited for Wendell and the Union rep to leave and, moments later, Dave, Cathy and Captain Hamilton came back into the room. "How much longer were you going to keep it a secret about someone coming after your father to get their money back?" Dave asked.

Paul shook his head. "I wasn't keeping it a secret, I just

didn't think about it until just now. Is it enough to keep me out of a cell tonight?"

Ted and the captain shared a silent communication and then Ted sadly shook his head. "I'm sorry, Paul, as Mr Wendell said, you're still under arrest. You'll have to be put in a holding cell until court tomorrow."

As Paul started to protest, Dave turned towards Captain Hamilton. "Come on, Cap, let him go home. He doesn't need to stay here. You know he'll be at the courthouse tomorrow first thing, it's not like he's going to flee the state – or even the country."

Captain Hamilton closed his eyes in sorrow. "I wish I could say yes, Dave, truthfully I do. But rules are rules and we can't be seen showing favor to a murder suspect just because he's a cop. Police all over the country are being blamed for getting preferential treatment on crimes a blind man could see they actually committed and I don't want to raise any suspicion here."

"Rules are made to be broken, Bob, come on!"

"It's okay, partner," Paul interrupted. "I'll go wherever's expected of me. I've been wondering how comfortable holding is since they did all those renovations six months ago. The bunks look nice and…um…supportive if you have some sort of chronic back pain." He looked up at Ted Reynolds. "I trust I'll see you at the courthouse tomorrow?"

"No, I'll be here first thing, around eight o'clock. I'll bring you something for breakfast and some decent coffee. I was subjected to what you try to pass off as coffee in here earlier and bringing you something nice is the least I can do." He gathered up his things, snapped his briefcase closed and bade his farewell.

Dave, knowing he had lost this battle, tried to remain calm, for Paul's sake. "I'll bring your suit, tie, shirt, and so on, in the morning, Paul. If you think of anything else, let me know."

"And I'll see Krista, keep her updated as much as possible," Cathy offered.

"Aren't I allowed my phone call? Can I phone her and tell her myself?" Paul asked.

Captain Hamilton didn't even hesitate as he took out his cell and selected Krista's number from his contacts list. When she answered, he passed the phone over to Paul and indicated to Dave and Cathy to follow him out of the room to give Paul some privacy.

Out in the corridor, Dave turned to Cathy. "When you were with him all that time, did you get something to eat?"

"No, didn't have time."

"Are you going to process him?"

It had never occurred to her and Cathy could only shrug. "I will if he wants me to."

Dave set his lips in a thin, grim line. "Laying it on thick, aren't you?"

"Excuse me?"

"You support the arrest, you bring him in for interrogation and now you're going to process him? Some friend you are."

The captain rolled his eyes. He had witnessed many a flare between Dave and Cathy over the years so he was used to them. But that didn't mean he wanted to listen to them. "Enough, Dave, I've been sensing this hostility between the two of you and I'm done with it. Go get Paul some food. Cathy, go ahead and process him and when you're done, come up to my office. There's something I need to talk to you about."

Her eyes opened in mild surprise. "Sure."

Dave threw her a wilting look and then stormed off. Captain Hamilton waited a few minutes and then went into Paul to retrieve his phone. "Sorry, Paul," he said kindly, knowing he'd cut a personal phone call short. "Dave's gone to get you something to eat, Cathy's going to process you right now and then we'll call it a night. I really am sorry about this but hopefully it can all be sorted out at your arraignment."

Paul was too emotional after the teary conversation he'd just had with Krista but he managed to nod his understanding and when Cathy came in seconds later, he stood up.

"Do I have to put the bracelets on him, captain?" she asked. She sincerely hoped the captain wouldn't be too strict at this stage of the game and she didn't want to put Paul through any more humiliation.

"Not necessary. Get done what you need to get done and then come up to my office."

"Can I forgo the strip search and the body cavity search?"

The captain knew she had to be teasing and he gave her a brief smile. "Again, not necessary. See you tomorrow morning, Paul."

Cathy took hold of Paul's arm and went through the motions of escorting him to the room on the ground floor reserved solely for processing. As a police officer, Paul's fingerprints were already on file but he insisted she take them to keep his arrest file separate from his work file.

Her hand was shaking as she placed his right thumb then his right fingers on the scanner and when she repeated the action for his left hand, she was visibly holding back tears. The photographer was waiting to take Paul's mug shot and at first he thought it was a joke. How could one of their own be getting processed? But one look at Paul, then at Cathy and he knew it was no joke.

After relinquishing his wallet, change, watch, belt and shoelaces, Cathy meticulously recorded everything down to the last dime. She then took him downstairs to the holding cells. She stopped first to talk to the sergeant on duty to see if they could get a cell furthest from the doorway and window; in other words, away from prying eyes.

These particular cells didn't have bars anymore. There was a row of six cells, all made from steel and individual doors. There was a small window made of safety glass on each door. The lock on the door was a heavy duty steel bolt and only the sergeant on duty had the key to it. The door itself locked as soon as it was closed behind the prisoner. In the event of a fire or other emergency, the sergeant was trained to open the doors and remove the prisoners as swiftly as possible. They couldn't be opened any other way.

Luckily, only one other cell was occupied tonight and the sole prisoner was leaning against the window, staring drunkenly into the hall. He blinked sleepily when he saw the man and woman appear and turned disinterestedly away.

Once Paul was inside, she leaned against the door to keep it open. "Well, this is it. This just isn't right. I know you've heard it a lot but I really am so very sorry, Paul."

He gave a brief glance around the six by eight room and turned to her. "Hey, little dude, it's fine. Thank you for making this easy for me."

She checked the cell and saw there was a single bed bolted to the wall, already made up, a hand towel, a bar of soap, a roll of toilet paper, a tiny sink, a toilet and a privacy curtain. "I'll make sure Dave brings your razor and so forth tomorrow." She grabbed a hold of his hand. "How was Krista?"

"Upset," he said with an unhappy shrug of his shoulders. "I told her you would see her in the morning, but she was crying all the way through the call so I don't know if she actually heard me or not. I was the cause of her tears and I felt so bad."

"I'll give her a call when I get home."

"No, let her try and get some sleep. I told her I would ask you to not phone her. It will be late before you make it home."

She nodded slowly. And then, pulling him into her arms, she hugged him as tightly as she could. "Good night, Paul. I love you to bits."

"Good night, Cathy. I love you too."

She reluctantly released him and when she stepped back, the door slammed shut. She turned to the sergeant on duty, who was trying to be discreet but was obviously waiting to hear what was happening. "Detective Dave Andrews is bringing Detective Cameron something to eat, he should be here soon. Please allow him entry."

"I will, Detective Andrews. I heard what he's been charged with and, for what it's worth, I don't believe it for one minute."

"Thanks, Ryan, that means a lot." She hurried away before she lost it completely and by the time she made it to the captain's office, she was in control again. She sat down in front of the captain's desk and waited for him to acknowledge her presence, which he did a moment later.

He looked troubled and she felt the first finger of unease trickle down her spine. "What is it you wanted to talk to me about?" she asked uncertainly.

His next words took her completely by surprise. "I have been asked by the commissioner to look into your conduct today."

"My conduct? About what?"

"About how you have handled Paul's arrest. I'm sorry, Detective Andrews, but he has voiced concerns that you handled the arrest with gross incompetence. You overrode the arresting officers for no clear reason, you promised you would have Paul here by eight o'clock and you were over an hour late. You then breezed in with no explanation and no apology as to why you were so late."

Although she tried not to let it happen, Cathy felt herself go on the defensive. "I did what I said I would do. We did get held up, and yes, I should have phoned or something to let you know we were going to be late, but Paul was pouring his heart out to me and we lost track of time."

"The commissioner doesn't care about that. He is appalled that you dismissed the arresting officers and for not getting Paul here when you said you would."

"Okay, so what can I do to make this right?"

"You can't. After much deliberation, we have agreed the only course of action is to place you on one month's unpaid suspension."

Cathy felt as if she'd just been kicked in the stomach and she expelled a long breath. "Wh-what? Suspension?"

"You heard me. Detective Cathy Andrews, you are no longer entitled to carry a firearm or your shield. I am formally asking you to hand over your badge and your gun. You are hereby under suspension, without pay, until January eighth 2021. It is also my duty, as your superior officer, to inform you that after the suspension you will be on report for another four weeks. If you step out of line even once, you will be faced with disciplinary action, which could include further suspension and or a demotion. I will save you the indignity of being escorted from the building but it is recommended you leave now."

By the time he'd finished, her cheeks were burning in humiliation and anger. She sat on a for a long moment, too stunned to move and trying to process what she'd just been ordered to do. She couldn't comprehend the fact that the captain was actually suspending her, but the more she searched his eyes for an explanation the more obvious it became that he meant what he'd said. She realized he was looking at her calmly, patiently, as if he was waiting for her to say more in her own defense, but she wouldn't give him the satisfaction. A line had been drawn.

She stood up and released the holster from her belt. Then she took her badge out of her back pocket. She held them both for a few seconds, their weight in her hands as familiar to her as ever. Then, with a heavy sigh of defeat, she placed them on his desk, turned and walked out of his office without so much as a backward glance.

She couldn't believe it. She had just been suspended. For a month. How was she going to be able to help Paul if she was under suspension?

# CHAPTER SIXTEEN

It was close to eleven o'clock by the time Dave made it back to the station. He was surprised to see Cathy's car was gone but he didn't give it much thought, he would deal with her when he got home. He had a burger and fries each for him and Paul, as well as two large sodas and he gave the food a quick blast in the canteen microwave to make sure they were hot when he got them to Paul. Retrieving the steaming burgers and fries, he went to the holding cells and greeted Ryan.

"Your wife said you'd be dropping by," he said, standing up and opening the door to the cell. "You know you're really not supposed to be here so just do me a favor and don't stay too long."

"No problem, Ryan, just let us have our meal and then I'll be out of your hair."

Paul had been in the cell barely twenty minutes when Dave joined him. He had been lying on the bed, the thin mattress doing nothing to cushion him from the stainless-steel frame, but he sat bolt upright when Dave entered.

They didn't embrace, they didn't say anything, they just locked eyes for a long moment and then Dave held up the bags of food. "Thought you might appreciate something to eat," he said casually.

Paul hadn't realized how hungry he was until he smelled the tantalizing aroma of the greasy fast food and he accepted the it gratefully. Apart from toast earlier that day, he'd had nothing to eat.

There was nowhere for Dave to sit except on the floor and he made himself against the wall. They ate their food in relative silence and when Paul finished the last bite they moved on to a more serious conversation.

"It's amazing how things can change through the course of one day," Paul said. "This time last night I was drinking my way to the worst hangover of my life, twenty-four hours later I'm eating fast food burgers and greasy fries in the holding cell of the station I work in."

"It's hard to take in. I still can't get my head around it. I could tell Jim and Mark were upset but they did you proud."

"They did. I feel really bad they had to go through that. Veteran interviewers they might be, but I can only imagine how difficult it was for them to interview someone they know so well."

"Jim told me he and Mark are going to the motel first thing to check over the crime scene. They double checked to make sure forensics had told the motel manager to leave everything as is and they also placed a uniform down there to stand guard. I wanted to go, too, but I wanted to be with you at the courthouse more. I figured you'll need to see at least one friendly face."

"Even if it's yours," Paul said with an easy smile.

"Luck of the draw. I'm sure Cathy will want to see Krista first thing but she'll be at the courthouse too. Maybe Krista will be getting out tomorrow so hopefully you'll be reunited sometime not long after the hearing."

"God, I hope so, I miss her and need to be with her."

"You will be. I promised Ryan I wouldn't stay long but I wanted to be sure you got something to eat. Try and get some shut-eye, you need to be at your best in front of the judge tomorrow."

Paul felt a shiver go up and down his spine. "I just want to get tomorrow over and done with. I want to get home, take a long shower and crawl into bed for a year...hopefully with my wife by my side."

"Good, positive vibes, Cam. Do you need to talk or do you mind if I go home and get some shut-eye too? I want to be on full alert tomorrow, too."

"You've been awesome, Dave, get on home. Oh, and kiss and make up with Cathy. Remember this, you were against her taking over my arrest, but I'm glad she was the one who did it. She made the whole process smooth for me and for that, I'm grateful."

Dave regarded him skeptically. "Whatever, Paul. Whether I kiss and make up with her is not your concern." He pulled his friend close and gave him a tight, back-slapping hug. Then he gathered up the empty food wrappers, knocked on the window to attract Ryan's attention, and left Paul alone to spend his first, and hopefully last, night in a jail cell.

He was bone tired by the time he got home. He knew Cathy was home too because her car was in its usual parking spot. The living room light was on and he went to stand in the doorway, half-expecting to find she had fallen asleep on the sofa. However, the living room was empty and he figured she had left the light on for his benefit.

When he made it upstairs a few minutes later, he found her lying wide awake in their bed. She wasn't under the covers, instead she was wrapped in a thick, terry cloth bathrobe and what looked like track suit bottoms. Her hair was piled high on her head, but despite her relaxed outward appearance, there was a look on her face he'd never seen before.

It was evident she'd been crying too and all at once, any animosity he still held towards her completely dissipated. Driving home he'd put himself in her shoes and realized she really had only been thinking of Paul and wanted to make the arrest a little bit easier for him. The least he could do was support her instead of be hostile towards her.

When she saw him in the doorway, she shot him a filthy look and then very deliberately turned away from him. He reckoned he deserved it but he was more concerned about the tears than her wrath against him. He approached her cautiously and sat down beside her. Her back remained stubbornly turned towards him.

He laid a hand on her shoulder. "Hey, what's wrong?" he

asked gently.

"What do you care?" she retorted.

"A lot, as you well know." He couldn't see all of her face, just her profile but he could see a little pool of tears collecting in the corner of her eye. "Why are you crying?"

"Because I have a horse's arse for a husband."

He carefully bit his lip to refrain from laughing. "I have to agree with you on that one. Really, Cathy, something's wrong. Is it Krista? Were you speaking to her?"

"No, it's not her. It's just…it's just…" She felt what little reserve she had managed to build up since those awful moments in the captain's office start to ebb away and she turned her head towards her pillow. She was sobbing, again, and was only dimly aware when Dave came round to her side of the bed and scooped her up into his arms. She didn't try to resist.

"It's just what, baby? Come on, talk to me."

The fact that he sounded like his usual loving, caring self wasn't lost on her and she buried her head against his solid frame. She struggled for control and, while he waited patiently, she managed to retain her composure. "You're not going to believe what I'm about to tell you," she said with a quivering voice.

"Try me," he said, gently wiping her tears away. The concern on his face was real and she felt her strength return, knowing she would have his full support.

"After I booked Paul, got him settled in lockup…" Her voice was still broken but was slowly becoming steadier. "… Captain Hamilton had asked me to go up to his office when I was finished."

Dave nodded slightly. He vaguely remembered hearing the captain tell her to go see him but he'd forgotten about it. "Yeah, so?"

"So…" She paused to push herself up into a sitting position. The tissue she held in her hand had already been half-shredded and she nervously started to shred the rest of it, her fingers trembling. She suddenly burst into tears again "Oh

Dave, I'm on suspension!" she wailed. "For a whole month."

"What?" He held her at arm's length so he could search her face for any hint of a joke or even a lie, but the devastation in her eyes was too real to ignore. "Suspension? What for?"

"For overriding Williams and Hernandez. For taking matters into my own hands and for not getting Paul to the station when I said I would."

"And you were suspended for that?" he asked incredulously. "Has he lost his mind?"

"Apparently. Him and the commissioner both."

"Oh, so it was the commissioner's idea and the captain had to do his dirty work for him. Really Cathy, he should have known better."

She blinked her tears away and eyed him cautiously. "You're on my side on this?"

"Of course I am. I may have been nasty and unsupportive towards you earlier – for which I humbly apologize – but I certainly wouldn't have wanted this as your punishment." He pulled her back into his arms and rocked her slowly back and forth, rubbing her back and soothing her in the way only he knew how. "I'll talk to him in the morning; find out what the hell is going on."

"Leave it, David, please. I'm out for a month – without pay, by the way, just to rub salt into the wounds – but the worst part is, he was adamant about it. If he'd been anyway against the commish, he would have fought to keep me on. I am now officially just a regular citizen, no gun, no badge, nothing. But on top of all that, I'm more upset that while I'm out, I can't do anything to help Paul."

Dave set his lips in a hard line. He hadn't thought of that. "Jesus, and with Krista out of action for who knows how long, we'll have to rely more on Jim and Mark to help with a lot of the leg work for us. Which would be fine under normal circumstances but I know they're already working a couple of hard cases down at the docks."

She looked at him miserably. "I didn't mean to cause all

this, honest I didn't. I truly thought I was doing it for Paul. If I'd known this was going to happen, I would have let Williams and Hernandez do their thing."

"What's done can't be undone," he reminded her.

"I can at least go to the courthouse tomorrow, after I've been to the hospital to see Krista. *She* doesn't even know I've been suspended, I didn't have the heart to call her to tell her and end up upsetting her more than she already is. Oh, and after the month-long suspension, I'll be on probation for another four weeks and if I step out of line even a little bit, it'll mean dismissal or a demotion."

He gently stroked her tear-stained cheek and planted a kiss on the tip of her nose. "It's way too harsh a punishment, baby. When I speak to the captain in the morning, I'll demand a reconsideration. He can't afford to lose another officer."

She wanted to believe it would be that simple to change the captain's mind but she was too upset and tired to get any good vibes going. "Come on, love, get into bed, it's awfully late and we've got another long day ahead of us tomorrow. You need to go to Paul's apartment and get his suit, remember. Don't forget his shaving stuff too, I told him I would remind you."

Despite the emotional upheavals of the day, and despite everything going through Dave's head, he managed to fall asleep almost immediately and stay asleep until the alarm woke him at six o'clock. He was surprised to find the bed beside him empty. But the usual morning smell of bacon cooking tantalized his nostrils so he got up, showered, shaved and dressed as quickly as he could and went down to the kitchen.

He might have had a reasonable night but it didn't look like Cathy had. She was pale and drawn as she moved slowly around the kitchen preparing breakfast. She was wearing her bathrobe, which was unusual for her. She never came downstairs in the morning unless she was showered and dressed.

"Morning," he said, pouring his coffee. He saw she already had a half-empty cup setting on the counter so he topped it up for her. "You doing okay?"

She was buttering toast and she shrugged. "Couldn't sleep. And the more I couldn't sleep, the more I got pissed at Captain Hamilton." She stirred the eggs in the frying pan, then lifted two plates down from the cupboard. "He's never spoken to me like that, and whether I deserved it or not it still doesn't give him the right to be that aggressive."

He watched as she spooned the eggs onto the plates and arrange bacon and toast beside them. She hadn't poured orange juice yet so, before he sat down, he did that while she carried the plates to the table. "He'll be answering a lot of questions," he informed her as he salted and peppered his eggs. "Will you be coming to the courthouse after you see Krista? I haven't heard yet what time the arraignment is but Paul will be there with the lawyer by nine o'clock. Hopefully he won't have to wait too long until he's called."

"Yes, I'll be there. I do want to see Krista first, of course. Maybe I'll hear if she's getting out today. I'm sure she would love to be able to be at the courthouse so hopefully that can happen for her. I know Paul would love her to be there."

"Without a doubt." He noticed she hadn't touched her food yet, not even a nibble of her toast. "Less talk, more eating," he said casually. "Eggs are getting cold."

She had a history of not eating when she was over-stressed and he didn't want to have to start worrying about her health on top of everything else. He was saved further concern when, without protest, she picked up her fork and ate silently until most of the food was gone.

Dave left to go to Paul's apartment at around seven thirty. He wasn't wearing a suit but he had deliberately worn dress pants and an open neck shirt, with black dress shoes instead of his usual sneakers. He wanted to look respectable in his support of Paul, who would be wearing a suit no matter what.

Cathy got showered and dressed after Dave left and got to the hospital just a few minutes after eight o'clock. She knew it was very early to be visiting anyone, and she couldn't flash her badge as an excuse to get to see Krista but she hoped the staff would recognize her and grant her entry.

Krista had just finished her breakfast when she saw Cathy walk in and she smiled in relief. "Cathy, I'm so happy to see you! I was wondering what's been happening. Is Paul okay? When he phoned me last night, we were both pretty upset and he told me he had to spend the night in lockup. I felt completely helpless stuck in here."

Cathy gave her friend a hug. "I'm happy to see you too, chum. I feel like I've been neglecting you. Texts and phone calls can't replace a proper face to face conversation."

Krista pushed her bed table out of the way and waited for Cathy to take her coat, scarf and gloves off before sitting down beside her. "You look tired, you okay?"

Cathy gave an awkward smile, shifting uncomfortably in the chair. "I'll get to me in a moment. Yes, it was unfortunate Paul had to be put in lockup and there was nothing anyone could do to stop it from happening. Ted should be with him now before going to the courthouse, Dave is bringing him his suit so he will be more than presentable and they will be at the District Courthouse by nine o'clock. Tell me about you, have they said anything about you getting out today?"

"The nurse this morning, before breakfast, said my vitals are all fine and within normal range. I've no more headache and ever so slightly diminished pain in my ribs. What do you think, does my face look less swollen?"

"Definitely around your eyes, yes. Your eyes look more open now, which is great."

"Then I really don't see why they would need to keep me here another day. The nurse said she would talk to the doctor and she would send him in as soon as he's done his rounds."

"Fingers crossed." Cathy smiled again, a real one this time. One of the things she had always loved about Krista was how upbeat and positive she could be about anything and everything. "Did Dave tell you I was the one who processed

Paul?"

"Yes, and he also said he was pretty pissed with you about it. For the record, I didn't like it either when I heard at first but I was able to realize you were doing it for Paul. I'm not mad at you anymore, I promise. Please tell me you and Dave are good too."

Relief flooded over Cathy's face. "Thank God, I couldn't bear it if you were mad at me too. Dave and I are fine, I promise, he eventually came round to the same way of thinking as you did."

"That's good. Will you be able to stick around to see if they'll let me out today? Or do you need to go to the courthouse or the precinct too?"

Cathy gave a short, bitter laugh. "I won't be going anywhere near the precinct. I'm waiting for a text from Dave to let me know what time Paul's hearing will be so I'll be going there."

"Okay, so if I get out of here before that, will you be able to take me home and help me wash my hair? They've only given me sponge baths here and I can't wait for a shower and to get my hair washed. And..." Krista trailed off for a moment and tilted her head inquisitively. "What did you mean there?"

"About what?"

"You said you wouldn't be going anywhere near the precinct. I know you've a lot on your plate right now but it was the way you said it, not so much as *what* you said."

Cathy bristled at Krista's innocent question. She lowered her gaze and chewed on her bottom lip for a long moment. She didn't want to tell Krista about her suspension...but then again, she knew she would have to sooner or later. She also knew Krista was waiting for an answer and, taking in a deep breath, she started talking. "Things kinda went pear-shaped in Cathy Land last night, Kris."

Krista reacted immediately in alarm. "Oh no! What happened?"

"I would ask you to guess but not even you could come

up with the right answer for this one. Just promise me you'll remain as calm as possible, I don't want you getting all tense on me and hurting your ribs."

"You're scaring me here. Of course I promise."

Cathy fixed her eyes on Krista's and did her best to sound as upbeat and nonchalant as possible. "Captain Hamilton suspended me last night. I'm off the force for the next four weeks."

Krista stared in shock. "You're having a laugh! Aren't you?"

"I wish I was." Despite her best efforts, Cathy's face collapsed in frustration. "It's as well you're out on sick leave for a while now because you are officially partnerless."

Krista took Cathy's hand in her own. "This is awful, Cathy, I can't believe he would do that to you. On what grounds?"

Cathy told her and even telling it again didn't make it better, or easier. "I asked Dave not to tell Paul just yet, I don't want Paul holding himself responsible. Besides, Paul might be out by this afternoon and, if you're home too, we might be sitting in your place eating pizza or Chinese food, talking as we always do, having a glass of wine or two and maybe even laughing about these two or three god-awful days."

"Yeah…that might happen. Not!" Krista shook her head and patted her friend's hand. "Oh Cathy, I'm so sorry for this. I can't believe you, of all people, just got suspended."

"Yes, well, apparently the captain didn't take into consideration I always work by the book. I'm so angry with him right now I don't care I never see him again."

"Unfortunately, it's inevitable your paths will cross again."

"Well, if nothing else, after these couple of days, from here on in it can only get better. Right?"

Krista tried to agree. She tried to share Cathy's enthusiasm, even though the attempt was half-hearted. She had a horrible sinking sensation in the pit of her stomach that the streak of bad luck hadn't even gotten off the ground yet, that there

was a lot more still to come.
 A lot more.

# CHAPTER SEVENTEEN

As planned, Dave brought Paul's suit and toiletries to him but was refused permission from the sergeant on duty to escort Paul to the locker room so he could have a decent shower and shave. No amount of pleading, threatening, begging or cajoling could change the mind of the hard-headed sergeant. If it had been Ryan still on duty, Dave was sure there would have been no problem.

Regardless, Paul was able to wash and shave in relative peace and when he was dressed, Attorney Ted Reynolds was escorted into the cell block to see him. It was then eight fifteen. Ted had told Paul the night before he'd be there at eight o'clock but a six car pile-up on the I-95 southbound had held him up. He did, however, come bearing gifts in the form of pancakes, bacon and scrambled eggs for breakfast, along with Dunkin' Donuts coffee.

Dave excused himself to let lawyer and client converse in privacy and went up to the fourth floor to confront Captain Hamilton where he promptly called his superior a callous, narrow-minded, intimidating bastard, who had let his better judgement be clouded by insensitivity. He said the captain had very clearly lost his rationality and decency and Dave was appalled at his so-called leadership. He spat the words out with as much venom as he possessed and, before the captain could even begin to admonish him, or try to placate him, he stormed out of the office. Although he'd always been one to speak his mind, no matter who it was, he had never spoken to his superior like that. He knew the captain wouldn't take the insubordinate behavior lightly but if he was in trouble, he didn't care.

He had a meeting next with Detectives Jim Turner and Mark Chipman who had just returned from the Blue Moon motel, after going over the room with a fine-tooth comb. They had found no further evidence that could either help convict Paul or clear his name. But the motel manager was able to produce CCTV footage that showed Paul clearly entering his father's room at twenty seven minutes past eleven in the morning and leave fourteen minutes later at eleven forty one. Paul's whole body language showed someone who was on the attack. However, all the footage did was prove Paul had told the truth about being at the motel and confirmed the times he had said he was there.

They had also stopped off at the county coroner's office to see if the autopsy report had been written up yet. The coroner was still working on it but was able to give them a print out that showed there was no evidence of skin or hair samples underneath Kenneth Cameron's fingernails. It was no wonder there were no samples; Paul had been videoed going into, and coming out of, the motel room wearing gloves and a mask.

Dave bemusedly read the report. He was hoping Ken's murderer had left some DNA behind so it could collaborate Paul's insistence that Ken had stated there were people coming after him. It was too bad there was no evidence to support that.

He told Jim and Mark about Cathy's suspension and earned their disbelief and support as he had known he would. He then went to see if Ted Reynolds was ready to go to the courthouse. Ted asked him if Cathy was going to meet them at the courthouse, or was she coming to the precinct. When he answered, Dave inadvertently let it slip, in front of Paul, that Cathy was on suspension and no one would see her until later, at the courthouse.

"She's on suspension?" Paul cried. "What on earth for?" At Dave's hesitation, he instantly knew the answer. "For what she did last night? Oh great! This is all my fault! I shouldn't have let her pull rank on Williams and Hernandez and I should never have kept her talking so long. How much more am I going to fuck up this whole fucking nightmare?"

Dave hated seeing Paul be so devastated and he moved quickly to try and console him. "She's fine, Paul, she's dealing with it, I promise you. She says it will give her more time to be able to help Krista get better. She's with her now, at the hospital and I'm expecting a text or call from her any moment."

Paul was too upset to listen and he turned away from Dave, feeling as if he was letting everyone down one by one. Ted let Paul digest the news and then told him he would have a quiet word in the captain's ear. The captain had an obligation to have as many officers as possible working on Paul's case. If he was willingly preventing one from doing so, he would have to come up with a plausible explanation or provide a suitable replacement. With Krista out of commission for a while, and Paul himself out indefinitely, there weren't many eligible replacements available.

Ted left the precinct at eight forty five. The District courthouse was approximately eleven blocks away and traffic should have eased by now. Paul was going to be driven in a squad car and Dave would follow in his own car. Before Paul was escorted to the police car, Cathy phoned Dave who immediately put her on to Paul so he could have a very quick word with Krista. It was against protocol but there was no one around to witness it and it gave Paul the chance to tell Krista he loved her. It also gave him the chance to tell Cathy he was so sorry for her suspension and he would do what he could to make it up to her.

Ted had managed to overrule the prosecution's request for the one and only eye-witness, Gabriella Rossini, the resident of the adjoining room, to attend an official police lineup. Ted's argument was that, because Paul had been wearing a mask, she wouldn't be able to positively ID a person based on half their face. For once, it was decided a lineup would not be necessary, despite the arguments from prosecution.

The arrest process in Massachusetts is such that when a prisoner is being arraigned, it is done so as quickly as possible after arrest. The case goes first to the District Court for the arraignment. There, the defense lawyer, in this case Ted Reynolds, would present his client's case in front of a judge and the District, or Assistant District, Attorney. It was up to Ted to provide as much information as possible to prove his client's innocence. It was also up to the DA to provide the court with sufficient evidence to hold the accused for trial. There were no jurors at arraignments – the decision was up to the presiding judge alone.

Dave was sitting in the corridor, alone, waiting for word that Paul's case was starting. Covid was responsible for holding up proceedings every day but rarely would a case not be heard, even if it took all day. While waiting, Dave was browsing through the internet on his cell phone, trying to distract himself when he heard his name mentioned. He looked up and instantly groaned. He didn't even try to hide his displeasure at the man standing in front of him. "Nikoli Ardolino," he said with a sneer.

"That's *District Attorney* Nikoli Ardolino," the DA said with a smirk. It was too bad he was standing far enough away that he didn't have to wear a mask so Dave could see every condescending expression. The man made his skin-crawl.

Dave suppressed a groan. He, Paul and Ardolino went back a long way and their history was anything but pleasant. In short, he and Paul hated Ardolino as much as he hated them. The fact that there was no love lost between them always made for fireworks when they were together. And then it hit Dave what Ardolino had just said. District Attorney. Which meant…

"You working Paul's case?" he asked through gritted teeth.

Ardolino was in his late forties and, despite his expensively cut business suits, imported Saville Row silk shirts, Italian leather shoes and briefcase, he always looked like a child dressing up in his father's clothes. It wasn't that he was short, or puny, or even not very handsome. He was six foot two, close to two hundred pounds and average looking. What he couldn't hide was, no matter how well he dressed, he was very effeminate in his actions and voice and not being married or having ever been pictured with a lady friend, his sexual orientation was open for debate.

It wasn't that which had caused Paul and Dave to detest him, far from it. A person's sexual orientation was for that person only and none of anyone else's business. What they held against him, but hadn't been able to prove, was the fact early on in his career Ardolino had supposedly accepted a bribe to overturn a case against a prominent business man accused of murdering his partner. A bribe had yet to be proved but getting elected to DA couldn't stop Paul and Dave from wondering who Ardolino had either slept with or done his own bribing to get the office.

Ardolino was still smirking at Dave's question. "Yes, I am happy to announce I'll be prosecuting your partner. It will be up to me to see he is put away for a very long time."

"Get lost, Ardolino," Dave commanded. "I can smell whatever you had for dinner last night. It's grossing me out."

Ardolino lost the smirk but only for a second. "I'll see you in court." And with that, he walked away, trying to be dignified but instead looking as if he had something stuck up his ass.

Dave returned to his cell phone again when a shadow loomed in front of him and, expecting it to be Ardolino back for round two, he looked up in anger. The anger didn't go away when he saw Captain Bob Hamilton standing in front of him. "Not in the mood for talking to you, Bob."

"That's okay, I don't want you talking, I think you did enough this morning. It's my turn to talk and you will sit there and listen. And yes, that's an order."

Dave glared up at him. "Sir, yes sir!" he snapped coldly.

The captain knew all about Dave's temper and knew he couldn't be intimidated just because it was a disgruntled superior officer in his face. "The way you spoke to me this morning was out of order, Detective Andrews, even for you. However, I'm not so insensitive that I didn't know you were doing it for Cathy and if I had to defend my wife, I would probably act the same way."

Dave slipped him an icy glance. "Yeah, so? I'm not about to nominate you for caring husband of the year, nor am I going to apologize if that's what you're expecting."

"Not at all."

"Are you going to suspend me too?"

"I'm very tempted, believe me. If it were different times and different circumstances, yes. But I realize Paul needs all the help he can get and to suspend you now would be to his detriment."

"Which is exactly why you shouldn't have suspended Cathy. She can't help Paul if she's suspended, can she?"

"No, and I took that into consideration before I asked her for her badge and firearm last night."

"You didn't consider very long. How is she going to help Paul? We need all hands on deck, she *wants* to help, she *needs* to help so how can she if you and the commish have her on a month long suspension?"

"She broke the rules, detective. She deserves the punishment."

"She didn't break anything and she certainly doesn't deserve what you gave her."

"She broke the rules."

"She bent them."

"Andrews!" Captain Hamilton was by nature a very placid person. He wasn't given to theatrics or unnecessary bouts of anger towards anyone, especially his detectives. He really did understand Dave's fury and animosity towards him but that didn't give Dave the right to be this defiant. "You and I are never going to see eye to eye on this and I get that. I just wanted you to know I was only acting on a direct order from the commissioner."

"You've ignored, or overturned, or certainly argued, the commissioner's orders before. *I've* done far worse and neither one of you have so much as batted an eyelid. What was so different about this one? Cathy did what she said she was going to do, she backed Williams and Hernandez to the hilt, let them keep the arrest on their record, and got Paul to the station. Okay, admittedly not when she said she would, but God, they were only an hour late. She processed him by the book, got him to lockup and handed him over to the sergeant as was her duty, so just what part of that warrants the suspension?"

The captain silently admired Dave his loyalty to his wife and took on board his frustration. "Look, Dave - "

"Oh, *Dave* now is it?"

"Dave, look, shut up and listen for one damn minute. We can't afford to lose Cathy, I know that. I don't think it's something the commissioner thought about, or else he forgot Krista is going to be out of action for a while. I saw you sitting here and I was going to let you stew in your own juice but I wanted to have my say. And since you wouldn't give me the chance this morning when you stormed out of my office -"

"It was warranted," Dave said softly.

"We'll agree to differ on that one. What I *do* want to say is this: Depending on how this hearing goes today, I will be talking to the commissioner again, face to face, not on the phone, and I will be pleading Cathy's case. I really didn't mean it when I said she deserved the suspension, of course she doesn't. However, I will do what I can to ensure she gets reinstated. As quickly as possible."

Dave recognized the olive branch and he looked up at his superior. He was still angry but he knew the captain was being genuine in wanting to help Cathy, and he closed his eyes briefly in submission. "I...she...*we*...would certainly appreciate it. Thank you."

The captain recognized that his olive branch had been accepted and he gestured towards the bench Dave was sitting on. "Mind if I join you?"

Waving a hand idly toward the empty space next to him he muttered, "Suit yourself."

Captain Hamilton eased his bulk on the bench and sat back for a long moment to observe the comings and goings around him. There was only a handful of people milling around but the numbers were greatly reduced compared to eight months ago. The district court building was three floors high and they were on the first floor, situated near the revolving main door. "Do we know yet when Paul's hearing is going to be?"

"Not yet." Dave looked at the time on his cell phone, shaking his head. It was already approaching noon. "Ted Reynolds is in the holding room with him, so at least he's not alone. Wish I could be there."

"Have you considered what to do if he's convicted?"

Dave shook his head. "Of course not. I know he's innocent, I haven't been able to make myself think otherwise."

"I understand. What about Krista? Is she still in hospital?"

"Yes. Cathy texted about half an hour ago, they're still waiting for the doctor to give Krista a final exam and then, hopefully, discharge her."

"I hope she gets out in time to be here for Paul, I'm sure she wants that more than anything."

"We all do. She still looks a mess but there's definitely an improvement since Monday." Out of the corner of his eye Dave saw Ardolino at the other end of the hall. He was standing talking to a man he assumed was another lawyer and he couldn't help curl his lip in contempt. "Oh, just when this day was shaping up to be one of my least favorites, I found out who Paul's prosecutor is going to be."

"Yeah? Who?" The captain followed Dave's line of vision and whistled long and low behind his mask. "Isn't that just wonderful? What did Paul do to end up drawing the short straw?"

"Beats me. I'm still trying to figure out how he got into the DA's office. Thank God we're not shaking hands these days, I can still feel the clammy slime from the first time I shook his years ago."

The captain chuckled. "I know what you mean. Hopefully his days of bribe taking are long gone."

Dave looked at him skeptically. "Yeah. Just like my temper tantrum days are over." He stood up and stretched. "I'm going to go find somewhere to get a bite. Want to come with me or do you want me to bring something back?"

"Thanks but I had a snack before I left the station. Cora has me on a strict diet and is making all these healthy little snacks now for me to take into work. I'm down ten pounds already so something's working for me. I'm good."

"No problem. If you hear anything about Paul, please let me know and I'll come straight back." With a heart that felt like a lead weight in his chest, Dave walked towards the main entrance and stepped out into the frigid air. Snow was forecast for later in the week and it felt like it might snow sooner.

If a snowstorm was the only thing on the horizon he had to worry about, he wouldn't have cared if two feet got dumped on the area.

# CHAPTER EIGHTEEN

Over the next two hours things finally started happening. Krista was discharged and Cathy got her home in record time to get her showered and dressed appropriately for the courthouse. Krista was still in a lot of pain and moved slower than she normally would but was grateful for Cathy's help. When she stepped into the courthouse, the timing couldn't have been more perfect. Dave had just received a text from Ted that Paul's hearing was up next and just after two o'clock, Dave helped Krista into the courtroom and positioned her carefully where she would be able to see Paul immediately, and he her.

Jim Turner and Mark Chipman followed them in. They each expressed their alarm at seeing how bad Krista looked. Now they could fully understand Paul's need to seek retribution for her. Seconds later, Captain Hamilton came in and sat behind them all. He tried to catch Cathy's eye and wasn't surprised when she didn't acknowledge him in any way. He understood why she was snubbing him, he would probably have done the same to her if their roles had been reversed. She also made a point of sitting as far away from him as was possible. He understood that too. He'd never been rebuffed by her before and just because he understood it didn't mean he had to like it.

Ted Reynolds and DA Nikoli Ardolino were already seated at their respective tables when Paul was escorted in by a bailiff. As his friends had hoped, Paul immediately saw Krista and as soon as their eyes met, they each felt a flow of strength pass from one to the other. He tried not to grin too broadly, she tried not to cry, but a smile lit up their faces, if only momentarily. It was all that was needed.

A court stenographer was sitting slightly to the left and

in front of the defense table. She was checking her equipment when the bailiff announced "All rise" and she stood up at the same time as everyone else. Seconds later, Judge Harold McNeill entered and sat down at the bench. While everyone was getting settled again, he took a few moments to read over the notes the court clerk had placed in front of him and then looked around the court room.

This was only a arraignment so there was no jury. However, as with all hearings and trials, it remained open to the public. Sometimes newspaper reporters and anchors from the local news channels were in attendance, circling like vultures for the next big scoop. The arrest of a police officer for the murder of his own father should be considered big news but for some reason, the only media presence was two or three reporters.

The judge looked over the small cluster of people seated behind the defendant. There were two beautiful women, one of whom seemed like she was sitting uncomfortably, and on closer inspection he saw her face looked like it was heavily made up. He wondered if that was the wife of the defendant, he remembered reading she had been badly beaten up. He also recognized Captain Bob Hamilton and assumed the other men seated close by were police officers.

Judge McNeill was renowned as a tough old buzzard but he was a veteran of the system who had earned the highest respect from every member of the Massachusetts Bar Association. He was close to retirement and didn't make many district court appearances but he had been approached to preside, at least for the hearing, over this particular case. If the case was bound over for trial, it was rare that the same judge would preside then.

"Mr Reynolds," he began, "your client is here today under arrest for the murder of his own father, Kenneth Cameron. Detective Cameron, this is a very serious charge. Are you aware of how serious this is?"

Paul stood up and cleared his throat. He was aware

umpteen pairs of eyes were on him, including the sneaky glare of his nemesis, Nikoli Ardolino. "Yes, Your Honor, I am aware."

"And how do you plead?"

"Not guilty, Your Honor."

The judge didn't seem surprised at Paul's answer and looked towards Ardolino for his comments.

Ardolino didn't waste any time getting right to the point. "Your Honor, we have an eye witness who not only places Detective Cameron at the scene at the time of the murder but she has been able to share with me the make, model and license of his car and CCTV footage places his car and the defendant himself at the motel at the approximate time of the crime. We also have Detective Cameron's police issue handcuffs that were found on the victim's body and Detective Cameron's fingerprints are the only ones on the cuffs."

Reynolds immediately stood up at that comment. "Your Honor, Detective Cameron hasn't denied those are his cuffs. However, the CCTV also proves he was wearing gloves so his prints would have been on the cuffs from anytime that he might have handled them prior to going anywhere near the motel."

"Your Honor," Ardolino rose halfway out of his seat. "There were no defensive wounds on Detective Cameron's body, which means he must have immobilized his victim – in this instance *his own father* – and how better than by using handcuffs?"

Judge McNeill looked from one lawyer to the other. "Mr Reynolds, why would your client, who I was told has been a detective for many years within the Bathville Police Department, go to the motel and attack his father so viciously?"

"Because, Your Honor, his wife, who's also a detective in the Bathville PD, was severely and brutally beaten by the deceased. Personal items were also stolen by the deceased at the time when he savagely assaulted and beat her. Detective Cameron was seeking retribution." Reynolds reached into a folder on top of the desk. "These are pictures taken of Detective Krista

Cameron upon her admission to hospital. She is a very beautiful woman but, as you can see, her injuries make her barely recognizable."

The judge looked at the pictures, four of them, carefully. As he studied each one in turn, he looked over to where Krista was sitting and couldn't seem to comprehend how she looked this good forty eight hours later. "I assume you are wearing a lot of make-up, Detective Cameron?" he asked her gruffly.

"I am, Your Honor. I also have broken ribs and bruising all over my body. Thanks to my father-in-law."

The judge shuffled the photos together and passed them back to the bailiff to return them to Reynolds. "A vicious attack indeed. Certainly gave your client a motive."

"Yes, but that would only be relevant if he killed his father, which he didn't. Hence his not guilty plea."

The judge turned his attention to Ardolino. "What evidence do you have to show me, Mr Ardolino?"

"The witness' statement. It is all there in detail what she saw and what she heard." He gave the bailiff the pages his secretary had typed up that morning. "I also have stills taken from CCTV footage that show Detective Cameron going into and coming out of his father's motel room." He passed them over too. "And these...I also have these." He handed over an evidence bag, in which there was a pair of handcuffs. "These belong to Detective Cameron." He gave the bailiff another sheet of paper. "This is the report that confirms Detective Cameron's fingerprints are the only ones on the cuffs." He reached into his brief case and brought out another report. "And finally, this is the preliminary report from the autopsy currently underway at the coroner's office. It confirms the cause of death."

Paul felt his spirits sink. Every piece of evidence Ardolino was handing over was enough to convict him. As he remained standing, he bowed his head. He wanted to get out of here. "What other evidence do you have, Ted?" he whispered.

"A pair of your jeans. Namely the pair you were wearing the day you attacked your father. The belt loop at the back is ripped. Isn't that where you usually hook your handcuffs?"

"Yes. I remember my dad grabbing me at the back when I was holding him against the wall. I didn't know he'd ripped my jeans. I slip the opened part of the cuff through the belt loop and close the cuff over without locking it, which gives me immediate access to them if I need to apprehend someone. Thing is, you can't prove that's where I had those cuffs or that the loop wasn't torn before I went to his motel room

"You're right, but hopefully it's enough to introduce reasonable doubt. We may not have as much evidence right now as Ardolino does but that doesn't matter. This is just a preliminary hearing and by the time this goes to trial, we'll have a lot more."

Judge McNeill looked over everything that had been presented to him. "There is a lot to consider here. I know this is just an arraignment, and we are already running behind schedule, but I would like to call a short recess so I can look over everything without interruption. I will be fifteen minutes."

"Just one second, Your Honor, if I may?" Ardolino interrupted smoothly. "I would like to bring your attention to the witness' statement I gave you a few seconds ago, in particular to the very first paragraph. It will tell you that not only did Detective Cameron murder his father, but the murder was premeditated."

Dave's head shot up and he stared at Ardolino in disbelief. What the hell was he playing at now? He had a feeling he wasn't going to like it.

"And how will that be?" The judge asked.

"Ms Rossini witnessed not just Detective Cameron going into his father's motel room on the day of his murder. The day before, she saw, and heard, someone else go into Kenneth Cameron's room. She heard the sounds of a struggle, of a physical fight. She heard the person say, and I quote, "If Paul doesn't kill you, I will" unquote. From as early as the morning *before* his wife was beaten up, Detective Paul Cameron had very clear intentions to kill his father and that particular paragraph is proof."

"Did your witness get a description of this visitor?"

"She did, also a vehicle description and license plate number for a black Camaro belonging to Detective Cameron's partner, Detective David Andrews."

Paul snapped his head round to stare at Dave in shock. Dave seemed as stunned as he was but when his eyes met with Paul's the exact same thought went through their minds at the same time.

Dave, for all his good intentions to scare Paul's father off, had unwittingly sold his partner out instead. And there was absolutely nothing he could say or do to argue Ardolino's words.

# CHAPTER NINETEEN

Ardolino achieved the desired effect with his last statement and while basking in the shockwaves he created, he swept his gaze over every one in the courtroom.

Suddenly on alert, the newspaper reporters were busily texting on their phones or talking into hand-held recorders. Both Paul and Dave's wives were seemingly trying to get some sort of an explanation from Dave, who had the deer-caught-in-the-headlights look on his face. Cameron himself looked as if he was about to pass out. Not even Ted Reynolds could get his attention, his client seemed to only have eyes for his partner, and his partner for him.

Perfect. Just what Ardolino wanted.

Judge McNeill had already called for a recess and as soon as he retreated to his chambers, Reynolds beckoned Dave to come over. He pulled Dave and Paul into a quiet corner, well out of earshot of reporters and spectators. And, most importantly, as far as possible from Nikolai Ardolino.

"Okay, guys, what's going on here?" Ted had always proved unflappable and even now, he seemed calm. But he did have a right to know about anything that could potentially harm his case.

Dave looked nervously at Paul and when he received a brief nod, he murmured, "Ardolino's telling the truth, Ted. I was at the motel that morning."

"And did you say what Ardolino said you did?"

"Unfortunately, yes. Paul, I'm sorry, I - "

"You think you sold me out, huh?" Paul interrupted.

"I don't think it, I know it."

"Bullshit. You did what you had to do that morning, I

appreciated it then, I appreciate it now."

"It's not that simple, Paul. With my so-called mission of mercy I have only succeeded in getting you into even bigger trouble." Turning his attention to Paul's lawyer, he continued. "Ted, what harm have I done?"

"Plenty, I'm afraid. You have quite literally corroborated the state's charges against my client. The only way I can clear this roadblock is to remind everyone that you, Dave, is not the one on trial. And your actions had nothing to do with Paul going to the motel the very next day. I just wish you had thought to tell me about this earlier. I would have had time to prepare a suitable rebuttal. Right now, all I can do is work the close partnership angle between the two of you, that you would never have done or said anything that might get Paul into trouble."

Paul shook his head adamantly. "What Dave did, or said, had nothing to do with me doing what *I* did. It's like you just said, Dave's not the one who's going to trial, Ted and yes, I know that's exactly where this is going." Paul fixed his gaze on Ardolino, who was sitting at his desk, casually shuffling papers as if he didn't have a care in the world. "Of all the hearings he had to be at, it had to be this one. How lucky can a guy get?"

"Unfortunately, he's still an excellent attorney, Paul."

"He's a dickhead, is what he is," Dave muttered.

"Enough about him," Ted said dismissively. "We have bigger problems to deal with. Paul, normally we'd have discussed alibis by now but you've already truthfully confessed to going to your father's motel at the time you stated. Indeed, there are CCTV stills, time-stamped, to prove that and they show you were alone. Have you been able to figure out who your father owed money to?"

"I know I have no alibi but Cathy, Dave and Krista knew before I went I wasn't going to rest until I'd seen him. They knew I was angry – *furious* - enough to want to kill him but at my wife and my friend's strong protests to not do anything foolish that would jeopardize my life, I promised them I wouldn't. Krista in particular begged me not to kill him, even though she was in a hospital bed, barely able to breathe because of the broken ribs *he* had given her. So, knowing how important this was to her, and to Dave and Cathy, I wanted to keep my promise that I wouldn't kill him. As for the money he owed, he told me it was thirty five thousand. He said he was desperate to get the money because he knew they were going to kill him. And I'm still thinking they are from Brooklyn and my father came up here to try and get away from them. Even though I was blinded with rage at what he'd done to Krista, I can say quite clearly that when he told me about them, I somehow knew he was telling the truth. For once in his miserable life, he was telling the truth."

"Okay, that's good, that's something we can work with. We'll go over the CCTV footage again, see if anyone else goes into your father's room."

"Why would the eye witness who recorded all our details not have come forward with details on whoever did the actual killing?" Dave asked.

Ted nodded sagely. "Good question. But I'm sure there are any number of reasons why not, such as she was in the shower, or had gone out...or they found her and threatened her. She will be questioned thoroughly on that point; I can assure you."

Paul nodded and glanced over towards Krista. He knew she hadn't taken her eyes off him since he'd huddled in conference with Ted. "Any chance I can go talk to Krista real briefly, Ted? I'm dying a slow, horrible death without her and all I want is one hug and a chance to tell her everything's going to be okay."

"You know that's not allowed, Paul. But I'll give the bailiff a head's up and distract Ardolino so he won't see and makes it worse by complaining. Go for it."

Dave watched his friend go to Krista and at Paul's hesitation to hug her, in case he hurt her, Dave sadly shook his head. "I hope looking for the guys who killed Ken Cameron isn't going to be like looking for a needle in a haystack, Ted. Paul's only assuming Brooklyn, they could be from absolutely anywhere, if they even exist."

"*Some*one killed his father, Dave. And Brooklyn is as good a place as any to start."

Krista didn't feel the pain when Paul gave her a hug. All she knew was the love of her life was next to her after what had seemed a lifetime and his strong arms around her felt like heaven. They didn't speak, they didn't have to, and Cathy stepped well to the side to give them a bit of privacy. She made a point of ignoring Captain Hamilton.

"I know you're not supposed to be doing this, my love," Krista murmured in her husband's ear. "But I'm so glad you are. Go back to Ted, know that I love you and I'm sitting right beside you, holding your hand."

He smiled into her eyes. "I love you, baby." He turned to go back to Ted and when Dave passed him, he gave him a playful punch on the shoulder. "We're good, Big D. We'll work this out."

Judge McNeill returned and banged his gavel to restore order, returning immediately to business. "Mr Reynolds, your comments please on Mr Ardolino's last statement."

"Detective Andrews does not wish to deny he was at the motel, nor does he deny saying the things Mr Ardolino's witness said he did."

Captain Hamilton sat forward in his seat behind Cathy and Krista, his eyes wide in surprise. He had been expecting denial all the way, but certainly not this. For the first time in his life, Dave had betrayed his partner, without even knowing it. So why the hell were he and Paul looking so calm?

"Detective Andrews and Detective Cameron," Ted continued, "have been partners for many years. They have enjoyed a rewarding career together and anyone who knows them will tell you they are as close as brothers. I think it is safe to say that Detective Andrews would never have gone to the motel if he had known a murder was going to be committed, that his partner would be implicated and his own actions could be used against him." He paused momentarily to lean down to ask Paul something and when he got the answer, he straightened to face the judge again. "The only reason Detective Andrews went to the motel was, in his capacity as a police officer, to warn my client's father to stay away from Detective Cameron and his wife. Detective Andrews was hoping a few choice words would be enough to scare the murder victim off. When that didn't happen, and after what happened to his wife, it was Detective Cameron's turn to warn his father off. As it turned out, Detective Cameron wasn't the only one who was at his father's motel room that day. At roughly twelve thirty, perhaps forty five minutes or so later, the real killers showed up and - "

"Wait a minute!" Ardolino interrupted, "There is absolutely no evidence to confirm what Mr Reynolds has just said and I want the record to show that this is pure speculation, concocted to try to clear an obviously guilty man."

"There may not be any evidence *yet*, Your Honor," Ted said smoothly. "My client just remembered late last night his father saying that he owed money to some people and he knew they were after him. We have not had the time to gather evidence but it will be our priority to do so."

Ardolino whipped his gaze over to the judge. "Your Honor, this is sheer conjecture."

"I don't agree, counsellor. This information sheds new light on this case. Defense, what are your intentions?"

"To have the eye witness interviewed again. And to have the CCTV footage from the motel viewed again in an attempt to identify Kenneth Cameron's killers."

The judge appeared uncertain how to deal with this. "All this might take time. Your client is here today for a preliminary hearing, not a trial. I think there is more to this case than meets the eye but I still have a duty to move this case forward as expeditiously as possible. Your client has pled not guilty. There is a lot of evidence against him, but now there is some level of reasonable doubt. Because of that, I will make my call now. Detective Cameron, please stand."

Paul raised himself from his chair, standing tall and proud.

"Detective Cameron, the charges against you are very serious. Your plea is that of not guilty, which means you are entitled and eligible to take this to trial. You are to be remanded to custody, without bail, until a trial date has been set."

Paul heard the gasps of shock behind him and felt his knees buckle but Ted was prepared for this and laid a calming hand on his arm. "Your Honor, Detective Cameron has the right to gather evidence to prove his innocence. He is a longstanding detective in the Bathville Police Department. He is a decorated officer, having saved the life of a fellow officer a couple of years ago, and for apprehending a serial killer who had killed several police officers. Any one of his fellow officers can testify what an upstanding officer he is. He should not remain in custody and I motion the court set a bail hearing as soon as possible."

Judge McNeill looked long and hard at Ted, then at Paul. The young detective had a shell-shocked look about him, certainly not one of a guilty man. The evidence against him might have been strong but there seemed to be other evidence that could come to light. "Very well, Mr Reynolds. Detective Cameron, you will be held until your bail hearing. It has been over forty eight hours since your arrest so the bail hearing will be either tomorrow or, if no time slots are available, the day after." And at that, the judge banged his gavel to end the session, stood up and retreated to his chambers.

Paul heard the words but he couldn't process them, never mind comprehend them. Although it was good he was getting bail, he would still have to spend another night in jail. Maybe even two nights.

He whirled round to face Krista and watched the tears streaking down her face as the bailiff clapped handcuffs on him. She knew he wasn't coming home with her tonight and her devastation was obvious. Dave was doing his best to support Krista on one side and Cathy was doing the same on the other but she only had eyes for him. He would never forget the look on her face. She was crushed.

He also knew that from this moment on, his joyride at the precinct lockup was now a thing of the past. This time he would be taken to the lockup at the city jail. If city was crowded, he'd be shipped to county jail. He gave Krista one last anguished look and, turning away, he let the bailiff lead him to the exit.

He didn't look back.

# CHAPTER TWENTY

It was a good thing for Ardolino that he left the courtroom as soon as the judge disappeared into his chambers. Dave didn't think he would have had the ability to hold back from punching the lawyer in his smug face.

He ushered Krista into the hall, the courtroom still had other hearings coming up, even though it was late in the day. He didn't want to hold up proceedings when the schedule was already behind. He settled her carefully onto a bench and Cathy sat down beside her.

Knowing Captain Hamilton was looking on, Dave made sure Krista was being tended to and then turned to his superior. Ted was standing beside the captain.

"I need to go with Paul," Ted said, rubbing his forehead to help collect his thoughts. "I want to make sure he's processed properly. I'll have my team get onto Gabriella Rossini so we can get a statement about whether she saw anyone else go to Cameron's room."

"I'll go with you, Mr Reynolds," Captain Hamilton offered. "I want to see how Paul is doing. And maybe help with the woman's statement. I want to see for myself how reliable she is and if I get even one hint that Ardolino has coerced her into giving a less than full statement, or has even altered one syllable of her words, I'll have his balls on a platter."

Dave nodded and glanced back at the ladies. He saw Cathy rub Krista's back, all the while holding her hand and shushing her gently. Both of them looked as shell-shocked as he felt. He couldn't get the image of Paul turning around as soon as court was adjourned, horror dimming his handsome features and his eyes seeking Krista's. The devastation on his partner's face had chilled him to the bone.

"What a cluster-fuck," he murmured to the captain.

"Paul doesn't deserve this." Captain Hamilton shook his head. "What are you going to do when his bail is set? If you'll need help financially, I can look into putting my house up for collateral if that will help. You know I'll do whatever I can."

Dave smiled grimly. "That's very kind of you, Bob. I don't know how I'm going to do it, it's not like I can take up a collection at the station. One million dollars is a lot of money and I have no clue how to get it."

Ted Reynolds caught the captain's eye. It was time to go. "Look after Krista. I'll be around to see her later to let her know how we got on."

Dave watched the two men walk away and then, glancing at his watch, went over to kneel in front of Krista. "How you holding up, sweetie?"

"How do you think?" she said, her eyes watering again. "Can't you get him back, Dave? Please?" She shook her head in despair, feeling herself choke up every time she recalled the look in Paul's eyes when the bailiff put the handcuffs on him.

"You know I would do that if I could," he said sadly.

"Not even for a moment? I just want to tell him I love him."

"He knows that already. You want to come back to our place or do you want to go home?"

"I don't care, I just want to get out of here." She rose stiffly and smoothed her blouse. She closed her thick winter coat, clutching it tight at her neck. "Can I come to yours?"

"Of course you can!" Cathy cried. "How about I take you to yours first so you can pack an overnight bag and stay with us? I don't want you moving around much, I want you close to us so we can look after you."

Krista's poor, swollen face crumpled again and she clasped Cathy's hand tightly in her own. "You're such a dear, Cath. Come on, let's get going."

"I'm here in my own car," Dave said, "I'll go home, make

sure the heat is on in the guest bedroom." He kissed both ladies and hurried out to his car. It was snowing lightly but it
didn't look like it was going to accumulate much and he made
it home in less than ten minutes.

The rest of the day passed in a haze. Krista's usually
cheerful manner was non-existent as she sat in the chair in
the Andrews' living room. She felt chilled to the bone and
even when Cathy carefully wrapped her in a navy blue throw
and gave her a hot whiskey laced with honey and lemon, she
still couldn't get warmed. It didn't take long for the whiskey,
coupled with the painkillers she was taking, to knock her out
but her doze was anything but restful.

When she woke, it was full dark outside but the three
lamps in the living room were on to chase away the gloom. Her
first thought was of Paul and her heart sank to the floor as soon
as she remembered he wasn't there. She could hear muffled
voices from behind the closed kitchen door and, carefully rising, she padded into the kitchen to join Cathy and Dave.

An extra-large pizza box was on the counter and Cathy,
when she saw her ashen-faced friend, indicated towards it.
"Hey, chum, I didn't want to disturb you. There's pizza there,
double pepperoni just the way like it, if you want me to heat
it?"

Krista grimaced. The very thought of food right now
was not her friend. "Maybe later." She sank into the chair beside Cathy and laid her weary head on Cathy's shoulder. "I want
to see him," she murmured. "I *need* to see him. Could Captain
Hamilton make it happen? Or Ted?"

Dave saw tears hovering behind her lashes and his heart
broke for her. "You know they can't, sweetheart. None of us
can."

She nodded miserably and stared off into the middle
distance, her brow furrowed in despair. "I guess I'll have to
wait until tomorrow. Hopefully his bail hearing will be early."

Krista only managed to sleep that night with help from
the painkillers. Otherwise, she would have tossed and turned

as Dave and Cathy were doing. Seeking comfort and support from each other, their hugs and murmurs of solace soon turned into embraces and soft sighs of pleasure. They submitted to the passion and made unhurried love to one another and even though it was sweet and filled with gentle words of encouragement and obvious desire, it didn't stop the worry about Paul taking over again almost as soon as they lay back on the pillows again.

The morning broke dull and overcast, as if reflecting their mood. Krista ate a bit of toast and drank two cups of strong, sweet tea. Dave and Cathy went through the motions of having a bit more sustenance in the form of scrambled eggs and toast but there was no idle chit-chat as there usually would have been during the meal. Each sat lost in their own thoughts and it was only when Krista's cell phone rang at nine thirty did it jolt them out of their reverie.

It was Ted Reynolds. "Good morning, Krista, I hope I haven't disturbed you."

"You're fine, Ted, you know you can call me anytime. Cathy and Dave are here too."

"That's good, can you put me on speaker?"

Krista did. "Can you hear us?"

"Loud and clear. I'm calling to let you know Paul's bail hearing has been set for eleven o'clock this morning."

For the first time, there was a spark of enthusiasm in Krista's eyes and she shot a look at Dave and Cathy. They were mirroring her expression. "That's great! Oh, that's so great, Ted. Can we be there? Can we come?"

"No reason why not."

The warmth in Ted's voice wasn't lost on them and she smiled through her tears. "We weren't expecting a result so quickly. How did you manage to get it so soon?"

"I called in a small favor with a bail commissioner and he shuffled his calendar around to suit us. He's right here in Bathville which means I hand delivered his forty bucks fee and reminded him I don't have to pay him any travel expenses."

Krista's sigh of relief was almost comical. "Unless you want to tack it onto our bill, I'll give you the forty bucks when I see you later, Ted, thank you. Have you seen Paul yet today?"

"Not yet, on my way there now but I've spoken to him and he's doing his best to keep his spirits up. Oh, he also said that if I was talking to you, to tell you he loves you."

Krista's smile became a chuckle. "Please tell him I love him too. We all do. Thanks, Ted, see you soon." She hung up and beamed at her friends. "Guess we'd better get a move on and get ready."

They were at the courthouse for five minutes to eleven. Appointments had already backed up but only by half an hour or so. At eleven forty five, they were seated in the same courtroom they'd been in the day before and waited as patiently as possible for Paul to appear.

Five minutes later, he was led in by the bailiff and his eyes lit up as soon as he saw Krista. He acknowledged Dave and Cathy's attendance too but, although he seemed like he was putting on a brave face, they knew he was wrought with emotions he'd never had to experience before.

"All rise," the bailiff ordered. A different judge came in from his chambers and when he sat, the bailiff gestured for everyone else to sit. "Bail hearing for Paul Cameron, Judge Caleb Dempsey presides."

Judge Dempsey took a few moments to read over the typed notes in front of him, then, taking off his glasses, he settled his gaze on Paul. "Will the defendant please rise and state his full name?

Paul got up from the seat and stood tall and proud, just as he had done the day before. "Paul Michael Cameron, Your Honor."

"You are here today to receive your bail amount, following your charge of not guilty in regards to the murder of your father, Kenneth Cameron. Do you wish to change your plea?"

"No, Your Honor."

"Very well. I have read the transcript of your arraignment very thoroughly and am in complete agreement with the case your attorney, Ted Reynolds, presented to the court yesterday. However, I cannot condone a murder charge. The murder of another human being is deplorable and without excuse. Because of the seriousness of the crime, it is my duty to demand the highest amount the Commonwealth of Massachusetts will allow and am hereby instructing that bail is set at one million dollars."

Massachusetts does not have private bondsmen, and, especially for a murder trial, the accused has to come up with whatever the bail amount is set at. One million dollars may as well have been ten million, or forty million, and as the figure slowly set in, Paul felt his heart sink. He, or anyone he knew, didn't have that sort of money.

Grim-faced, Ted Reynolds rose to his feet. "Thank you, Your Honor. We will await instruction from the court for the pre-trial hearing, the deposition and trial."

Judge Dempsey banged his gavel to end the hearing and, after he had retreated to his chambers, Paul turned round, immediately seeking out Krista again. She was about six feet away from him, her arm outstretched but he couldn't go to her. Already the bailiff was slipping the cuffs around his wrists.

"I'm sorry, baby," he said softly. He knew she could hear him and, as he was led away, he heard her say, "I love you." The further he was led away from her, the more his heart shattered.

Cathy sat holding Krista's hand, feeling the tension roll off her in waves. "It will be all right, Kris, we'll get through this."

"How, Cathy?" Krista asked dispassionately. "We don't have that sort of money. I'll never get him home."

Dave sat impassively beside them. His mind was going a mile a minute and, out of nowhere, he came up with an idea that could help Paul. It would mean a huge sacrifice on his part but, for Paul, he would do it, no matter what it took.

Krista stood up. "Can I bother you to take me home for a bit?" she asked in a shaky voice. "I don't want to go home to an empty house and I just wanted a couple of extra changes of clothes in case I want to stay with you longer."

"Not a problem, chum." Luckily, they had come in separate cars in case one of them needed to go somewhere the other didn't have time for. Cathy caught Dave's eye, not sure if he had been listening to the conversation. "I'm taking Krista home so she can get a change of clothes," she said. "Will you be okay to be on your own for a while?"

Dave had already formulated his idea into a doable plan and, putting a relaxed smile on his face, as much for Krista's benefit as for his own, he stood up. "Not a problem. I'll see you back at our place." He kissed both ladies and hurried out to the gray day. It wasn't far to his place and he took the time to rehearse what he was going to say but by the time he parked the car and went inside, his nerves were shot. He really didn't want to have to do this at all, but he really didn't have a choice.

As he settled himself on the sofa, his cell phone in his hand, he knew he was going to hate every single second of the conversation he was about to have. But it had to be done, he had to swallow his pride and, after that humiliation, he was going to have to do an awful lot of kissing up and maybe an awful lot of begging. But deep down he didn't care. This was the only way he could get Paul out of jail and he was willing to do anything for Paul.

Even this.

He thought long and hard about what he was going to say that would assure he would get the money. He knew he would have to make his story convincing, even touching, but most of all reasonable.

He looked at his phone as if it was suddenly the enemy and he felt his mouth go dry on him. Getting a hold of himself, he tapped on his contacts but his finger hovered over the number he wanted for a long moment. He knew he was being ridiculous, he was only making a phone call to help his best friend, there should be nothing to it. Then, taking in a deep breath, he pressed the dial button and waited for it to be answered.

After three rings, it was. He wondered if his name had popped up as the caller whose number he had just dialed but, regardless, he now faced with another problem: How should he address him? It was the same dilemma he had faced all of his life. To call him Anthony would have been an insult, to call him dad would have been a joke. Sir seemed a bit harsh and father too formal. He settled on what he had always called him when he was this unsure.

"Hello, sir."

Anthony Andrews opened his eyes wide in surprise. He had seen his son's name appear on this caller ID but the infrequency of his calls always caused him to feel like that. "David. To what do I owe this unexpected privilege?"

Dave mentally gritted his teeth. Why did he always hope that once, just once, his father would put a little bit of warmth into his voice when talking to him? Surely he would have forgiven and forgotten by now? But the habits of a lifetime were hard to break, even despite the fact they hadn't seen each other in over eight years.

Not that Dave had ever claimed he was the model son. Far from it. He only phoned his parents when he felt like it, which was rarely. They just as rarely called him. "I thought I would give you a quick call, see how you and mom are. If you're busy..."

"No, I'm not busy at the moment. I'm just surprised to hear from you, that's all. I assume you have fully recovered from that injury you had last year?"

*Injury*, Dave thought. A coma that could have stretched on for months, even years, was not an *injury*, it was a traumatic medical emergency. He forced himself not to bite back. "Yes, thank you. A few headaches and sleep disruptions now and again, but otherwise fine."

"And how is that wife of yours...um...Karen isn't it?"

"Cathy. It's Cathy." Dave closed his eyes and pinched the bridge of his nose. *Christ, he couldn't even remember his daugh-*

*ter-in-law's name.* He could feel one of his sudden headaches creeping over the top of his skull.

"Cathy. Right." Dave could already hear the impatience in his father's voice. "Are we going to exchange pleasantries much longer or are you going to tell me the real reason why you called? I have a busy schedule for most of the day."

Dave glanced at his watch. It was almost twelve o'clock on the east coast, which meant it was coming up to nine o'clock in the morning in Nevada. All he had to do now was open his mouth and say the words. "I need money."

There was a pregnant pause and then, "I thought so. How much this time?"

*This time?* His father had made it sound like he made this sort of request every week. Anthony seemed to have forgotten he had never once asked for any sum of money. "One million dollars, er, sir. Please."

"One million dollars?"

Dave supposed he couldn't blame his father for sounding so incredulous. "Yes sir."

"That's a hefty chunk of change. What would you need an amount like that for?"

Dave knew if he mentioned it was to bail Paul out, a man Anthony Andrews, for whatever reason, hated, he may as well kiss the money good bye. "Well, I…I don't quite know what to _"

"Oh. I get it. You got a young lady into trouble. Didn't you?"

Dave suddenly wanted to laugh, he really did. His father was such a stranger to him, he didn't even know his own son was incapable of impregnating anyone. Dave was completely sterile after the vasectomy he'd had performed not long after Cathy's miscarriage. Ah, the bitter sweet irony of it all. On the other hand, his father had just given him a good and plausible excuse.

"Yes, sir, that's exactly what I did. It was one night of foolishness, Cathy doesn't even know and understandably, I don't want her knowing. This girl is very young, barely nine-teen, she doesn't want the responsibility of a baby. She has no money, no insurance and she's terrified of telling her parents. So I told her I would try and help her. Abortions aren't that expensive but making sure she keeps her mouth shut is." He could almost picture his father right now, no doubt dressed in one of his habitual navy blue business suits and plain white shirt, with an exactly matching navy blue tie. The tie would be tied just so in a Windsor knot, his salt and pepper hair trimmed immaculately and no doubt his brow furrowed in disapproval. His deep blue eyes, eyes so like his son's only one shade lighter, would be ice cold. It was the same image Dave always carried of his father and he suspected he had it to a T.

"If you want the abortion done by a reputable clinic, I'm sure it can be expensive enough."

"I agree, but as I said, I need to make sure she keeps her mouth shut. If Cathy ever got wind of this..." He trailed off deliberately, knowing the implication wouldn't be lost on his father. "Could you and mother live through the scandal of yet another divorce in the family?" These were the magic words and he knew it. He waited patiently.

There was another pause, a longer one, and then, "How soon do you need the money?"

"As soon as possible. I have my bank account details right here, can you wire it through before the end of the day?"

"I can try. Give me your details."

Dave recited them, reading the numbers from his debit card, and just as he prepared to end the call, in the nick of time remembered his manners. "Thank you very much, sir. This means a lot to me." More than his father would ever know. Paul was almost home free. Literally.

"I'm very disappointed in you, David, I would have expected better from even you. Cheating on your wife, getting a young girl pregnant, asking me to bail you out to pay for your mistake. I thought we had raised you with better values that this. If this ever gets out it will break your poor mother's heart so I think it would be best if you and I just kept this between ourselves, don't you?"

"Certainly, sir, if that's what you want. And I'm sorry that I've disappointed you." Dave could afford to sound humble now, he had got what he had called for.

"You've been disappointing me one way or the other all your life. Let this be the last of it."

The same speech every time, all water off a duck's back now to Dave. "I'll try my best." He was about to say good bye when an idea sprang into his head. "Is there any chance I could use the apartment in New York if I need to?"

"I've never denied you use of any of our homes. Just give George a call before you go down, he'll want to have the place ready."

"George is still there? I thought he would have been put out to pasture years ago."

"Good, honest housekeepers are hard to find. Is there anything else I can do for you today?"

The beginning of a dismissal, if Dave wasn't mistaken. "No thank you. And thank you again for helping me out in the, huh, matter we discussed. Give my regards to mother. Good bye, sir." He quickly hung up and breathed a sigh of relief, as much as at the fact that the phone call was over as that he had accomplished what he had called for.

He sat back against the sofa and cleared the conversation with his father from his mind as best as he could. Then, re-membering he had to let the bank know to expect the transfer, he pulled up the app on his phone to get the number. After holding for a miraculous three minutes he got to speak to a live person and gave the necessary details to her. He then asked for the money to be made available as a cashier's check and was hit with the first hurdle. A money transfer as large as that would take at least twenty four hours to clear before the issuing of a cashier's check and the earliest he could collect it would be around one o'clock the following afternoon.

Not wanting to take his frustration out on the clerk,

he politely thanked her and requested she contact him if the transfer was cleared sooner. After receiving the promise she would, he hung up.

Everything was set, now all he had to do was wait. He hated Paul having to spend another night in jail but there was nothing he could do. At least he would be out tomorrow.

Cathy and Krista came home half an hour later. Krista looked pale and drawn but whether from pain or shock or both, it was hard to tell. Dave took her bag of clothing up to the guestroom and then hurried back down so he could share the good news about Paul.

Cathy was surprised to see Dave look so upbeat. His best friend had just been put in jail for Lord knew how long and there he was, standing in the doorway, a friendly smile on his face.

Krista noticed his excessively sunny demeanor and she eyed him suspiciously. "Why so cheerful, Dave?" she asked.

He sat down beside her and motioned to Cathy to sit down on her other side, which she did. He then took a hold of Krista's hand. "What would you say if I were to tell you Paul will be home by lunchtime tomorrow? Maybe even earlier."

"I would say you're crazy," she answered immediately.

"Oh, that's not the first time I've been told that," he said cheerily. He patted her hand again. "Really, Kris, please believe me when I say it's going to happen. I was hoping it would have happened today but it just isn't to be."

She somehow knew he believed he was telling the truth but she wasn't going to get her hopes up. There was far too much at stake and Paul's freedom was riding on it. "But how? We don't have that kind of money. It's a million dollars, Dave... a *million!*"

"Can I ask you to please trust me on this? You know I wouldn't give you false hopes, you know this has to be true."

"Please just tell me, Dave. Where are you getting this money from?"

"Never mind where. Just accept it."

Cathy carefully studied her husband's face, looking for a clue that might betray where he would get all that money from. He didn't know anybody with that kind of money...and then the penny dropped and her eyes widened in surprise. "Oh dear God. I know where you're getting it from," she said shakily.

He turned to look at her, his eyes dancing in amusement. He knew it wouldn't have taken her long to work it out. "You do, huh?" he said lightly.

Krista looked at the two of them in bewilderment. "Would one of you please tell me what this is all about?"

Cathy got the nod of approval from Dave and, still trying to process it all, she patted Krista's knee. "What he's being so secretive about is, he has phoned his parents for the money and they have agreed."

Krista sucked a sharp breath in and then grimaced at the pain in her chest. But she ignored it as she shook her head in disbelief. "You actually asked your parents? I didn't think you wanted any more contact with them after the disinterest they showed you when they heard about you being in a coma?"

Out of nowhere, he recalled part of a conversation he'd had with Paul, not that long ago. They'd been sitting in a restaurant, waiting for their lunch, when out of the blue, Paul had asked him what it had been like growing up rich. He couldn't recall every word of the conversation but he did remember saying his parents would need him before he would need them. How wrong had he been, he realized. Pushing the thought out of his head, he gave a nonchalant shrug of his shoulders. "I don't. But for Paul, I did it, I phoned my dad while you were getting your extra clothes. He's transferring the money to me and I should be able to pick up a cashier's check by lunch time tomorrow."

The ladies were stunned into silence. They each knew what it had cost Dave to do this and all they could do was accept it. Krista, predictably, started to cry. "This is too much, Dave, far too much. How can we ever pay you back?"

"Huh? What are you talking about? When his trial is over, regardless of the outcome, I get the million bucks back and I return it to my father. It's as simple as that."

"What reason did you give to get the money?" Cathy asked. "As I recall, Paul isn't one of your dad's favorite people."

He emitted a chuckle. "I got a nineteen year old girl I've been having an affair with pregnant and I needed to pay for an abortion as well as keep her mouth shut so you wouldn't find out."

It was so unexpected and outrageous, it tickled Cathy greatly and she joined him in his laughter. "Oh my, that's too funny!" she said.

Krista could see the funny side too and she smiled through her tears. But it was still serious and she tried to get her head around it. "Before you get the cashier's check, can Cathy and I go shopping first?" she quipped.

He kissed the back of her hand. "Sure thing."

She gently cupped his face. "You are an amazing man, Dave. I know this wasn't an easy decision for you but I am just so grateful you had the resources to be able to do this for Paul."

"For once, I'm glad too. I never thought it would ever pay off to have a wealthy father."

The unexpected news helped clear their minds and gave them a far more positive outlook toward Paul's future. And when Krista went to bed that night, totally exhausted both mentally and physically, she slept soundly and didn't dream, safe in the knowledge the next night she would be in her own bed with her husband lying beside her.

# CHAPTER TWENTY-ONE

Despite being on suspension, Cathy still arose early the next morning. Dave was sleeping soundly beside her and, although it was barely five thirty, she tiptoed into Krista's room to check on her. By the look of it, Krista was deep in slumber and Cathy gently closed the door to let her sleep on as long as she needed.

She took a peek outside the landing window and saw about an inch of snow had fallen sometime through the night. She shivered slightly and padded into the bathroom to take her morning shower. She wrapped her freshly shampooed hair in a towel and went through the motions of getting dried off and dressed before quickly running the dryer over her hair to loosen the curls up a bit. She pulled on blue jeans and a lightweight raspberry colored fleece and, after checking on Dave again, she figured she would give him another half hour before waking him. She had forgotten to ask him the night before if he was planning on going into work today or not.

Tiptoeing downstairs, she checked the fridge and cupboard and saw she had the makings for a pancake breakfast. It had been ages since she'd made pancakes from scratch so she busied herself doing just that, with scrambled eggs, sausage and bacon as accompaniments.

She felt like she should be hurrying to get it all made and eaten in time to leave for work and had to constantly remind herself that she had nowhere to go for the next month. To avoid getting upset about her suspension she busied herself putting on the coffee and just as it hissed and spat its final drops into the pot she was able to put everything in the oven to keep warm until either Dave, or Krista, or both put in an appearance.

She only had to wait barely five minutes when Dave came into the kitchen. She hadn't heard him up and about but she saw he was freshly shaved and showered and dressed in jeans and a navy blue sweater with an open-neck shirt underneath. He kissed her full on the lips when she came up to him for a cuddle.

"Morning, baby," he said softly. He felt her nuzzle his neck and he grinned down at her. "I didn't hear you get up."

"I was a quiet wee mouse," she informed him, kissing him again. "Mmm, you taste good."

He happily obliged letting her taste him as much as she wanted and they would have gotten carried away if they hadn't heard the not too subtle clearing of a throat behind them.

Krista was standing at the doorway, grinning broadly. "Get a room, you two," she said smoothly, sliding into a seat at the table. She saw three place settings and for the first time in days, felt like she could eat something.

Cathy placed a prim look on her face and turned back to the oven. Dave grinned at Krista and sat down facing her. "How you feeling this morning, sweetie?" he asked.

"Better. My chest still hurts but I think the swelling on my face is coming down quite well. At least I can see clearly through both eyes now."

"You do look better," he agreed.

Cathy set a plate laden with pancakes, eggs, bacon and sausage in front of each of them. She was about to pour the coffee when the doorbell rang and, wondering who it could be so early in the morning, and because she was closest to it, she answered it.

She pulled back in surprise when she saw Captain Hamilton standing on her doorstep. "Bob," she said stiffly. In all the time she'd known him, not once had she addressed him by his first name. As he was the one who had placed her on suspension, as far as she was concerned, he technically wasn't her superior officer at the moment. She didn't want to call him what she normally did.

Captain Hamilton kept his expression neutral. "May I come in?"

"If you wish." She stepped back to let him enter and pointed towards the kitchen. "Dave and Krista are in there, go on through."

Dave looked up in amazement when he saw the captain come into the kitchen. "Captain! What brings you here?" He saw Cathy was hovering on the threshold, unsure what to do so he waited for the captain to let them know why he was calling.

"Would you like some coffee?" Cathy asked politely.

He knew she was just playing hostess and he nodded his acceptance. He was painfully aware he still wasn't one of her favorite people. "That would be lovely, Cathy, thank you. Strong and black, please, I've been up all night." He waited for her to pour him a mug and indicated to Krista and Dave to carry on eating. "I didn't want to come so early, but I just got finished and since I was passing your door on my way home, I thought it would be best to talk to you face to face. Please, don't let me interrupt your breakfast."

"There's plenty of food," Cathy said, "I'd be happy to fix you a plate. If you were up all night, you must be hungry."

"I appreciate the offer but no thank you."

Kathy put a forkful of eggs in her mouth and waited for the captain to settle. He looked exhausted as he took a few sips of his coffee. "Why were you up all night?" she asked.

"I wanted to oversee the last of Ken Cameron's autopsy, to make sure every possible detail was covered and there was no evidence of any DNA that might be Paul's on him."

Cathy picked up her coffee and moved towards the door. "It sounds like you're about to talk shop," she said. "Which means I, as an ordinary citizen, should not be listening in on official police business. I'll be in the living room if you need me."

"Cathy, wait." The Captain looked at her as calmly as he could. He was too tired to play any mind games. "I'd like you to stay and hear this. Just because you're on suspension doesn't mean you're not still a cop."

She glanced at Dave for some form of direction and when he gave a terse nod, she went back to the table to sit beside her husband. "I'll listen and try not to intervene," she said coldly.

"Stop looking at me like I'm the enemy, Cathy," Captain Hamilton said with a weary sigh. "Contrary to what you might think, I don't get a kick out of suspending one of my officers. I did what I had to do and unfortunately it just happened to be at your expense."

"I'm not looking upon you as the enemy," she retorted icily. "Just someone I thought I could trust to make the right decision and stand up for his officer when she makes a simple error in judgement."

The captain's eyes clouded over. He was hoping she wouldn't still be this upset. But then again, who could blame her? "Okay, Cathy, let me tell you the report and I'll be out of your way."

"As you wish."

"The coroner was very thorough, I'll give him that. He knows this is an official murder case so he wanted to make sure he performed a complete autopsy and got everything recorded. The definite cause of death was a broken neck. He went over the whole body with a fine toothcomb but he didn't find any foreign skin or hair samples under the fingernails. It seems he didn't struggle with whomever killed him, nor did he struggle with Paul. The only other hairs they found were red female pubic hairs mixed in with his own, indicating he'd had sex with someone within twenty four hours prior to being murdered. Assuming he didn't shower, of course."

"Where is this getting us?" Dave asked.

"Not sure yet. Krista, when he beat you up, did you fight

back?"

"I tried to, but he was freakishly strong – and agile."

"Did you kick him at all? Like in the groin?"

"Not so much a kick, but I kneed him as hard as I could. It clearly wasn't enough to stop him. Why?"

"Because his penis and testicles had been mashed to a pulp."

"Oh. Well, I don't think I got him that badly."

"Do you think Paul could have?"

"Paul's usually a clean fighter," Dave said. "He goes for the jugular, not the balls. However, as angry as he was, he was capable of anything."

"That's what I figured. I'll have to ask him."

"Could Ken have been murdered by whomever he had sex with?"

"Possibly, but not probably. An unidentified redhead was caught on CCTV leaving his room late on the night before he was killed. She looked like she was a hundred pounds soaking wet and, unless she's had martial arts training, she didn't look strong enough to break a man's neck. Her pubic hair was used to get a DNA sample but the results are still pending. However, gut instinct is telling me she was just a random woman. If she's a hooker, her DNA will match in the system, but only if she's had any other priors."

"Okay then, we'll have to come up with some sort of angle here." Dave felt a tap on his shoulder and turned towards Cathy. "What, love?" She leaned in against him and whispered something in his ear and when she finished, he looked at her in amazement. "That's a good idea, Cath. Cap, did the ME find any drugs in Ken's system?"

"Cocaine, yes. And alcohol. Apparently he was in the early stages of alcoholic cirrhosis of the liver. I know a full toxicology report can take a while to come through but alcohol and a few of the more common drugs can be easily detected. What have you come up with?"

"*I* didn't come up with anything, Cathy did. As Paul

testified yesterday, his father had confessed there were men coming after him because he owed them money...thirty-five grand I believe. I think it's safe to assume these men were drug lords, or more than likely worked for drug lords. What if the damaged sex organs and or the broken neck are their calling cards? That those methods are the way they get rid of their victims instead of a bullet to the skull, or a pair of concrete shoes or whatever. Plausible?"

"Very. But how can we come up with the proof?"

"Aren't Jim and Mark checking the CCTV at the motel again for anything that might have happened after Paul was there?" Krista asked. "Do you know if they've had the chance to go to the motel yet?"

Hamilton nodded. "Yes. I texted Chipman for an update just before I left the morgue but haven't heard back."

Just to be sure, the captain checked his cell phone in case he'd missed a message but there wasn't anything new showing. He was about to pocket the phone again when it rang and the caller ID showed him it was Detective Chipman. "Mark, was just talking about you. I'm at the Andrews' and Krista is here too..." He paused to listen when Mark interrupted him and he rolled his eyes. "No, I haven't reinstated her...yes, I'll be sure to tell the commish he's an asshole. Enough. Tell me what you and Turner found at the motel." The captain listened for a long moment and it was hard to read his reaction to Mark's words. He murmured a thank you and hung up.

Krista didn't like the defeated look in the captain's eyes. It wasn't a look she saw often and she felt her heart sink. "Doesn't look like good news," she said.

"For whatever reason, the CCTV camera was disabled right after Paul left," he said-shaking his head in disbelief. "The motel manager wasn't made aware of it until late last night so Mark and Jim think whoever came to murder Ken knew the camera was there and disabled it to make sure they weren't filmed."

A heavy silence descended on the room. Now they

wouldn't be able to prove someone had gone into Paul's father's room after Paul left, which meant they were going to have to find the proof from somewhere else.

Cathy looked meaningfully at Dave and he nodded. When she had whispered to him a few moments earlier, she had said more than just to check about the drugs in Ken's system.

"There might be a way we can come up with some proof," he said.

"And how is that?" the captain asked.

"You let us go to New York."

"Just like that? I am as anxious as you are to get some proof but going down there would more than likely be nothing but a wild goose chase. You could be down there for a weeks, or even months, and with even more budget cuts, the department won't be able to fund it for you. There'll be your accommodation for starters, flights…"

"We can drive down. We'll take one car and even spring for our own gas. As for accommodation, my father has a Penthouse down there, big enough to house twelve people comfortably. Paul knows Brooklyn like the back of his hand and he can strike up a rapport with his buddies at the Brooklyn PD. Any investigations we can do ourselves and because it's official police duties we'll get paid as if we're doing our job. I have no way of knowing how long we'll be down there, but at least you can rest assured we're not costing the department anything extra other than the pay we're entitled to."

The captain mulled over that information, stroking the stubble on his chin. He could see the determined light in his detective's eyes and he knew there was no reason why the commissioner or anyone else would stop them from doing what they had to do to prove the innocence of one of their own. "I'll see what I can do," he acquiesced. "I'm going home for some shut-eye first but I'll go into the office this afternoon and set the ball rolling." He drained the last of his coffee, grateful for the caffeine hit. He was still tired and knew the coffee wouldn't hold him for long. "Any word on how we can get Paul out of jail?" he asked.

"The bank will be notifying me within twenty four hours to let me know I can go down to pick up a cashier's check."

"For a million bucks?" the captain asked in astonishment.

"That was the bail amount."

"Where are you getting the money from?" Before Dave could say anything, the captain answered his own question. "Your father, right?"

"Right."

"That must have hurt."

"It was worth it for Paul."

"I understand. I was going to speak to Cora for us to put our house up for collateral. Now we won't have to. She wouldn't have had a problem." He gave Krista a tired smile. "She really wouldn't have - don't know why but she has a soft spot for all four of you."

The kindness Krista had been shown over the last couple of days continued to amaze her and she returned the smile. "Thank you, captain."

"I'll see myself out. Cathy, thank you for the coffee. Krista, Dave, one of you guys let me know when Paul's out."

The front door closed softly and when the captain got into his car and drove off a few moments later, his thoughts returned to a conversation he'd had with the commissioner late the evening before. He had pled Cathy's case as best as he could and he was hoping he had been able to convince the commissioner into lifting her suspension.

He knew how much she was hurting, and although he couldn't blame her, he wasn't able to tell her he was completely on her side. Maybe when he spoke with the commissioner later it would be to hear good news.

He could hope so anyway.

# CHAPTER TWENTY-TWO

Dave picked up the cashier check at around one thirty the following afternoon. The bail payment rules in Massachusetts are such that, regardless of the amount, the money is returned to the payer at the end of the trial. It doesn't matter if the person is found guilty or not, the bail is simply a guarantee the accused will show up in court.

He handed the check over to the county clerk at the jailhouse without fanfare. After everything was rubber-stamped and recorded, and he had signed his name more times than he thought necessary, he was told to wait. The waiting area was depressingly gray and soulless and, thankfully, no other patrons were about. He waited for what felt like an age and was just about to go and ask what the holdup was when a buzzer sounded and he looked expectantly towards a grey steel door in the far corner.

A few seconds later, the door opened, and through it came a tentative Paul. He paused for a moment and when he saw Dave coming slowly towards him, he strode over to him. The two men embraced and when Dave released him, he gave his friend a critical once over.

"You look like shit, bro," he stated cheerily.

Paul knew he wasn't going to be winning any beauty contests and couldn't refrain from smiling. "Still better looking than you, bro." He had spent three nights in a jail cell and it had taken a dramatic toll on him even in this short space of time. He was pale and drawn, needed a shave and even his eyes, usually so full of life and sparkle, were dull and empty.

"Come on, let's get you home. I know a certain young lady who is probably wearing a path between the living room and the window looking out for you to come home."

"How is she?"

"She looks lots better but her ribs are still tender." Dave handed Paul a thick jacket. "Here, you'll need this, it's freezing out there and it's starting to snow."

Paul gratefully pulled the coat on and followed Dave outside. He didn't look back, he kept his head down and slid into the front seat of the car. As Dave settled himself and started the engine, Paul gripped his arm. "Who paid the bail?" he asked.

"Later, Cam, I'll tell you later. I just want to get you home."

Paul narrowed his eyes thoughtfully. Dave didn't usually stall and would normally have given the information over easily. Which meant he was stalling for a reason. And suddenly Paul knew why. "Oh, Dave…no…please tell me you didn't go to your father for this?"

Dave concentrated on keeping the car from skidding when he pulled out into the main road. Thankfully, traffic was at a minimum. Knowing Paul was waiting expectantly, he mentally gritted his teeth. Paul's apartment was twenty minutes away and there was no way Dave would get out of telling him during that time. "Okay, seeing as how you asked…yes, I went to him. I really had no other choice."

Paul threw his head back against the headrest. "Jesus Christ." He didn't know whether to be angry or upset or grateful or what, and he turned to stare out the window. "You did have a choice. Ask him or let me stay in jail."

Dave nodded. "Exactly. I had no other choice. Did you really think I was going to let you stay in jail? You know how long these things can take to come to trial. Did you really think I could do that to you *and* to Krista? I had the resources and I used them accordingly."

For once, Paul couldn't tell if Dave was on the defensive. He did know Dave was at least trying to remain calm and act like it was no big a deal. The problem was, it was a *huge* deal but it had been a completely selfless act on Dave's behalf. He had done what he did to help his best friend. Paul also knew it had probably caused Dave a lot of angst to go to his father so he reckoned he should at least show his gratitude. "Bet you didn't tell him it was to bail me out of jail," he said, tongue-in-cheek.

Dave heard the light-hearted tone and he inwardly relaxed. "Oh no, not at all. He thinks I got a nineteen year old girl pregnant and I'm paying for an abortion and to keep her mouth shut so she won't tell Cathy."

Paul spun his head round to look at Dave in astonishment and then, out of the blue, he realized the bitter irony of that story and he started to chuckle. "Are you serious? You, the Sunkist orange?"

"Sunkist orange?"

"Yeah, all juice no seed." The shared laughter eased the slight tension and Paul thumped Dave playfully on the arm. "Thank you, Dave, I know asking your father can't have been easy for you."

"He'll get it back after the trial, you know that. Think I'll hold it in the bank for a while, collect some interest and then get Cathy the house by the sea she wants so badly."

They lapsed into a companionable silence for the duration of the journey. There was no need for words, Dave sensed Paul needed to get his head around being free. It might have only been seventy-two hours but it must have felt like a year to Paul.

When they got to the apartment, Paul was barely out of the car when he saw Krista hurrying down the path towards him, her arms outstretched, tears of happiness in her eyes. He folded her carefully into his embrace, mindful of not to hurt her and he buried his face against her neck, smelling her, wanting her, needing her.

"Let's get inside," she said softly, keeping a tight hold of his hand. "Cathy wants to say hello, then I think she said she and Dave will leave so we can be alone."

Paul turned to look at Dave, who shrugged. "If that's what the boss has said, then I guess we will."

"Come over for dinner, please," Paul said as he entered the warmth of his apartment. "Chinese, my treat."

Cathy didn't give Dave a chance to answer as she flung herself into Paul's arms. "Thank God you're home," she said softly. "You have been much missed."

"Thanks, little dude. And thank you for looking after Krista."

"She makes it easy for me but you're welcome."

He shepherded them into the living room, wanting them to leave him alone with Krista but wanting their company as well. Five minutes wouldn't hurt. Krista was still holding on to his hand anyway so at least he still had physical contact. "So, what about Chinese later?"

"Depends on how much snow we get," Cathy said quickly. "I've a feeling we shouldn't be out and about later. We'll play it by ear."

"No worries. Has anybody said anything about new findings at the motel or anything else?"

"We'll talk shop tomorrow," Dave said. "Right now, we want you to relax, with your beautiful bride by your side and not think about a thing except being together. Deal?"

Paul didn't get the sense he was being stonewalled. In truth, he didn't want to talk about himself or his case for a while yet and he looked down into Krista's eyes. "You up for being by my side, beautiful bride?

"Try and stop me," she purred.

Cathy caught Dave's eye and nodded towards the door. "On that note, we'll get going." She hugged Paul again and then Krista. "Call me if you need me, okay chum?"

"You know I will. Love you."

Dave embraced his friends too and gave Paul a fist bump. "Really glad you're home, partner."

When the Andrews left moments later, Krista quickly snuggled in against Paul. "You okay, love?"

"Perfect now. Except I would really love to get out of these clothes and have a long, hot shower. Can you give me about fifteen minutes?"

"I can give you as long as you need. If you don't mind, I won't be joining you, but I'll wait right here for you."

He understood she was sore and therefore not looking for anything strenuous and he kissed the tip of her nose. "I won't be too long."

After hanging up his suit and throwing his other clothes in the hamper, he stayed under a steaming shower for as long as he could bear it. He could feel the hot water hitting his skin like tiny pin pricks and felt his tensions slip slowly away. When he stepped out and wrapped a towel around his waist, he reached over to the mirror and, using a hand towel, wiped the steam away so he could see to shave.

There was a spotlight on the ceiling above the mirror to help whoever was using the mirror see their features clearly. Krista loved it when she was applying make-up but now, as he peered at his face, he inwardly groaned. The stark light showed every line of fatigue and strain and even he could see his eyes had lost their spark.

He applied shaving cream to his cheeks and chin and although he was far from over the horrors of the last few days he wasn't surprised to see his hands were still shaking. He knew it probably wasn't the best time to shave but he needed to because it always helped make him feel more human, and certainly more clean.

He willed his hand holding the razor to stop shaking but it wouldn't co-operate and he let out a hiss when he ended up nicking himself pretty badly on the chin. He stared miserably down at the droplets of blood hitting the globs of shaving cream in the sink, turning them an interesting shade of pink. He grabbed a tissue from the box on the shelf beside him and winced at the sting when he held it to the cut.

He sat down on the closed toilet lid and stared off into space. He felt strange, as if he was floating outside of his own body and looking down at himself from a great height. He didn't like what he could see in himself: a man who had lived a relatively good life for a long time and who was now broken, with no clue how to put himself back together again.

He faced a turbulent sea of life-altering choices but he didn't know where to begin in making the right choice. He wanted to hear the autopsy reports, the crime scene reports and anything else his fellow officers had been able to find out for him. He wanted to place the biggest ad he could in the newspaper and declare his innocence. He wanted to run away with Krista and stay away for a very long time. Just go somewhere no one could find them. He wanted his name cleared but didn't know how to clear it. He wanted to turn back the clock and start it again a week ago and make sure none of the events of the last four days ever happened.

With a deep sigh of despair, he came back into himself and when he took the tissue away, he saw the cut had nearly stopped bleeding. His literally felt sick and his emotions were all over the place and he knew there was still a long road he had to travel before he would find anything close to normal again. He felt helpless and hopeless and knew he had to adjust his attitude if he was going to begin to put the pieces together again.

He stood up, washed the blood and shaving cream down the drain, checked to make sure he hadn't left any towels lying around, if only to please Krista, and went into the bedroom to get dressed.

When he went downstairs a short while later, dressed in jogging bottoms and a Bathville PD sweatshirt, he found Krista standing at the living room window. She was staring out at the snow accumulating thick and fast but she heard him come in and turned towards him.

"What happened?" she asked, pointing to his chin.

"Razor cut." He pulled her into his arms and rubbed her back. "I missed you, baby," he murmured.

"Not as much as I missed you."

He pulled back slightly so he could study her face better. The ugly purple bruises were slowly fading to a yellowish tinge and the swelling was definitely down. He laid a kiss on her forehead. "I want to make love to you," he whispered, gently pushing an errant strand of hair away from her cheek. "I want to take you to bed and make love to you…and I can't."

"You can't?" She shook her head in bewilderment. "Why not?"

"You have broken ribs. You got kicked all over. You're in pain even when you're sitting still. No, I just want you to know that I want to…but I can't. And I won't."

She loved him for taking her injuries into consideration. She loved him for everything and her heart swelled with emotion. She had wanted even a tiny embrace from him and now that she had him right in front of her, she felt more relaxed than she had in days. She gently traced the outline of his lips, her eyes full of adoration and yearning. "Hopefully it won't be too long before you can. Maybe in a day or two we can find a way that will be gentle and careful and yet totally mind blowing."

"Baby, I like the way you think." And as he kissed her softly on the lips, he knew he had found the first step in getting his life back to some sort of normal.

Anything he had to do would be for Krista, and because of her. She was his life and with her strength behind him, he would be able to get through anything.

# CHAPTER TWENTY-THREE

The snow stopped falling around eight o'clock that evening and by the morning, Bathville woke up to temperatures in the mid-forties and the snow melted or melting. It was only the second week of December but it felt almost spring-like so, if nothing else, it would be a welcome respite before winter kicked in for real.

Dave had every intention of going into the office early. However, he slept through his alarm and had to hurry through his shower and get dressed in record time. Cathy woke up with him, saw how late it had gotten and, pulling on her bathrobe, hurried downstairs to make breakfast while he got ready.

Half-way through eating, the doorbell rang for the second morning in a row. Because he was closest to it, he answered it and was surprised to see Captain Hamilton there. Again.

"Bob," he said crisply. "I know I'm running late but I didn't think they had to send the cavalry."

The captain gave a tired smile. "Not here for that at all. May I come in?"

"Well, Cathy's here and you know how she feels about you right now."

"I'll only keep you a moment," the captain persisted.

Without a word, Dave stepped back to let the big man enter. He pointed him towards the kitchen. "She's in there. If you prefer we can go to the living room, it's up to you."

Cathy appeared at the kitchen door, wiping her hands

on a tea towel and she froze when she saw the captain there. She pulled the front of her robe more tightly to her neck. "Er, please excuse my appearance, if I'd known you were coming I would have gotten dressed."

"It's not a problem. I've been married nearly thirty years, I've seen a woman in her bathrobe before."

"Would you like a cup of coffee?" she asked politely.

"That would be most welcome, thank you." Following Dave's gesture for him to sit at the table, he slid into a chair. "I've come for a couple of reasons this morning," he said. "I spoke with Paul last night and he said you'd told him to wait until today to talk about your plans to get his name cleared. From that, I take it he doesn't know you intend to go to New York?"

Dave sipped at his coffee and shook his head. "Not yet. He was exhausted when I picked him up at the jailhouse, and I know he needed to get his head around what's happened these last few days. I told him we would talk today."

"That's fine, I don't blame you for wanting to wait. I have it cleared with the commish that you can go down to New York. I've applied for the necessary paperwork and the only thing I need to do today is let the DA and Ted Reynolds know I'll be applying for the paperwork to allow Paul to leave the state while he's out on bail. They can't stop him from leaving if he's working in his capacity as a police officer. And they definitely can't stop him if he's trying to get evidence that will clear his name. The DA might be opposed but that's because he's an asshole. He can't do anything to stop the investigation from happening."

Dave nodded his head in appreciation. "That's great, captain, thank you for doing that for us. We might be gone a few days but hopefully we can be back before Christmas with the evidence we need to clear Paul."

The captain looked into the dark depths of his coffee. He remained silent for a long moment, then turned to Cathy. "I take it you'll be going down to New York too?"

She faltered and looked over at Dave, who immediately stepped in with a reply on her behalf. "Of course she's coming with us. I thought I might treat my wife to a little bit of sight-seeing down there. If there's anywhere open, of course. Too bad we can't take in a Broadway show."

"You needn't try to pull the wool over my eyes, Dave. I know she'll be helping you with the investigations. Which is the other reason why I'm here today."

"Are you going to try and stop her?"

"Nope. I'm here to give her these." The captain reached into the pocket of his winter coat and brought out a gun and a badge. "These, I believe, are yours, Cathy. And as of seven o'clock this morning, your suspension has been lifted."

"It has?" she asked breathlessly.

"It has," he confirmed. "I'm still not saying I was wrong to impose the suspension but I will concede that agreeing with the commissioner so quickly was not one of my finest moments. The suspension was harsh, even the commissioner agrees with me now." It had taken him most of the previous day before he had been able to get through to the commissioner but he didn't tell Cathy that. The important thing was, he had. "However, he and I are in full agreement that if you step out of line even once within the next two weeks – either here or in New York – the suspension will be reinstated. Is that clear?"

"Yes, sir," she said and carefully took her badge and gun from him. "Thank you very much," she added, remembering her manners. "This means a lot to me because now I can fully help Paul again." She looked at Dave, her eyes sparkling and he tipped her a wink of congratulations.

The captain drained his coffee and stood up. "On that note, now you're *both* late so I won't keep you any longer. I'll see you at the station."

Dave closed the door after him and turned to Cathy with a chuckle of delight. "You're back on the force, baby. I'm really glad for you. I knew it was only going to be a matter of time before the captain came to his senses. And not a moment too soon."

"I was hoping." Suddenly, she glanced at the clock on the kitchen wall. "Oh goodness, the captain is right we are both going to be late. I haven't finished my breakfast, I need to shower and dress. My car needs petrol in it too -"

"Gas, love," he corrected her. "Your car needs gas. I'll take your car and fill it up, you go ahead and get showered and you can go to work in my car. I'll clear up in here too." He turned her around in the direction of the stairs and patted her rear end. "Get going, and I'll see you at the station."

While he was filling the tank on Cathy's car, Dave mentally went over a plan of attack for the day. He knew Paul wasn't expected to go into the station but he really wanted to talk to him about New York and, after hanging up the pump and getting the receipt, Dave got into the car and pulled over to the side so he could make a phone call. His phone contacts weren't on Cathy's Blue Tooth. He called Captain Hamilton and told him of the change of plan, then he called Cathy, who had showered and was already almost dressed. He told her to meet him at the Camerons', then he called Paul.

"Yo, Dave," Paul sounded sleepy but cheerful. "It's seven fifteen, are you okay?"

"Yes, great, just wanted to run something by you. First, you'll be pleased to know Cathy's suspension has been lifted."

"Aw, that's great man, happy for her."

"Thought you might be. Second, rather than talk to you on the phone, can you get your ass in gear and be up and about in about ten minutes? Cathy and I need to talk to you and Krista."

"Sure, I wasn't sleeping anyway. I'll shower real quickly and I think Krista's already downstairs so she can let you in. She's feeling a lot better today, which is great."

"Sounds fantastic, man. Want anything from Dunkin's?"

"Yes, but no thanks, I think Krista said she wanted to

make breakfast this morning, get back into some sort of routine and normalcy again."

"No worries, see you soon."

Krista was happy to see her friends when they arrived within a couple of minutes of one another and they each congratulated her on how well she looked. She was moving less stiffly too, which pleased them immensely, and Krista gave Cathy a huge hug to congratulate her in getting her job back.

Paul came downstairs a short while later and after the customary greetings and the initial joy at being in each other's company again, they sat down at their favorite meeting place in the kitchen. Krista had made a fresh pot of coffee and made sure everyone's cup was filled before they started talking.

"I was on the way to the station," Dave began, "but I wanted to come and see you first. I'll still be going to the station sometime today so I can talk with Mark and Jim, see if they have any new angles that might be of help to you. But first, I believe Captain Hamilton phoned you last night, probably to see how you are?"

Paul was buttering a slice of toast and at the mention of his superior, he paused. "Yes. Why?"

"The other morning, when he came to our house, he asked what we were planning to do to get your name cleared? We all agreed we should go to New York."

Paul looked down at his toast and set it back on the plate. "New York? Why?"

"Because you seem to think the people who murdered your father come from there. I know we can't confirm that and I also know it will be like looking for a needle in a haystack but we have to start somewhere, right?"

Paul carefully considered and nodded. "Right. But I'm probably not allowed to leave the state so does that mean you and Cathy are going to go down there on your own?"

"Nope, you and Krista will be coming with us. The captain has it cleared with the commissioner and he's approaching Ardolino and Reynolds today. The DA can't stop an investigation in progress."

Paul looked at each of them in turn. "You think we might find something down there?"

"Only one way to find out."

He returned his attention to his toast. His eggs were getting cold but he didn't care. He took a few bites just to settle his hungry stomach but he knew they were all waiting for some sort of response from him. He hadn't considered for one second going to New York, he had assumed he wouldn't be allowed to leave Massachusetts but after being told it was possible, and even getting his superiors' backing, he allowed the first stirrings of excitement. He wanted to be cautious, though, he didn't want to get his hopes up but he knew he had just been given an answer to one of the many dark doubts he'd been experiencing since being released.

"This is a wonderful plan and I really can't thank you all enough for wanting to do this for me. But, really, New York? Where can we stay? Are hotels even opened down there? Even if they are, they're ridiculously expensive and we could be down there for days, weeks, who knows how long. I'm sure the department won't pick up our tab and I just can't justify you having to waste your money on what could be a wild goose chase."

"We've got the accommodation sorted," Dave said matter-of-factly. "My father has a penthouse apartment on Park Avenue and I asked him permission to use it when I was asking him for the million bucks. He said I was welcome to use it anytime I wanted."

Paul baulked at that final bit of information and suddenly felt at a loss. "Dave, no, this is all getting a little bit ridiculous, don't you think?"

"Huh? How so?"

"The bail money, the use of an apartment – on Park Avenue, no less! I just keep taking and taking and giving nothing back."

Krista could see the wounded pride lurking behind

Paul's eyes and she reached over to hold his hand. "I really don't think Dave is expecting you to give anything back, love," she said softly.

Picking up on her cue, Dave nodded enthusiastically. "All I want is for you to agree to this. The department might not be picking up the tab, but you do have their full support behind you."

"It just seems that you're putting way more into our friendship than I do - and now this."

"You give me more every day than I'll ever be able to return," Dave said slowly. He was trying not to sound exasperated but he could understand where Paul was coming from and he didn't want to chastise or ridicule him.

Paul shook his head. "You bought me a beautiful guitar the first Christmas you and I became partners. Then when that asshole Chuck Ericson damaged it beyond repair, you bought me a new one. One that was more expensive than the original. On top of that, you gave me a solid gold guitar pick. Those aren't like giving someone a sweater or a pair of shoes, those are big ticket items."

"Paul, really, you know material things don't mean anything to me."

"I know, but that's not the point. Then, not long after we came back from Belfast, I find out when I was doing a routine check on my bank statement, that you had paid the last six months of my car loan. And your answer was, you had been given a lot of money for your birthday a few years back and you were able to buy your Camaro outright. You didn't like the idea of me making payments on my Mustang so you helped me along. You know I was shocked when I found out what you'd done, you know I even got angry with you but you also know I was eternally grateful."

Dave squirmed uncomfortably. He didn't like being reminded of the generosity he sometimes showed to people. He bought them a gift, that was the end of it as far as he was concerned. "Yeah. So? What does all this have to do with us going to New York?"

Paul stared moodily down at his coffee. He could feel Krista's hand in his and he sought comfort in her touch. He lifted his gaze to Dave. "I suppose it doesn't have anything to do with us going to New York," he said eventually.

"Then we'll go?"

"Uh huh. I suppose I should be grateful we have the means to save us some money."

Cathy and Krista shared a glance of relief. Cathy had seriously thought Paul was going to reject the whole idea. "It's okay, Paul, we want to do anything, and go anywhere, if it will help clear your name. This is the real reason why we're doing it."

Paul nodded slowly. "Okay, but please, Dave, no more."

"Hey, I can't make any promises but I'll do my best."

There was a moment of silence as they gathered their thoughts and tried to ease the built-up tension. Eventually, Paul broke the tension with one of his unexpectedly offbeat comments. "Say, Big D, just how many homes does your father own anyway? I might want to plan my next vacation in one of them."

Grateful for the levity, Dave grinned. "He has four, if you must know...no, wait, he has five. One in Vegas, one in Reno, one in Carson City, Nevada one in the Bahamas and the one in New York. Oh, he also has a place in Big Sur, California. So I guess that makes six."

Having not expected such an impressive answer, Paul stared at his friend in shock. Then he quickly composed himself. "Well, in that case, when the pandemic is finally over and world travel is allowed again, I vote we go to the Bahamas."

"You did ask, Paulie," Dave reminded him smugly. "But as long as you're on board for the New York trip, I'll phone the housekeeper and tell them to expect us in a couple of days."

"Does anyone know what the quarantine rules are for New York?" Cathy asked.

"It won't matter. We all get tested regularly because of

our jobs, we've always tested negative, if we prove we're down on official police business, that should keep us in the clear," Krista stated.

Paul lapsed into silence and concentrated on finishing his breakfast. Here was yet another choice he had made that was going to help shape his future in the way he wanted it to be. Going to New York might prove futile, but at least it was something concrete to focus on.

If he dared believe it, maybe, just maybe, everything else would fall into place and his future wouldn't be so uncertain after all.

# CHAPTER TWENTY-FOUR

Dave and Cathy went into the precinct mid-morning. They hurried up to the fourth floor and, as they made their way to their desks, they passed several people, some of whom gave Dave peculiar, side-long glances. Some were even scowling, a few downright hostile. He thought it had something to do with Ardolino having brought up the fact he'd been at the motel and had maybe inadvertently jeopardized Paul's case. That sort of thing he could handle. But when he got to his office, he witnessed more of the same from the few detectives in the squad room. He really had no idea what he'd done to deserve the looks but he had a feeling he wasn't going to like hearing it.

Cathy looked around them slowly, mentally taking a note of who seemed friendly and who didn't. She had no clue what was going on but then she saw the friendly faces of Jim and Mark, who were already on their way to her and Dave's desks.

"Are you back with us, Cathy?" Mark asked, slipping her a warm smile.

"For another while." She looked back towards the squad room and jerked her thumb in its direction. "Why were a lot of people looking at Dave as if he had done something wrong?"

Dave had taken off his jacket and was hanging it over the back of his chair. "Yeah, what gives?" he asked, rolling up the sleeves of his shirt. "Was it my turn to bring the donuts or something?"

Jim and Mark looked at each other, trying to decide who should tell him, and what they should say. As close as they were to Dave, they had both been momentarily thrown for a loop when they'd heard the news because they simply had not heard anything about it before. However, they had reckoned it was just one of those matters Dave wanted to keep private and the news certainly wasn't going to be enough for them to write Dave out of their lives.

Jim flopped down at Krista's desk. He linked his fingers over his trim waist and put his feet up. "Well, Andrews, it's like this. It seems that for all the time we've known you, you've been a dark horse."

"Okay," he answered slowly, a frown of confusion wrinkling his forehead. "In what way?" In his peripheral vision, he saw three detectives come to the doorway of the office but he ignored them as he kept his attention on Jim. He could see Jim was struggling to find appropriate words. Or maybe he was trying to think of what to say that wouldn't hurt Dave's feelings.

"We didn't know you had a Daddy Warbucks," Jim volunteered at last.

At that, although slightly out of context, Dave knew what Jim was referring to. He let out a sigh of exasperation. "Right. Paul's bail money. How did you find out?"

"Someone...and I won't say who...overheard the captain telling the commissioner yesterday about Paul's release and who had paid the bail and where the money had come from."

"I see." He turned towards the officers loitering in the doorway. "Anything you want to add to this, boys?"

One of them marched meaningfully into the office. Detective Peter Holden, ten years Dave's senior, squared his five foot nine frame up against Dave's six foot three. "Daddy pay for everything in your life, Andrews?" he asked snidely.

Dave could have chosen to be sarcastic, or angry, or apathetic, or even non-committal. Instead he looked Holden up and down and then, with a smirk, turned away and sat down at his desk. "I assume you have work to do? I know I do."

Cathy went to stand beside Dave. She was angry Dave was being singled out like this. She knew Holden well, but didn't particularly care much for him. "Just leave him alone, Holden. His private life has nothing to do with you."

"It does when I find we have a little rich boy in our midst, pretending to earn an honest living when all he has to do is phone his Daddy for any amount of money he wants."

She let out a long, low breath. She felt Dave tense beneath the hand she had placed on his shoulder and she pressed down slightly to stay him. "Are you jealous or something?" she asked icily.

"Not a bit. Any money I have I have gotten honestly."

"So has Dave. And as his wife I have first-hand knowledge of what his bank account is. You keep up this little... *meeting*...and I will have to report you to HR for interfering in a colleague's personal life."

"Go ahead. Will you also tell them you married Andrews for his money?"

Cathy chuckled at that. "You absolute moron. First of all, I fell in love with him *before* I knew of his family money. Second, it's not *his* money, it's his parents'. And lastly, he wanted to get his partner out of jail so he swallowed a lot of pride and went to the only source he knew where he could get the money from." She flicked a glance at Mark. *Get rid of him,* was her silent message to him.

Mark understood and shepherded Holden towards the door and closed it behind him. He turned to Dave and Cathy and raised his hands in an apologetic gesture. "Sorry, buddy, I knew they were a little disgruntled, but I didn't realize Holden, at least, is downright jealous."

Dave shrugged. "No one was supposed to find out. But since it's out in the open, are you guys cool with it?"

Jim nodded without hesitation. "It surprised me, which you can understand, but it doesn't bother me. I'm glad you were able to do this for Paul."

Dave relaxed. Having the backing of Jim and Mark on anything was important to him. "Thanks, Jimbo. Mark?"

Chipman shrugged noncommittally. "No worries, Dave. Like Jim said, I'm glad you could do this for Paul. We had no idea...*none* of us had any idea...you had that type of upbringing."

"What did you want me to do, come in every morning and throw money around?"

"No, but you can start if you wish. You know where my desk is."

Dave grinned. "Asshole. Okay, now that we got that out of the way, any news from the motel?"

"I got the guest list from the manager," Jim said. "For such a sleazy place, their computer software is impressively state-of-the-art but not used to its fullest potential."

"In what way?" Cathy asked.

"He gave me a printout of the people who were registered at the time of Ken Cameron's murder. However, the information on these people is scant at best. First and last names and the state they're from. No credit card information, no address, no license plate number, no cell phone."

"One of the guests came from, of all places, the Yukon. You know, in Canada," Mark continued. "He was, apparently, in a Winnebago and why he was staying somewhere like the Blue Moon when he had a sixty thousand dollar RV to sleep in, we're still trying to find out."

"If the motel only registered his name and state...or in this case, territory, how did you know he was in a Winnebago?" Cathy asked.

"The CCTV showed it parked a few doors down from Cameron's room and it even caught the license plate. We've been on with the Canadian equivalent of the DMV and they're trying to get us more contact details."

"Good job," Dave said. "Thanks, guys. I really appreciate your helping out with this investigation. I haven't been able to do much for Paul, which I'm going to rectify, and now with Cathy back on the force, we'll be able to give it our all."

"We want to help Paul just as much as you do," Jim said. "What are your plans?"

"We've been granted permission to go to New York. To Brooklyn to be exact where, as you know, Paul hails from. We're thinking the people who were supposedly after his father are operating out of Brooklyn."

"You want to go down there in the middle of a pandemic?" Mark asked in surprise.

"No choice, Chips. When we left Paul and Krista this morning, she was begging for something to do so I tasked her with checking the Covid rules and regulations both for Manhattan and Brooklyn.

"Hotels are ultra-expensive down there," Mark said.

Dave had the good grace to look sheepish at that. "I know...which is why we'll not be staying in a hotel. We'll be staying in my father's Park Avenue apartment."

Despite his matter-of-fact tone, Jim and Mark looked at him in astonishment. And then they started to laugh. "Jesus, Andrews, you're just full of surprises."

"I try," he said, in his best 'aw shucks' manner. He glanced over at the captain's office. The door was open and the blinds were too, letting him see that the captain wasn't there. "Any idea when the big man will be back?"

"We weren't here when he left," Mark said.

"Doesn't matter, we're not going anywhere. I just wondered if he'd found anything out about Paul's permission to go to Brooklyn. Oh, speaking of Paul, he was going to arrange a Zoom meeting with one of his colleagues in the Brooklyn PD to try and put some feelers out about drug families down there. He's going to see if there is a particular family who use pulverized genitalia and or a broken neck as punishment for people who wrong them."

"At least that helps narrow the field," Mark mused. He sat down heavily on Paul's chair. "Man, I can't believe this is

*Paul* we're talking about. What did he do to deserve this?"

Cathy's face clouded over. "He didn't do anything. All he wanted was to avenge Krista's beating, he certainly didn't murder anyone."

"Although I was shocked when I saw her physically in the courtroom, those pictures we saw when Ardolino produced them showed just how badly she had been beaten," Jim said, "I couldn't believe it was Krista."

"Believe me, when I took those pictures, seeing the bruising and marks and cuts up close made my stomach churn," Dave said. "She's a very lucky young lady to be as well as she is today when she looked that bad five days ago."

"She's the only person I know can get beat up like that and still remain as beautiful as ever. And I'm not jealous at all." Cathy chuckled warmly. "She remains in good spirits, which is just like her. We've been told she won't suffer permanent damage, no scarring, nothing."

They settled down to start work and were going over their respective reports for Paul's case when Captain Hamilton returned. He walked determinedly through the office but indicated with a jerk of his head for Dave and Cathy to follow him to his office. Inside, he closed the door and the blinds, indicating he was in a private meeting.

"Before I get down to business, do either of you have anything new to tell me?" he asked.

"Just that there seems to be some displeasure at the fact my husband is going to be rich some fine day in the distant future," Cathy said.

"Displeasure from who?"

"A few people, Holden being one of them. Who overheard you talking to the commissioner yesterday about the paying of Paul's bail?"

Captain Hamilton slowly shook his head. "I honestly have no idea. This going to be a problem for you, Dave? I remember way back in the beginning, when you were fresh off the plane from Vegas, you asked me not to tell anyone about your background. You made it clear it was a part of your life you didn't like, didn't want and didn't want broadcast. I have to admit, not once have I ever thought of you as a rich boy. I've never seen you flaunt your money."

Dave rolled his eyes. "That's because I don't have any money to flaunt. That's my father's wealth you're talking about, not mine."

The captain gave him a slow smile. "Yeah, I understand the difference. But when the time comes, if I'm still around, I want a brand new, shiny black Beemer as a gift for putting up with you and your temper all these years."

Dave chuckled. "I'll keep that in mind."

"Now, down to business. Ardolino demanded a face to face meeting. I reminded him about social distancing and would rather conduct a meeting on the phone, or Zoom. He reminded me we could do the social distancing in a wide open conference room near his office. He fought me every step of the way but Ted Reynolds was there and shot him down every time. In the end he had to agree, knowing it wouldn't look good if he tried to obstruct the course of justice. Reynolds was already way ahead of him anyway. He'd presented a petition to the judge who, after careful deliberation, granted permission. It seems the judge was won over by Paul's track record, being a decorated cop and, believe it or not, being one of the best players he's ever seen on the Bathville Blazers."

"His hockey prowess helped sway the judge?" Dave asked incredulously. "That's great, good for Paul."

"Indeed. So, without further ado, get your affairs in order and get yourselves down to Brooklyn," Captain Hamilton said.

It really was going to happen. Not just because they wanted to, but now with the backing of the courts, they were going to Brooklyn in a move that would hopefully clear Paul's name.

# CHAPTER TWENTY-FIVE

The next day, Paul tried again to set up a Zoom meeting with his old friend and mentor in the Brooklyn Police Department. Harry Pedowski had been a detective when Paul, still in uniform, had worked alongside him. He had risen in the ranks to Captain, which was why it was hard to get a hold of him but finally, after emailing the meeting invitation for the third time, Pedowski finally flickered on Paul's laptop screen.

"Yo, Harry!" Paul said in genuine delight.

"Hey, hey, it's Paul Cameron, as I live and breathe!" Pedowski greeted him warmly, a broad smile creasing his weathered face. "You're a sight for sore eyes."

Paul grinned at the thick New York accent. Krista was lying down or else he would have had her sit in on the meeting, but he knew she would meet Pedowski when they were in New York. "Thanks for agreeing to this, Harry, I really need to talk to you."

"Your email didn't give much away. Want to fill me in?"

Paul remembered Harry always got right to the point and he was prepared for the question. "Short story, I've been arrested for murder."

The picture on the screen was crystal clear and Harry furrowed his brow in alarm. "I reckoned it had to be something serious. But not this. What the hell happened?"

Paul told him as much as he could, right down to the fact he would be in The City in two days. "What I need to find out is if there is any gang or drug family who destroys a person's genitals and breaks their neck as punishment. The broken neck was the cause of death for my father but his entire groin area was an absolute mess."

Harry listened without interrupting and Paul could see him scribbling down notes every so often. "I might have a name in mind here but I'll run this through the database and get back to you as soon as I can. Nothing else ringing any bells with me but that doesn't mean there isn't anyone." Harry Pedowski looked pensive for a moment. "I'll check with vice, homicide and narcs and I'm sure we can dig up something of use to you. I did a search on you a couple of years back, just to see how my protégé was handling himself. Way to go on the Medal of Honor, you certainly deserve it. Who was the fellow officer you saved that day?"

"My partner's wife. *My* wife's best friend and partner. She's a dear friend of mine too."

"You're married now? *You*? The Playboy of the Eastern Seaboard?"

"I was just waiting to meet the right woman. She's all that and more, you'll get to meet her when we're down there. In fact, you'll get to meet my partner too, and his wife, we're all cops and we're coming down together."

Despite seeing Paul's eyes light up when talking about his wife and friends, Harry couldn't fail to see the fear lurking there too. He wanted to do all he could to help clear Paul's name and already his mind was working overtime trying to come up with a suspect whose *modus operandi*, or MO, met Paul's parameters. "You'll be allowed into the precinct as long as you've gotten tested recently," Harry said, steering the subject to something more neutral. "Unfortunately, Brooklyn is way ahead of the rest of the city as far as opening up stores and businesses goes. Frankly, I think we opened up too soon and I see all kinds of trouble in the not-to-distant future. If you weren't coming down to find evidence to clear your name I would suggest you stay away until this whole mess disappeared – or at least we got it under control. The lunatics here don't seem to know what social distancing is - so a word of caution about that." Harry leaned a little closer towards the camera. "We'll get these scum bastards, Paul, don't you worry. We'll get 'em and your name will be cleared. I just want you to know I'll do whatever I can to help you and I'll put my best team on it, too. We'll get 'em."

Paul could hear the reassurance in his friend's voice and knew he had done the right thing in contacting him. Yet another choice he had made that was proving it had been the right thing to do. "I hope so, Harry. Hey, I know you're a busy man now *Captain* Pedowski so I'll let you get going. Email me your cell number, I thought I had it but I don't."

"Will do. Take care, young man. See you soon."

Paul pressed the "Leave" button and Harry's face disappeared from view. He sat back against the sofa, feeling considerably more light-hearted than he had before the Zoom meeting. He knew Pedowski was as reliable as you could get and Paul trusted him implicitly. He could only hope Pedowski would come through for him but there was no way of knowing until they got down there and started their investigation properly.

He went up to their bedroom to see if Krista was awake yet. She had been napping for over an hour and, although she was still asleep, it looked like she was slowly returning to the land of the living. His assumption was correct because she stirred when she felt him sit on the bed beside her. He hadn't wanted to disturb her but he wanted her to be able to sleep when she went back to bed at a more normal time. While she slowly came around, he took a moment to study her face. It was a face he knew every square inch of and his heart soared with love and gratitude in the way it always did when he looked at her.

It had now been a full week since her attack and she really was doing much better. Her bruises were fading quickly and the swelling was all but gone. Cathy's regime of using Vitamin K cream, ice packs and rest had done wonders. She could now easily cover the bruises with make-up and in a few more days they would be gone completely. She could take in a deep breath now without it hurting much and she could even laugh comfortably which would make their trip to New York a lot easier. A few days ago, she might not have been able to travel, and do what needed to be done, without some level of discomfort. He assumed the beds in Dave's father's apartment would be comfortable for her body pains.

"Hey, sleeping beauty," he said softly when he saw her eyes flicker. "You doing okay?"

She nodded in way of an answer. "I just feel so tired all the time," she said in mild exasperation. "I don't like sleeping through the day and yet lately that's all I've been doing."

"I know but you obviously need it. Your body went through a lot and you're still recovering, of course you're going to be tired and off-schedule for a while."

She closed her eyes again and, just as he thought she was going to drift off, she said, "Did you get your friend in Brooklyn?"

"Yes, we hooked up. He's shocked at the wrongful arrest and promised to do whatever he can to help. He's looking forward to meeting you."

"I'm looking forward to meeting him, too. I'm glad you got a hold of him."

He leaned over and kissed her forehead. "Go back to sleep, baby. I'll check on you in an hour. You want me to ask the Andrews' if they'd like to join us for dinner tonight?"

"Sure. I haven't seen Cathy since yesterday."

"I'll see if they're free." He reached for the cell phone in his back pocket when he felt it vibrate and saw he had a text from Captain Hamilton. He read it without saying anything and returned the phone to his pocket.

"Who was that from?"

"My girlfriend."

"Which one?"

"A new one." He grinned. "It was Captain Hamilton, my request to leave the state has been signed, sealed and delivered.

I'm official now."

"That's really good news, I know it was worrying you in case you were going to be denied."

"Nah," he said with pseudo nonchalance, wrinkling his nose and shaking his head.

She turned so she could face him better. "I have a good feeling about this trip, Paul," she said softly. "We're going to work together and get the answers we need. Then we can tell the courts to go stuff themselves, return the money to Dave's dad and let life return to normal."

"Sounds like a plan," he said.

She looked at his watch to check the time. "What time are you going to ask the Andrews' to be here?"

"After work, presumably, and if they get held up, they'll let us know."

"Then we've got a little time to ourselves," she said, holding his eyes.

"We do."

"I know something else I'd like to get back to normal."

A flicker of a smile danced on his face. "And what would that be?"

"This," she murmured and placed his hand inside her blouse. "I'm up for normal, if you are."

He didn't need much persuasion and, at her gentle coaxing, everything quickly felt more than normal. Everything felt perfect.

# CHAPTER
# TWENTY-SIX

The day they left for New York dawned bright and clear. Temperatures were mild and, because a lot of people were not working, or working from home, the usual early morning traffic was reduced greatly. Knowing the drive from Bathville to New York City would normally take nearly four hours, they set off in Dave's car at seven thirty. The luggage was stored in the trunk of the Camaro, except for one medium sized case that rested in the back seat between Cathy and Krista. They drove through Rhode Island on roads that were as light in traffic as Massachusetts had been and it enabled them to catch the I-95 in Connecticut at just after nine thirty.

A pit-stop for a late breakfast and coffee refills, as well as to refuel the car, put nearly an hour onto their journey but that was fine. They wanted to arrive in The Big Apple well-fed and as relaxed as possible.

Dave had spoken to the housekeepers at the apartment a few days before to tell them he would be coming down with three other people. He had nothing but fond memories of these wonderful people and he couldn't wait to show Cathy off and introduce them to Paul and Krista. He had texted them that morning to say they were on their way and would see them soon.

Shortly before noon and after leaving the I-95 to take a more direct route into the city, hopefully avoiding the worst of the traffic while they were at it, the familiar New York sky-line appeared in the distance. The Freedom Tower, built next to where the Twin Towers had soared high and proud until their shocking destruction nearly twenty years ago and the Empire State building were easy to identify. So was the Chrysler building.

Krista and Cathy were excited to see as much as they could, having never been to New York before. To let Dave concentrate on the escalating traffic, Paul happily pointed out as much as he could to the ladies.

The traffic was horrendous, and several different routes he could have taken were blocked off for construction but at last, Dave turned on to Park Avenue. His father's apartment was located roughly four hundred yards from the Empire State Building and less than half a mile from Grand Central Station and Times Square. One thing about the apartment Dave had always appreciated was its convenience to mid-town amenities.

He pulled up outside a forty-story high building constructed of a mixture of red brick, sandstone and glass. It was a narrower, less bulky building than some of the others surrounding it, but it was no less as striking. Some of the apartments overlooking Park Avenue had balconies outside them. A lot of them had floor-to-ceiling windows that reflected the sun and provided twenty-four-hour privacy. As New York high-rise apartments go, it was one of the nicer looking ones and also one of the more recently constructed.

Dave turned to Paul, then looked back at Krista and Cathy. He seemed a trifle embarrassed. Or maybe he was nervous. "Here we are. We leave the luggage and a porter will bring it up. You're staying in PH 1, that's all the porter and doorman need to know. If they persist and ask for a name, say you're a guest of Anthony and Joyce Andrews."

A doorman, resplendent in a dark green coat with gold epaulettes, black pants, green peaked cap and shiny black boots, and, of course, a black face mask, was already at his side of the car, his hand reaching out to open the door. Dave stepped out and introduced himself and as soon as the doorman heard the name Andrews, he almost tripped over himself.

"Yes, sir, very good sir. You have three companions, I see, do you also have luggage sir?"

Dave was already tired of being called 'sir' but that was how the staff operated in this establishment and he would have to grit his teeth and try to ignore it. "Yes. Three suitcases in the trunk and one in the back seat. Please park the car in my father's space and arrange for the luggage to be brought up to PH 1." He slipped the doorman a ten dollar bill for five seconds of work and gestured to Paul and the ladies to follow him.

The foyer was ultra-chic, in Italian marble, glass, highly polished tables and soft leather chairs and sofas. Fresh cut flower arrangements were placed strategically on end tables, shelves or windowsills and the air smelled sweet and clean. Despite the opulence, it felt welcoming and Dave led the way to the rows of elevators.

"Did you really ask that man out there to bring up our luggage?" Paul asked.

"I did."

"We could have handled it ourselves."

"I know. But they're paid to do that and it's easier to let them do what they have to do." The elevator dinged to herald its arrival and they all stepped inside. Dave selected the button that said PH1 on it. "Believe me, last time I was here, which was about ten years ago, I tried to carry my own suitcase and was almost ostracized from the community. It's not worth it trying to fight them." Although he could see her reflection in the smoked glass walls of the elevator, he turned to look at Cathy properly. She hadn't said a word since he'd pulled up outside the building and he thought she looked uncomfortable. "Okay, love?" he whispered.

"Uh huh," she answered absently. And that was all she was willing to say.

The elevator stopped after only a few seconds and they stepped out into an ornate gold, glass and marble hallway, with plush dark teal blue carpeting. They turned right from the elevator and the door to penthouse one was in front of them. Dave didn't even get to ring the doorbell when it was flung open and there in front of them stood a seventies-something black man.

"George!" Dave said in obvious delight. He wanted to hug the man but because of social distancing couldn't and, on seeing George was wearing a mask, the one he'd been wearing and had just taken off in the elevator was hastily pulled out of his pocket and put back on. They all followed suit.

"Mister David!" George returned happily. "Are you a sight for sore eyes." He stepped back and ushered them all inside. "We can do the hugging and the hand shaking and the no-mask wearing and the back slapping when we've out of the prying lens of the security cameras, if that's okay. But in the meantime, introduce your guests to me before Hannah comes in and takes over like she normally does. Oh, you don't need to wear your masks indoors, unless you want to. I don't know what the rules are up in Massachusetts, but at least in this house, we wear them if we're admitting someone at the front door and when we're outside."

Dave grinned and, peeling his mask off, turned to Paul first, who was standing closest to him. "This is Paul Cameron, my best friend and my partner. This beauty by his side is his wife, Krista Cameron, a very dear friend. And this other beauty by *my* side is Cathy Andrews, my wife and my rock."

George's warm brown eyes danced merrily during the introductions and finally settled on Cathy. "It is a pleasure to meet you, ma'am. When I heard David had gotten married again I knew it had to have been to someone pretty special."

Cathy faltered just a bit. She wasn't used to being addressed as ma'am. Aware that George was expecting some sort of response, and knowing she was being rude, she gave a nonchalant shrug of her shoulders. "Thank you, but he made it easy for me to fall in love with him."

Paul and Krista knew this was Dave and Cathy's moment and they intentionally kept quiet until the preamble was over. They were still standing in the entrance hall and they couldn't help but notice that it seemed bigger than the entire downstairs of their own apartment.

George seemed to approve of Cathy's answer and he tipped Dave a wink. "He has certainly shown remarkable good taste."

Dave could sense Cathy wasn't entirely comfortable and he put a protective arm around her waist. "George, less of the 'Mister David' and 'ma'am', please. I'm all grown up now, it's Dave, Cathy, Paul and Krista, okay?"

George gave a slight bow. "As you wish, Dave." His smile without the mask hiding it lit up his eyes and Cathy could at least see he had a genuine fondness for Dave. It helped relax her a bit.

"Before we meet Hannah, can we at least move on to the living room?" Dave asked.

George clicked his tongue in self-irritation. "Of course. Where are my manners? I was just so happy to see you, I didn't think." He gestured ahead and, knowing Dave knew the way, let Dave lead them down the black and white tiled hallway that opened up into a huge living area.

The living room was huge and tastefully decorated in muted tones but with splashes of color to add character and style. Monet, Cezanne and Manet paintings hung on the walls, spot lights placed just-so to enhance every subtle detail of the priceless works of art. Limoges, Spode and Villeroy & Boch chinaware were sitting on end tables and highly polished credenzas. Despite the sheer exuberance, the room looked lived in and felt warm and welcoming.

Windows took up two walls, with views that offered Central Park, the city skyline, and snatches of the East River. They let in lots of natural light and a quick check by Cathy told her there were carefully concealed drapes to pull for privacy. They were on the fortieth floor but surrounded by other buildings, some much taller, and she appreciated they could close the rest of the city out if they wanted to. It was beautiful and relaxing and George gestured they all sit and make themselves comfortable while he went to get some refreshments. He promised Hannah would be along momentarily and warned Dave she was bursting with excitement to see him.

"This place is...is...awesome, Dave!" Krista said in delight. "I was expecting a mausoleum, certainly not this. It's beautiful."

Dave sank into the nearest Italian leather easy chair. It was cherry red and as soft as silk. "They've had the place renovated since I was last here. I have to admit they've done a great job."

Paul strode over to the largest window and looked towards the river. He hadn't seen this stunning city in a long time and it always made him feel good to see it. "Nice view," he said light-heartedly, making an understatement.

Dave was looking covertly at Cathy. She hadn't sat down and hadn't said a word and he wondered what was going through her head. She still looked pensive and more than a little uncomfortable and he began to worry. "Hey, Cath," he said cheerily. "What do you think?"

She turned in a slow circle, taking everything in. There was a two ton elephant in the room and she didn't know how to acknowledge it, or even if she should. "It's very...nice," she said eventually and inwardly cringed. She knew Dave was looking for some sort of affirmation that told him she was cool with her surroundings but she didn't feel it yet. It wasn't the abundance of richness hitting her at every turn that was bothering her. She had never been one to seek happiness in material objects. So what if there was a real life Picasso hanging next to what could be a Turner or a Dali? What did bother her was all this was one day going to be Dave's. Which meant it would be hers too. She didn't want to hurt Dave's feelings, she knew all too well he was uncomfortable showing off his parents' wealth and she forced herself to relax. "No, honestly, it's quite lovely. I just didn't know what to expect and I'm still taking it all in."

He relaxed slightly but was spared further comment

when he heard a high squeal behind him and, leaping up, he saw Hannah, George's wife, hurrying towards him, her arms outstretched. Without thinking about restrictions, he went straight into her arms and held her close for a very long moment. She smelled exactly as he remembered her, of violets and roses, and he was promptly swept back twenty-five years when he would receive a hug from her when she thought he needed one. Which he often had back then.

"My boy!" she cried. "Look at you, my handsome boy!"

Dave had the good grace to blush but he let Hannah make a fuss of him. He loved this elderly black woman dearly and, although now he towered over her by a foot or more, he always felt loved and comforted in her arms. "Hannah, so lovely to see you."

Hannah stepped back but held on to his hands. "I'm so glad you're here. George is fixing a light lunch for you so he shooed me out of the kitchen, told me to come see you." She seemed oblivious to the other three people who were looking at them curiously but then she remembered her manners. She may have had a hand in raising Dave but she had to remember her place too. Not that Dave would have cared her overstepping the mark, but for this first meeting she would do what was expected of her. She was wearing a spotless white apron over a navy blue short sleeved dress, her face was free of make-up and her gray hair swept back in a rolled bun at her neck. She straightened up to her full height and smiled at Dave's friends. "Welcome to New York," she said warmly, "and to the apartment. I'm sure Dave will have told you to treat this place like your own home but if he hasn't, please do. George and I are here at your disposal. Anything you want, just ask."

"Thank you," Cathy said, "that's very kind of you."

Hannah faltered a bit at Cathy's voice and then she rolled her eyes in faint amusement as she put two and two together. "Are you Dave's wife?" she asked.

"Yes."

"Then that explains it. He phoned me a couple of years

ago to tell me he'd gotten married to a lovely young lady from Northern Ireland. For some reason, I hadn't expected an accent." Again throwing virus protocol out the window, she came over to Cathy and shook her hand. "He was certainly right, you are quite lovely. I am so pleased to meet you."

Cathy's heart was already won over, not by the woman's words, but the genuine way they were delivered and she smiled. "I have been looking forward to meeting you and your husband. Dave has told me a lot about you."

Hannah threw Dave a warning look. "Better have been nothing but good, boy," she said.

"Couldn't have been anything but," he said. "The gentleman to your left is my police partner and best friend, Paul Cameron. And this is his wife, Krista. We're all really close, Hannah so be careful about badmouthing me to them."

Hannah chuckled good naturedly. "Pleasure to meet you both."

They returned the greeting and now that the initial introductions were over, they could begin to relax properly. A low ringing heralded someone was at the door but George was there in seconds. It was the porter with their luggage and George instructed him towards the bedrooms, in the opposite direction of the living room. After the porter left, George returned to the kitchen.

Dave steered Hannah to the sofa and gestured she should sit for a moment. "Just want you to rest your weary feet for a bit," he said. "Because if I know you, you've been baking and cooking all morning."

"Maybe," she said coyly. "Wanted to make some of your favorite things. Restaurants were given the go ahead just last week to remain open but to operate at a fifty per cent capacity and I hear it's murder trying to get a table booked. A lot of retail stores are closed but you can still do a fair bit of shopping, if that's your thing. No tourist attractions open, though. I phoned this morning to find out for you but got a taped message saying that due to Covid restrictions, everywhere will remain closed until Governor Cuomo decides to have them reopened. But I am more than thrilled to cook for you and your friends." Then, after a pause, she added, "You can still get delivery and curbside pickup, if you prefer some restaurant cooking."

"We don't want to be giving you any bother," Krista said.

Hannah realized Krista had an accent also and she nodded with a smile. "No bother for me, child. I'll be happy to do for you what you want. Usually got nobody to cook for but me and George, and I do love to cook."

"Guys, Hannah is one of the best cooks in the whole wide world..." Dave trailed off with a mischievous grin, "... my favorite things you said? Uh...um, please tell me that includes your fried chicken?"

"You know it."

Dave rolled his eyes in pleasure. "That's my supper sorted. Guys, trust me, you haven't tasted fried chicken until you've tasted Hannah's fried chicken."

Hannah laughed at his enthusiasm and she grabbed a hold of his hand. "I can't believe you're here. At last. And with your beautiful bride." She looked at him pointedly. "*At last.*"

Dave threw his hands up. "Guilty. When this whole virus mess is over, I will bring Cathy down for a proper visit, I promise. And, if Paul and Krista like it here, they can come too. Lord knows there's plenty of room here and we promise we won't be too much of a burden."

Hannah smiled at the man she loved like a son. She instinctively felt the close-knit relationship of these four people but she also sensed an underlying tension. Something dark and menacing was rolling over them and threatening to envelop them.

Dave had been vague on the phone; he hadn't gone into any detail why they were coming down but he had promised he would fill them in when they got here and she planned on holding him to that promise.

She had a feeling she wouldn't like what she was going

to hear.

# CHAPTER TWENTY-SEVEN

Later on in the afternoon, Paul asked George if there was a room in the apartment he could use to set up his laptop. He had texted Harry Pedowski an hour earlier and arranged a Zoom meeting and he wanted it to be in relative privacy.

George led him to a flight of stairs that went down one floor and going down them, Paul caught the distinct whiff of chlorine. They descended to a level that had slip-proof tiles on the floor and several doors along a wide corridor. Paul felt like he was in a gym and, although the surroundings were spotlessly clean, they were in sharp contrast to the gold, marble and priceless paintings one floor up.

"If you wish to use Mr Andrews' Olympic sized pool, it's right through there," George told him, pointing towards the last door on the right. "It's climate controlled and tested regularly to make sure it's up to code. There are towels and noodles and anything else you might need right at your disposal. Here -", he indicated to a door to his left, "is the weight room and here," he pointed at a door to the right of that one, "are your Nordic tracks, treadmills and other gym equipment. Please feel free to use them, Mr Cameron, any time."

Paul tried not to gawp. He was suitably impressed and quickly shook his head to bring himself back to reality. "Uh, please George, it's Paul. And thank you for showing me what you have available here."

George nodded and held up a finger as if to indicate something else he wanted to show off. "You asked for a room to have a meeting in. Please, follow me." He led Paul to the furthest end of the corridor and opened a door. He stepped aside to show Paul the interior. "I hope this will do?"

The room was as large as a boardroom in a blue chip company. There was a highly polished conference table, soft leather chairs, a credenza that had gleaming glasses and empty water jugs on it and a static screen on the wall for power point presentations. There were several wi-fi routers and phone points scattered around the room and even a table that had legal pads and a container full of pens and pencils on it.

"This is awesome, George," Paul said, getting the feeling he was making yet another understatement. "My meeting is at three o'clock and I will come down at around two forty five to get set up. Do I need a key or a pass or anything?"

"Not at all. The rooms throughout the unit, except the bedrooms, are kept unlocked when we have guests. Can I fix you a snack or a beverage to have during your meeting?"

Paul patted his full stomach. "After that awesome lunch you made us, I think I'm good but thank you. Maybe some water?"

"Certainly." George smiled directly into Paul's eyes. He had taken a genuine liking to this young man, and not just because he was a close friend of Dave. "Please relax and make yourself at home, Paul, you're under no restrictions here."

Paul nodded. "Thank you, I appreciate that." He glanced at his watch. It was only two o'clock. "Shall we go back upstairs to the others?"

"As you wish."

Paul found Krista in the living room, looking out at the rooftops and skyscrapers surrounding them. The weather seemed gloomy, as if it was about to rain and Krista seemed pensive as he slipped his arms around her. "You okay?" he asked, with a soft nuzzle at her neck.

She smiled and sank in against him. "I'm fine."

Not sure if he was reading her right, he moved in closer against her. "You sure about that?"

"Oh, yes, I was just thinking that here we are, in the most exciting city in the world, and we can't even go anywhere to sightsee or see a show."

"Yeah, it kind of sucks. Next time, though, when this whole mess is over, we'll come back." He planted a gentle kiss at the back of her earlobe. "Where are Dave and Cathy?"

"Haven't seen them for about five minutes."

"I'd like him to be in on the Zoom meeting with Pedowski. Hey, you should see downstairs, there's a huge pool and a complete gym too, it's awesome. I'm glad I brought my workout gear."

"Wow, this place has got everything. Cathy will be glad to hear about the pool, she loves to swim."

"She won't be disappointed."

"Why won't I be disappointed?" Cathy said, walking in on the last of their conversation. Dave was right behind her and when she heard about the pool, she clapped her hands in delight. "That's great! Except… I didn't bring a swimsuit."

"Yes you did," Dave said with a twinkle in his eye. "I wanted the pool to be a surprise for you so I packed a couple of your suits when you weren't looking."

Cathy grinned and threw her arms around him. "You're just the bestest husband in the whole wide world."

"I know," he said, returning the grin. "Paul, did you get to see the gym?"

"I did, and the boardroom. Both very impressive. Are you joining me on the Zoom meeting at three, with Pedowski? I'd really like you to be there."

"Then I will be."

Paul looked at the two ladies in turn. "Just the guys this time, okay?" he said apologetically. "Harry is looking forward to meeting you all but he specifically requested this meeting with just Dave."

"Sure, that's fine," Krista said. "I don't mind sitting here with my feet up. Cathy and I can have a coffee and a natter."

"Just for a change, huh?" Dave said sardonically.

"Can we ask Hannah or George to bring us coffee?" Cathy asked uncertainly. "Or do we go and get it ourselves?"

Dave shook his head. "Only if you want to give them apoplexy. Sweetie, Hannah and George will be more than happy to bring you whatever you want. They are literally expecting you to ask them for whatever, so just do." He saw her hesitancy and buffed her cheek. "It's fine, I promise. It's their job."

"Okay. But what's apoplexy?"

At exactly three o'clock, the Zoom meeting commenced. Harry Pedowski's face pixelated on the screen then smoothed out to a good quality image. Paul made the introductions between him and Dave and the two men gave each other a friendly greeting.

"When you planning to come over to the real world and see Brooklyn?" Harry asked.

"Tomorrow, early. I'm not sure which station we're closest to but we'll get the subway. Remind me again which train to catch and which station is closest to you?"

Harry told him. "I can send a squad car to pick you up, if you want, save you the bother."

"There'll be four of us. Too many people. We'll drive or take the sub."

"Four of you?"

"My wife, Krista. Dave's wife, Cathy. We're all cops. I thought I told you we were all coming down?"

Harry raised an amused eyebrow. "Keep it in the family, huh? Maybe you did tell me they were coming. I'm looking forward to meeting them."

"This is Krista's first time back on the job. She's mostly recovered from broken ribs – courtesy of my father. She says she's ready for some field work, but I don't know, it still hurts her sometimes to just bend over and tie her shoe lace. I'd rather she took it easy for a while yet."

"Problem is, she won't go easy," Dave said, "she's determined to help Paul find someone who can clear his name.

Whether she's injured or not, she's still a valuable member of our team. She's super smart and might see things we don't."

Harry nodded slowly, digesting all this information. "We're all anxious to get Paul's name cleared. Which brings me to the reason for your visit. When we spoke last week, I wasn't able to bring anyone to mind who does the type of mutilation that was done to your father, Paul. However..." Harry leaned to his left, and slapped a file down in front of him which he opened and read the first few lines. "A week ago, there was a hit on a victim exactly the same as your father. Two nights ago, the same thing. We've IDed the victims but, other than the fact we know they were both from Brooklyn, there's no connection to one another. There were significant levels of heroin in both bodies, one of them had severely damaged nasal passages due to overuse of cocaine." Pedowski glanced up from the file to Paul. "Damn lining of his nose was eaten clear away. We're waiting on an analysis of the heroin to see if it came from the same source.

"Sounds like you have a possible suspect," Paul said.

"It's not written in stone yet, I'm expecting the final report by maybe, hopefully, tomorrow morning. You remember the Romano family?"

Paul thought for a moment but shook his head. "Doesn't sound familiar. Unless..." He trailed off, searching for a memory and then nodded. "The Romanos...Right... drug lords."

"Exactly. From right here in Brooklyn and going by what you've told me about the condition your father's body was in, they certainly fit the MO, right down to the damaged genitals. Mega-rich today, they started out back in the eighties as art traders, based mostly in Manhattan, Paris and Milan. They're second and third generation American - the grandfather was born in Sicily. He came to the US in the mid-fifties when his son was nine. In the nineties, the art corporation became a front for their drug dealing business, which, no surprise, is where they get most of their money from."

"Have they had any arrests?"

"Nope, and that's what makes me think they have at least one judge in their pocket. They live right here in Brooklyn, Cobble Hill to be exact. A veritable fortress – apparently close to fifty million dollars forty years ago, which was high then, even for Cobble Hill - set in its own compound. High walls, security system, guards, lasers, trip wires, silent alarms, and, oh yes, even man-eating guard dogs, the works. It's cut off from the outside world and you can only gain access if you're a personal guest of one of the family. It's estimated to be worth somewhere north of a hundred and fifty mil for the property alone. Not even a warrant could get you access."

"Then how do we get in to interview them?" Paul asked.

"You don't. No one can."

Paul and Dave shared a baffled glance at one another. "What makes them above the law?" Dave asked.

"Money."

"That's all? Surely after all this time, the authorities would have figured a way to get in at least for an interview."

"The DEA is keeping their eye on them. Right now they have nothing concrete to go on but they claim they're close to indicting them." He shrugged. "Who knows. All I know is that so far we haven't been able to get a charge against them, at least not one that will stick. Hence they're all still running around as free as a bird. Untouchable."

They sat in silence for a few moments, their minds working overtime, trying to find a way to gain access. "So I couldn't try to set up an interview, even on Zoom or Skype or whatever their video chat of choice is?" Paul said.

"An interview about what?" Harry asked with a scornful laugh. "What do you say? How many murders have you guys committed in Massachusetts recently?"

"Of course not, but I – *we* – can figure something out. I can try and negotiate."

"Negotiate? For what? Their confession for a false promise of amnesty?"

"As I said, we can work something out."

"Bullshit. You'll come out of there with your balls kicked all the way up to where your tonsils should be and that's only if they decide to take pity on you."

"I have to do it, Harry, I have no other choice. The foreseeable future and possibly my whole life are literally on the line here, which means I have to do whatever I can. My wife, my partner here, his wife – three *excellent* cops – can be my backup. If I can get in, I'll go in wired, with a concealed weapon or two, I can -"

"Bull*shit!*" There was a loud slapping sound as Pedowski brought his fist crashing down on the desk. "For one thing, they search everyone who goes into their premises, no matter who they are. A strip search, body cavity search, you name the type of search, they do it. One sniff of you being a cop, you're dead. You're gone."

"Then it seems we have no choice but to break into their place and see if we can find any sort of evidence on my father's murder."

"*Now* what are you talking about? Are you crazy, man? They have that place more secured than Fort Knox. I didn't mention electric fences earlier but they have those too – mounted on top of ten-foot stone walls. If you so much as breathe within five hundred yards of the fence, they'll have you caught, bound, beaten up and missing your family jewels before you can cry 'help'. I mean it, Paul, they're dangerous people, you shouldn't try messing with them. Getting close to them could mean destroying months of hard work and covert operations within the DEA *and* the FBI. Then you're on their shit list, too."

Paul scoffed at that. "The Romanos are little league compared to what I've been up against in the past. Like the Free the North party, a dangerous paramilitary organization in Northern Ireland. We brought them to their knees just over a year ago."

"Listen to me, Cameron. Dangerous is dangerous is dangerous, on whatever level. I don't care you've fought one-on-

one with Kim Jong-un himself, you can't go anywhere near the Romanos."

"Damn it, Harry, I *have* to. Don't you understand what I'm saying? I'm facing life for a crime I didn't commit unless I can come up with some solid evidence that will clear me. The Romanos definitely fit the MO and are the only lead I have. If I head back to Bathville without the chance to clear my name I may as well just take a gun and shoot my own head off to save myself from getting bumped off by my cellmate when I'm convicted. You know what happens to cops in the joint. I'm desperate here, literally desperate and I'm prepared to do whatever it will take."

"At the risk of your own life?"

Paul gave a tired, resigned laugh. "I'm damned if I do, damned if I don't. But I have to at least try."

"Jesus H Christ, how old are you now, thirty, thirty one? You're still a baby, you shouldn't have to be making decisions like this."

"Well, I am, Harry, because I have to."

Harry Pedowski leaned over, his head in his hands, his face partially obscured. "Okay," he said hoarsely, "okay, you've convinced me. I'll get the blueprints of the house, find a sewer line or something and we'll go in that way. I'll even figure out how to cut the power to the tripwires, lasers and electric fence without cutting power to the house." He looked from Paul to Dave and cocked his head in Dave's direction. "You look like you're trying to figure something out, Dave."

"Just that...well...Paul's father said he owed "some people" close to thirty five thousand dollars. If the family is that rich, why would they bother over a paltry sum like thirty five thou? To even follow a man up to Massachusetts and kill him for that amount of money just doesn't make sense."

Pedowski pursed his lips. "You're right, it doesn't. But they do shit like that just to make a point. Nobody messes with the Romanos, not even a little. They'd kill you for half a buck to make a point. They're not a family you fool around with.

Maybe Cameron did more than just owe them money, maybe he stole from or accosted one of their own? Who knows? All I know is we have to do what we can to find records or something. Although, you do have to admit it's a long shot thinking they keep books on who owes what but we have to find something."

"If we have to go in under cover of darkness," Paul said slowly, as if he was thinking out loud, "what can you give us to facilitate our actions?"

"In terms of back up? Two-way wires, silencers for your guns, fully automatic weapons, flick knives. Anything you need."

"Thought you'd say that. Hold on a sec, Harry, I'm going to put you on mute for just a second while I run something by Dave." He clicked on the microphone button and turned to Dave. "I have a bad feeling about this one, Dave, I really don't want the ladies involved at all. Only problem is, we can't keep them out, it's not fair. When we do our brainstorming tomorrow, I want Harry to make it sound as dangerous as possible and he will want as few people going in to investigate to cut down on casualties. Not that I'm saying there'll be casualties, but you never know. I think it best we organize the whole thing with Harry right now, get him to tell the ladies we're going to the Romano household hopefully tomorrow night but they're going to be our getaway drivers. We'll need someone to monitor our whereabouts and listen to what we're saying so they'll need to be in a van or something with surveillance equipment." Paul chewed thoughtfully on his bottom lip for a long moment. "I really don't want Krista caught up in what could be a shoot-out, and I'm sure you feel the same way about Cathy. But since we know we can't stop them, at least they'll still be involved if they're on surveillance."

Dave mulled it over, his eyes narrowed. "Much as I know they're more than capable of taking care of business, I agree with you, I don't have a good feeling about this either. Yes, let's tell Harry."

"So…You in?"

"Keeping the ladies safe, you bet. They'll go nuclear though, you know that. They'll want to be in the thick of it."

"Chance I'm willing to take." Paul clicked on the microphone button again to bring Harry back in. "Sorry about that. This is what we were talking about…" He filled Harry in on what he and Dave had discussed and, as expected, got his reluctant approval and promise of cooperation.

"It won't be a problem. No matter what we come up with tomorrow morning, I'll have something worked out for tomorrow night. I'll email you anything else I can think of."

"Great, Harry, thank you."

"Don't thank me. If the shit goes down, you're on your own. The department can't help you."

Paul nodded "We understand. See you tomorrow morning, buddy."

"Looking forward to it, Paul. Nice meeting you, Dave, it will be a pleasure doing business with you."

They said their farewells and Paul reached over to close the video meeting. When Harry's face disappeared, he shut the laptop down. "I'm really glad Harry's on board with this. What can we say to sweet talk the ladies into taking the low road on this one?"

Dave grinned in genuine amusement. "I have a great idea what I can do to make Cathy nice and mellow."

Paul returned the grin. "That's because you're a perv."

"That's why she loves me."

"Then she's a perv too."

"That's why I love *her*." Dave moved to get up but Paul caught his arm to stop him. "What's up?"

"Tomorrow night, are you sure you want to get involved with a family like that?"

"Are you serious? Paul, I'm hoping we can get answers tomorrow night, I'm more than sure I want to get involved."

"Even if it's dangerous?"

"Even if."

Paul let out a long, shaky breath. "You're a true pal, Dave. You've been there for me every step of the way in this… this…nightmare. Lesser people would have bolted by now."

Dave gave him a playful punch on the shoulder. "I'm not lesser people, Paul. And I know you'd do the same for me. Come on, let's go see what Cathy and Krista are doing."

They spent a tense rest of the afternoon talking over with Cathy and Krista what their plan, such as it was, was for the following night. As predicted, the ladies were none too pleased about being kept on the periphery while Dave and Paul entered the Romano house and put their lives in immediate danger.

It was only when Paul told them about the state of the art security at the Romano household that he managed to get their attention. He stressed, repeatedly, it would be best for all to have as few people as possible going in and, at last, he got them to calm down a degree.

They didn't want to go out for dinner, instead Dave got his much-anticipated fill of Hannah's fried chicken and it was well worth the wait. Hannah beamed with pride when all four guests wanted seconds and when they also got to sample her Dutch apple pie for dessert, and wanted seconds of that too, she happily obliged. Cooking for multiple people had always been a passion of hers and cooking for Dave was a labor of love.

Wanting the parental substitutes from his childhood to get to know his wife and friends better, Dave invited Hannah and George to keep them company after dinner. Soon, both of the servants, George especially, had them all enthralled or in stitches regaling them with tales of Dave as a young boy, then as an awkward teenager.

The jovial atmosphere and continuous laughter were the right tonic for what the next day was going to bring. Even when Paul and Krista retired to bed, he had to admit it was the most relaxed and normal he had felt in a long time.

It was a good thing this night had worked out so well and had been so enjoyable. Paul had a feeling the following night was going to be anything but pleasant.

# CHAPTER TWENTY-EIGHT

Despite numerous protestations about her not having to get up at an ungodly hour to make them all breakfast, Hannah insisted. As a result, they came down at six thirty to find a sumptuous breakfast of Canadian bacon, sausage, a choice of scrambled or poached eggs, toast, fresh fruit, orange juice and coffee. The elderly lady seemed as fresh as a daisy and it was obvious she was happy to do what she could to look after her guests. Their gratitude only served to widen the smile on her face and gave her another opportunity to hug her beloved Dave. He was happy to let her.

Dave decided he would dispel the myth that nobody in New York actually drove anywhere and volunteered to take them to Brooklyn. He put the address of Pedowski's precinct into his GPS and gave Cathy and Krista their first experience going over the Brooklyn Bridge. It was barely seven thirty and a stiff, cold breeze rolled along the East river as they crossed from Manhattan into Brooklyn. Traffic was predictably heavy but they had left in plenty of time - they hoped - to meet Pedowski at eight thirty as scheduled.

The further into Brooklyn they drove, the quieter Paul became. He hadn't been to the city of his birth in nearly nine years and, although he didn't see much change, he felt an uneasiness in his stomach as the surroundings started to become familiar.

The precinct wasn't too far from the rundown apartment block Paul had grown up in. He was hoping by now it would have been torn down but, as Dave drove along, he saw it looming ahead. If anything, it was even more dilapidated than when he'd walked away from it for the last time sixteen years ago. It was still surrounded by the same tired looking brownstones, liquor stores, Italian delis and other establishments that all had bars protecting their windows and doors. At this hour of the morning, there weren't many people on the streets but if there had been, Paul knew they would have received more than one curious look and not just because of the Massachusetts license plate on Dave's sleek, black car. In this neighborhood, a stranger stuck out like a sore thumb.

It was a weird coincidence that Dave was forced to stop for a red light directly in front of Paul's former home. Paul fought the urge to look up towards the second floor but it was a losing battle and as his reluctant eyes fell on the window he knew to be the one to the living room, he barely suppressed a shudder.

Memories, none of them good, flooded his thoughts and suddenly his mind was pulled back in time. He was a little boy again and his father was beating him, right behind that very window.

"*No, daddy, no,*" his seven year old voice haunted him. "*Stop...please, stop.*" Tears that had always threatened, but had never been allowed to flow, stung his eyes, the effort not to cry hurting his chest. One single tear would have meant victory for his father. He had learned that at a very early age.

"*You no good, worthless piece of shit!*" His father's voice, ringing in his ears with as much clarity as if it was happening right now. "*This'll teach you to take it like a man...*"

"*No, daddy...no...*"

Paul did shudder then and, knowing Dave had caught it and had turned to look at him quizzically, he swallowed the lump in his throat. He pulled himself together, reminding himself he was away from all that now. "That, er, that's where I grew up," he said hoarsely, jerking his head in the direction of the apartment.

Sitting in the back, Krista and Cathy heard his hushed words and Krista sensed her husband's discomfort. She looked through the window and carefully kept her expression blank. "Thank God you're out of that sort of environment now," she told him gently, reaching over to place a hand on his shoulder. "Thank God you're with me, with us."

He tried to smile at her kind words but the memories lingered. It also wasn't lost on him how sharp a contrast his childhood home was to *one* of Dave's childhood homes.

"Light's taking a long time to change," Dave murmured. "If I'd known where we were, I would have jumped the light." He cast Paul a sideways glance and gave a half smile. It was his way of saying he understood why Paul was upset.

"The cops will ticket you for that," Paul said, feeling his humor slowly return.

"Pussy cops in Brooklyn," Dave said smoothly, the sideways glance slipping up to the light just as it turned green.

It was enough to make Paul chuckle and, as they drove past the apartment building, he didn't turn to look back. He let it disappear in the rear-view mirror.

Less than five minutes later, Dave pulled into the parking lot of the precinct where Paul had started his police career. It was a huge, six story building that stretched half a block. It had security cameras placed strategically every fifty feet or so along the front but otherwise it was a non-descript red-brick and concrete structure that had started life in the latter half of the nineteenth century as a wallpaper manufacturer.

The interior on the ground floor had been modernized since Paul had last been there and the desk sergeant looked at them with a stony expression when they approached him.

"We're here to see Captain Harry Pedowski," Paul said.

"And you are?"

"Detectives Cameron and Detectives Andrews." Paul gestured at Dave, Cathy and Krista, not taking his eyes off the gruff sergeant. "He's expecting us."

The stony expression changed to that of disinterest and,

leaning over to his phone, he punched in a five digit number. "Captain Pedowski, you have visitors. Where do you want them?" He listened and, with a grunt, hung up. "He says I'm to take your temperature and then send you right up." He held the contactless forehead thermometer up to each of them and after receiving four normal temperature read-outs, he indicated a set of stairs behind him. "You can either go on up to the fifth floor, or take the stairs to the second floor and get the elevator. He's in room five two one B."

They took the stairs, then the elevator and the doors opened onto a wide, airy office. There were open desks and cubicles, and roughly a dozen people milling around, some wearing masks, some not, none paying attention to the strangers who had just stepped out of the elevator.

"Bring back memories?" Krista asked Paul.

"Not really, I was mainly on the second floor and only came up here if I needed to talk to the detectives. It certainly has been spruced up since I was last here."

"Paul Cameron?" Boomed a voice from their left and they turned toward the sound. A tall man with a buzz cut, piercing blue eyes and wearing a dark gray business suit that didn't disguise his muscular physique, was hurrying towards them and Paul's face instantly crinkled into a smile.

"Captain Pedowski!" They couldn't shake hands or hug so they did an elbow bump, and then Paul stepped back so he could introduce his wife and his friends.

Pedowski was in his early fifties and had taken Paul under his wing when he was a rookie fresh out of the academy almost thirteen years ago. Pedowski, then a detective looking to make sergeant in a year or two, had seen the potential in Paul and, like Captain Hamilton, had showed him the ropes as best as he could. Paul had always been a quick study and his ability as a top notch cop still carried through to this day.

Pedowski turned his attention to Krista. "Very nice to meet you. Sorry you wound up with this jackass."

"I took pity on him," she said with a chuckle.

"You're beautiful *and* you got an accent?"

"Sure. Why not?"

Pedowski looked pointedly at Paul. "You did good, Cameron."

"Told you she was beautiful," he said proudly. "You met my partner, Dave, yesterday on Zoom and this other beauty is his wife, Cathy."

"Lovely to meet you, Captain Pedowski," she said.

Pedowski shook his head in bewilderment. "I'm hearing an accent again?"

"Yeah, we're a veritable United Nations," Dave said jovially.

Pedowski kept the grin on his face as he looked at each of them in turn. He could sense their easy going, comfortable way with one another and, trusting Paul to be friends with good people, he relaxed. "Come on," he waggled his fingers, "let's go to my office. You want any coffee or anything?"

They shook their heads and followed him to the back of the room. They passed several detectives who were all either on the phone or scrutinizing their monitors. Not one of them looked up as the five people passed them, instead remaining engrossed in their work.

It was a bit of a tight squeeze inside the captain's office but they settled in and shared a bit of friendly banter for a few moments. Then, as was Harry Pedowski's style, he got right down to business.

"Yesterday afternoon, I broke the rules and got a drone to go on a little recon over the Romano house. Luckily, no one has reported it and it managed to get a few nice bird's eye images of the house and grounds. I'll let you see the video in a little while. I also got the blueprints and, as I've already told you, the interior is huge. A shit load of rooms, ante-rooms and corridors. It's a fucking maze." Instead of unrolling the paper copy of the blueprints, Harry turned his monitor around and, after bringing the screen to life with a click of the mouse, he showed them what he was talking about. "As you can see, there are two floors and the second floor is accessible by a flight of stairs from the main hallway, located in the center of the first floor at the front door. There is another flight of stairs accessible from the extreme left of the building and yet another flight to the extreme right. If I haven't already said it, I will say it again: This place is *huge*."

It took them a while, but they were finally able to figure out where the weak areas were in the security system: namely a sewer line that was accessible about half a block away from the south corner of the house; another sewer line coming in from the east; and a maze of ventilating ducts in the walls and ceilings. They couldn't find anywhere that would provide easy access to the ducts so it looked like they would have to use the sewer line.

Harry clicked on a minimized page on the browser and it revealed the electrical system. "I'm waiting on our electrical expert to get here so he can determine where to cut the wires for the lasers, trip wires and silent alarms. When I was talking to him, he wasn't sure he'd be able to disable all of them but he assured me he could keep the power for regular lights, appliances, televisions, and so on running without disruption. With luck, they won't know the security has been disrupted." He slipped Paul a glance and gave a surreptitious nod towards the ladies, as if to ask if it had been decided how much were they going to be involved.

Paul had no problem understanding the action. "Cathy and Krista know we intend to go in tonight," he said. "They have agreed to remain as our getaway drivers and to help you with surveillance."

Harry suppressed a sigh of relief. "That's good, I'll need all the eyes and ears I can get. And speaking of which…" He leaned behind his desk and pulled up a huge canvas bag. "Here are your two-ways, ear buds, flick knives, silencers, and automatic weapons. The mini cameras are set to record images only if there's motion. It conserves storage space and battery life. I have them programmed to feed to my cell phone as long as you're within two hundred yards. I suggest you keep them off until you get inside the house, then do a quick test to see if we're connected. Clear?"

"We've used something similar in Massachusetts on a couple of drug raids," Dave said.

"That's good. There are utility belts in there too. Waterproof coverings for your shoes for the sewer and flashlights. Oh, and a few treats for the dogs in case they sniff you down. They've been laced with a sedative that will knock 'em out cold in seconds but not do them any harm. You can pick up bulletproof vests on your way out, I'll sign them out for you. I'm assuming you have your own Glocks?" At his guests' nods, he indicated towards the canvas bag again. "I assumed you'd have them so the silencers are designed specifically for Glock-17s."

Paul and Dave didn't try to hide their gratitude at the equipment Harry had gotten for them. "You've managed to get all this stuff in such a short space of time, Harry, well done you." Paul enthused.

"It pays to know people in high places," he said cryptically. "Right. Now that we have the equipment sorted, let's get a plan formulated. None of us are leaving this room until we know exactly what we'll be doing tonight. Clear?"

So they brainstormed and talked and argued and haggled and after nearly an hour, they came up with what they hoped would be a doable plan.

They would rendezvous at the precinct at ten o'clock. Pedowski would drive them, in an unmarked van loaded with surveillance equipment, to the sewer to the south of the house. They would be able to pull up a floor plan of the house from the file Pedowski sent to their cell phones. Since they didn't have the time or capability of getting in ahead of time and planting bugs to pick up conversations, or heat sensors to pick up where people were, they had to do the best they could with what they had.

It looked like two rooms on the second floor could be studies or offices and one room on the first floor an office, and these rooms would be their goal. Stealth and speed were the key. There was to be no dallying, no second guessing and at the first sign of being discovered, they were to do what they could to leave without getting caught. Only when they had devised a plan they all agreed would work did they decide to get off site and return later that night at around nine thirty.

Harry could feel their determination and he knew they were all doing it for Paul. If he couldn't agree with their commitment to what could be a suicide mission, he could at least admire them for their loyalty. It wasn't lost on him how their body language indicated they were used to moving, talking and thinking as one entity. They each had their individual ideas but they delivered them the same way and usually earned each other's approval. That they were as tight knit as any foursome could be was easy to see. Now he could truly understand how much they wanted to do this for Paul and he admired again the loyalty and devotion shown to his old friend.

Wanting to ensure he had covered every little base he could think of, he realized he had left something quite important out. He had already checked with the precinct's stores and found out there were no spare manhole keys. He needed to speak to the city's Public Works to check he could pick up the necessary tool so they could open any manhole cover they needed to.

With nothing else left to talk about, they parted company and got back to the penthouse before lunch time. The weather had turned chilly and there was a threat of snow. The skies were gray and heavy and the wind was picking up to add to the misery of the day.

They wanted to rest and relax and, after partaking of homemade broccoli and cheese soup and ham salad sandwiches for lunch, they gathered in the living room to discuss what they wanted to do.

"I think I'd like to do a few laps in the pool," Cathy said with a hopeful look at Dave. "If I would be allowed?"

He admonished her with a wry shake of his head. "This

is your home too, Cathy, you don't need to ask permission. None of you do. Krista, if you get the munchies as you normally do and want to go to the kitchen to see what there is, I expect you to do it. If George or Hannah are there, just smile and ask how they're doing, then go right over to the fridge or the pantry and help yourself. I guarantee you'll find just about anything and everything you could possibly want or need. Paul, you want to try the gym, go ahead."

Cathy blushed slightly, still trying to get her head around the fact this wasn't George and Hannah's property, it belonged to her husband's family. But she didn't want to make a big deal out of it, she knew to do so would only hurt Dave's feelings and she didn't want to do that. "I'll try and remember. Anyone else is welcome to join me."

Krista caught Paul's eye and gave him a slight smile. "I think I might like to lie down for a while," she said sweetly. "Then I might do what Dave suggested and go raid the fridge."

Paul knew full well what she meant and his interest, among other things, piqued, he stood up with an exaggerated, exuberant stretch. "Yes, good idea, seeing we were up so early this morning and have a seriously late night ahead of us."

Dave shot them both a grin. "You go do what you want to do," he said cheerfully. He watched them start to walk away but something came into his head and called them back. "Oh, Paul, while I remember, later on, if you like, I can take you down to the garage and show you some of my father's cars."

"Your father has cars, not just car, but *cars* in New York City, where you so aptly pointed out this morning nobody drives?"

"He does...and I did. He has a Bentley...and a stretch Mercedes Limo... and a Lincoln Town Car...oh, and another little one you might be interested in...a Ferrari in, what else, Ferrari red."

" A F- a what? A *Ferrari*? For real?"

"For real. Tomorrow, when we're winding down from whatever happens tonight, we can take it for a spin. Just us guys. And you can drive if you want."

Paul felt the butterflies of excitement flutter in his stomach and his whole face lit up in a way it hadn't in ages. "You *know* how much I want that, partner. That would be *awesome.*"

"Then we'll make it happen. I'll ask George to make sure there's gas in it and to have it ready for us in the morning."

But the following morning, the idea of taking a pleasure ride in one of the world's most fascinating cars would be the furthest thought from their minds.

# CHAPTER TWENTY-NINE

Now that Krista was feeling so much better physically, she was back to her passionate self again, and able to show Paul just how ready, willing and able she was to have him make love to her. Or her to him. Knowing the visit with Pedowski had been a good one, and their plan held a lot of promise, she was eager to let the positive vibes continue flowing. Barely had they gotten through the doorway to their bedroom when she turned around, pushed him gently against the door and pressed her body against him.

He let her take the lead and when she had kissed, or licked, or touched every part of his body until she knew she was driving him completely crazy with desire, only then did she lead him towards the bed. She watched him peel off his clothes, and let him watch as she shimmied out of her jeans and panties and when she held her arms out to him, he obliged and slid into the folds of her waiting sex.

"God, Krista, what you do to me…"

Her breathing quickening, she sought his mouth and kissed him fervently, "Oh boy, what *you* do to me…Christ…Do it, Paul, just…do it…"

Within moments, he could feel her tense beneath him. That she was this ready this quickly only added fuel to his already burning fire. When her breath became whimpers of deep passion, he let her ride it out before joining her in reaching the apex that only hot, quick sex could bring.

He collapsed on top of her, feeling every little movement inside her as she came down from her high point and, although their interlude had been hurried, he didn't feel cheated. He loved her so much and he never could quite understand how she always seemed so eager to take him to her bed but he was eternally grateful that she did. He knew this wasn't the only time this afternoon they would make love and the next time they would be able to take it more slowly.

Cathy had stayed in the living room for a while after Paul and Krista had taken their leave, reading a mediocre story on her Kindle. She wasn't used to idle time like this, especially during the day and, giving up on the storyline for now, she went to the bedroom she shared with Dave to get changed for the swimming pool. She had stripped down to pull on her one piece swim suit when she suddenly felt Dave's hands steal around her from behind. He cupped her breasts and kissed her neck.

"Uh...hello," she murmured. "Can I do anything..." Her breath caught when she felt his hardness pressing against her buttocks. "...um...anything to help you?" She managed to finish.

"I came in to change my top and saw you standing there, beautiful and naked," he said, his hand smoothing down her flat belly to the vortex between her legs. Already he could feel a reaction from her and he pressed even tighter against her. "God, baby, seeing you like that, so hot, not knowing I was even here and looking at you, I knew I just had to have you."

"Did you now?" She ducked under his arms and turned to face him. She returned his fingers to where they had been a moment before. "So, have me." She invited.

He didn't need to be asked twice and, although she was a few beats behind him in her arousal, it didn't take long for her to catch up. He could never get enough of her, she was his soul-mate and his lifelong love. Although he hadn't come to their bedroom just now with the intentions of making love to her, he simply hadn't been able to resist. She had been so innocent and vulnerable standing there, and that was all it had taken.

They didn't move from where they were. He was strong enough to support her as she guided him inside her and he let her set the pace. There was nothing innocent about her now as her breathing became urgent. It didn't take long for him to feel the pressure mounting in his groin and he tried to slow down to make sure she was ready. He truly did try but she was too hot and too sexy and at her guttural words of encouragement, he soon felt himself explode inside her.

"Oh...fuuuu...ck...baby," he whispered as she shuddered and cried out his name and when she buried her face into his neck, he could feel her heat and her pulse and he couldn't remember loving her more than he did at this moment.

When he gently laid her on the bed, she reached up and cupped his face. Her eyes were bright with desire and shining with love. "My amazing man," she said softly. "What would I do without you?"

"You won't have to find out." He lay down beside her and held her close. The room temperature was comfortable but he was still mostly clothed and she had nothing on. He pulled the throw from the bottom of the bed up and draped it around her. "Next time you tell me you're going for a swim, give me a heads up so I can be here and help you take your clothes off."

She snuggled in against him and chuckled. "Now that I would like. As long as you do it nice and slow."

An hour later, Cathy was swimming contentedly in the perfectly heated swimming pool. She had always been a strong, keen swimmer and she cut effortlessly through the water doing her preferred front stroke. She could feel the tensions of the day slipping further away with each slice of her arms and kick of her legs. Dave had come to watch her for a little while but when she came up to the top end, he had caught her attention and told her he was going to go and visit with George for a bit.

Krista had come to the kitchen a little timidly half

an hour before and immediately saw she'd had nothing to be timid about. The welcome from Hannah was warm and friendly. Krista had taken a true shine to the old woman and, always a good judge of character, she knew the woman's smile and greeting to be genuine.

Hannah had waved in the direction of the huge, hotel-sized fridge and then to the walk in pantry and told her to help herself. She even set down a tray for her to use.

When Krista had gone back up to the bedroom, she woke a dozing Paul and showed him her goodies. Cookies, chips, dip, chocolate dipped strawberries, cashew nuts, crackers, three different types of cheese, bottled water and Fresca. She had contemplated beer for Paul and wine for herself but she wanted to ensure they both had clear heads for their mission.

After their snack, Krista had snuggled down for a nap and Paul wanted to get up for a bit. He wanted to go to the gym and work off some of the sugar he had just ingested. Even if it was just a five mile jog on the treadmill, he would be happy.

He started downstairs but as he was passing a room where the door was slightly ajar he heard his name being mentioned by a voice he recognized as George's. A second later, he heard Dave's voice responding.

"...you have to understand, what we have to do tonight is very important. It's more than important, it's absolutely vital. We have to do what we can to spare Paul from being sent to prison for a crime he did not commit."

Paul didn't like eavesdropping and normally he would have continued on his way but he hadn't failed to catch the desperation in Dave's voice and something compelled him to listen for a while longer.

"Let me ask you something, David," George continued. "First, I and Hannah were talking last night and we both agreed all four of you seem very close. Your wife is absolutely adorable, very sweet, but I think there's a bit of a fiery nature there too, am I right?"

Dave chuckled. "She isn't afraid to put me in my place, that's for sure. But she's honestly the best thing that has ever happened to me. I couldn't do this thing we call life without her. And, before you ask, she fell in love with me before she knew a thing about my parents' money. When she found out, she almost walked away, but luckily, I convinced her to stay."

"That's good to know. And your friend Paul?"

"What about him? As you and Hannah have already figured out, we're all very close."

"Yes, but you also told me he's from an abusive, very poor family. Do you think he's so close to you because of your inheritance?"

Paul closed his eyes and leaned heavily against the wall. Nothing good ever happened to those who eavesdropped and he knew he should walk away right now. If he heard Dave admit to something bad or negative he hadn't known anything about, he would be devastated.

At George's question, Dave emitted a clearly amused laugh. "Absolutely not. No, George, Paul is my best friend. My *best* friend. I can't be without him either. Not once has he ever asked me for money and even when he found out I'd asked my dad for his bail money, he was fit to be tied. Grateful, yes, but not happy."

"I can see in your eyes how you feel about him, boy. I just needed to make sure he wasn't a gold digger."

"He is the furthest thing from a gold digger, I can assure you. He has a loving, beautiful wife who is the one of the most adorable people I know, he has a good life and a stellar career, he doesn't need money and he certainly doesn't want mine."

There was a brief silence and then George said, "You've always told me the truth so I have every reason to believe you. Forgive an old man's suspicions, and I know it's not my place, but realize where I'm coming from. You phone out of the blue, say you're coming down to New York City – in the middle of a pandemic, I remind you – and then tell me the reason for your visit is to try and get your partner's name cleared. The very partner who has been arrested for the murder of his own father. I think you can understand my skepticism."

"I do, George, I totally get it. I don't want you worrying unnecessarily. He's a good person, the best, and if this is what having a brother is like, then I'm glad it's Paul because that's what he feels like to me. He keeps me right, he's the most level-headed person I know."

"And you are absolutely, one hundred per cent certain he didn't kill his father."

"I am totally one hundred per cent sure. Are you through with the third degree or is there more?"

"I'm through. I just didn't want to see my boy getting used or taken advantage of, especially by the people closest to him. You're too giving, you wouldn't always see something bad if it was standing right it in front of you. But I believe you, you might be too generous but you're not stupid. Now, when are Hannah and I going to get the news there's to be an addition to the family....And, uh oh, seems I've hit on a raw nerve with that comment. What's up?"

Paul was reeling from Dave's words. If ever he'd needed proof Dave was the best and most loyal friend he could ever wish for, he had just gotten it. But now that George had unwittingly brought up an innocent but very painful subject, Paul knew it was his cue to leave.

It was only three in the afternoon, they still had six hours to kill before crossing back over the Brooklyn Bridge. As he jogged along on the treadmill, Paul could only hope it would be a life-changing experience tonight, one for the better. He couldn't face it if the mission turned out unfruitful because after this, he had absolutely nothing to work with. It was hard enough knowing he was endangering not only his own life but that of his partner's and if something were to happen to Dave, how would he ever be able to forgive himself?

# CHAPTER THIRTY

When they met up with Pedowski at the precinct just before nine thirty, the snow that had been threatening all day still hadn't put in an appearance. The strong, gusty wind had increased, bringing with it frigid windchills. They considered the wind as a blessing, it was strong enough to rattle window frames, blow debris around and provide cover if they made a noise and someone in the house heard it.

In Harry's office, they looked over the blueprints one last time. They needed to know what area of the house the sewer would lead them to. There were two possible locations, one was the middle of an underground room, presumably a cellar or boiler room, from which a flight of stairs led to the back of the kitchen, which in turn was close to the stairwell in the middle of the building. The second was to the left of the house, close to the stone wall enclosing the grounds. The sewer cover sat roughly a hundred feet from what looked like a side entrance that seemed close to a stairwell on the far right of the building.

They also needed a quick escape route and Paul pointed at what looked like a gate cut into the perimeter wall. It was also close to the sewer tunnel. "Is that wired like the rest of the fence?" he asked.

"According to my guy, the power going to the gate can be cut same as the tripwires and lasers." Harry looked up when the wind outside swept by in a long, mournful wail. "Wouldn't it be great if the wind tore down the powerline to the whole house?"

"It would save a lot of guesswork for your guy," Dave nodded, grinning.

Cathy had been looking over the blueprints as intently as the rest of them and something suddenly occurred to her. "Um... don't know why this has just come into my head but I think it deserves checking. Is it possible to open a manhole cover from underground? I would assume yes, because of the safety factor, but it would be nice to know for sure. Wouldn't want Dave or Paul getting stuck down there, especially with all this rain that will have the storm drains flooding in no time, and there's no easy way out for them."

Everyone turned to look at her in surprise. It was clear it hadn't occurred to anyone and with a low rumble deep in his throat, Harry snatched up his cell phone and selected one of his contacts. "Jorge, Pedowski. How hard is it to open a manhole cover if you're underground, instead of above ground?" He listened intently for a few minutes then, with a gruff "thanks", he disconnected the call. "Shit. Good thing you brought that up, Cathy," he said. "Quick answer is, you *can* open a manhole from underneath it, however you need a special tool that is only available from the water company and has to be ordered in advance. It's practically impossible for a man, or in this case two men, pushing up on it to open because it will be locked from above. It's also incredibly heavy to raise manually. We can get the rod to unlock the manhole on the street, but getting the one in the grounds open isn't going to happen because we'll we underneath it. That's why, if servicemen are going in, they have their entrance and exit covers opened before they make their descent."

There was a long, tense silence as each realized their mission might be over before it had even begun when, suddenly, Krista grinned.

"Who says they have to go through the sewer or water line?" she said. "If that gate is disconnected, they can get in through that way. They can get to the house quickly and undetected if all security has been disabled."

Paul looked proudly at his wife. "Told you she was smart, Harry," he said smoothly.

"*Both* ladies were smarter than the three of us," Harry said good-naturedly.

"You would have figured it out," Cathy said. "Krista was just quicker."

Blowing a sigh of relief, Dave tipped Krista a wink before looking back at Pedowski. "When is your guy going to disconnect what he needs to disconnect?" he asked.

"He's waiting for my call. We'll pick him up on the way. He's already sourced the power supply and the only tricky part for him will be making sure he disconnects that gate first." Harry looked at the four of them in turn and glanced at the clock. It was five minutes to ten. "Are we good or do we need to go through this one more time?"

Paul and Dave passed a silent communication and Paul nodded. "We're good. Let's roll."

Harry led them to the basement garage where a black Chevrolet van stood waiting. He opened the back doors and showed them the equipment inside. Along one side was a desk type bench, with three black office chairs bolted to the floor in front of it. There were two, twenty-four-inch monitors on brackets mounted above the desk. Overhead, and down each side of the monitors, audio equipment was bolted to the walls of the van. The banks of electrical panels had rows of flick and toggle switches, some of which were labeled, some not.

Harry informed them that the camera equipment could pick up long range motion, as well as provide infrared and night vision. The audio surveillance could pick up conversations up to a thousand yards via Wi-Fi or LAN. That should enable them to hear everything Paul or Dave were saying. Although manufactured to filter out weather interference, such as wind or thunder, there was no guarantee the audio would be able to pick up other conversations inside the house. Paul and Dave were advised to be mindful of that. One thing Harry tried to instill was, that although this surveillance van was good, and loaded with equipment, systems were prone to fail and any part of the gear could fail at any time.

Harry showed them how to connect their cameras to the van's system, as well as to his cell phone, the latter would serve as their back up if the primary system failed. Their earpieces were connected also. Then he gave Cathy and Krista a quick tutorial on how to zoom in on an image on the monitor, or use the night vision function. They had been joking about it earlier, but now the wind really was so strong it could topple a power line or two. For now, the power was still on and they couldn't rely on Mother Nature to turn it off.

Once all the instructions had been explained and demonstrated, it was time to leave. Harry got into the front seat, Paul in the passenger seat beside him and Dave strapped himself in between Cathy and Krista on the chairs in front of the monitors.

It took ten minutes to get to the home of Brooklyn PD's electrical expert. Errol Simmons was a black man in his mid-thirties. Built like the proverbial brick shit house, he had a shaved head and a huge scar that ran from his right cheek up to the middle of his skull. But he seemed friendly enough and his dark brown eyes danced in good humor.

Errol was carrying a large, hard-shelled briefcase and a utility belt filled with all types of tools and equipment was secured around his waist. At Harry's request, before they drove off, Errol opened the briefcase to explain his tool kit. There was a black box about the size of a pack of cigarettes, with a gauge on it. It was a stud finder and would detect were the electrical wires were behind a wall. There was also an electrical tester and a wire tracer. He showed them a small monitor that would help him determine what each wire was for when he located the junction box. He had already pored over the blueprints earlier in the day and, because he had the advantage of working for the electric company, he was able to pull up the information for the property on his computer and locate everything he needed.

A building the size of the Romano house had at least two junction boxes, one of which was outside and, mercifully, close to the gate Paul and Dave would be using. Errol explained he had studied the wiring for the security fencing by relying on what he had been able to find online. He said he knew exactly where he needed to put a jammer on the outside of the fence that would cut the power. He assured them that the power for lights, heat and electrical appliances wouldn't be jeopardized and he was pretty sure the people in the house wouldn't even know their security system had been compromised.

Convinced the man knew what he was talking about, Harry got back into the driver seat. It was a bench seat and Paul slid along so Errol could get in beside him.

When Harry pulled up on a quiet, residential street five minutes later, the men in the front got out of the van and went around to the back. Dave and Paul tested their camera and audio equipment one last time and when the monitors displayed a connection had been made, they knew they were ready.

Unconcerned about privacy, Paul and Dave pulled their respective wife into their arms. They held each other close, whispering soft words of love and encouragement and, when they stepped back, they noticed Errol's eyes were as wide as saucers.

"Man, the po-lees force is *very* friendly up in Massachusetts," he said with a grin.

"We like to spread the love around, Errol," Dave said lightly and then, with one last look at Cathy, and a kiss on Krista's cheek, he jumped out of the van and, seconds later, Paul and Errol joined him.

Harry stood in the doorway. "We'll be watching, we hope, and listening. Any sign of trouble, haul ass out of there. If you haven't got what you want, that's too bad. I have no intention of phoning your captain to tell him to prepare a memorial service."

Paul and Dave looked around them. Several houses stood in the distance on their left, all good-sized family abodes. Ahead of them, about fifty feet away, there was a high, stone wall that seemed to stretch on for ages. Above the top of the wall, through the strands of electrified razor wire they could just about make out the roof of a massive building. The sheer size of the Romano house, even from this distance, was daunting.

Errol reached into his briefcase and extracted the gadget that would jam the signal. The gate they were going to use as their entrance and exit point was on the other side of the wall but, by their calculations, it was not far along the perimeter.

They were all dressed in black and Paul had pulled on a black ski cap to cover his blond locks. Moving slowly to their left, they located the gate a few dozen yards along the perimeter and, after taking a careful look all around them, checking for any cars or someone out for a late-night jog, or even someone out walking their dog, Paul and Dave stepped back and let Errol do his thing. They could only hope everything would run smoothly from this point on.

Errol turned the signal jammer on. "When I jam the current to this gate, it should release the locking mechanism too," Errol whispered. "According to my notes, there are no lasers or tripwires between here and the house but there is at least one security camera. It rotates a hundred and eighty degrees and takes twenty five seconds to complete the arc. Once I get in past the gate, I know where the camera is situated so I'll wait for it go to the opposite side, then we can make a sprint for the side door. Cool?"

"Cool," Paul and Dave said in unison.

"What about silent alarms?" Dave asked.

"They'll be disabled same time as the tripwires and lasers. This ain't my first rodeo, guys but I appreciate your concerns."

"Hey, Pedowski trusts you," Paul said, "that's good enough for us."

Errol held the gadget a half inch from the lock on the gate and pressed a switch. A second later, the gate clicked, as it unlocked itself. Without hesitation, Errol reached out, pressed the lock-button on the gate and it sprang open. There were no sirens, no alarms, no flashing lights, nothing and, in unison, they exhaled a deep breath they hadn't realized they were holding.

Errol pointed toward the overhead camera. It was about midway in its sweep, headed away from them. "Okay, good, we have about thirty five seconds to get to the side door. You can't see it because it's dark, but underneath and behind the camera is the junction box and soon as I open it, I'll be able to disable the sensor lights – as long as I don't trip the sensor first!"

The easy part was getting across the grounds to the door, the hard part was waiting for Errol to study the maze of wires and cables and decide what he needed to cut. While waiting, Dave and Paul studied the entrance door, looking for a sliver of light along the bottom or top to indicate they weren't going into darkness. The door was a sturdy oak structure and had a complicated looking lock operated by a keypad.

Errol snipped and cut and, after about thirty seconds, stepped back to study his handiwork. He held the prong of the multimeter to check the circuit and smiled when he saw there was no voltage running through the wiring. Just what he wanted. He turned to the door and couldn't help but smirk when he saw the keypad's interior lighting had disappeared.

"You have anything in your bag of tricks that can crack the code?" Dave asked. From where he was standing, he couldn't see the now dark keypad.

"Who needs anything to crack a pussy code?" Errol said. "It's already disabled, did it right there at the junction box. Some people, when they're putting together the most sophisticated of systems, think no one knows how to disable the system from the junction box. Easiest thing in the world."

Paul gave Errol an air high five and went to the door. He put his ear against it, listening for any sign of life on the other side. They couldn't tell if there was a light on inside, or not, the door was too well sealed, but he couldn't hear anything and looked inquisitively at Dave.

"I'm ready if you are," he said.

Dave quickly nodded. "Let's do this." He turned to Errol. "Everything we need disabled has been disabled? Tripwires, lasers, motion sensors?"

"Yes, sir. As long as you're quiet and don't let anyone see you, they won't even know you're there. I was instructed by Pedowski to wait here for you so I will. He'll text me if I need to abandon ship. Good luck, guys, I hope you get what you're looking for."

Paul put his hand on the doorknob, twisted it carefully and pushed. The door opened. A rush of warm air hit him in the face but he didn't care, he was relieved to be walking into dark silence. He knew Cathy, Krista and Harry were watching and listening and even though the distance between them was barely a hundred feet, they could have been an ocean apart.

They had entered a utility room. An industrial sized, washer and dryer took up about a quarter of one side of the room. There were two huge chest freezers on the opposite wall and floor to ceiling cupboards covered the remaining walls. At the far side was a door standing wide open. Assuming this was the way to the stairwell, they crept towards it.

They stood in the doorway for a few seconds to get their bearings, and were about to turn to their left when, from their right, they heard a low rumbling sound.

"Even you couldn't be hungry at a time like this," Dave hissed.

"It wasn't me. I don't know what made that noise."

Dave took the penlight out of his back pocket and shone it downwards and behind Paul. "Oh...shit...Er... Paul, if you had a pet Rottweiler, what would you call it?"

"Sir, probably."

"No, seriously."

"I don't know...Satan? Or how about Zeus?" The growling behind Paul sounded again and he slowly turned around to face the source. "Oh sweet Jesus, definitely Sir."

"Sir works for me. Now what do we do?"

In the van, Cathy pointed at a heat source that had appeared on the monitor. She hadn't heard the growling but understood by the men's conversation what the heat source was. "Er, guys, we can see what you're seeing, don't forget. Can you immobilize him?"

"Yeah, if we shoot the sonofabitch - um, no pun intended," Dave said, his eyes riveted on the dog as it started to inch closer.

He was one hundred and thirty pounds of sheer muscle and no doubt trained to attack intruders. Standing rigid, his razor sharp teeth were barred and ready to use.

# CHAPTER THIRTY-ONE

Paul tentatively put his hand out in an attempt to let the dog smell him and hopefully realize he wasn't the enemy. The dog snapped his jaws and Paul snatched his hand back, the dog's teeth missing his fingers by barely an inch.

Dave suddenly remembered the treats Harry said he'd put in their utility belts and, reaching into one of the pockets, he felt the rubbery surface of a dog treat. "Good dog," he said softly, "good, *good* dog." He held the treat towards the dog, who didn't seem interested in any way, shape or form. "Here you go," he encouraged, "a yummy treat, all for you. It will help you have a good sleep. Good boy!"

The dog didn't even blink at the treat being dangled mere inches from his nose. His stance hadn't changed, his low growling continued unabated and when Dave let the treat drop at the dog's feet, the dog snapped and snarled at Dave's hand instead.

"Uh, plan B anyone?" Paul asked.

"Give me a moment," Dave said. It felt like ages since the dog had made its presence known, but in reality was only a few seconds. "I got nothing. You?"

"Oh for Christ's sake. If you want to get him to roll over and play dead or tickle his tummy, go right ahead, pal. Me, I'm just going to stand here and try to stare him to death."

"Brilliant plan, Paul, definitely one of your better ones." Dave had already reached behind him to where the silencer for his gun was. He quickly screwed it on the nozzle and took a step backwards.

The dog, whose name wasn't sir, or Zeus, or Satan, was called Hercules and was getting restless. He backed up five feet and lunged forward again, his powerful back legs propelling him upwards, his teeth barred as he prepared to go for the throat of an intruder, just as he had been trained.

Paul was the unfortunate victim and, as Cathy, Krista and Harry looked on helplessly, Hercules hit him with so much force he was pushed backwards until he slammed against the wall. He could feel the dog's claws digging into his chest, he could see the evil in the dog's eyes, only inches from his own, he could smell the raw-meat smell of the dog's breath and a split second after the impact, he felt the knife-like teeth biting into his throat. He was only dimly aware of a dull *thunk!* and after that, the pressure on his chest lifted. When he opened his eyes, he saw Hercules lying on the floor, the bullet hole in the side of his skull already oozing blood out onto the carpet.

"Oh Jesus, oh Christ, oh Holy Mary Mother of God!" Paul gasped in fright and accompanying relief. "Did you see that, Dave? Did you *see* that?"

"I saw." Dave had already holstered his gun and came to his friend. "Let me have a look at you, see what damage has been done."

"Yes, Dave, please look," Krista's anxious voice came through their earpieces.

Paul pulled down the collar of his heavy sweater. He didn't feel any pain but he could feel the warm blood trickling towards his chest. "Well?" he asked impatiently.

"It doesn't look like he got his teeth too far into you," Dave said, again using his penlight so he could get a better look. "There's broken skin, though, and a little bit of bleeding, but nothing too deep. You might consider a tetanus shot."

"Got a booster last month when I got shot."

"Then when we get back to the Penthouse, we can raid the medicine cabinet, I'm sure we can find some antibiotic ointment. You going to be okay?"

It felt a bit ridiculous they were standing in a house they had just broken into, with a dead dog at their feet, discussing treatment for dog bites but that's exactly what was happening. Getting back to their mission, Paul impatiently rolled his collar back up. "I'm fine. Let's get going."

"Wait, let's put the dog where no one's going to trip over it."

They stored Hercules behind the door. Collecting their bearings, they moved cautiously into the hallway. They reckoned Errol had done a stellar job in disconnecting all the safety equipment. Unless there were silent alarms they knew nothing about, if there had been lasers or tripwires, where they were now in the entrance hall would have been the first place for them to go off.

They came to a stop at the foot of the stairwell that had been shown on the left of the hallway in the blueprints. This was how far they had gotten before the demon dog from hell had appeared. On the bottom level there were several doors to their right and left but there was no telling what was behind them.

"Harry, remind us again exactly where the studies and or offices are," Paul said. All he got back was a hiss of static and he tried again. "Harry, do you read me?"

"Harry, come back?" Dave said. Nothing but static for him too. Harry would have been listening to the same receiver Cathy and Krista were listening to, and if he couldn't hear them, neither could they. He looked at Paul and grimly shook his head. "We've lost them. Must be out of range. Harry said he wasn't too confident in the power of the surveillance equipment, especially if we got over a hundred yards from them. If it's an equipment error, chances are Harry can't pick us up on his cell phone either."

"We can't hear them, but can we see them?" The camera was on a lanyard around his neck and when he turned it around there was nothing but snow. "Oh great. Maybe the dog jumping on me like that has dislodged something."

"Then why wouldn't mine be working?" Dave looked all around him and shook his head. "No, I think it's this place. The walls are probably six feet thick and are blocking the signal." He looked back up the stairs. There was no sign of life anywhere, which unnerved him. It wasn't lost on either of them there could be someone watching their every move right now from one of those rooms up there, or down here, where they were. But a family like this, presumably with staff and security personnel, would have someone floating around, surely? They'd been inside the house for a total of five minutes and there wasn't even the sound of a television, radio or a toilet flushing anywhere.

"How do you want to do this?" Paul asked softly. "You want to split up, you take down here, I'll take up there?"

"I don't like going in blind," Dave said hesitantly. He was still trying to hear anything that would indicate there was at least one human around somewhere. Sometimes, silence was a bad thing.

Outside, as soon as the monitors displayed snow and the audio system turned to static, Harry tried to get the tuner to pick up a different signal. Nothing. He looked grimly at Cathy and Krista, who were in turn looking at him in concern. "Not looking good, ladies."

"Can we fix it?" Cathy asked.

"I don't think it's an equipment malfunction, I think it's one of the things I was afraid of would happen and why I didn't want this mission to take place. The walls of that house are solid masonry, probably three to six feet deep. We can't pick up them, they can't pick up us."

"Would Errol be able to do anything?" Krista asked.

Pedowski shook his head. "Not unless he's got dynamite in that black box of tricks of his and blows the walls to smithereens."

"So what do we do?" Cathy said, her eyes darting from Harry to the monitor, in the vain hope the latter would magically spring back to life.

Harry blew out a long breath of derision. "We wait, ladies. And pray."

Knowing every second they stood there doing nothing brought more danger, Paul and Dave knew they had to come up with a plan. Fast. They stood for a few seconds, weighing their options and came to a decision.

"I'll stay down here," Dave said. "You go up. We take fifteen minutes, no longer, then we get the hell out of here. If one of us gets caught, the other gets out. No stupid heroics. At least we will have the full backing of the Brooklyn PD to help rescue whichever one of us it is."

"The Romanos won't care. If we're caught, that's it. End of watch."

Dave shook his head. "Positive thinking, my friend, that's all we need, positive thinking." He checked his watch. "Eleven ten. We rendezvous back here at eleven twenty five. Okay?"

Paul nodded and gripped Dave's arm before he took off. "Take care."

"You too." Dave paused long enough to search his friend's eyes. This might be the last time he would ever see him alive. This might be the last time Paul would see *him* alive.

"I know, Dave," Paul said softly, knowing what was going through his mind. "But this isn't good bye, this is..." He trailed off deliberately to let Dave finish the sentence.

"...see you later." Dave smiled sadly. "Get going," he murmured. He watched Paul walk away, pulling on black leather gloves as he did so, and when Paul turned back one last time to give a thumbs up, the gesture was immediately returned.

The two men had parted company unaware that only a few yards away, in a room that would have done NASA proud, an alarm heralding their intrusion had already gone off. The security room was filled with computers and cameras and timer-controlled monitors that viewed every room in the house. It was the only room that had escaped being disconnected by Errol, because whosever idea this room had been, had had the foresight to keep it separate from the rest of the power supply. The only areas the equipment didn't monitor were the bathrooms, the cellar, and certain areas of the grounds.

The equipment was watched over by a sharp-eyed security guard, who was paid handsomely by the family for his services and discretion.

On an instrument panel, a little red light flashing on and off that warned of an intrusion in the hallway was unnoticed, at least for now. The security guard was in the kitchen, on the other side of the building where Paul and Dave had come in, trying to sweet talk Carmen, the eighteen-year-old maid, into going on a date with him the following night. She was flirting with him, batting her long-lashed lids over eyes that were mischievous and sultry. She was playing hard to get, driving him crazy with her thirty-eight-inch chest pushed out to tantalize him further. Keeping him preoccupied, and practically drooling, as he plied her with compliments and begged her to go out with him seemed like second nature to her.

The twenty-four-year-old security guard would return to the carefully concealed room that wasn't shown on any blueprint, within five minutes of the time Paul and Dave had parted company. The contented smile on his face and the raging hard-on in his pants would disappear the moment he realized there were intruders in the house.

Dave had checked out two rooms downstairs and was on his way to the next. He moved stealthily along the corridor, never knowing what he was going to find when he opened each door. So far, he had unearthed nothing of importance. He had come across a huge dining room that, after a quick check through the credenzas and buffet tables, didn't reveal any relevant paperwork. Not that he had expected anything like that in a dining room, but he couldn't discount it. He touched each picture on the wall to see if they hinged open to reveal a safe, but no such luck.

The next room was a cozy little sitting room. There was nothing in it except for a two-seater sofa, a large rocking chair, a coffee table, a medium sized television and a small bookcase. He'd cast his eyes over the book case, but there was no paperwork there either and no other furniture that had drawers in it for him to check. Again, he checked the pictures, and even an ornate rectangular mirror. Again no safe.

Suddenly he remembered the two-way, hand held radios Harry had shown them earlier, in the van. He put his hand on his utility belt where he thought he had slipped it in and froze for a second when he realized the pouch was empty. Harry had handed the radios to Cathy to synchronize the channels. Dave had watched Cathy do that and then she had placed them on the table beside the back door so they could be retrieved when they got out. She had even made a point about telling them they were synched and the battery level at full, then told them not to forget them on the way out.

Clearly they had left the van without the two-ways. Definitely not one of their brighter moves. With a curse of irritation, he checked his watch. It was eleven fifteen, which meant he had ten minutes before he had to meet up with Paul so he hurried on his way.

Once again, he was struck with how quiet the house was. He still couldn't hear anything, no clock ticking, no background music, no phones ringing and it gave him an uneasy feeling. It wasn't just quiet here, it was eerily so, as if a vacuum from another world had sucked all the noise out.

He stood in the deep shadows of the long hallway, feeling his skin rise in goose bumps. The sensation wasn't just caused by the unearthly silence, it was also because the atmosphere in the house didn't feel right. It was thick and cloying, heavy and oppressive and, Dave ventured to think, menacing.

It was the same sort of feeling he got if he was standing too close to electrical pylons. He did a slow, three-sixty-degree turn, his eyes searching for cameras or electrical equipment that would produce this sort of feeling. The mahogany paneled walls were mostly bare. There were only one or two pictures scattered around and he went through the motions, checking behind them for a safe, or concealed camera. Again, nothing.

He angled his penlight towards the ceiling to see if there was a dent or a groove in the plaster work, indicating a hidden camera. The ceiling appeared smooth and unflawed. The ceiling was too high to check if there was anything embedded in the recessed lighting so he could only hope there were no cameras up there either.

Maybe Pedowski had gotten it wrong, he mused, maybe the security in the place was minimal. Maybe the Romano family had only started a rumor with the intention of foiling the police or anyone else who might think it a novel ideal to break into a notorious drug lords' abode.

But he couldn't afford to think like that, he couldn't afford to relax. This house was dangerous, he could *smell* it. And the Romanos themselves, the father and his five sons, were each as dangerous as the other. The difference was, a house couldn't kill people. But people could kill people. He kept that in the fore of his mind and crept along to the next room.

As Dave moved along the hall, the security guard, twenty-four-year-old Bruce Fennell, who topped the scales at two hundred and forty pounds, returned to his post with nothing on his mind except getting into little Carmen's panties the next evening. When he realized four flashing red lights had come on during his ten-minute absence, one upstairs and three downstairs, he thought there was a malfunction. The lights indicated an intrusion of some sort.

Fennell knew it could only have been Hercules who had set off the ones downstairs. That stupid dog was forever doing that when he was locked indoors. On a night like this, with a frigid, howling wind, the boss had insisted the dog be allowed to stay inside. Maybe he had set the other alarms off too, but Fennell knew Hercules rarely, if ever, came upstairs.

Not wishing to take any chances, he switched on one of the screens showing the lower hallway - just in time to see an unfamiliar figure enter a room just three doors from where he sat. He didn't see much, only that the figure was tall and dressed all in black.

With a curse, he reached over to a switch, picked up a microphone and buzzed Julius Romano, patriarch of one of the most dreaded families in Brooklyn. He was at home tonight, deep in business discussions with three of his five sons, even at this late hour.

"I said no interruptions, Fennell," the old man said gruffly.

"I know sir, but I think you'll appreciate why I'm ringing you. It looks like we've got ourselves an intruder." Fennell blinked in surprise when another alarm went off, this time in the upstairs study. "Make that two intruders, er, sir, one is in your wife's dressing room downstairs even as we speak but he's already been in three rooms before that. And one just now upstairs, in the study."

Julius Romano heard the excited tones of his employee, as did his sons, and he narrowed his brown eyes in irritation. "How did they get this far, Fennell?" he demanded coldly in a faint Italian accent.

"Er, well...I've had an upset stomach, sir and I -"

"Never mind. We're coming down." Romano turned off the intercom and looked at each of his sons in turn. Markus, Pieter and Julio were just like their father: dark-haired, dark-eyed, tall, heavy set and mean. "Well, boys, you heard him. Time to dispose of our uninvited guests." He settled his gaze on his youngest son, Pieter, his pride and joy, the son he was always prepared to do that little bit extra for, and his eyes softened. "You stay here, Pieter, you can be our backup in case something goes wrong. Turn on the screen and keep an eye open for danger. Markus, Julio, are you both armed?" At his sons' quiet nods, he arose from the leather smoking chair. "Let's not waste any more time. Julio, lead the way."

Dave really didn't know what hit him. One minute he had been standing in an empty room, trying to force his way into a locked filing cabinet, the next he was being pinned against the wall, held in such a way he couldn't turn around to see his assailant. In five seconds flat, he was stripped of his gun, his semi-automatic, his flick knife, his camera, flashlight and earpiece. Only when his captors were convinced they had retrieved everything was he released from the iron grip and forced to turn around.

He barely gave the two apes at his side a second glance, his eyes were fixed on the old man who could only be Julius Romano. He smiled his most disarming smile. "Mr Romano! Such a pleasure to meet -" He was silenced by the ape on his left who used a sneaky undercut punch to the stomach to shut him up. It wasn't enough to wind him, just enough for him to take the warning.

He knew he was in deep trouble.

# CHAPTER THIRTY-TWO

Julius Romano looked at the items on the floor, his attention taken in particular by the semi-automatic rifle and the wire. "Quite the hardware you have there," he commented. "The cat burglar business must be pretty good."

Dave was torn between remaining silent or talking. He chose the latter. "You've got it wrong," he said, trying to wrench free from the iron grip of his captors. "I'm not a burglar, cat or otherwise."

"No? Then whatever you are, you're pretty stupid, coming into my house, snooping around where you have no business being. We have a way of dealing with people like you."

"I'm sure you have." Dave glanced at the clock on the wall. Ten minutes had passed since he left Paul. "Look, why don't you forget you ever saw me and I'll just leave right now with a promise not to breathe a word of this to anyone. What do you say? Sound like a plan?"

Romano smiled, a cold, reptilian smile. "I don't think so. That wire tells me you're not alone, that there's someone else here or is waiting outside for you. Whatever it is, if my sons can't find him, Hercules will."

"Hercules?"

"My dog. Trained to kill on sight."

"He wouldn't happen to be a big-ass black and brown Rottweiler with horrendous bad breath by any chance, would he?"

"Oh? Have you met him already."

"You could say that. I hate to tell you but he's in hell right now, running around with all the other demon dogs, his little stubby tail on fire and his paws burning." For that information, Dave was rewarded with another blow, this time to the solar plexus and one that did wind him. He doubled over, using his captors as support, gasping heavily.

Romano sneered in contempt. "You're going to pay for that. But before I dispose of you, tell me who you are and where you come from."

"Come from? Nevada, originally. If you want me to go back further, you'll have to let me speak to my psychic channel, he can give you all my past existences, as far back as the time of Moses."

"Being a wise-cracking smartass is not going to earn you any favors. What is your name?"

"From which life?"

Julio, on his right side, grabbed Dave by the hair and forced his head back. "Answer my father, moron."

Dave hated not having some kind of an advantage and he felt his blood simmer. "The name's Tony, pleased to make your acquaintance. Only my friends call me Dave though, so you may call me Tony." A stinging slap sent his temper soaring and he stared in hatred at the man on his right. "Hit me again and I'll break your neck."

"You're hardly in a position for threats," Romano reminded him. "For your own good, tell me where your accomplice is."

"I don't have an accomplice, I work alone."

"Then why did you have a two way wire on your body? Why all the weapons?"

"Hey, a guy needs to keep his ass covered, doesn't he? And the wire is just a front, it doesn't even work."

"It's only there for show?" Romano smiled again. "I don't think so. Are you going to tell me why you're here or are we going to have to beat it out of you?"

"I'm here because I'm trying to get the name of your

interior designer." Out of the corner of his eye, he saw one of the son's fiddling with the controls on the wire and camera. He hoped that whatever he was doing would coax one of them into working again. Either one would do, all he needed was for Harry, Cathy and Krista to see or hear something that would tell them he was in trouble. He knew they'd come running in, guns blazing, despite Harry's words to the contrary.

The son handed the wire and camera to his father, shaking his head. "He was actually telling the truth, these are for show, they're not working."

More than anything, Dave wished he could break free from the death-grip he was being held in. He didn't particularly enjoy being rendered powerless. His usual first intention in circumstances such as this was always to be in a position where he could call all the shots. "Told ya they weren't working," he said with an indignant sneer. "Hey, while I'm here, I thought I would drop off a Resumé cause I'm looking for a new job. Any offers?"

"You're not looking for a new job. Nor are you trying to get the name of my interior designer. You got your chance to tell us and you blew it. Julio, Markus, take care of him."

Dave tried to brace himself but the first blow caught him completely off guard, mainly because it was delivered below the belt. Literally. He felt the fire in his testicles rise as far as the pit of his stomach and he hurriedly bit down on his tongue to give his brain another area of pain to think about. That trick only worked until the second punch to the same area landed and with the sheer agony that followed, he couldn't hold back a grunt escaping from his throat.

"Bastard!" he hissed at the one called Julio, who had punched him. "Now you're going to pay." With all his strength, he pulled himself free and delivered a swift kick to Julio's groin. "See how *you* like it, dickhead." He drew great satisfaction when he saw the young man double over, his hands protectively covering his crotch, his mouth open in an O of surprise and pain. Dave lunged forward, intent on retrieving one of his weapons, but his attempt was foiled by the other brother who sent him sprawling to the floor with a hard kick to the back of his legs. He landed heavily on his side, too far away from the weapons.

After that, Dave although he fought valiantly, really didn't stand a chance. It was two against one and when the uniformed security guard came charging in, it became three against one. Dave was a powerful man and an excellent fighter, who knew every trick in the book to not let anyone get the better of him when it came to physical combat. But, already on the floor and therefore at a disadvantage, not even he was any match against the three strong, sturdy men.

He knew he didn't have a hope in hell of getting out of this one and he did what he always did when he needed a distraction, in this case from the pain being inflicted on his whole body. He brought up an image of Cathy, this time from the day before when she had walked into his father's apartment for the first time. The look of awe and bewilderment on her face, that quickly turned to acceptance, for his sake, and then the smile she kept strictly for him when she wanted to make him feel special.

The vision of her sweet, dazzling smile and the dancing of her beautiful azure blue eyes remained constant in his mind until the torture his body was being put through became too much for him to handle. He was close to blacking out and he prayed he would and he also prayed that if he was going to die right here, in this room, it would be swift.

Upstairs, Paul had just finished going through paper files he had found in what had to be the main study. Although the majority of the paperwork proved a lot of illegal activities, he wasn't interested in anything he saw. He was only interested in finding something that would prove the Romanos had a file on his father. A file that would tell him what he needed; that they had put out a hit on Kenneth Cameron and would stop at nothing to eliminate him.

Despite a lot of incriminating evidence about one crime

or another, there was nothing that had his father's name on it. In frustration, he went from one filing cabinet to the next, knowing he was running out of time. It had been ten minutes since he and Dave had parted company.

His eye fell on a monitor that was blinking red and, out of curiosity, he moved toward it. He didn't know it, but this was the only other room in the house that was directly linked to the control room the security guards worked from. No doubt whoever worked in the study wanted round the clock security when they were doing their wheeling and dealing. Paul brought the monitor to life and as soon as he did, he pulled back in shock.

At first, his brain wouldn't let his eyes accept the frenzied attack he was witnessing but eventually he was able to gain control and he gasped aloud in horror. Dave was being punched and kicked and tossed around as if he was nothing more than a rag doll. He was receiving multiple kicks to the groin and stomach and vicious blows to the head and upper body. His face was covered in blood and Paul was certain Dave was either dead or close to it.

He saw two of the attackers raise a barely conscious Dave to his knees, force his arms up so his hands were behind his head, and then forced his head forward. The other man took out a gun and pressed it against the back of Dave's skull.

It was then Paul noticed a microphone with a switch that was currently set to mute and he tapped the button on the keyboard to unmute it.

"...tell us who you are, prick," The one on Dave's left demanded.

Dave managed to lift his gaze to the one who had spoken and even on a screen with poor picture resolution, Paul couldn't fail to see the hatred and the fury in his friend's eyes.

"Fuck you," Dave said, staring at someone who was off camera.

At that moment, Paul broke his promise to his friend, a promise that had been made in haste only ten minutes ago. A promise that had sounded good at the time, but was right now proving to have been a completely foolish idea. A promise he had made in good faith that he would get out, regardless of the danger his partner was going through.

# CHAPTER THIRTY-THREE

Paul ran noiselessly down the stairs. Beneath the monitor he had watched Dave getting beaten to a pulp on, a tag had read DOWNSTAIRS LIBRARY. Although he had no clue where that was, at least he might identify his destination by the sounds emanating from beyond the correct door.

When he got to the corridor, he turned left and forced himself to think the way Dave would. Dave was usually methodical when he was on a search, he wouldn't have gone haphazardly along the corridor, he would have taken each room as it came. Paul barely gave the first two rooms he passed any consideration. Dave would have had the time to already check them. It was at the fourth door that Paul paused. The door was slightly ajar and, from behind it, Paul could hear muffled voices and the unmistakable sound of flesh slamming against flesh. If they were still beating Dave up, the threat of a gunshot to the head had obviously been a scare tactic.

Paul put his handgun away and took out a thirty round clip which he snapped into the semi-automatic. It was bigger and faster than his Glock and Paul intended to put it to good use. He released the safety, took a deep breath, counted to three to steady his nerves and burst into the room.

Dave was in the same kneeling position Paul had observed on the screen, which meant he was still alive. In living technicolor, he looked much worse than he had on the monitor. But he was still alive. There were four other men in the room, two of which Paul was unaware of. He guessed all the men except the uniformed security guard were the family Romano.

They had all turned at the sound of the intrusion but Paul was ready for them. "Nobody moves, nobody gets hurt. Dave, can you stand up?"

Dave, through the fog of mind-numbing pain, heard and acknowledged his partner's voice, but he didn't move. He couldn't move. But a faint smile flitted into his eyes. "Sonofabitch," he said weakly, "you broke the promise. God will bless you and your children a thousand times."

Every muscle and nerve ending in Paul's body waited for trouble. He didn't have long to wait. The man he had seen point the gun at Dave's head swung round, the gun in front of him as if seeking its next victim. Paul fired five quick shots first and watched the blood spurting from every impact point. One bullet went into his left eye, the eyeball exploding in its socket, spewing blood, gore and tissue down the man's face and unto the rich, cream colored carpet. Another bullet went into his throat nearly severing his head from his body. Another struck his right chest and two more into his heart. He died instantly.

Part of Paul's brain realized Dave had yet to get to his feet. The remaining part told him to worry about his friend later and concentrate on the other men in the room. The old man stared at his dead son in a mixture of fury and disbelief. The security guard was standing uncertainly, alternately training his gun on Dave, then Paul. Clearly he had no idea how to handle this sort of situation.

Another of the younger men was seriously contemplating avenging his brother but the old man didn't give him the chance to do anything. He snapped his fingers and his son and the security guard reluctantly but obediently stood down. They came to stand on either side of him.

"Look what you did to my son!" Romano roared at Paul. "You bastard! You killed my son."

"Well, I did tell him not to move and he did."

"Nobody crosses the Romanos and gets away with it.

You killed my son and now you have to be killed."

"Yeah, whatever. All three of you go stand in the far corner. I want to check on my friend. If either one of you tries something stupid, you'll join Romano junior on the floor there."

But Paul didn't get a chance to take one step towards Dave. Pieter Romano, having watched his brother being killed, ran from his room and crept noiselessly up behind Paul. The butt of a .38 slamming into the back of his skull sent Paul crashing to the floor.

Outside, in the surveillance van, Harry, Cathy and Krista were growing increasingly impatient. Paul and Dave had been gone for twenty minutes which was far too long, especially with no communication to keep tabs on them.

"Something needs done, Harry," Krista insisted. "I have a bad feeling about this."

He nodded absently, his mind working overtime, trying to figure out how to make Paul and Dave magically reappear. If only they hadn't lost contact with them, at least they would have known what had happened. He took out his cell phone and sent Errol a quick text

Errol read the text with mixed feelings. *Lost contact with P & D 15 mins ago. Return to van right now.* He could have decided that technically Pedowski wasn't his boss and therefore he didn't have to follow his orders, but Errol was sensible enough to know Pedowski always knew the right thing to do. If he was being recalled, he would have to do what was asked of him.

The power to the gate was still off but, as he went through it, and knowing the power could literally come back on again any minute, he wedged a rock against the frame to stop it from closing and locking. A minute later, he tapped lightly on the back door of the van and Harry swung it open to let him enter.

"What's happened?" Errol asked. He could feel the tension and see it on their faces and he immediately wanted to help.

"We lost contact, both audio and visual. We think it's the building itself, the walls are too thick."

Errol nodded slowly, his technologically advanced mind working overtime. He had no doubt there was a ton of wi-fi and Bluetooth equipment in a house like that. He also knew he had only disconnected what could well be a small percentage of whatever gear was there. He had told Pedowski that at the beginning of this mission but Pedowski had assured him anything he could disarm would be a tremendous help.

"Do you want me to go in and try and get them out if they've been caught?" he offered.

Krista looked at his kind, concerned face and gave him a warm, rueful smile. "Thanks, Errol, but that will be our job. We just need to come up with a suitable plan to execute it."

"Did you try their cell phones?"

"Yes. They have them on silent and they haven't responded. We noticed about ten minutes ago that the two-way radios Harry got for them were left behind. Which means if they went in and split up, they can't even get in touch with one another to warn of danger."

Errol felt the cloak of despair and hopelessness fall around them. "I could go to their door and tell them I work for the electric company – which isn't a lie, I've got ID and everything on me – and tell them the wind has downed a power line nearby and we need to check their electrical supply."

Harry looked at him thoughtfully but then shook his head dismissively. "You're not in uniform, no hard hat, nothing. They'll see right through it. Besides, you can't just walk right in and up to their front door, the fence and entrance gates are wired, remember?"

"If I disable them again, that will prove there's a problem. They won't know any difference."

"It's just too risky, Errol," Cathy said. She could see how much he wanted to help and hated shooting him down. But he was a civilian and if anybody was going in, it was going to be her and Krista.

In the house, Dave couldn't cope with the physical trauma any longer. He had been fighting waves of nausea and pain in his groin and lower back for what now felt like an eternity. But the time had come for him to give up. If he passed out, he wouldn't have to feel the pain anymore. Maybe while he was out of it, the pain that was in his head would leave so when he came to, he could help Paul.

He couldn't see Paul; his eyes were nearly swollen shut and caked with drying blood. And even as he struggled to block the pain, he was aware Paul's voice had gone silent.

Unable to help it, he slumped to the floor but just before whatever vision he had in his eyes glazed over and his eyes began to close he saw Paul had hit the deck.

There was nothing he could do as his world faded to black.

# CHAPTER THIRTY-FOUR

Julio Romano came over to put his hand on his youngest son's shoulder. "You did good, Pieter. Thank you." He then went over to the mangled carcass of his dead son, his whole body slumping as he looked down at him. He couldn't help it, he was hoping he would see some indication Julio was still alive; a twitch of his eye, a guttural breath, something. But even as he stared in hope, there was no doubt he was dead and Romano's heart twisted with grief and rage. How was he going to explain this to his beloved wife, who hadn't been in the best of health in a long time?

Pieter looked down at Paul in disdain. "I saw what he did to Julio, Father. I had no other choice."

"Julio..." At the mention of his dead son's name, Romano's head bowed lower. He knelt stiffly beside him, his eyes awash with sorrow. He wiped some of the blood off his son's face and let his fingers hover over him for a long moment. "Julio...my son..." He stood up again, slowly and painfully, the sorrow in his eyes replaced by outrage and hatred. "Kill them," he commanded. "Kill them both." He watched Pieter and Markus position themselves over the unconscious bodies of the intruders, their guns already cocked and ready but he suddenly held a hand up to stop them. "Wait! We'd better see who they are first. Search them for identification."

Pieter found Paul's ID first, in the back pocket of his jeans, and let out a soft curse. "He's a cop, Father, he's a goddamned cop. Detective Paul Cameron of the Bathville Police

Department."

"Cameron? Bathville? I wonder if he's related to that deadbeat we wasted up there last week? Whatever. We'll find out soon enough. Markus, the other one a cop too?"

"Detective David Andrews."

"Then that presents us with a problem, doesn't it? We can't waste two cops; we'll have the entire police force all over us like a bad rash. We're too close to completing the order for next month's shipment to risk having cops breathing down our neck. The entire police department probably knows they were going to be here tonight and if they go missing, the police will know where to look. The Bathville PD must have planned this in conjunction with the Brooklyn PD, No, we can't risk it, not at all."

"So what do you want us to do?" Markus, the impatient, impulsive one of the family asked.

"We dispose of them, but we don't kill them. We take them into New Jersey, then we get off the highway and find a nice quiet road in the Garden State and dump their bodies." Romano Senior looked down in disgust at Dave. "He doesn't look like he's going to be around much longer anyway." He paused for a second to consider his plan. Then, satisfied it would work, he nodded. "Once the shipment arrives, we can finish them off – if they survive – up in Massachusetts, if need be. Fennell, go start up the Cadillac, we'll meet you down in the garage."

Less than ten minutes later, Pedowski was going over a plan with Cathy and Krista when he suddenly stopped. A massive gate further along the Romano's stone wall had just opened and he pointed towards it. "Activity." He and Errol climbed through to the front and Harry started the engine. They hunkered down in the seats so as not to be seen but Cathy and Krista could see out into the sleek, black vehicle as it passed them. As soon as they saw the occupants of the Cadillac, they let out a cry.

"I saw Paul!" Krista declared. "Three other men too, but definitely Paul."

"I couldn't see Dave," Cathy said frantically, "but there was a shadow against the back passenger door that looked big enough to be a man." She snatched the binoculars and trained them on the passenger's side rear door. She could see something hanging outside the door and when she was able to focus, she thought at first it was the seat belt. On further inspection, she realized it wasn't the seat belt at all. It looked like the utility belt Dave had worn.

Harry waited for the Caddy to move past, counted to ten, then pulled into the street. He maintained a discrete distance to avoid arousing suspicion. Traffic was uncommonly light, even for this time of the night so maybe the weather was keeping a lot of people home. The wind hadn't abated and sometime during the long wait for Paul and Dave to appear, a slamming rain had started. It was mild enough for it to be just rain, which was fortunate; they didn't need ice, sleet or snow. The rain, however, was torrential and relentless. When they reached Canal Street in Lower Manhattan, it didn't take Harry long to figure out they were taking the Holland tunnel into New Jersey. Sometimes it could take an hour to get through the tunnel but tonight they zipped through in ten minutes. The Cadillac was keeping a steady speed of thirty-five miles per hour. Because they were leaving the City, they didn't have to pay the toll. Returning, they would.

"Why can't we just radio ahead to the New Jersey Police and have them pulled over at the end of the tunnel?" Krista asked. "Or somewhere in Jersey City? God knows where they're heading for."

"If it were that simple, I'd do it," Harry said. "You really have no idea what this family is like, Krista. Your husband asked the same question yesterday. We try to arrest them, their hitmen will have us and our families murdered in no time. I know that sounds like we're scared of them, we're not. They have no qualms killing people, cops included. Trust me, we learned that lesson the hard way."

Exiting the tunnel, the Cadillac led them beyond Jersey City, off the highway and eventually on to country roads. They were roughly five miles out of the city when the Cadillac slowed down slightly to about thirty miles an hour and a second later, Harry watched as the passenger rear door was opened. He had the good sense to kill the lights and drop back so the Cadillac wouldn't see him.

Dave was the first to be thrown out of the vehicle. He was still unconscious but he landed on the ground on his shoulder, dislocating his right collarbone, the second time in his life he had received an injury like that, which jarred him awake. His eyes semi-focused in time to see Paul being thrown from the car and at the sight of his friend hitting the road, his mind started playing tricks on him. Hadn't he already witnessed Paul lying on the ground just a few seconds ago? Was this what was meant by déjà vu? He didn't know and he didn't have the strength to care. His mind was seeking the pain free haven it had found for itself and he let himself drift off to Neverland again.

Paul was aroused by the feel of something cold and wet on his face and a loud roaring in his ears. It was the rain, falling on him and rushing down the gutter beside him towards the storm drains. His head was thumping sickeningly, the feeling only intensifying when he opened his eyes and tried to get up.

He heard, or thought he heard, the opening and closing of several car doors and seconds later, what could only be a mirage: Krista's beautiful anxious face peering down into his. "K-Krissss...."

"Yes, it's me...Are you hurt? Can I move you?"

He tried to shake his head no and fresh pain exploded and ricocheted inside his skull. "Head..."

It was all she needed to hear and, gently lifting his head off the ground, she felt around and quickly located a golf ball sized bump just above his occipital ridge. "You know what day it is, baby?"

"Sure...Wednesday...no, Thursday. Yes, Thursday."

"And your birthday?"

"March sixth, every year."

"Who's the president of the United States of America?"

"Trump. But not for much longer."

She noticed he was answering the questions so far without any hesitation and she forced levity into her tone to see if he would act appropriately to a little bit of humor. "Your wife's bra size?"

"Forty four double D."

She grinned. He was fine. "Only in your wildest dreams. Want me to help you up?"

He gripped her upper arm, his face twisting in pain. "Dave," he said hoarsely, "where's Dave?"

When they'd all jumped out of the van, about ten yards from where Dave's motionless body lay, Cathy and Errol had sprinted towards him. Krista and Harry had carried on to Paul, but Harry had stopped roughly half way between them, ready to see who needed the most assistance.

"Dave's up the road just a bit," Krista said reassuringly, "Cathy and Errol are with him. What I saw of him, he didn't look good."

"And Harry?"

"Right here, Paul," Harry's gruff voice came from somewhere behind her. He came into his line of vision. "Want to try and stand? I'll help."

Paul ignored the jackhammering pain behind his eyes and, holding on to Krista and Harry, let them help him to his feet. He swayed uncertainly, for a few moments, feeling his stomach somersaulting and back flipping and he willed the nausea to die down. He stared up the road at the dark form lying on the side and his heart sank.

Cathy was obviously crying, Errol was patting her shoulder and Dave... well, Dave was just lying there.

"He got beat up pretty bad, guys," he said softly, "I watched it and I couldn't help him. It will be a miracle if he's still alive."

"There's only going to be one way to find out," Krista

said, "Come on…"

Dave was still lying face down in the gutter. He was soaked through, barely breathing, still unconscious and, according to Cathy, had a barely traceable pulse. He didn't respond to any of the commands to open his eyes, he didn't moan to indicate he could hear what was being said to him, he just lay there, unable to move and unaware of what was happening.

"Dave, come on," Paul persisted, "don't do this to me, open your eyes." Getting nothing, he straightened up and as he looked down at his friend, he noticed the awkward positioning of Dave's right arm and shoulder. "Oh terrific, looks like he's dislocated or broken something. You got anything in the van I could use as a splint or a sling, Harry?"

"Best to just immobilize it," Krista said, keeping a careful eye on Cathy while giving Dave a quick examination. Cathy was clearly very distraught. "We need to get him to a hospital."

"His head, Kris," Cathy said, "Please, check his head. There's an awful lot of blood on his face from I think a head wound."

Usually, Cathy was calm in the middle of a crisis, she didn't often let a situation get the better of her. But now, with that statement, Krista could understand why she was so upset. Seeing Dave like this was clearly bringing back memories of the night he had been attacked and shot in a street in Belfast. The night he had been put into a medically induced coma to cope with a serious head injuries. The doctors in the Royal Victoria Hospital in Belfast had realized his brain was swelling but, instead of removing part of his skull to relieve the pressure, they had drilled a tiny hole just behind his ear instead. The result had been swift but effective as the blood causing the swelling drained away. The drain had been kept in place for a few days to make sure he didn't have another bleed that would cause another swelling and it proved to have been a lot kinder on Dave's system. But it had still been touch and go and now Cathy was reliving that night all over again. Right down to the rain swept streets.

Krista kneeled on the ground and gently felt all over Dave's head. His hair was soaking wet and the rain had washed away a lot of blood but she could feel several areas where there was a small bump. "I don't think it's serious, but I still insist we get him to a hospital. Harry, Errol, I need you to help me lift him in one steady motion. Paul, you'll need to hold his injured arm against his body while being lifted. Cathy, go check the van, see if there's a blanket or something we can lay him on."

Cathy started to turn away but stopped when she heard Dave suddenly let out a low moan of pain. He had been jolted awake when Harry had put his arm underneath his body. She was sorry he was in pain but the sound had been music to her ears. Being able to respond to anything, even pain, was a good sign.

"P-Paul...what...?" He stammered through chattering teeth. "What's...?"

"Ssh, buddy, don't try to talk, just relax."

"Cathy...I want Cathy...to see her..."

Cathy immediately leaned over him. "Hey, baby, it's me, at your service."

"Hey you..." He trailed off into semi-consciousness again and Harry and Errol took the opportunity to lift him again.

The pain he was being subjected to was heart wrenching to watch. They had to ignore his feeble struggles against the torture to get him settled in the van. They hadn't found a blanket or first aid kit so they made him as comfortable as possible on the floor.

After careful deliberation, they decided to return to Manhattan. They reckoned that if the Romanos wanted to finish what they'd started, they might call the hospitals in and around Jersey City trying to find them. The Romanos would have searched Paul and Dave for their ID and–found their names so it would have been an easy search. They wouldn't have been able to tie Paul and Dave in with Park Avenue.

Getting back to New York was the most sensible answer.

Digging in his pocket for the six dollar toll, Harry got into the driver's seat, turned the vehicle around and headed back the way they had come.

Paul was sitting up front with Harry, Krista had insisted upon it as the seat itself would have given Paul better support so as not to aggravate the bump in his head. At least if they were going to the hospital, Paul could get checked out too.

It took nearly an hour to get back to the city and was nearing two a.m. before Harry drove up to the entrance of the emergency department. They were all running on adrenaline and showing no sign of crashing just yet. Dave was slipping in and out of consciousness but to complicate matters, he was also in shock. Even when the ER team rushed to get him on a gurney and inside, he didn't stir or come to.

Cathy followed them in and refused to leave his side unless it was absolutely necessary. Only when they took him away for a head, chest and abdominal CT did she hold back. A quick x-ray confirmed his dislocated collarbone and the CT would determine if there were more serious injuries to his shoulder and collarbone.

Harry and Errol went to find some coffee. At this time of the night, the cafeteria wasn't open but there had to be at least a drinks machine, or even a soda machine somewhere. Anything with caffeine would do.

Krista waited with Cathy while Paul, too, was taken for a CT. He wasn't showing any signs of concussion but he clearly had a pounding headache and they wanted to make sure he had no subdural hematomas or anything that could be life-threatening. The ladies found two seats in a quiet corner and held onto each other's hands. They didn't speak, they didn't need to. They had rescued Paul and Dave and that was all that mattered.

Krista sat up straighter when she saw Paul being wheeled back into the examination room. At Cathy's gesture for her to go to him, she hurried towards the room and heard the doctor give Paul a rundown on his injuries. He stopped and looked expectantly at Krista when she came in.

"Mrs Cameron?" he asked. At her nod, he continued. "As I was saying to my patient, he was very lucky. He has no signs of concussion and the swelling should go down within a day or two. I'd rather we kept him in for forty-eight hours, but he insists he doesn't think it necessary. I assured him it is."

Krista looked sympathetically at her husband. He looked fine, he seemed alert and oriented and she could understand why he wouldn't want to be kept for observation. However, she knew head wounds could be sneaky, he could feel and act fine and then all of a sudden, keel over with a brain bleed or worse.

"Sorry, Paul, if the doctor wants you to stay, that's what you're going to have to do."

"But I'm fine!"

"You can be good support for Dave, he won't be going anywhere either for a few days."

At the mention of his friend, Paul backed down a bit. He slapped the pillow in frustration. "How is he?"

"Getting a lot of tests even as we speak. Nobody knows anything yet."

"Are Errol and Harry still here?"

"They are. Did you want to see Harry?"

"I'd like a private word with him, if that's okay?"

The doctor went to the door to leave. "I'll have you moved to a private room, Mr Cameron."

Krista thanked him and turned her attention back to Paul. "I'll get him in a few minutes. I just want you to tell me, with no bullshitting, how you're really feeling."

"My head's sore, I won't lie. Other than that, honestly, I'm fine. They even cleaned my wound."

"Your wound?"

"A very minor bite from the dog."

She rolled her eyes and leaned over to give him a kiss. "Please try and rest, I'll go and get Harry and then you promise me you'll get some sleep."

Harry was pleased to hear Paul wanted to see him and when he left Errol and Cathy, Krista sat down beside her again.

"I feel bad you're still here, Errol," Krista said.

"No worries, Krista. Harry told me when he's spoken with Paul, he'll take me home. I offered to take the subway but he insisted."

Cathy suddenly let out a groan. It was well after three o'clock. "We won't be back at the penthouse before Hannah or George get up to make us breakfast. We'll have to let them know we won't be there."

They all looked up when Cathy's name was called by one of the doctors who had been with Dave earlier. The doctor was Asian and she put him in his early forties and she could see the fatigue behind his eyes. Krista stood up with her. "Go ahead, go see him. I'll text George and ask him to phone either you or myself when they're up."

Cathy nodded her gratitude and then, with trepidation, hurried towards the doctor. She had a horrible feeling she wasn't going to like what he was about to tell her.

# CHAPTER
# THIRTY-FIVE

Cathy was expecting to be taken to where Dave was, so when the doctor opened a door and ushered her inside, she was surprised to see Dave wasn't there. Instead, she was in a room with a desk, three chairs and an examining table. Charts on the wall showed various drawings of the human Musculo-Skeletal system with the muscles and bones named on the legend on the side.

There were anti-violence to women pamphlets stuck on the wall as well as pamphlets on what to do if you had been diagnosed with cancer/dementia/ STDs. The expected Coronavirus pamphlets were there too and instructions on social distancing and what to do if you develop a fever and a sudden dry cough.

The fact that she was in this room, and not with Dave, filled her with apprehension. She waited as patiently as she could while the doctor produced a tablet and brought up what she assumed was Dave's electronic medical record on it. He was wearing a mask, as was she, and there was a safe distance between them.

"Doctor, please, when can I see my husband?"

"In a little while. I wanted to go over the results with you, to bring you up to speed. You told me earlier your husband was in a coma roughly fourteen months ago? And this was in the United Kingdom?"

"That's correct."

"Can you recall how long he was in the coma?"

"Eleven days." She could feel her stomach tightening. If she heard the words "....we've had to medically induce him..." she would die.

The doctor quickly typed something into the notes. "And you're saying he's like this tonight because he got beaten up?"

Cathy shifted uncomfortably. She didn't know the full story so she had improvised and, since Dave certainly showed all the evidence of a brutal beating, it made sense she could say what she did. "That's right."

"His body shows signs of a kicking. There are what looks like boot or shoe marks all over, including his head but aside from what looks like a couple of bruised ribs, he seems to have got off really light. We've also been able to rule out internal bleeding. His lungs don't sound compromised in any way, he's breathing fine on his own and, aside from a slightly elevated blood pressure, no doubt because of his pain levels, he seems to be doing okay. So far."

"That's good...right?"

"Of course."

Cathy waited for more. He seemed to be figuring out what to say and she knew what his next word was going to be before he even said it. *However...*

"However...the good news is, there is no cranial involvement, aside from very minor swellings in several areas. The dislocation of his collarbone happened at his AC joint. It's been re-located - not without a great deal of stress to your husband. We're going to put him on anti-inflammatories as well as get him fixed up with physical therapy. He'll no doubt have to wear a sling for a couple of weeks, but there shouldn't be any lasting effects." Here, the doctor paused and consulted his notes again. "The bad news is...he took a severe kicking to his genitals, bladder and kidney area."

The news shouldn't have surprised her. The Romanos' calling card was mutilating the genitals of their captives. But as it sank in what the doctor was trying to tell her, she felt as if the air was being sucked slowly out of her lungs.

"H-how bad?"

"He's passing blood in his urine. I've paged the lead Urologist on call and I think he'll want to do a special x-ray where he'll insert a dye to determine where your husband might be cut and therefore producing the bleeding. He's badly bruised around his testicles and we'll apply ice packs for that. I'm only going by what the CT showed so the extent of the damage to his kidneys might be causing the hematuria."

Cathy knew that meant blood in the urine and she nodded. She was trying to process all this information. "What is his treatment going to be?"

"Rest, ice, anti-inflammatories, physical therapy. So far, he's not a surgery candidate but he has a rough few days ahead of him. The pain in his groin, and anywhere else on his body for that matter, will be vying for his attention as much as the trauma to his kidneys."

"How long?"

"Hard to say…a week, ten days? It will depend on him."

"Will he have to stay in hospital all that time?"

"Again, it will depend on him. And for your next question, when will he be able to have a normal sex life again? When the swelling, inflammation and bleeding are gone and he has complete feeling again without it hurting then there is no reason why there would be any problems. The Urologist will do thorough tests on him and will explain the road to recovery but, as I said, it will depend on him."

Cathy lowered her gaze, her mind working overtime. It was a lot to take in but she was eternally grateful there was no evidence of any head injuries. "Can I see him?" she asked timidly. "I mean, if his tests are done, can I please see him?"

"Of course. They were taking him up to the semi-private room his friend, Detective Paul Cameron was admitted to, just before I came to talk to you."

She gave him a smile. "That will be great."

"He's full of pain killers right now, I should warn you he

may not be very coherent and the best thing for him right now is sleep. I just didn't want you worrying if he wasn't responding to you."

"That's fine, doctor, thank you."

There were two beds in the room Dave had been put into, the other was occupied by Paul. He was lying on his side, facing his friend, doing his best to watch over him while he fought exhaustion and the need for sleep. He brightened a bit when Cathy came in and she smiled a hello at him before going to the side of Dave's bed. She positioned herself so she could see Paul too, so as not to sit with her back to him.

She looked carefully down at Dave. He was out cold but at least he didn't seem to be feeling any pain right now. His face was a mess, and, lying bare-chested as he was, she could see the contusions and bruises on his upper body. She was tempted to lift the sheet to see how bad his groin injuries were but she refrained. She would wait for Dave to show and tell her himself. "How are you, Paul?"

"High if you must know. Flying like a kite but I *think* I'm on the same planet." He indicated his IV with a tired roll of his eyes. "Don't know if this is saline or a painkiller or what but they insisted in putting it in. I'm sleepy, Cathy. Deathly worried about him. No one would tell me anything because I'm not family but I'm encouraged, other than the IV which I assume is some sort of painkiller, he's not hooked up to any monitors or anything. And to answer your next question, Krista went to find some coffee and bottled water, she should be along very shortly."

"Good, I want to see her too. So we can all be together. Apparently, apart from the dislocated collarbone, his groin and kidneys are the worst affected."

"His groin?" Paul let out a groan. "That's right, it's what the Romanos do to their victims."

"They're waiting for a Urologist to come so they can do some sort of an x-ray that will determine where the blood in his urine is coming from." She looked down at a catheter bag hanging over the side of the bed. There wasn't a lot of fluid in it but what she could see was the color of a rusty nail. She reached over and stroked Dave's bruised face. "First you, Paul, then Krista, now you again and Dave too. It's usually me who ends up in the hospital."

He smiled tiredly. She looked and sounded as exhausted as he felt. "You got lucky this time."

"Have Harry and Errol left?"

"Yeah, Harry wanted to get Errol home. I'm to call him in the morning...or whenever I wake up, seeing it's morning already. We have a lot to discuss and I need him to do me a favor."

Before she could ask what it was, she felt movement beneath her and looked down to see Dave trying to focus on her. "Hey, Cathy," he said softly. His voice was very weak but he sounded otherwise okay.

She looked down at him in surprise. "Hey you," she said tenderly, feeling a lump form in her throat as she stroked his face. He looked so vulnerable lying there, beaten and bruised, and her heart twisted with love. "How you feeling?"

"Light," he managed to say, which could be interpreted as he was feeling a little high.

"Do you know where you are and how you got here?"

"I k-killed...Hercules," he said cryptically.

"Hercules?" She looked over at Paul for an explanation but he shrugged he had no idea.

"Yeah...sonofabitch."

Paul clicked his tongue in realization. It was funny Dave was focusing on that now. "He must mean the Rottweiler we had a run-in with. We didn't know his name but he must have heard it being mentioned. If he told the Romanos he killed their dog, that would have been enough for them to beat him like that."

"He got like this because of that *dog* we saw on camera?" she asked incredulously.

"That dog was a demon dog from the depths of hell. But I don't think that was the only reason."

Somewhere through the fog that was his mind, Dave heard Paul's voice and he turned towards it. He could make out a shadowy figure lying on the bed beside his and he blinked to try and clear his vision. "Paul?...you're okay," he said.

"Hey partner, how you doing?"

"Light." He clearly didn't remember saying that to Cathy a few seconds earlier but that was okay. If light was the new high, he was doing fine.

Krista returned and she summed up what was happening. "Hey Dave, glad to see you more awake than you were a little while ago."

"Thank you." But he was clearly struggling to stay awake and, within moments, the strong painkillers did their duty and pulled him under again. He didn't put up a fight.

Krista handed Cathy a cardboard cup filled with what Cathy hoped was coffee and to Paul she gave a bottle of water. She had a selection of chocolate bars to give them all a boost and by the look of it, she'd already started on one of them. Half of a Milky Way was clutched in one hand. "I would feel a lot happier if you would stop fighting it and just lie back to get some sleep, Paul," she said.

"I didn't want to in case Dave needed me," he said.

"Now you've no excuse. Cathy and I aren't going anywhere, so please, do your old lady a favor and just sleep."

He didn't need much coaxing as he downed half the bottle of water, then settled more comfortably on the bed. He realized, although he had told Pedowski the bad news, neither Cathy nor Krista knew their mission tonight had been a complete bust. He grabbed a hold of Krista's hand as she sat on the chair beside him but he turned to include Cathy too.

"I'm sorry, ladies, you know how much we wanted to get a positive result by going to the Romanos tonight. Harry did the best he could by providing us with whatever information he had on their house but he underestimated – we *all* did - how sophisticated their security system is. No wonder even the police don't want to touch them. They're afraid of no one."

"So everything was in vain?" Krista asked. The realization of what that meant now, that they had tried, and failed, to find something or someone who would clear Paul's name, slowly sank in. Instead, they were no further forward, had nowhere else to turn, they had narrowly escaped with their lives and now Paul faced a bleak and hopeless future.

"I'm sorry, but yes." Paul held her gaze, hating the despair flooding into the clear green of her eyes. He turned to Cathy to gauge her reaction and saw she was staring down at Dave, her whole expression telling him how appalled she was that Dave had ended up like this, and all for nothing.

For the first time in his life, knowing he was responsible for this whole sorry mess, Paul felt self-loathing pour into his very soul. Nothing was ever going to be the same again and he could feel the tenuous grasp he had on his idyllic life with Krista start to give way.

# CHAPTER THIRTY-SIX

A week before, the whole world had watched the United Kingdom proudly demonstrate the first Covid vaccination being administered to a senior citizen. Now it was the United States' turn as it celebrated the first vaccination given to an intensive care nurse, right here in New York City. It was the first time since the pandemic had begun that there was a chance this nightmare might come to an end.

Paul was discharged the next day. After the vaccine announcement, he had felt the slight shift in attitude in the hospital staff, all of them overworked and exhausted to the point of collapse. They could now begin to hope that soon their lives would return to some form of normal. He was pleased for them and he hoped it wouldn't be too long before all health workers and first responders, himself and his entire circle included, would receive the much anticipated vaccine.

The doctors had been pleased with his progress. He had no real complaints other than a mild headache that was easily controlled with over the counter painkillers. But Krista being Krista, she only agreed to his release after insisting he return to the penthouse and lie low until the next day. After that, he was free to do whatever he wanted, as long as it didn't involve slipping and falling and banging his head.

He hated leaving Dave. He had witnessed Dave's personal nightmare still holding him in its grasp as he lay writhing in agony between bouts of fitful sleep. Dave's diagnosis was hematuria caused by severe bruising to his kidneys, which was now exacerbated by a nasty bladder infection. He was spared painful urination by the catheter but sometime in the early morning, he developed a kidney infection that sent his temperature soaring.

Three days had passed with little improvement in his condition. The broad-spectrum antibiotic he was placed on did little to control the infection but by the fourth day, there were signs he was on the mend.

Cathy barely left his side, only returning to the penthouse at night when Dave was sleeping. She would sit with George and Hannah and tell them of how he'd been that day and she hated upsetting them but they insisted they be told.

"We helped raise that boy," George had told her in anguish, "he's as close to us as our own children, we want to know what's going on with him."

"We love him," Hannah had told her, wringing her hands and using the edge of her apron to wipe away tears. "Can we see him?"

"Right now, he's too uncomfortable, and sleeping a lot," she had told them. "When he's feeling better he will love to see you both. I will make it happen. I don't know what the hospital rules are for visiting but we can say we're in the same household. If they get picky, I'll flash my badge."

"You're a good girl, Miss Cathy," Hannah told her often, always holding her hand or patting her arm. "You are right for him, he needs someone like you, someone who will love him, no matter what."

"We need each other," she had replied.

"Mr Paul wants to get over to Brooklyn, he says Dave's car is at a precinct there," George said. "He refused my offer to drive him but it's the very least I can do for him. That boy is so genuinely concerned about Dave and I feel bad for him, so can you please talk him into accepting my offer?"

"I'll see what I can do. I'll be leaving soon to go back to the hospital and I haven't heard him or Krista up yet."

"You'll give our boy our love, won't you?" Hannah said pointedly.

"Of course I will."

"Good girl. Now eat your breakfast, make an old woman

happy."

Cathy looked down at the plate Hannah had set in front of her a few moments before. Pancakes, bacon, scrambled eggs, hash browns and toast, enough food to sink a ship. She really didn't have an appetite but she didn't want to hurt Hannah's feelings either, so she picked up her knife and fork.

In the hospital, Dave had spent another restless night. The dull ache in his groin was still there, the throbbing in his flank on both sides also still there and when the nurse had come in to take his temperature, he had learned he still had a low-grade fever.

He hated the fact that Cathy was wasting her day with him but he couldn't keep her away. He wanted to feel better and get discharged so he could recuperate in his dad's penthouse. At least there he'd be more comfortable and if George or Hannah tried to kill him with kindness, he would have Cathy intervene. He realized he was only kidding himself; no one killed him with kindness more than Cathy, especially when he was poorly.

Before leaving for the hospital, Cathy had a little pep talk with Paul and finally convinced him to let George take him over to Brooklyn. Krista encouraged him to go, she said she was going to go to the hospital with Cathy and then they could all meet up again later for their evening meal.

Crossing the Brooklyn Bridge this time felt like a huge letdown to Paul. The last time they had done it, they had all felt the surge of excitement that came when a job was going down. Hope and expectations had been running high. This time, Paul felt like a failure but he kept up a pleasant conversation with George and, when he was dropped off at the precinct, he thanked him sincerely and promised to see him later.

He had texted Harry to let him know to expect him and Harry was openly relieved when he saw Paul come into his office.

"You're a sight for sore eyes, Cameron," he said warmly. "How are you feeling? And Dave?"

"I'm fine, Harry…Dave, not so much. He's still got a temperature and an infection he can't seem to shake."

"Hope he gets better soon. Tell him I send my best."

"I will." Paul nodded at the offer of a coffee and when he had it sitting in front of him, he absently stirred some cream into it. "I know I've already said it but on behalf of us all, thank you for everything you did for us the other night."

"I didn't do much, Paul, certainly nothing that helped you."

"You were great, Harry, really. I take it you haven't come up with any new suspects?"

"Nothing, Paul, I'm sorry. Plenty of drug lords out there, but none who punish their victims in the way your dad was."

"Did you extend your search? Go into the other boroughs? Connecticut, New Jersey?"

"I included the whole eastern seaboard and all of New England."

Paul set his lips in derision. "What about a list of employees?"

"With what for a job title? Personal hitman?"

"Come on, Harry, there has to be something we can tie in with them."

"I'll do what I can to get you a payroll list, but don't hold your breath. They think they're above the law, what makes you think they'll have legitimate records of their employees?"

"Can't you check with the IRS? What about USCIS?"

"You want me to check with the immigration service? What is that going to do?"

"You think their minions are all born and bred American citizens? I can almost guarantee their maids and house staff originate from south of the border, without papers. We don't have to go back to the Romano house, but if we can get names of people who are remaining under the immigration radar, we can interview them at their homes. Their loyalty to their employer might not be as strong when they're threatened with deportation."

Harry looked at Paul long and hard. He knew how much this meant to Paul and he couldn't blame him for coming up with any angle he could think of.

"I'll see what I can do," he relented softly. "I'll pull a couple of men to work on it if I get anything."

"Thank you, Harry, that's all I can ask." He took a sip of his coffee. He felt tense, and impatient and he wanted to get going. "You got me that address I asked you for the other night?"

"Maria Cameron? She a relative?"

"My sister."

"Yeah, I got her. She's living life now as Maria Taylor and is still right here in Brooklyn." Harry reached into a drawer and took out a sheet of paper. He handed it over. "Four husbands behind her. All ended in divorce. Changed address nine times in seven years, each locale worse than the one before. Seems she's fallen on hard times."

Paul looked at the address and knew what Harry meant. "I have a feeling she never really left the hard times behind. Any rap sheet?"

"Nothing major, picked up for loitering a couple of times."

Without another word about his sister, Paul folded the piece of paper up and slid it into the back pocket of his jeans. "Any backlash from the Romanos after me killing one of the sons?"

"Not yet. After four days, I have to admit I'm surprised. But that doesn't mean I'm not waiting for something to happen. Maybe we'll get lucky, maybe they'll have realized you and Dave are cops and will leave well enough alone. We have our ear to the ground nonetheless. Just tell me again, reassure me, it was self-defense, wasn't it?"

"You know it was."

"That was just for the record."

Paul drained the last of his coffee and stood up. "Thanks, Harry. I want to do whatever I can to help and if you can think of any other angle, let me know."

"I will, you know I will."

Paul took his leave and when he got out to Dave's car, he looked at the address Harry had given him. He had a vague idea he knew how to get to it but he punched it into the GPS system to make sure.

Twenty minutes later, he pulled up outside a sand colored apartment building. The neighborhood he'd driven through for the last five minutes had been rundown and seedy and the building fit right in with its surroundings. There were probably thirty apartments in this building and what he could see of the outside filled him with regret and sorrow. Filthy windows, dirty outer doors, cracked paving and crumbling concrete steps were commonplace. Graffiti was everywhere. Those that had balconies were laden with cracked patio furniture and discarded toys. Some had washing hanging over the rails. The neighborhood was, in short, awful.

Getting slowly out of the car, he made sure he locked it and put the alarm on. Last thing he wanted was to try and explain to Dave his car had been hijacked. He looked up at the building and, steeling himself, went to the front entrance. He wasn't surprised to see that, instead of having to get buzzed into the apartment he wanted, the door was propped open, the lock hanging by a dirty, frayed shoestring.

The interior wasn't any better than the exterior and carried a hodgepodge of smells, only some of which were identifiable. Urine, cabbage, sweat, weed, nothing pleasant. He went up to the second floor and located apartment 2B to his right.

The green paint on the door was cracked and peeling. Graffiti on the walls told a multitude of tales: *For the best blow, call Mary-Jo.* It was hard to tell if it was an advertisement for oral sex or cocaine. *Cum with me and I'll take you to paradise* promised another. Paul read a few of them, showing neither amusement nor disdain. Then, taking a deep breath, he knocked sharply on the door to his sister's apartment and waited.

From within, he could hear the sound of a radio or the television. It sounded like a commercial jingle. He wondered for a moment if the volume was up so loud his sister hadn't heard his knocking. Or maybe she simply wasn't home. It was eleven o'clock in the morning, maybe she was at work. If she had a job, of course. Or she could be out getting groceries. He knocked again, more loudly, and after waiting a full minute was about to walk away when he heard soft, shuffling footsteps from behind the door.

Seconds later, the door swung open.

# CHAPTER THIRTY-SEVEN

For the first time in sixteen years, Paul came face to face with his sister. She was barely recognizable, but he knew instinctively it was her. The years had not been kind to her, not at all. At thirty-five years of age, she looked ten years older. The once lustrous long blonde hair Paul remembered had been cropped short and been dyed a shade of ginger that hadn't come from Mother Nature's color palette. At five foot seven, she was rail thin and couldn't weigh more than a hundred pounds. Her face, once beautiful, had taken on a hard edge, with tiny permanent lines around her mouth and dull brown eyes. Her cheeks were hollow and dark smudges rimmed the bottom of her eyes.

Paul stared, momentarily speechless, at this woman who was his own flesh and blood. He hadn't known what to expect, but he certainly hadn't been expecting this. She was dressed in a grubby imitation silk kaftan and he felt his stomach crawl in sorrow for what might have been if she hadn't been subjected to the childhood she'd had.

The memories and scars ran deep. He had seen it too many times and his heart broke that she had continued living a life like that.

There was a scowl on her face when she yanked the door open, until she saw who was standing there and her eyes lit up. "Oh, a new one, and a mighty cute new one you are too. Did Eagle send you? You bring me my blow, sugar?"

Paul suddenly felt like crying. His sister was doing

drugs. Not that he hadn't expected it but he had chosen, for whatever reason, to believe otherwise. And there hadn't been one spark of recognition in the murky depths of her brown eyes. Strange, even after all this time and even with the vast difference in her physical appearance, he would have recognized her anywhere. He would have been able to pick her out of a crowd.

"No Maria," he said softly. "Eagle didn't send me and I didn't bring you any blow."

"Then who...?" Wariness invaded her expression. If this was some trick she had turned recently, surely she would remember a body like that. She tilted her head to one side and eyed this stranger in a mixture of contempt and curiosity. "Hey, I paid my rent in advance..."

"Maria, it's me, it's Paul." When he still didn't get a reaction, he added, "Your brother."

"Paul?" she repeated. Realization dawned slowly and her eyes darted nervously behind him to the top of the steps before settling on him again. "What you doing here?"

"I came to see you."

"Why?"

"Why? Because you're my sister and I wanted to see how you were doing. May I come in?"

"No, I, er, I'm sort of busy right now. I'm, er, waiting for someone."

"Your contact from Eagle? He can wait. I can't. Please, Maria." He didn't give her time to protest further, he simply pushed back the door and stepped inside. He took it as a good sign when she didn't put up much of a protest. He did a quick survey of the room.

There wasn't much to look at in this tiny apartment. The living room was bereft of furniture, except for an unmade sofa bed, a thirty inch television sitting on a cheap, scratched table and a small dining table with three mismatched plastic chairs. At the far side of the room, there was a small fridge, something that looked like a toaster oven, a microwave, a teakettle and a tiny sink. There were two cupboards above the toaster oven and to the left of that, a door that led presumably to the bathroom. He shuddered to think what the toilet was like because if it was anything like the rest of the place, it would be filthy.

On the dining table, tubes and pots of makeup were strewn all over it, as well as a couple of packs of cigarettes, a lighter, an overflowing ashtray, a couple of bottles of vodka, one which was full, the other half full and a box of condoms.

There were a few dirty plates and mugs by the sink, as well as a few chipped glasses. A garbage can by the door to the bathroom was overflowing with empty TV dinner boxes, fast food wrappings, soda cans and God knew what else. A stifling aroma that was anything but pleasant-was just now starting to reach his nostrils. The garbage can was sitting on a ripped linoleum floor and what looked like rodent droppings were visible around it. No wonder, with wide open garbage like that, it was a veritable buffet for the rats and mice that no doubt frequented the apartment.

He went over to the grimy, nicotine stained windows to look down at the street. He was checking on Dave's car and was pleased to see it was still intact and no one was hanging around looking at it the wrong way. He turned back to Maria, who was watching him suspiciously, her skinny arms folded across her chest.

"You waiting on someone?" she asked sharply.

"No, not at all." He forced a smile on his face.

"You want that I should clear a space on the bed to give you somewhere to sit?"

Paul glanced dubiously at the bed. God alone knew what sort of horrors were lurking unseen on the crumpled sheets and he tried not to wrinkle his nose in disgust. "It's okay, I prefer to stand."

"Suit yourself." She had caught the carefully veiled look and offered him a smirk. "Bit of a step down from when we were kids, huh?"

"I've seen worse." He watched as, undeterred, she

flopped down on the bed and made herself comfortable. "Bet you're wondering why I'm here, out of the blue?"

"More to the point, little bro, what made you think I would *want* to see you? You missing your big sister all of a sudden?"

"I just wanted to see you, see how you were doing. You working?"

"You could say that. Flat on my back, legs spread wide open, bumping and grinding for forty bucks a fuck. Sixty bucks sometimes. Easy money."

Paul looked down at his hands, feeling his skin crawl in anger and revulsion. Not only was she a junkie, she was also a prostitute. "There's better ways of making a living Maria, you know that. Besides, don't any of your four husbands still support you?"

"How did you know about them?" She asked sharply. "You been checking up on me?"

"Had to, to find out where you are. Why four marriages, Maria?"

"Never did find true love, I suppose. Not one of those four deadbeats did anything for me expect give me grief and try to treat me like a breeding machine. First there was Jim, nice looker, great bod, but a real lousy lay, then came Stanley, six foot five of muscle and determined to become a father. Only problem was, his lover Jeremy got jealous of old Stan exploring his male side and gave him an ultimatum. Guess who he picked? After Stan came Brett, a jealous sonofabitch who banged anything in a skirt and left nothing for poor old wifey. And last, there was Dwight. A good guy, I suppose, but a terrible bore, in and out of the bedroom. He's got the kids now and he don't let me see them no more."

"Kids? You've got kids?" *Oh Jesus, he was an uncle and he hadn't even known.*

"Yeah, I've got kids. Don't sound so surprised. Two of them, two girls, Josie four and Emma two. Brats is what I call them, spoiled saucy brats, who deserve the boring life they're going to get with their old man. He keeps them somewhere upstate, Syracuse, I think. Maybe Buffalo. I don't remember and I certainly don't care. Daddy's girls the pair of them, and I say good riddance to all three of them."

Paul began to feel genuinely nauseated. He had just found out he had two little nieces, who surely couldn't be as bad their mother was making them out to be. Maria was talking about them as if they were no better than two pieces of garbage. Maybe it was just as well their father had custody of them, and yet it was still so ironic that God, in His infinite wisdom, had blessed Maria with the sweet gift of motherhood, not once but twice when there were women like Cathy who would sell their soul to become a mother. "I'm sorry it didn't work out for you," he heard himself say. "Congratulations on your two daughters, I'm sure they are as beautiful as their mother. I hope I get a chance to meet them some day."

"Don't care if you do, certainly don't care if they get to meet their uncle. I'm free of all of them and I'm having a ball."

He looked at her incredulously. "Doing drugs, turning tricks, living in squalor like this? How could you be having a ball, Maria?"

She didn't answer, instead curling up on the bed. Eagle was long overdue and she needed her next hit of cocaine real bad. Her head was starting to pound, her joints were starting to ache and her stomach was upset. Soon, the shakes would start, then the sweats. She shivered, absently wiped her nose with the back of her hand and reached for her packet of cigarettes.

Nicotine helped, but not much. She lit one up and inhaled deeply, only to break into a long, rasping cough. She needed cocaine, or crack, or, if Eagle was feeling generous today, maybe a little H. A little bit of anything would make all her aches and shakes go away in no time.

Paul looked sadly down at her, recognizing the onset of withdrawal all too well. "Come on Maria, why are you doing this to yourself? You're going to end up like mom."

"So what? At least she had the sense to get out of it when she did. In fact, taking that overdose was probably the most sensible thing she ever did for herself."

"You can't mean that. There's more to life than wondering when you're going to get your next hit. Mom could have had a half decent life if she hadn't fallen into the trap she did. The same trap you're sinking into now."

"Hey, who died and made you a know-it-all?"

"Nobody. I just know what I want out of life and I know I don't have to put it up my nose or in a vein to get it."

Maria shrugged one bony shoulder. "I like my life as it is, thank you very much. At least I still have my freedom, which is a lot more than some people have." She squinted through the thin trail of blue-gray smoke rising from the cigarette, taking in Paul's appearance. "Must say, you're looking good, little bro. Bet your pecker's getting plenty of exercise these days."

"You could say that. I'm married now, have been closing in on three years."

She threw her head back and laughed. "You're married? *You*? What ya do, knock her up?"

"Nothing like that." He was uncomfortable bringing Krista into this conversation. The mere mention of his wife was inappropriate in a place like this. "We want to concentrate on our careers for a while and when the time is right, we might start a family then."

Maria bounced off the bed and glided over to where Paul was standing, displaying a cat-like grace that defied her hard-nosed appearance. She squeezed his upper arm. "Let me guess, you're a construction worker. Gotta be, with muscles like that."

"Wrong." He smiled faintly. He was about to shock her but he reckoned it was his turn after the bombshells she had already dropped. "I'm a cop, Maria. Detective Sergeant Paul Cameron at your service."

"Yeah, right," she said disbelievingly after a moment of a heavy silence. "Good one, Paul, telling me you're a cop. Come on, tell me, what you really do?"

"I already told you. I'm a cop."

Uncertainty flicked into her eyes and then fright. "You here to bust me?" she asked breathlessly. Without giving him time to answer, she clenched her hand into a fist and punched him as hard as she could on his upper arm. Despite her small frame, she was deceptively strong and he suspected he would have a bruise by the end of the day. "You back stabbing little fuck!" she screamed, "You're not here to see me at all, you're here to take me in. Well fuck you, I ain't going nowhere!"

Paranoia was the norm for drug users and Paul waited patiently for her to calm down as she went off on a long, red-faced, fist-clenched barrage of verbal abuse. Her voice rose to a high pitch in her fury. He closed his eyes in disgust to her strong language, subconsciously comparing her with Krista. And Cathy too, for that matter. Those two ladies, although prone to letting loose from time to time, deplored really foul language, especially from a woman. Paul was no saint himself, neither was Dave; they had turned the air blue many a time in each other's company. But, like Krista and Cathy, they too hated listening to a female go off on a rant like this.

He listened to his sister yell and scream and berate him until he could take no more and, grabbing her by the arms, he unceremoniously forced her back on the bed.

"Shut up!" he ordered. "Just shut up and listen to me for one minute. It was because I am a cop it made it easier for me to find you. If I'd been an ordinary citizen, Lord knows when I would have found you. But just because I'm a cop, doesn't mean I'm here to bust you...although God knows I should with some of the things you've just told me. I'm here to see how you're doing, that's all. My God, Maria, it's been sixteen years since I last saw you, *sixteen years*, and in all that time, there hasn't been one single day that's gone by that I haven't thought about you, worried about you or wondered what you were up to. Maybe you don't want me here but *I* want to be here and I'm not about to leave until I can get some sort of guarantee that you're going to do something to clean up your act."

Maria's temper outburst had sent her spinning into withdrawal far quicker than she would have wanted. She crouched away from Paul, hugging herself tightly and trying to quiet her trembles. "Go away, Paul...I don't want you here no more. Eagle's comin', I know he is...Oh Jesus, make him come... hurtin' now..."

It wasn't the first time Paul had been in the presence of a drug user coming down but he was rendered powerless to do anything because this wasn't just some anonymous junkie, this was his *sister*. "I'm sorry, I - "

"Make him *come*, you fuckhead!" she cried shrilly, approaching panic. She hated these experiences her body was forced through from time to time and Eagle was going to pay for keeping her waiting. Her telephone request an hour earlier had been simple enough and with just the right amount of urgency to her voice, so where the hell was he? No sexual favors for him this time, he could keep his miserable dick in his pants, for sure...

A sudden sharp tap at the door heralded the answer to her prayers and when it was followed by two more taps, she knew it was the signal she had been waiting for. With morbid hope in her eyes, she pushed Paul roughly away and ran to the door, almost falling over herself in her haste to get there.

Paul was too dumbfounded to do anything to stop her and he watched helplessly as Maria opened the door a few inches, mumbled something to the unseen dealer, produced three twenty dollar bills from a pocket in her kaftan and received in exchange a package of white powder.

"Maria, don't," he pleaded when the door was closed. "You don't need to do this. You can get help. *I* can get you help, starting right now."

She turned towards him, triumph showing in her eyes. "This is all the help I need, little brother."

He watched her go into the bathroom and when he heard the door being locked, his reflexes kicked in. He ran to the door, pounding it with his fists. "Open the door, Maria," he roared. "Open it right now." As expected, he got no reply and, stepping back, he opened the door with one brutal kick. Mere seconds, no more than half a minute, had passed since she'd locked herself inside but he saw immediately he was too late. Obviously an expert at this terrible game, Maria had already snorted a line of cocaine and was hurriedly lining up her second. Of the rest of the dangerous package there was no sign, it had already been carefully concealed. Tears of despair flooded into his eyes as he stared sadly at his sister. "Oh Maria... why...?"

She had her eyes closed, a gentle smile twitching at the corners of her mouth. She was swaying slowly, as if to some soft music only she could hear. The drug was taking its sick hold and when she opened her eyes again, she seemed like a totally different person. Certainly nothing like the shaking, edgy, pain-riddled wreck she had been only moments before. "Bliss, Paul, sheer bliss, you should try it some time, if you haven't already. I know what they say about cops, doing their beat high on anything they can get their hands on."

"Not all cops are corrupt, Maria," he said softly. He knew the right thing to do now would be to hurry after her dealer, handcuff him, call it in and make him the Brooklyn PD's problem. He knew he should march Maria off to the nearest rehab facility. He also knew he'd have a hard time getting her admitted but he could at least try. And then he could help her straighten out her life. She was too young to be this old.

Defeated, he started to turn away. He knew a hopeless case when he saw one. But he had one thing left to say, and then he would leave. "Maria, if this will make you face up to your problems any better, I want you to know that Pops is dead. This is one of the reasons why I came here today, to tell you he's gone, sis, for good, and I bet you he's burning in hell right now for every time he beat me and raped you. If you're still having the nightmares you used to have when you were a little kid, maybe knowing of his death will help put them to rest. I hope so, because you're the only blood family I've got left now, and I love you. I also care what happens to you. I want you to get help for what you're doing to yourself because...Maria...because you're worth it. You can be better than mom and all you have to do is reach out and get that help. That's all it's going to take. Will you do that?"

Her expression had barely changed through his impassioned speech and she looked at him calmly. "Brother dearest," she said, in a tone normally used for someone very young or very stupid. "You seem to be under some misguided illusion that I *want* help. Well...surprise!... I don't. I told you, I'm happy with the way things are going for me and the last thing I need is some long-lost brother turned cop coming into my home unannounced, uninvited and *very* unwelcome. Feeding me bullshit about love and how much he cares for me. You and I were going our separate ways even before mom's suicide, that suited me fine then, it suits me even better now. And as for the news on the old man? What makes you think I care if that sonofabitch is living or dead? I haven't seen him, or even thought about him for years. He was nothing but a bastard and not worth thinking about. The nightmares stopped a long time ago and when they did, that's when I got my freedom." She looked him critically up and down. "What do *you* have"?

"A drug free, non-abusive life. A happy marriage with a loving wife. A career I truly enjoy."

"Boring!" she said dismissively. "Sounds like you live in Boresville, little brother."

Paul stared hard into her watery eyes. "I can honestly say I've never had a boring day in my life. I live the life I do with my head held high. I coped with my childhood by facing up to it and telling myself I could make something of my life. You think you've managed to free yourself of your upbringing, then think again. You're burying yourself in drugs and self-abuse because you can't cope with what you went through as a kid. Some great freedom you have, Maria. Try telling me you're truly happy and I'll call you a liar to your face."

The drug was now taking full hold, relaxing her, giving

her a buzz and making everything in her world seem just peachy. Even what Paul had just said to her couldn't upset her. How could it? She was feeling too good. One of her regulars was due for his lunchtime screw and he had promised he would bring "a little something" to help spice up the sex. If she was feeling this good, maybe she wouldn't need it...

"You know what I really want from you right now, Paul?" she purred. "I want you to take your mission of mercy, shove it up your ass and get the fuck out of my apartment. And my life. And don't come back here, ever, you're not welcome."

Paul knew how much she meant it and he tensed, trying to hold back a roar of frustration. He knew he had no choice but to go. "Sure, sis, if that's what you want." He reached into his wallet and saw that he had eighty seven dollars in cash on him. But if he offered her money, he knew it would end up going up her nose or into her arm. Instead, he pulled out one of his cards. "I want you to at least take this," he said, slipping it into the groove of the frame of the grimy, cracked mirror on the wall. "If you call and ask for me, they'll get a hold of me somehow. Or you can ask for Krista, she's my wife, and a cop too. I really do want to help you, please know that, so if you need me for *any*thing, you can call me. Or her. I mean it, Maria." He knew she would more than likely throw the card out as soon as he left but he had at least tried. He backed to the door, sorry he couldn't even give her a hug but before he opened it to leave, he turned back for one last long, searching look. He knew in his heart he would never see her again. The knowledge saddened him to a degree he found overwhelming and, with a whispered "Good bye," he hurried from her filthy, stinking apartment, down the steps and out to the car.

He was so overcome with helplessness and grief, he wouldn't even remember his drive back to Manhattan.

# CHAPTER THIRTY-EIGHT

The turning point for Dave came that evening. His fever broke, his bladder infection seemed to have cleared and the dull ache in his side was all but gone. A combination of the fever and the antibiotics had left him with a killer headache and he was advised to stay in hospital one more day for further observation. He asked if the catheter could at least be removed and after much pleading and arguing back and forth, his wish was granted.

The morning of his release, which was the day after Paul had been to see his sister, Dave woke up at around six thirty. There was barely a sound to be heard, which was unusual because there had been some sort of activity going on around him twenty-four seven. And then there was a clash and jingle of cutlery and crockery that signaled the arrival of the breakfast cart and the silence was shattered once more.

The housekeeping staff were doing their rounds quickly and efficiently. A friendly forty something black lady brought his breakfast on a covered tray and beamed a huge smile at him.

"Morning, my sunshine," she said cheerily. "You're looking a lot better today than you did yesterday."

He returned the smile. "Feel it too. You got any coffee?"

"It'll be right along, Suzannah is doing the coffees this morning. Can I get you anything else?"

"No thank you." He waited for her to leave and, after sneaking a peek at the pile of what he thought was scrambled eggs with a side of burnt-to-a-crisp bacon, he dropped the lid back on the plate and pushed the table away.

He threw back the bed sheet and swung his legs out of bed. The world went a bit askew but only for a moment. Days of fever and an infection had taken their toll and he knew he would be lightheaded and out of sorts for a while but at least he was on the mend.

He went to the toilet and groaned when he began to urinate and saw the bowl start to fill with blood. The pain in his left flank was throbbing again too. Even as the stream started to taper, he could feel a sting, as if he was peeing rusty razor blades. He waited until he had finished urinating, gasping in pain and trying not to tense, but he was starting to feel awful again and he just about made it back to the bed before he collapsed on the floor.

The night before, he hadn't felt anywhere near as bad as he did now and he argued with himself about pressing the call button for the nurse. He didn't exactly relish the thought of being poked and prodded anymore, he certainly didn't want the catheter reinserted but, if he was going to be released later on today, he wanted to be sure he was fine.

Nurse Sheila came in a few minutes later. She had been working all night and it hadn't been an easy shift but she did her best to retain a professional smile and manner. At least this patient was easy on the eyes, especially with his facial bruises and contusions starting to heal. "What's up, Mr Andrews?"

"I woke up feeling fine," he said, suddenly shivering. "But I just went to use the toilet and there was a lot of blood and real bad pain towards the end, and pain in my left side again."

She reached into her pocket, brought out a forehead thermometer and took his temperature. "Your temp was normal last night, this morning it's a hundred point one." She wiped the thermometer with some sanitizer and pocketed it again. "I'll speak to the doctor, see if we need to give you a new antibiotic. I know you're itching to get out of here and we don't want to hold you any longer than we have to so hopefully by lunchtime we will have you on the mend."

Feeling lousy and in rotten form was how Cathy found him when she came in at around nine o'clock. She was alone this time but she noticed immediately he didn't look too well. He all but scowled at her when she came in.

"And a very good morning to you too," she greeted cheerfully, giving his unyielding lips a firm kiss. "What's wrong?"

"More bleeding, more pain, more fucking temperature."

"Aww, I'm so sorry to hear that." And she genuinely was, so she sat down beside him and laid her hand on his arm. "I can't believe you're feeling so unwell again after feeling so good last night. I didn't think an infection could return after an antibiotic has killed it."

"Obviously it wasn't killed, it was just recharging itself."

"Have they said what they're doing for you?"

"They wanted to reinsert the catheter. I told them only over my cold, dead body. They couldn't explain the relapse, said something like 'it could have been because of having the catheter in so long' and 'it's unusual but not unheard of'. Yeah, yeah, yeah, yadda, yadda, yadda. They decided a change in my antibiotic would be the best thing. I told them it damn well better be a miracle cure that will get me out of here today."

His tone was moody and churlish but it didn't deter her. She would empathize and sympathize and cajole and look out for him and generally just love him until he felt better. Even if he was rude and refused her efforts to make him more comfortable or got him fresh cold water to drink, she would still do what she could.

By two o'clock that afternoon, and many texts and calls with Hannah, George, Krista and Paul, it was announced Dave could finally get out. His temperature was normal, his last two trips to the bathroom had been blood-free, there was no more of the peeing over rusty razor blades sensation and even his mood had lifted. Whatever had caused the return of an UTI, including the hematuria and then have it vanish as quickly as it had reappeared, was something that would forever remain a mystery.

The brutal beating to his groin showed signs of improvement. A chat with the urologist assured Dave he should be back to normal but advised them both to leave a return to a sex life for a few more days. If there was any difficulty in performance, and certainly if there was any pain, or bleeding, he was to call immediately.

When the doctor left the room, Dave looked sheepishly at Cathy. She had remained calm through the consultation but he could tell she was disturbed with the possibility sex could hurt him. She assured him she would be happy to wait until he knew he returned to normal.

George was waiting outside at the pickup point at precisely three o'clock and when Dave was wheeled up to the car door, with a jubilant Cathy by his side, George got out and dutifully held the door for them both. George was grinning from ear to ear, so obviously happy to see Dave out and about again and he took them straight home to the penthouse to let Hannah fuss over him in the way only she knew how.

Krista was clearly delighted to see Dave home, as was Paul, and after the welcome home hugs, they settled in the living room. Hannah hugged Dave as tightly as she could, then clucked around him, fluffing his cushions and making sure he was comfortable. She was driving him crazy with her motherliness but he loved her for it too. She brought in a tray of coffee and homemade chocolate chip cookies for everyone. She had been busy that morning baking a gingerbread Dave had always loved as a child. As soon as he saw it, he scooped up a piece and delighted Hannah by telling her she hadn't lost her touch.

After Cathy checked to make sure he wasn't starting to flag, and getting the expected impatient confirmation he was fine, Dave motioned they should discuss what their next step was going to be to help Paul. Paul hadn't yet told Dave of his visit with his sister the day before, but Krista and Cathy knew, so he filled Dave in.

"Not that her being in the quagmire she's in has anything to do with my upcoming murder trial, but I went to see her because I thought she had a right to know our father was dead."

"I get that," Dave said. "I'm sorry she was so unreceptive. That had to burn."

"It wasn't one of my finest moments." Paul stared moodily into space for a moment, reliving the conversation with his sister. "Anyway, that's why I went to see her. I'm sorry it turned out the way it did but at least now I know."

"And the Romanos still haven't made it public their son is dead?"

"Nope. Pedowski didn't seem surprised. After four days...five now, you'd think they'd make some sort of statement."

"Must be something going down, they're keeping below the radar."

"The ports are on alert for any tankers coming in from France. That's been their MO in getting their drugs in, apparently. They use their art containers and shipments as a shield. Harry is going to check the employee records, see if we can get someone, maybe an illegal alien or two, interviewed to see if they can relate any conversations overheard about how they've gotten rid of their victims."

"I think that's a bit of a reach," Cathy said. "I have a feeling the employees are either too hardnosed to break their employers' confidence, or too scared to do the same."

"Maybe," Krista said slowly, "but I've a better idea. Why don't we find someone we can build up a trust with, someone who works in that household, someone who the Romanos probably don't even see are in the room, and have them check for records?"

It took a few seconds for that suggestion to sink in. Then Paul reached out to grab a firm hold of Krista's hand. "You never cease to amaze me, my love," he said softly, his voice breaking with emotion. "I've been looking for an easy fix and couldn't even think to take this route. I don't know if I would ever have thought of that."

"You would have eventually. I just said it out loud first." She gave his lips a soft kiss. "We all want to do anything we can to help you, I can't tell you that often enough."

Cathy and Dave exchanged a look. "Does that mean we get to stay in New York longer than we anticipated?" he asked.

"Hopefully not too much longer," Paul said. "I'd really like to be home in time for Christmas, which is only nine days away."

"Then we'd better get busy, get some sort of plan formulated, get in touch with Harry and see what he can give us as soon as possible."

Paul was about to respond when his cell phone rang. When he looked at the caller ID he smiled. "Speak of the devil, it's Harry Pedowski himself." He opened the call. "Hey, Harry, was just talking about you."

Harry looked around the tiny, filthy apartment he was phoning from and at the body of the woman about to be zipped up in a black body bag. His heart was heavy, as it always was delivering news like this.

"Paul, I've got some bad news for you, I'm so sorry. Are you alone?"

Paul recognized the business tone and glanced briefly at Krista. "No, all of us are here, Dave just got out of hospital."

"Are you in a safe area?"

"We're in the penthouse, as safe as we can get. What is it, Harry?"

"Paul, I'm at a murder scene right now. There's no easy way to say this. It's your sister, Maria Taylor. I'm so sorry, but she was found in her apartment, around mid-day, she'd been beaten up, severe bruising around her genitals but the cause of death is a broken neck."

Paul felt as if the air was being slowly sucked out of the room. His chest tightened as he absorbed Harry's words. "A broken neck?" he managed to repeat.

Krista narrowed her eyes in suspicion as she watched Paul reacting to what was being said to him. At his last words, she looked at Cathy and Dave in alarm. Paul was clearly becoming upset but they didn't yet know who Harry was talking about.

"Yeah. ME said it was quick."

Paul arose and walked over to the window. He knew everyone was looking at him but he needed to process this before he could offer them any explanation. "Do you know who did it?"

"Where were you around nine o'clock this morning?"

Stunned at the question, Paul felt his fury build. "Are you fucking kidding me, Harry?"

"Just asking, Paul. Questions are going to be asked that you're not going to like, but I'm asking them first. You asked me for your sister's address, you confided in me you hadn't seen her in over sixteen years. I assume you came here yesterday after you left the precinct, to see her." It was a statement but the question was implicit.

"I did."

"You couldn't deny it anyway, your card was found stuck to her mirror."

Paul pinched the bridge of his nose. It was no comfort whatsoever she hadn't thrown it away. "Yeah, so, I'm up front about asking for her address, I tell you immediately who she is to me, I leave my card, you think I'm going to be so open if I had anything to do with getting her killed?" He was aware Krista had made a squeal of alarm behind him but he couldn't even turn to look at her. "Come on, Harry, you're reading the scene, I assume?"

"You didn't answer my question. Where were you at around nine o'clock this morning?"

"I was right here, having breakfast with my wife."

"So aside from Krista, any other witnesses?"

"George and Hannah Waite, the housekeepers."

"And they'll testify to your whereabouts?"

"No reason why not."

Harry watched as the body of Paul's sister was put on a gurney. She was wheeled away and he let out a long sigh. What he'd seen of the pathetically thin body had saddened and sickened him. She didn't look like she'd put up much of a fight, there were no obvious signs of a struggle. "Okay, Paul, interrogation over, I'm not pinning this one on you, just asking the questions to put you in the clear."

"Who found her?"

"911 got an anonymous tip. Caller ID didn't register."

"Have the uniforms ask around for someone known as Eagle. No idea if he's black, white, or Asian or whatever else but he's a dealer, or at least a runner. Someone's bound to know his real name."

"I don't think he's the one who did it."

"How can you tell?"

"Think about it, Paul, come on. Beaten up. Broken neck?"

"Shit...you think the Romanos did this?"

"Looking that way. We're guessing in retaliation to what you did to Julio Romano."

"But how did they know where to find my sister? Assuming they knew Dave and my names, she has a different last name than me. Unless...you think I was followed from the precinct yesterday?" He recalled being on automatic pilot on the drive from the precinct to his sister's. He had gone through the motions of checking his mirrors, using his directional signals when appropriate and getting from A to B without noticing anything suspicious. He also recalled looking outside the window at his sister's apartment, checking Dave's car hadn't been vandalized in any way. He was almost a hundred per cent certain he hadn't seen anyone paying him any attention when he'd gotten in and out of the car.

"It's the only connection we can make. But your card on the mirror would have been all they needed to confirm it."

Paul would have laughed at the bitter irony of it all, if it hadn't been so serious. He had been placed at his father's room, just before he was murdered. Now he had been placed at his sister's apartment shortly before she had been murdered. At least this time he had witnesses. "Do you need me to come over to Brooklyn?"

"We're still trying to find her last ex-husband."

"Dwight Taylor."

"Dwight? That's great, that helps. If he doesn't claim next of kin, you might have to come and ID the body."

Paul felt his stomach churn. "Let me know. I'll also see about funeral arrangements."

"Might be a long wait, because of Covid. City's using refrigerated trucks as temporary morgues. I'll see what I can do. Paul, I really am sorry, man. She looked like she had a hard life but she certainly didn't deserve this."

"Thanks, Harry. Keep me posted. I can be over there as soon as you need me." He disconnected the call and stood for a moment looking out the window at the street below. Then he turned to face Krista and his friends. He shrugged helplessly. "My sister's been murdered," he stated simply, even though he knew they'd probably figured that out already.

Krista got up to hug him fiercely. He was understandably shell shocked but even as he accepted her hug, his eyes locked with Dave's and Dave read something in them he didn't like.

"What was the COD?" Dave asked carefully.

"Broken neck. She was also...um...badly beaten up...her body...and around the genitals."

"Oh God," Cathy said, "The Romanos?"

"Certainly sounds like it, doesn't it?"

"In retaliation for you killing their son?" Dave asked.

"No other reason I can think of." Paul felt his chest tighten. As if hearing his sister had just been murdered wasn't bad enough, now they had no other reason but to accept his killing of the Romano boy had caused it.

He turned away, feeling helpless and hopeless and so dreadfully sorry for a wasted life that could have been so much better if he'd intervened years ago.

Across the East River, in the Romano fortress, Julius Romano held the hand of his seventy three year old wife. They were in a private room, with rows of chairs set out. On the raised platform, a bier was positioned against the wall, a highly polished mahogany coffin with a huge spray of lily of the valley and white lilies on top of it.

His wife was weeping softly, her black veil hiding her outward display of grief. Julius blinked back his tears as he sat in quiet reflection, staring at the coffin holding the body of his beloved son, remembering happy, childhood memories. At seven years old, Julio running to him on a beach in the Bahamas, a conch held out in front of him, getting him to hold it to his ear and listen to the sound of the ocean. Julio at his First Communion, his face serious as he received the Eucharist for the first time. Julio passing his driving test and thanking his parents for the gift of a black Porsche Carrera.

His thoughts and memories were interrupted by a bodyguard coming up to him and leaning over to talk to him quietly.

"Is it done?" he whispered back.

"She is dead." It was affirmed.

"Does Cameron know?"

"He has been informed."

Julian looked at the clock on the wall. The funeral was scheduled for four o'clock that afternoon, in barely fifteen minutes time, and soon the guests would be arriving. No waiting for a funeral home for the Romanos, not when they had their own chapel right here and a priest on their payroll. He nodded absently at the bodyguard. "Good. He or his partner will be next. I will decide where and when. Right now, let us grieve in peace." And with that, he turned to his wife, put a comforting arm around her shoulders and returned his attention to his dead son.

# CHAPTER THIRTY-NINE

Dave phoned Captain Hamilton to bring him up to speed and, on Paul's behalf, told their superior about the murder of Paul's sister. The captain was understandably shocked and granted them all permission to stay in New York for as long as they needed. If DA Ardolino started making noise about the length of time they'd been away, especially if he knew their mission had been unsuccessful, there was nothing he could say or do to protest time away for a family bereavement.

"I'm glad you're out of the hospital, Dave," he said, "and I'm sorry things didn't work out with the Romano family. That was a great idea Krista had of getting someone on the inside to check the files. I hope it works out for you this time."

"It has to because after this, we got nothing."

"And Captain Pedowski is absolutely certain Maria's murder can't be pinned on Paul?"

"Even if he tried, Paul has three rock solid alibis."

"Thank God for that, had a sort of déjà vu feeling there."

"Yeah, I know what you mean. Thanks, Bob, we'll be in touch soon. Our best to Cora." Dave disconnected the call and returned to the living room.

Paul and Krista were huddled in one corner, talking quietly, with a lot of touching and hugging. Dave didn't want to interrupt them and beckoned to Cathy so he could run something by her.

"I feel so bad for him," Cathy murmured. "How dreadful

to see your long lost sister and then the next day hear she's been murdered." She stole a glance at her friends and saw Krista cupping Paul's face, loving him and comforting him as best she could. She turned back to Dave and saw him looking unhappily towards their friends too. "Hey, you doing okay?" she asked softly.

"I'm a little tired," he confessed. "Should I tell Hannah we'll order in tonight and take the burden off her?"

"Sounds like a plan. Come on, I'll go with you. We'll need to tell them what happened to Maria anyway, see if they can suggest a funeral home."

As she started to get up, he held her back. "There's something I want to talk to you about first. Krista and Paul are saving as best they can for the lawyer fees so they don't have a lot of spare cash hanging around. Funerals are costly enough, funerals in New York even more so."

"Oh, I never thought of that."

"Right. So...would you mind if we used some of the money from the deposit for the house to help them out?"

She looked at him wide-eyed but then a slow smile spread over her face. "You are an incredible man, David Andrews."

"I know *that*," he said flippantly. "Is that a yes?"

"Of course it is. I haven't been so sure about the last few houses we've looked at anyway and I don't want to settle just for the sake of settling. Covid is really messing up the property market so I was going to suggest we wait until the market is in a better place before we start looking again."

He kissed the tip of her nose. "Thank you, my love. We'll tell them later, now let's go talk to George and Hannah."

The housekeepers were understandably upset for Paul when they heard the news and immediately offered their help. "We can use the limousine if we need to transport people around," George said quickly.

"That will be great, George," Dave said, "but I have a feeling it will be a very low-key affair. His sister...well...let's just say she'd fallen on some hard times and with Covid, not too many people are allowed to attend a funeral. Last time I heard, in Massachusetts, the limit was twenty five. I doubt there will be even half that many people there, Covid or not."

Hannah looked so sorrowful her eyes filled with tears. "That poor child. George and I will attend, we'd like to pay our respects."

"Thank you, Hannah. Oh, I just realized, we didn't bring suitable attire for a funeral. Does my dad have any clothes here?"

"You know he does," George said. "You and Paul are roughly the same size and you're about the same as your father, so there shouldn't be a problem getting the right clothing. I'll pick out two dark suits for you and have them cleaned and pressed in time for the funeral."

"I think Krista and I brought dresses, in case we were going to have the chance to go out for dinner. I'm sure we can improvise with what we have," Cathy stated.

"That's that sorted," Dave said. "You haven't started anything for dinner yet, have you, Hannah?"

"Was just about to. Why, do you want something special made?"

"I don't know if Paul will be up to eating but I was just going to suggest ordering something in tonight. I think it will make it easier on us all."

"As you wish," Hannah said. "Let us know what you want and George can either go and collect it or we can have it delivered."

"Oh, delivered, please," Cathy said quickly. "Let's all just have an easy night."

Paul was subdued but open for company, and even though he only picked at the sumptuous Chinese food, straight from Mott Street, he at least ate enough to keep him going. Afterwards, when George and Hannah had cleared everything away, Dave reckoned it would be a good time to bring up the subject of the funeral costs.

"I know what you're going to say but, please, hear me out first before you fly off the handle. Cathy and I have talked about this and we really want to do it for you so I really hope you'll accept."

"Accept what?" Paul looked at Krista for some sort of help but she seemed as in the dark as he was.

"Cathy and I, we want to pay for Maria's funeral. We have the cash and we know you are cutting costs all you can for the lawyers' fees so it makes sense to let us contribute."

"Makes sense?" Paul cried. "Dave, when are you going to just *stop*?"

"Stop what?" he asked in genuine bewilderment.

"Giving! It's all just too much."

Cathy reached over and linked her fingers with Paul's. "No one expected this to happen, Paul. It's an expense you don't need right now and we want to do this for you. We didn't know Maria, we never met her but we know she was troubled and we know how much this is hurting you. This is our way of helping, that's all."

Krista looked from Paul to Cathy to Dave, unsure of who to stand up for first. She could understand why Paul was upset but she could also understand why Dave and Cathy wanted to help.

"Where would you and Dave be getting the money from?" Krista asked. "Please don't say from your father again, Dave, because then it would be a flat-out no."

"No, we won't be asking Dave's father this time. It will be coming from our house money. We had been toying with the idea of waiting a while longer before setting down roots when, hopefully, the market will be better. It's just money sitting there doing nothing. We can't even take a vacation somewhere on it because of the lockdown, certainly not home to see my mum and my niece because the UK is supposedly closing its borders to certain countries. Plus the self-isolation before and after the holiday. So, Paul, please let us do this for you."

Paul could feel tears threatening. It had been a terrible,

screwed up, emotional few days for him and witnessing his best friends' heartfelt generosity yet again was more than he could bear right now. He looked down at Cathy's hand still clasped in his, then over at Dave. Dave's face was still a mess of bruises and he seemed very tired. All at once, Paul decided that if he refused their offer, he would only end up hurting them both. He blinked away the tears and forced some semblance of a smile on his face.

"You guys are just too much," he said, his voice quavering. "And I love you both. Thank you for wanting to do this for someone you've never even met, it means more to me than you'll ever know."

Dave breathed a sigh of relief that it hadn't taken too much coaxing for Paul to take the money. "We love you too, man. We're not just doing it for her, we're doing it for you."

He stood up and came over to hug them both. "Thank you," he whispered into Dave's ear. There was no need for any more words.

# CHAPTER FORTY

Paul didn't have to ID his sister's body after all. According to her medical records, her ex-husband, Dwight Taylor, was still listed as her next of kin. He drove down from Buffalo, confirmed it was her when he saw her lying on a stainless-steel slab in the city morgue and left as abruptly as he came. Paul never got to meet him.

Funeral arrangements were made and Pedowski was able to pull a few strings to guarantee that the service would be held within a couple of days. He used Paul as an excuse, saying he had come from out of state and needed to get home as soon as possible.

The funeral had pathetically few mourners. Pedowski came in support of Paul, and Errol was there too. Paul was as touched by the electrical specialist's presence as he was by Harry Pedowski's and, although the service was short and impersonal, Paul figured they had done his sister proud.

Unknown to Paul, Pedowski had posted a couple of uniformed officers outside the chapel. As lazy snow flurries flew around them at the gravesite, the officers remained out of view but kept a careful watch. Suspicions the Romanos were responsible for Maria's murder were still high and, fearing further retaliation, Pedowski had ordered the guards for as long as Paul stayed out in the open.

As the tiny clutch of mourners started to walk away, Paul excused himself from Krista and came over to talk to Harry. "Thanks for all you did, Harry. Want to tell me why you had the uniforms watching my every move?"

Harry gave a short laugh of embarrassment. "Was hoping you wouldn't notice. They're new to the force, don't know how to blend in yet."

"Uh huh. You think the Romanos might come after me?"

"No reason to believe otherwise. We've got the name of one of the servants who works for the Romanos. She's been in the States for three years, has only worked for them since she arrived from Nicaragua. She's willing to help but only if I can get her immigration papers through."

"Can you do that?"

"I might have a favor or two to call in. Leave it with me. Let me talk to her, tell her what we need, she's skittish enough as it is without adding new faces to intimidate her."

"You know I want this to be mine, Harry, the less people involved, the better."

"I do know, but this one…trust me on this one, okay?" Harry fixed him with one of his no point in arguing stares and Paul reluctantly nodded. "I really am sorry about what happened to your sister. I had no idea they would go after her, especially considering you've been spending most of your time in Manhattan."

"People like them can stretch their tentacles far and wide." Paul glanced at Krista and his eyes softened. "She has been so supportive of me, I couldn't do this without her. She never even met Maria and yet she's the one who did most of the funeral arrangements."

Pedowski smiled and nodded. "She really is something, man."

"I think so. And as for Dave and Cathy…amazing people." Paul shifted his attention to Dave and saw him support his arm to take the weight off of the sling as if he was in pain and trying to find relief any way he could. It looked like he was trying not to grimace or bring Cathy's attention to it and Paul felt nothing but sympathy for Dave. He had tried so hard all along to help Paul, not just physically but financially, and yet he was the one who was hurting the most. "Dave looks really tired. That infection really took it out of him. I think I'll suggest we all return to his dad's place so we can relax. You're welcome to join us for dinner tonight."

"Thank you, but Noreen wants me to help her trim the tree. I've let her down two nights in a row and for my own safety, I don't dare do it again. Besides, it's sort of a tradition for us."

"Then we'll take a raincheck. Give Noreen my best. Let me know if you need me to help out with the employee you think can get us some answers."

"I will, I promise. I've told her I would be in touch today and would expect results within three days max. I'm heading back to the office to call in that favor from immigration. Take care, Paul." Harry waved at Krista, then at Dave and Cathy and, with Errol in tow, took his leave.

George was standing by the limo, waiting for instruction on where they were going. It was midafternoon and the light was already fading. Paul knew they were waiting for him to dictate their next move and, putting his arm possessively around Krista's shoulders, he gestured towards the car.

"Let's go back to the penthouse. Is that okay, George?"

"Of course, Mr Paul."

The drive back to the city took over an hour and when they got into the penthouse, Paul excused himself to be on his own for a bit. He was tired and depressed and he couldn't lift his mood at all, not when he knew if it hadn't been for him visiting his sister she would more than likely still be alive. It was a realization he had shared with Krista the night he'd learned of his sister's murder and she had been quick to convince him if it was anybody's fault, it was his father's. Although he couldn't argue with that, he still felt responsible.

He loosened the black silk tie that belonged to Dave's father and carefully folded it up. Then he stripped down to his underwear and pulled on his track suit bottoms and a t-shirt. Feeling better just by getting out of the suit, he sat on the edge of the bed and went through his cell phone, checking for texts or emails.

Captain Hamilton had sent a text, expressing his and

Cora's condolences. Likewise Jim Turner and Mark Chipman. There were no threatening texts, no threatening emails, no warnings on messenger, nothing that would indicate anything from the Romanos.

He was about to pocket his phone and join Krista and his friends when he inadvertently clicked on his phone's contacts. His eye fell on a name that stirred nothing but fond memories and, without a moment's hesitation, pressed the call button.

He stayed on the phone for fifteen minutes, accepting condolences about his sister in the good faith they were offered and listening to pearls of wisdom from a man and woman he, as a child, had wished a thousand times were his real mom and dad. When he hung up, he felt a lot better, at least emotionally, and when he joined everyone again, he allowed himself to feel their love and support lift his spirits further.

He told them what Harry had found out about the worker from Nicaragua and that he had been promised he would be contacted as soon as she got in touch with Harry. Although they were all on the same wavelength about wanting to interview her, they could understand Harry wanting to keep this within his own jurisdiction. At least, as Paul pointed out, with Harry on the job, he would stop at nothing to get what they needed.

The next morning, after breakfast, Dave and Cathy seemed at loose ends. Apart from a physical therapy appointment at noon, Dave really had nothing to do. George was going to take him to the hospital as Dave wasn't yet able to drive, and probably wouldn't be able to for a few weeks yet.

Paul still hadn't told Krista he had made plans for the two of them but when they were getting dressed, he sat her down and explained there was something he needed to do and he really wanted her with him while he was doing it.

When she heard what it was, she looked down at her jeans and t-shirt in panic. "Oh no, I should change!"

"What on earth for? You look great. You could wear a

sack and you'd still look great."

"Not when I'm going to meet Mr and Mrs Benetti, two of the most important people to you when you were growing up." She got off the bed, already stripping off her t-shirt and going to the wardrobe. She didn't have a lot to choose from and wondered if she should ask Cathy if she could borrow a blouse. But then her eyes fell on a deep mauve silk top with three quarter length sleeves, a v neck and a loose bottom and she triumphantly pulled it out. She held it up in front of her, and pivoted to show it to Paul. "Will this do?" Before he could answer, she hung the hanger on the handle of the wardrobe, her tongue clicking in irritation. "Except now I have to change my bra because this one's too white against such a dark color."

He watched in faint amusement as she unclasped her bra but she was driving him crazy with her antics and he grabbed her wrist to pull her towards him. The bra slipped off and fell to the floor and he immediately took advantage of her toplessness.

She arched her back as his tongue and mouth did what they did best but before she could get too distracted, she pulled away from him. He looked at her in surprise. "What's wrong?"

"I've just done my hair and my make up."

"So? It's never stopped you before."

"No but I've never been about to meet your surrogate parents before."

He detected a slight lack of confidence, which was very unusual for her and he pulled her back towards him. "Baby, they will love you, no matter what you're wearing, no matter what your hair is like and no matter what your make up is like. Trust me. They are so looking forward to meeting you and certainly wouldn't want you getting stressed like this."

She looked at him dubiously and then gave him a slow grin. "I might have to change out of my jeans too." To prove her point, she stepped back, unbuttoned and unzipped them and slid them slowly down her legs.

"Uh…right…will you have to change your panties too?"

"Well I wouldn't want to get any wrinkles in them, would I?"

Never having heard of anyone ever getting wrinkles in their panties, and choosing not to waste time contemplating whether anyone actually *could* get wrinkles in them, he grabbed her again. This time, she didn't pull away and happily let him do whatever he wanted to her, as long as he let her pay him back in kind.

Afterwards, when she had showered and gotten dressed again, she was standing in front of the mirror reapplying her make up when he came up behind her and nuzzled her neck. "Do you need to change again?" he murmured.

She chuckled throatily. "Later, baby, I promise."

He inhaled her familiar Chloe Rose perfume and stole his hands round to her breasts. "God, I can't get enough of you today."

"So I can feel." She had been about to apply lipstick but turned round to face him before she did. She kissed him deeply. "Hold that thought, okay?"

He could tell she was torn but she also had started to feel anxious again and, visualizing himself jumping into a freezing cold pool, he did his best to reassure her it was going to be okay. "Rosa and Santo Benetti will love you," he said, smiling into her eyes. "They will see how happy you make me and that will be good enough for them."

"I hope so. Are you going to tell them about what happened with your dad?"

"Yes. I owe that much to them. I was tempted to tell them when I called to let them know Maria was dead but I changed my mind, decided to wait until we were face to face."

"Okay. Now please, be honest, do I look okay?"

"Better than okay. Good enough to eat...which might happen later."

"*Might*?" she cried derisively. She smiled her special smile at him and then, trusting him when he said she looked great, she took his hand and let him lead her out of the bedroom.

When Paul entered Brooklyn, he knew this would be the last time he would be here. Krista was strangely subdued as they came off the bridge and when he gave her a quick scrutiny, he saw her expression matched her mood. She was usually chatty, upbeat, pointing out landmarks or things that caught her eye, or she would be humming along to a tune on the radio. But right now, she was looking out the window, not paying attention to anything.

"You okay, love?" he asked casually.

She didn't answer him, instead she checked her purse for her wallet. "Can we find somewhere I could get Mrs Benetti some flowers or chocolates or something? I don't want to arrive empty handed."

"Sure, there's bound to be a mini mart around somewhere." He waited for a count of five, then tried again. "You sure you're okay?"

She chewed pensively on her bottom lip. "I keep going back to the visits your father kept paying us before...well, before he came back that morning and attacked me."

"Why are you wasting time thinking about him?"

"I'm not really thinking about *him*, I'm thinking about the visits. He kept saying how he wanted you to forgive him, to let him back into your life. You, rightly so, turned him away. And now here we are, in Brooklyn, trying to clear your name for his murder."

"Are you saying I should have welcomed him back with open arms?" he asked incredulously.

"No, no, not at all. I'm just saying if he hadn't shown up then or any other time, we wouldn't have to be here."

"My father...the gift that keeps on giving." He snorted in disdain. "Enough about him, I want to be in a good mood when I see the Benettis."

"You will be in a wonderful mood," she assured him, her mood already lifted and her clear green eyes sparkling again. "Is that a mini mart up there?"

It was and he dutifully pulled in so she could purchase a gift for a couple she had never met. But he knew they had earned a place in her heart because of how they had looked after him as a child. She knew they were largely responsible for him being the remarkable man he was and he couldn't wait for them to meet her.

Ten minutes later, his wish came true.

# CHAPTER FORTY-ONE

Paul rang the doorbell. When the door opened, he beamed a smile at the elderly, silver-haired woman, dressed all in black, eyeing him suspiciously. It had been many years since she had seen him and only vague recognition flicked into her coal black eyes. And then she broke into a long spiel of excited Italian, her hands clasped in front of her in glee when she realized who she was looking at.

Even still standing on the stoop, Paul couldn't stop smiling, he really couldn't. And when a tall, gangly white-haired man appeared from a room down the hall, a room Paul knew to be the cramped but cozy living room, his smile widened. "Hey, Mama and Papa Benetti. Long time no see, huh?"

Santo and Rosa Benetti, two of the nicest, kindest people Paul knew, stopped their excited babbling long enough to draw their prodigal fostered son into their embrace. Paul had the foresight before coming to find out if he would be breaking any coronavirus rules. He and Krista had taken their temperature that morning and he had texted that information to Rosa. She had replied they were negative too, thanks to a routine doctor's appointment they had each had that morning.

He only knew he couldn't have come all this way without at least one hug from these two lovely people and when he sank into Rosa's mothering arms he felt, at last, at peace. Dave may have had George and Hannah to give him love and guidance and self-esteem, but he had had these people. They had opened up their home and their hearts selflessly, their only reward being that they could watch him grow and mature into a fine, loving, honorable young man. He loved them well and now he felt he had come home, to his proper home. This was the home that had nothing to do with his mother, or his father. Or Maria.

"Pauly! My boy," Rosa welcomed, her eyes awash with tears of happiness. "Look at my wonderful, beautiful boy, how you've grown. Let me hug you, then you can take off that mask and come in." She had been so caught up in seeing Paul, she suddenly realized he wasn't alone and looked to his right. "This must be Krista...oh sweet Mary, you told me she was beautiful but that's an understatement. She is absolutely *gorgeous.* Divine. Welcome, my child, welcome."

"Let them in, Mama," Santo said gently, "I don't want a reunion on the stoop."

Rosa dutifully stepped back, shepherding them in, clucking around them as she led them to the living room. She waited patiently as Santo relieved them of their coats and clasped her hands to her chest again when Krista proffered the beautiful mixed bunch of flowers. "Lovely, just lovely, thank you, thank you."

Santo took the flowers and disappeared into the kitchen. He returned moments later with the flowers in a vase and let Rosa arrange them to her satisfaction. "Again, Pauly, our deepest sympathies for your sister," Santo said sincerely. "We are both so sorry for your loss."

"Thank you, Papa, much appreciated."

"You have a lovely home, Mrs Benetti," Krista said politely as she sat down. She had already taken in the numerous framed pictures of, she assumed, family members dotted around the tables and credenza. Paul had told her this was a large family and it certainly seemed that way. The pictures were of different times throughout the years, young children, the same children grown to adulthood, the adult children holding babies of their own. She recognized a young Paul in a couple of them and her heart swelled with gratitude for Rosa and Santo for including him in their family gallery. Then one particular picture caught her attention above all the others. It was set in the middle of a table with a tealight burning in front of it. It had to be of their deceased son, Frankie, and she smiled sadly.

Rosa beamed her pride at Krista's words. "We will eat in a little while," she said. "And please, it's Rosa and Santo, or Mama and Papa, whichever you prefer. Pauly is our son, you are our daughter."

Krista clutched a hand to her chest, her smile widening. "Grazie, Mama, significa che il mondo per me." *Thank you, Mama, that means the world to me.*

Santo and Rosa looked at her in astonishment. "You speak Italiana?" Santo said in awe while Rosa beamed her pride at her new daughter-in-law.

Krista chuckled. "Unfortunately, only a little. I can listen better than I can speak it."

Paul grinned at them all and then, in an exaggerated stage whisper, said to Krista, "You've won them over already, baby."

Rosa was laughing merrily and she clutched Krista's hand in her own. "I knew as soon as I saw you that you were the right person for my Pauly. Now, as I said, we will eat in a little while."

"Aww, Mama, you didn't have to make us anything to eat," Paul scolded gently. "I told you not to go to any bother."

"It's nothing, some lasagna, some good Italiano bread, perhaps a Tiramisu."

"And you made them all, I bet."

Rosa nodded absently. She was a large-framed woman who had lived her life raising children and making a home for them all. She had spent much of her life in the kitchen and her cooking and baking were legendary around the neighborhood.

"First, you tell me, how you two meet. And bambinos, any bambinos?"

Paul chuckled. "We met at work, we're both cops. And no babies. Don't know if we'll change our minds on that or not, we're happy together the way we are."

"Career people," Rosa said in an aside to Santo but she wasn't being unkind. "You are both so beautiful," she said, her heart swelling with love. "I am so happy to see you, Pauly, and to meet your lovely Krista at long last."

"I am so happy to meet you too," Krista returned, the feeling genuine. She knew Paul had been right when he'd told her she had nothing to worry about. She knew the little bit of Italian she'd spoken had been the right thing to do. It had helped her feel more relaxed, knowing it would have gotten the reaction it did.

"Why did you come to New York, Pauly? In the middle of this horrible virus," Santo asked. He had just come back from the kitchen again, this time with a tray laden with cups of coffee and a plate of homemade cookies. He passed them around and settled down to listen to his beloved boy but couldn't understand the look that passed between him and Krista.

Krista nodded her encouragement and Paul slipped his hand into hers. "Well, we're here on official police business," he began slowly. "And, I'm sorry, what I have to tell you, it's not going to be easy to hear."

Santo slipped Rosa a nervous look. Paul's eyes had clouded over and it was obvious something big was hanging around his neck. "You tell us in your own time, boy," he said. "We're here for you."

"Just like you always have been." Paul looked down at Krista's hand. Her nails were beautifully shaped and had a coating of a light pink polish on them. "I ran into my dad a while ago...a couple of weeks before Thanksgiving."

Rosa's lip curled in contempt. "What that man want?"

"In short, he wanted money. He didn't get it, although

he tried. Came to our home – I wasn't there – and beat Krista up, got away with some jewelry, car titles, that sort of thing but…" he trailed off, re-living the moment he had come into Krista's hospital room and seen the damage his father had done. He suppressed a shudder. "But I couldn't let it go, I couldn't let him harm her like that and not seek retribution. So I found him and beat *him* up…and the very next day I was charged with his murder."

Santo and Rosa sat staring at him for a long moment, looking as if they were expecting to hear him say something along the lines that it had been a misunderstanding, a case of wrong identity, his father was still alive. Something. Anything.

And then Santo realized this was it, this was why Paul was back in Brooklyn, his roots, to try and clear his name. Santo let out a gasp, his bony fingers gripping Rosa's shoulder. "I don't need to ask, I can see it written all over your face. You didn't do it."

"I really didn't, Papa. I wanted to, I won't lie, no one hurts my Krista and gets away with it, but I truthfully didn't do it."

Rosa's wrung her hands in anguish. "My poor boy…what can we do to help?"

"Unfortunately, there is nothing. Just your prayers."

"You will have those no matter what. You have any evidence at all? Anything to clear your name?" Santo asked.

"Very little, none from here. And the DA is out to crucify me, so my lawyer – who luckily has the savvy to defend me to the hilt – is doing his best to get my name cleared but he has an uphill battle ahead of him."

Although he was trying to downplay the whole thing, Santo could hear the underlying despair and his deep brown eyes suddenly filled with tears. Seeing them both so distressed had shocked and upset Paul. Santo had always been the stoic one, the parent who had given the best advice, who kept his emotions in check. But to see those tears, Paul's heart shattered.

"You will keep us informed?" Rosa asked shakily.

"Of course I will. No doubt you'll hear about it on the news. I haven't heard about a deposition yet but it's ahead of me and we might have a better idea of where we stand."

"I do a rosary for you and pray every night," Rosa promised, dabbing at her eyes. "Please ask for our help if you think we can."

Their love and loyalty were as strong now as they had been when he'd been a child. "I will, I promise but, unfortunately, there's nothing anyone can do. We had a lead down here but so far it's amounted to nothing. We have one more thing to try and, if it doesn't pan out, we go back to Bathville and try to think of a new plan of attack."

"If we can find a way to help you, we will," Santo asserted.

Paul took a sip of the strong, Italian coffee. With a half-smile, he got up and went to the window, to look out into the backyard. The old swing set was gone, probably long gone and retired gracefully after ten little Benetti children, and himself, falling off it, skinning their knees. Only to get right back on it again in the devil-may-care attitude children have. In its place was a sandpit and a climbing frame, no doubt to entertain the fifteen grandchildren Paul knew of. He had spent many happy hours out there, fitting in with the family, letting them treat him like any other sibling and the memory made his heart give a melancholy twist.

"I wish I had been your real son," he announced softly.

"To us you were," Santo said, as surprised as Rosa at the admission. "And you still are."

Paul turned slowly to face them again, catching Krista's look of appreciation at what they had just said. "And you are my real parents. Not Eva Cameron and certainly not Kenneth. Both my parents are dead and I have yet to shed one single tear over them. And yet if something were to happen to either of you…" He didn't finish the sentence, he didn't need to and he turned back to the window again. It was a bright sunny day but the December air lacked any real warmth. "Anyway, enough of this, tell us what's been going on with you."

"No, no, you tell us about your lovely bride here," Rosa said, forcing a happy smile on her face.

"Now *there's* a subject I could talk about all day," he said, much to Krista's chagrin. "As you know, she is beautiful. She can also speak Italian, at least a little." He tipped Rosa a wink to show he was teasing her by telling her what she already knew. But then he grew serious and proceeded to tell them about how they had met, their first case together, how he hadn't believed in love at first sight until he'd set eyes on her. He told them she was as beautiful on the inside as she was on the outside and, when Krista playfully tried to cover his mouth with her hand to shut him up, he grabbed her hand instead and kissed her fingertips.

"I'll pay you the twenty bucks for those nice words later," she joked, which earned a hearty laugh from both Santo and Rosa.

The subject of his dad and his pending trial was set aside for now, and, with the mood lifted, Krista proceeded to tell them what Paul had been up to. She had learned Santo was the one responsible for putting his first pair of ice skates on him and how the local team in Bathville had snapped him up after the coach of the club he'd played for in Brooklyn had suggested they should.

She proudly told them how he had earned a Medal of Honor for his part in ending the life of a serial killer, and saving the life of her best friend at the same time. She also told them how his cases were usually solved quickly and efficiently. She wanted them to know that, although he had a badly broken childhood, he was the man he was today thanks to them putting him back together.

Paul was touched by her words but made a point of telling them he would pay *her* the twenty bucks later. He knew Krista had won them over and he was pleased she was always so friendly and easy going, even with strangers.

It was after one o'clock and Rosa threw her hands up in dismay. "Look at me, listening to you talk and you with empty stomachs!" she scolded herself. "We will eat. Santo, you help?"

"Oh, let me," Krista insisted. "Can I at least set the table?" it means the world to me

Santo nodded and pointed at an antique sideboard behind the dining table. "Thank you, Krista, that's very kind of you. The silverware and anything else are in those drawers."

Ten minutes later, they sat down to Rosa's heavenly smelling lasagna. There was a side salad of romaine lettuce, plum tomatoes and crunchy croutons with homemade Italian dressing and homemade crusty Italian bread. It was a small feast but a truly delicious one and Krista, who loved authentic Italian food, had two huge helpings of the lasagna.

"She tends to eat a lot," Paul said dryly, mopping up the sauce with a slice of the bread.

"She's too thin," Rosa scolded, happily placing the second helping on her plate.

"She eats like a horse. What's that saying you have, Kris, when it's been more than an hour between meals?"

"My stomach thinks my throat's been cut," she dutifully responded, getting ready to tuck in. "Rosa, this is easily the best lasagna I have ever tasted. Thank you."

"I hope you have left room for her Tiramisu," Santo said dubiously. He couldn't quite grasp how someone who was so slender could eat so much. "It's to die for."

"I always have room for dessert," she said happily.

"And she's not kidding," Paul interjected.

Krista insisted on helping with the clearing up and when they returned to the living room, they had just settled with fresh coffee when the doorbell rang. Seconds later, Santo and Rosa's oldest son, Santo Junior, and third son, Antonio, came in from their shift at the gas company. They couldn't believe they were seeing Paul and greeted him like the long lost brother he was.

Rosa clucked around her chicks and Krista was once

again impressed by how close and loving the family was. Paul felt like he truly had come home, just as he had mentioned earlier, and he and Santo Jr easily slipped into a conversation about the New York Rangers mediocre performance this season. Not that many teams, in any sport, had been playing to their full potential because of the pandemic.

They chatted and laughed and grew serious again when Antonio asked what had brought Paul back to Brooklyn. When growing up, he had been the one closest to Paul because of their similar personalities and tastes and when Antonio heard of the pending trial, he, like his parents, immediately offered his help.

"Ay, you know, as a character witness or something," he'd said in this thick Brooklyn accent.

Paul thanked him for the offer and promised he would be in touch if he thought there was anything they could do.

The mood was lightened again and then, with regret, as late afternoon approached, Paul and Krista announced they should leave. The drive back to the city was going to be long and slow at this time of day.

They thanked Santo and Rosa for their kind hospitality and they all hugged tightly at the door, pandemic be damned, as they bid the Benetti family farewell. Although Paul had kept in touch over the years since leaving Brooklyn, sometimes a long time could pass between his calls or texts. Rosa and Santo were always glad to hear from him no matter how much time had passed and he knew their acceptance of how he lived his life was genuine. He vowed he would keep in better touch and keep them updated with how the trial was progressing. Krista backed him up by reassuring them she would make sure Paul phoned when he could.

In the car, they were still buzzing from the feel-good vibes and then, as they crawled along the Brooklyn bridge, Krista slipped her hand in his.

"Thank you," she said softly.

"For what?"

"For sharing your family with me. I love them and I love them even more for loving you."

He didn't need to say anything to that. Her words had said it all.

# CHAPTER FORTY-TWO

It took another two days of anxious waiting and endless text messages and calls between Paul and Harry before they got a result from the Romano maid. The only problem was, it wasn't the positive result they'd been hoping for.

The day before Christmas Eve, after breakfast and before Dave was scheduled to leave for yet another physical therapy appointment, Paul's cell phone rang and when he saw it was Harry Pedowski he answered it immediately. Within a few seconds, he knew he wasn't going to like the conversation but switched the phone to speaker so everyone could hear.

They had gone to the living room to let Hannah and George clear up in the dining room. Dave had been exercising and moving his arm in the way the physical therapist had taught him to do and he felt there was some improvement in the range of motion compared to the day before. Cathy was half watching him, half reading her Kindle. Krista was sitting on the window seat looking out at the city below, wishing she could be part of the hustle and bustle down there. The city had been forced into another lockdown mere days before but it didn't seem to stop anyone getting out and about for Christmas shopping in whatever stores remained open.

They turned as one towards Paul when they heard his phone being switched to the speaker and waited expectantly for what Captain Pedowski was going to tell them.

"It's not good news, Paul," Harry said. "In fact...I'm sorry, man, it's the worst."

"What is it?" Paul asked apprehensively. Already his heart was hammering against his ribcage and he didn't even know why yet.

"Consuela Espanoza was our contact in the Romano household," Harry said slowly.

It was Krista who picked up on it straight away as she got up from where she was sitting to come and sit beside Paul. "*Was*, Harry?"

"Exactly...sorry, don't know if that was Cathy or Krista because I can't tell the difference with your accent."

"It was Krista," Paul said. "Is she no longer working for them?" At the too long silence, Paul let out a groan. "Jesus Christ, they got her?"

"I'm afraid so. Her half-naked body was found early this morning down by the river. Time of death is yet to be confirmed but preliminary time was around eleven o'clock last night."

Paul pinched the bridge of his nose, his eyes closed tight as he tried to keep it together. "Cause of death?"

"Same as your sister, right down to the broken neck."

This time the silence was communal as they all tried to piece it together. Their emotions, already raw and overly sensitive were back on overdrive again.

"It's Cathy, Harry," she said, "did she leave any family?"

"A six year old boy. And a sister. We're trying to locate the sister to see if she has the boy. He wasn't at Consuela's residence. I'm really sorry, Paul - sorry to you all - I know you were counting on a positive result," Harry paused for a second, he hadn't told them the worst yet. "There's something else you need to know. There was a note taped to her body. I'll send pictures through after I hang up but the note said it all."

"Which was?" Dave asked.

"Nothing good. It said, 'Leave us alone, Cameron. You're not going to find what you're looking for'."

"Jesus..." Paul hissed. "They knew it was me who got Espanoza to do this?"

"Certainly sounds like it. Although how they could have known I still haven't figured out."

"You think you might have someone on the inside?" Krista asked.

"I haven't ruled that out, especially after the Romanos finding Paul's sister so quickly. Leave this with me, guys, I'm looking for answers and won't stop until I get them. Sorry I had to be the bearer of such bad news, I know how much you were counting on a positive result."

"Why can't we go after these people?" Dave asked in agitation. "What is it about them that keeps the cops from getting anywhere near them?"

"It started back in the nineties, the Brooklyn PD foiled a drug shipment coming in from Europe destined for warehouses belonging to the Romanos. The fallout was horrendous. The lead narc detective was murdered right in front of his seven year old daughter when he went to pick her up from school. The day after his funeral, the daughter was found at the babysitter's. Both were dead – broken necks – and a note pinned to the little girl's jumper said 'For every shipment you stop coming through, we will kill the ones responsible and their children.' Because of that threat – and we have no reason to believe it's an idle threat, we can't, and we don't, go near them."

"So we let them bring their drugs into this country, this city, and let them get distributed around the playgrounds and malls and street corners and Brooklyn PD can do nothing to stop it?" Paul cried in disbelief.

"We can't stop the Romanos. We have made a lot of headway cracking down on the dealers. It's not enough but it eventually trickles up to the Romanos and hurts their pockets. Hey, I appreciate your disgust, and I can see why you can't understand why we handle it this way, but there are a lot of children out there who have Brooklyn PD cops as their parents. Another way to look at it is an awful lot of Brooklyn cops have children. We're hoping we can just swoop in one day and throw the lot in jail. We're hoping the DEA, in conjunction with the FBI, can help us with that and there's every sign to indicate it's going to happen in the foreseeable future. In the meantime, we have no choice but to wait. Besides, what makes you think the Romanos are lying? Or trying to bluff? Do you really want us to take the chance?"

"No, I suppose not. But something you said the other day, about the Romanos having a judge or two in their back pocket...if the Brooklyn PD can't touch them, why would they need a judge?"

"They've committed other felonies, Paul. Misdemeanors too. A family like that will always need the services of a lawyer, which means they'll need the support of a crooked judge or two."

Paul locked eyes with Dave. They could hear the frustration in Harry's voice but couldn't fathom how a force as powerful as the Brooklyn PD hadn't been able to stop a family like the Romanos. This was a feud that had been going on for over twenty years and the Romanos still called the shots.

"I suppose you're right," Paul said evenly. He was trying to keep his temper in check and it was getting harder to do so.

"There's more," Harry confessed. "One thing Consuelo was able to relate back to us. She phoned me last night to tell me she had found some paperwork in the office – by what she said and what you told me previously, I think it was the one you were in that night, Paul. She couldn't talk loud, and she sounded scared, but she gave me a date of January fourth, in the new year. I got the feeling it was a docking date. Unfortunately, something spooked her before she could give me a name of the container ship. And probably not long after that call, the Romanos must have realized what she was up to. The rest you know."

"Yeah, and even if you did get the name of the ship, you're too afraid to do anything about it," Dave said.

"That's not fair, Dave."

"Neither is letting the Romanos bring their poison in to

sell to kids and ruin their lives."

A long silence followed and Paul could picture Harry on his end trying not to retaliate to Dave's words. Dave may have been harsh, but what he had said was sadly true. "I'm not disagreeing with you," Harry said eventually. "Let me know if you come up with a plan for an ideal world where people like the Romanos don't exist and drugs are no long available. Paul, I'll be in touch if I hear anything new."

Paul murmured a thanks and disconnected the call. He got up immediately and strode toward the window. Although he was looking out, he really wasn't seeing anything.

Dave put his sling on and went to stand beside him. "I'm really sorry, partner. I didn't mean to say what I did."

Paul nodded, his jaws clenching and unclenching. "You only said what I was thinking. Our investigation into the Romanos is now officially closed," he said tersely. "We've endangered our own lives too much and for our troubles have now got a second innocent woman killed."

Krista heard his words, as did Cathy, and they looked at him in dismay. "We can't leave it like this!" Krista cried. "There has to be something else we do. A court order, a raid, something."

He turned to look at her and sadly shook his head. "It's over, Kris. You heard how the Romanos control the cops. I can't have any more deaths on my watch."

"Did you want to wait a couple of days, see if Harry can come up with something else?" Dave asked.

"We can wait but I don't think he'll be able to come up with a new angle. Besides, it's Christmas day after tomorrow. It all depends on where you want to spend it?"

"That's up to you. I know Hannah would love to make Christmas dinner for us but if you want to get back to Bathville we can leave tomorrow."

"I'll think about it. I don't think I want to go back to Brooklyn. I'm done with that city, except to see Rosa and Santo. Don't you have an appointment you need to get to?"

Dave glanced at his watch. "Yeah, in half an hour. I'll ask George to take me." Cathy started to get up but he stopped her. "Keep Krista and Paul company, love," he said. "The less time we spend in public places, the better."

She understood his meaning. He wanted her to make sure Krista wouldn't take this latest setback hard and she gave him a soft kiss on his lips. "Just be careful. We'll be here for when you get back."

Fifteen minutes later, after Dave and George's departure, Cathy asked Hannah if she would mind bringing some coffee through to the living room. Paul had slipped into a pensive mood and Krista knew it was best to let him get his head around the situation in his own time.

He was grateful for the coffee, and the Christmas cookies Hannah had piled high on a plate. As he reached for his second one, he reached a decision for the immediate future. He knew by this time next year he might no longer be a free man so he might as well make the best of this Christmas while he could.

"Shall we tell Dave we would like to stay here for Christmas?" he asked Cathy.

She looked at him in surprise and then at Krista for her reaction. "I think he would love that. Krista?"

"Sounds good to me. Only…"

"Let me guess. No gifts?"

"For no one, not even Paul. The few bits and pieces I've been picking up since August are all up in Bathville."

"I think we're all in the same boat. I think we should check what Amazon has to offer and if we can get it delivered for tomorrow." Cathy looked in the direction of the kitchen. "I think also we should get something really special for Hannah and George, they have been so sweet and eager to make us feel welcome and comfortable while we've been here."

"Great idea," Paul agreed. "I hope Dave can give us a few clues on what to get them."

When Dave returned over an hour later, he found them

all still in the living room. Cathy was on her laptop, Paul and Krista were on their cell phones and each seemed in deep concentration.

"Hey guys," he greeted. He looked strained; the therapy today had been intense and had left him with a gnawing pain deep inside his shoulder. But he believed the therapist when he'd told him there was definitely progress being made and another appointment had been made for the next day.

Cathy quickly minimized the page she was on and jumped up to give him a hug. "How'd you make out?"

"Too bad I can't arrest a physical therapist for beating up on a cop," he said, sitting down and easing out of the sling. Sometimes it helped, sometimes it didn't. "What are all of you doing?"

"We were wondering if you would be on board to ask George and Hannah if we can stay for Christmas?" Paul said.

Dave looked at him in bewilderment. "Sure, but what made up your mind?"

Paul didn't want to mention it was because this could be his last Christmas as a free man and he wanted to make the most of it. But the murder of the young Nicaraguan woman had taken the wind out of his sails, as it would have even if he wasn't fighting to prove his innocence. It had hit him about half an hour ago how that young woman had died, leaving behind a six year old son. He didn't know their family or financial situation but he could only assume the little boy and his aunt would have a miserable Christmas. At six years old, the boy would be old enough to understand his mother was never going to be home again. There'd be no more mommy kisses, no more mommy hugs, no more Christmas presents from her. And no matter what anyone said, it was entirely his fault. He had been too enthusiastic at Krista's idea to get someone within the household staff to spy for him and they had paid the ultimate price for nothing. His eagerness to get some sort of result, *any* sort of result, had overridden his common instinct to protect the public, at any cost.

As he thought it all through yet again, and realizing Dave was looking at him, waiting for an answer, he gestured to Dave to come to the far corner with him so he could talk more openly.

"I want to repay your kindness for one thing, Dave," he said in a low voice. Out of the corner of his eye he saw Cathy and Krista had resumed their online shopping. Not that Amazon needed it but it certainly looked like their coffers were going to be boosted greatly from this one zip code today.

"My kindness? What are you talking about?"

"For everything you've done for me. I know how much you love George and Hannah, and they clearly worship you so I think it would be nice if you got to spend Christmas with them."

"That's very kind of *you*, partner. Thank you, I am sure they'll be thrilled to hear they'll have guests. Although, to be fair, I don't know what their plans are, I don't know if dear old dad gives them time off over the holiday so they can spend it with their family."

"Oh." Paul's face fell. "None of us thought of that. We just assumed they were here no matter what."

"It's no problem, I'll ask them if they have plans. If they do, the least we can do is let them keep them." Dave glanced at Cathy to see her studying her laptop screen. "I recognize that look. She's having a little bit of retail therapy, isn't she?" And then the penny dropped and he rolled his eyes. "For Christmas presents. Which I will have to take care of too."

"I tried to tell them we could wait until we got back to Bathville but my protests fell on deaf ears. I've at least told them not to finalize any orders until they know what address to get them sent to."

"Okay, in that case, let me go ask George and Hannah right now." Dave paused for a second to put his sling back on. It was getting on his nerves but it wasn't worth the nagging he would get from Hannah for not wearing it. He was about to turn away when a look came over Paul's face and he stopped to ask him what was wrong. Paul didn't seem to want to divulge but he didn't have to, Dave could read him like a book. "I know you're thinking about that little boy and how tough this is going to be on him."

"It sucks, Dave. I can't get it out of my head."

"What do you want to do? Have Harry get up a collection?"

"Oh yeah, that sounds really good," His voice dripped sarcasm. "'Here, little boy, sorry for getting your mom killed. Here's some money and some toys. Merry Christmas'. Yeah, real good."

Dave could take the sarcasm, what he couldn't take was the despair and self-loathing lurking behind Paul's eyes. "You know I didn't mean it like that, pal," he said gently. "Unfortunately Consuela Espanoza is collateral damage. All we can do is hope the little boy gets to stay with his aunt, if she's in the picture, or is placed quickly with a suitable, loving foster home."

Paul mulled over that but, although it had been the right thing for Dave to say, the words didn't make him feel any better. "I know…it's okay, I'm still trying to process all this. Go ask George and Hannah."

Dave found Hannah alone in the kitchen, adding something to a huge pot of soup simmering on the stove. "Smells good, Hannah," he said.

"It had better, it's your lunch," she chuckled.

"You know we're just about done with what we came to New York to do, don't you?" he said slowly, testing the waters.

Hannah laid the spoon down and turned to look at him in shock. "Does that mean you're leaving?" she asked.

"We were going to be leaving sometime," he reminded her. "What plans do you and George have for Christmas? You going to be with Zeke or Camella?" Her son and daughter, both of whom were a few years older than he was but he had grown up with them too and had nothing but fond memories of them.

"Zeke's out in California and because of these no household mixing or no flying to certain states rules, New York being one of them, he can't come home this year. Pretty much the same for Camella, she's in Michigan and can't come. As you know, she's a nurse and can't get any leave anyway. Too many sick people."

He could see the sorrow and regret in the old woman's eyes and his heart broke for her. He knew she hadn't seen her 'babies' in quite a while and, having always been a close knit family, it had to be hard on her. "Well, in that case, would you like to spend Christmas day with us? Here? And I bet Cathy would love to help you make dinner – she's very good in the kitchen – Krista too, for that matter."

She barely suppressed a squeal of delight and flung her arms around him, forgetting his injured shoulder area and only pulling away at his hiss of pain. "Sorry, Mr Dave, so sorry, but you gots me so excited now. Of *course* we'd love you to be here with us, we wouldn't have it any other way. You know we love you like one of our own and to spend the holiday with you..." She stopped and clasped her hands together at her chest. "You've just made an old woman very happy. But Miss Cathy and Miss Krista are not here to be in my kitchen, you tell them Hannah will be doing the cooking."

"They'll want to help but if it's this important to you, we'll figure something out. You sure now?"

"Positive. Thank you. I'll let George know, he was going to do a grocery shop online this afternoon so I'll make sure he orders plenty."

"Oh, that's great, Hannah. And make sure you charge this to my dad's account."

"I will. The booze too?"

"There's going to be booze?" Dave asked in wide-eyed innocence and earned another hearty chuckle from her. "Oh, which reminds me, as part of Paul's Christmas present, from me to him, could you ask George to ask the valet service to make sure the Ferrari is cleaned, polished and vacuumed for first thing Christmas morning? Paul would love to take it for a test drive so I'd like it looking the best for him."

"I will ask him and it will be done. Now shoo, I need to finish making lunch. Oh, and Dave?"

"Uh huh?"

"Thank you again for making an old woman happy. I know George will be tickled to death when he hears you'll be here for Christmas. This is great news. He and I thought we were going to be spending Christmas alone for the first time in years and now we won't be. You've made our day."

Dave kissed her smiling cheek and returned to Cathy and his friends to let them know Christmas was being spent on Park Avenue this year.

Krista got on the phone to Captain Hamilton to let him know of their plans. She had phoned him earlier to tell him about the Espanoza murder and he could tell from her tone how rattled they were. He had said then he would be glad to let them have a few days to regroup and hopefully come up with another plan of attack, but to confirm as soon as they could what they would be doing. Knowing they had his full support, she had promised their superior they would be home between Christmas and New Year's and that was all he'd needed to hear.

# CHAPTER FORTY-THREE

Christmas was as pleasant as it could be considering there was a world-wide pandemic, a loved one had been wrongfully accused of murder, and he had just buried his estranged sister and knew he was the one responsible for the death of an innocent woman. Not to mention a six year old boy was now an orphan. But it was still pleasant and it helped being in the company and loving arms of people who cherished him and wanted him with them.

Paul adored the ride in the Ferrari 812 Superfast. At Dave's mysterious urging, he went with Dave to the lobby and when he stepped outside and saw the beautiful car, shining and sparkling and waiting for him, he let out a whoop of joy. Now he could understand why Dave had barely been able to contain himself with excitement on the way down from the penthouse and Paul high-fived him in sheer happiness. It was still early in the morning and, although the sun was mostly up, the streets were relatively quiet. Dave handed him the keys and encouraged him to hit the highway once he'd gotten the feel of it around the city streets. The Superfast might be a luxury car, with its V12 engine and ability to do zero to sixty mph in under three seconds, but Paul still had to abide by the speed limit. But the sheer power purring underneath him as he cruised along the deserted streets was intoxicating and as soon as he hit the nearly empty interstate, he floored the accelerator. For a mile, anyway.

He took the first exit and double backed but it was clear

he was thoroughly enjoying the ride, whether at high speed or within the speed limit. When he reluctantly turned towards Park Avenue, he almost shyly asked Dave, if they were to come down here again, could he have another drive in what was now officially his dream car. Dave, who was delighted his friend was as thrilled as he was, was glad to tell him yes. Anytime he wanted.

After the thrill ride of his life, Paul tried his best to keep the festive spirit going, he really did. There were a few moments of genuine levity when he ate heartily of the feast Hannah had lovingly prepared, enjoyed the giving and receiving of gifts, drank the wine and beer "just to be polite" and grabbed Krista at random moments to kiss her under the mistletoe. She happily obliged, even when there wasn't any mistletoe overhead.

But when the day wound down, when he could be coaxed no more with cookies or candy, when even an ice cold beer sat untouched on the table, he wished more than ever his life hadn't taken the turn it had. Krista was so happy, spending time with Dave and Cathy, including George and Hannah as much as she could in anything they did, and the thought of losing her filled him with so much dread it was like a punch to the solar plexus. She was so beautiful, so sweet, so loving and so funny and she was his whole life and now...now he might have to give her up, perhaps for good.

When they retired to bed, he held her in his arms, smelling her special scent, feeling the softness and smoothness that was her. She knew he was standing on the rim of a deep, dark hole, and she understood why, and her heart broke into a million pieces. She had enjoyed the day very much. She had loved seeing Paul be so relaxed and seeming to have fun, despite his recent tragedies and personal loss. But for now, grateful it was just the two of them, she wanted him to talk, ease his burden by sharing with her what she knew anyway but what she wanted to hear from his lips.

He idly stroked her bare shoulder, unaware what she

was thinking. He wanted to talk but he didn't want to kill the relaxed mood.

"Just talk to me," she said eventually.

He couldn't help smiling. He should have known she knew what he wanted to do. "I nearly got him killed," he said.

It hadn't been what she'd expected but that was beside the point. "Who?"

"Dave."

"But you didn't."

"No, but that's the worst I've ever seen him get beat up. And all because he wanted to help me. I watched him today when I knew he wasn't looking, and I know he's still in a lot of pain."

"The physical therapy is definitely helping him."

"I know. But the painkillers aren't." He pulled her closer and entwined his legs around hers. "He has given so much of himself since this whole ordeal began, both monetarily and materially. And, of course, physically."

"He's your partner. You know he wouldn't have it any other way. He doesn't want anything to happen to you anymore than I do."

"I know. I just feel bad for him, I don't like seeing him in pain."

"Nobody does. We'll just have to remember he will get through this."

"He will. I need him to be in tip top shape."

"For what?"

"For looking after you when I'm not here."

She pushed herself up on one elbow and searched his face. She didn't want to resort to platitudes about his uncertain future but neither did she want him to start talking like that. "We have to have faith in the system," she reminded him.

"A system where our fellow cops lets the likes of the Romanos practice their own brand of the law? That's sick, Krista."

"It is. I've been wracking my brains, trying to think of a

way to get past their front door, without fear of retaliation, and I've come up with nothing."

"Yeah, we all have. Dave and I were talking about that last night. If we were to go back in, either undercover or right out in the open, the end result would be the same. If we get a warrant, to make it legal, then I can almost guarantee I have signed, sealed and delivered a death warrant on someone in the Brooklyn PD, or their family. I don't think I could stomach another death at my hands, it's bad enough there have been the two already. I don't want anyone else meeting their untimely demise. Besides, if they have judges in their back pockets, what judge could we trust to issue a warrant for us?"

She nodded pensively, her mind automatically turning towards a plan of attack. Nothing came to her. "Maybe when we get home we can talk with Jim and Mark, see if they've come up with something from the motel."

"Yeah, except if they'd found something, they would have called to let us know."

Krista flopped back down again and laid her head on his shoulder. Every time she thought of something, if no one else reminded her, she would realize the possible outcome would be nothing but *im*possible. Although she had tried her best to remain upbeat and positive, since Maria's murder she had felt her fortitude start to weaken, strand by delicate strand.

For the first time, she started to feel scared. Maybe she had been burying her head in the sand, maybe she had believed too much in the system, maybe she had even let herself be naïve and think no one could tear her and Paul apart. And yet, here they were, on Christmas night, maybe their last one together, trying to convince one another that not all was lost.

Although she tried hard not to, she started to cry soft tears that puddled on his shoulder and made him feel like his heart was being ripped out of his chest.

"Don't, baby, please," he said, drawing her close.

"I'm sorry," she said shakily. "I feel like we're all letting you down. We're supposed to be the power team in the seventh precinct and not one of us can help you."

He turned on his side so he was facing her and gently wiped away the tears. "No one's letting me down, least of all you and Dave and Cathy. I've been bowled over by how much you're all doing to try and save my hide. We might get lucky, we might find something, we just have to - "

" – remain positive," she finished for him. "Hey, how about we bite the bullet and give Romano senior a phone call? A good will gesture. Promise him immunity if we ask him if he was responsible for your dad's murder."

He looked at her slightly bemused. "It's not like you to think up something like a simple phone call will work."

"It's the best I could do. I think I shouldn't have had that last glass of wine."

"Oh, so now you're blaming the wine, huh?" He was glad she had at least stopped crying, but when he stole a glance at her he couldn't fail to notice how incredibly sad she looked. He also noticed another look about her, a look he had never seen on her before, a look he thought he never would. She looked defeated. She had exhausted every avenue, every thought, every probability and now knew she was beaten. There was nothing more she could give. He tamped down his despair and carried on with the conversation they had turned to. "Want me to go get you another glass? Or some other kind of nightcap?"

She considered his offer then shook her head. "No, I think instead I would like you to just hold me, and maybe, hopefully, please, you might want to give me some hot jungle-loving."

"A perfect end to Christmas day," he said, pulling her to him to kiss her deeply.

At the same time, across the East River, in Cobble Hill, Brooklyn, Julius Romano sat beside the crackling fire in his drawing room, swirling brandy around in a snifter in his hand. He watched the dark amber liquid catch the yellow and orange flames of the fire and was about to indulge in a sip when he heard the door softly open. Moments later, his sons Markus and Pieter were sitting opposite him.

Christmas for the Romano family had been subdued this year. Julius' wife was still in heavy mourning for their son Julio and Julius himself had spent the day withdrawn and morose. He looked at his two sons and knew they were waiting for him to speak.

"Did Consuela's sister take the money?" he asked gruffly.

"She did," said Pieter. "Half a million dollars to set up home for her and her nephew should go a long way."

"And she has no idea it was you who killed her sister?"

"None, she was too grateful for being given the opportunity to provide for the boy. She just assumed it came from us because we were Consuela's employer."

Julius nodded his satisfaction. "And Cameron?"

"Our source says he's still in Manhattan. As well as Andrews. You want us to take care of them tomorrow?"

"No, I've had a better idea. I'm sure they'll be returning to Massachusetts soon. I want our boys to go up there again, track them down – it shouldn't be hard if they're cops – and get rid of them. Let them be Massachusetts' problem, not New York's."

Pieter and Markus exchanged a look. They wouldn't question their father's change of plan. There was no need. The cops who killed their brother would be eliminated and that was all that mattered.

Pieter got up and poured himself and Markus a brandy. Then, with a *Salut!* they toasted one another, satisfied there was a now a plan.

# CHAPTER FORTY-FOUR

Leaving for home was difficult. It was two days after Christmas and they had exhausted every possible scheme for getting evidence against the Romanos. Harry had talked extensively with Paul on the phone, and the evening before had promised him he would continue to do his best to find a way to infiltrate the Romano stronghold.

Even though they had known all along Dave would be leaving soon, George and Hannah still took his departure hard. Dave had always hated goodbyes and holding Hannah in his arms as she cried sorrowful tears against his chest, he was reminded exactly why he hated them.

He knew their sorrow to be genuine and felt his heart swell with love. "I'm only a four-hour drive away," he reminded them solemnly. "And I'm always only a phone call or a Skype call away. I promise I won't leave it so long until the next time I see you. Thank you for looking after my wife, my friends, and me so well, I will always remember your kindness. Remember that I love you both."

"We love you too," George said, his brown eyes awash with tears. He had an arm around Hannah's shoulders, trying to comfort her when he needed comforting himself. "It is our pleasure to take care of you, anytime, David. And in the meantime, take care of yourself, no more getting that pretty boy face of yours messed up like that again. That's an order from old George here."

Dave drew him into his arms for one more hug then,

with one last look, he turned away, closing his ears to Hannah's soft sobs and trying not to recall the look of devastation on her warm, loving face.

The valet was waiting at the front entrance to help him into the car. Paul was driving and Krista was in the front with him. Dave had told them to sit together in the front so he would have more room to move about in the back if his shoulder caused him discomfort. They had all already said their goodbyes and expressed their heartfelt thanks to George and Hannah and the elderly couple had made them promise to return soon.

They got into Bathville mid-afternoon and stopped at Paul and Krista's apartment first, via the grocery store, where they got a few essentials. Cathy took over the driving to get her and Dave home and, ignoring his protests, carried their bags upstairs.

She tasked him with sorting through the mail and putting the groceries away while she unpacked. Hannah had thoughtfully done all their laundry, including Krista and Paul's, and thanks to that gesture, all she had to do was put their clothes away.

When she got downstairs again, she found Dave sitting on the sofa, staring moodily off into space. He hadn't bothered putting on the television, he hadn't even gotten himself a beer and she sat beside him to see what was wrong.

"They are such lovely people," he said after a few moments silence. "Hannah and George. I hope my dad pays them appropriately and will set them up for a happy retirement."

"They were so awesome," Cathy agreed. "When I was Skyping with mum and Avril on Christmas day, Hannah was cooing and laughing at our little niece. Catherine was taken with her too, there was no doubt."

Dave smiled at the mention of his niece. "I remember the look on Catherine's face. She's such a smiley child. And it was neat she remembered her 'Auntie Caftea'."

Cathy chuckled at how her twenty-month-old niece had

tried to say her name. The little girl didn't seem to have quite grasped they had the same name, just in a different way, but that was okay. Hopefully someday soon she would realize the connection and would be happy. "You want something to eat? Hannah sent home a ton of food for us. Turkey, stuffing, cookies, chocolate cake, ginger bread. I think she thinks we're starving up here. She gave the same to Paul and Krista."

"I'll get something later." He gestured for her to come closer and, since she would be leaning against the shoulder that wasn't injured, she slid in against him. "We'll go down at Easter, pandemic allowing. Maybe with this vaccine that's available now, we'll be back to normal by then."

"I would like that. You want to phone the captain and let him know we're back?"

"Not really, right now I'm enjoying just being with you."

"I'm anxious to get talking with him, and Mark and Jim. Jim's text this morning wasn't too encouraging but maybe next time when we're all together we can brainstorm better."

Dave lazily buried his face into her hair. He had a lot on his mind but being here with her like this, alone for the first time in a while, helped mellow him. He knew she was mulling over what Jim had texted that morning but his thoughts turned to something far more intimate. Since receiving the injuries to his groin at the beating in the Romano household, he hadn't been able to contemplate sex for the first week afterwards. His kidney and bladder infection hadn't allowed him to feel amorous and he accepted it was all part of the healing process.

Not once had Cathy tried to coax him, she had been very sweet, not to mention patient, understanding that he might not be able to perform to his usual high standards. The bruising to his genitals had taken a while to heal but he had to admit that now he could seriously contemplate a little bit of action. He wasn't surprised when even the very thought of making love to his wife again sent a reaction to his groin and, hiding a grin, he pulled her closer to him.

"Um...Cathy...?"

"Uh huh?"

"You know how you like to kiss things to make them feel better?"

"Huh?" She looked up at him in bewilderment and when she caught the naughty twinkle in his eye, she immediately picked up what he meant and the broad grin made her eyes crinkle. "Yes, I *do* like to kiss things to make them feel better," she agreed. "Do you have something that is hurting you?"

He could feel the sudden rush of blood and was relieved everything felt normal. "Yes. Something that's positively *swollen* right now...and..." He paused because her hand was already slowly lowering the zipper of his jeans. "And...uh...I wasn't sure if I would need a little bit of persuasion but... oh, sweet Jesus, don't stop...whatever you do, don't stop..."

All things considered, their first foray back to a normal sex life was better than either of them had anticipated.

# CHAPTER FORTY-FIVE

As it turned out, and not to anyone's great surprise, finding any new evidence to exonerate Paul had produced nothing. While they'd been in New York, Captain Hamilton had Jim, Mark and a couple of officers working solely on whatever evidence they had already gathered, following up on it, checking it was solid and making sure it would be admissible in court.

It took a few days poring over everything their colleagues had gathered but they soon learned everything that could possibly be checked had been checked. More than once. It was unfortunate they hadn't yet realized there was a major screw up in their investigations. That would be discovered soon and would set off another chain of unpredictable events. Nonetheless, knowing there was nothing new and no prospects of finding anything more was a bitter pill to swallow. It was just as hard hearing from Brooklyn that no one had been able to approach the Romanos, never mind get information that would help Paul.

New Year's Eve was a quiet affair. The usual outdoor festivities and gatherings had been canceled. With such a rotten 2020 now in their rearview mirror, but the pandemic still holding the world captive, no one was in the mood for celebrating. The new year started with a small pop rather than with a loud bang. Maybe 2022 would be better.

Or maybe Paul would see it in from the confines of a prison cell. Anything was possible.

Two weeks into 2021, Dave and Paul were in the captain's office, going over the evidence one more time. The whole country felt tense, anticipating trouble at the inauguration of the new president on the twentieth of January. The storming of the Capitol and the subsequent rioting on the sixth of January had stunned the nation and the world. And through all the unrest, Paul and Dave were still striving to clear Paul's name.

"The only thing I can suggest you do is you go back to the Blue Moon motel and get a list of everyone staying there the day of your father's murder," the captain said.

"We've done that," Dave said impatiently. "Jim and Mark have done that."

"I know, but there will be no harm in doing it again. Then follow up with the phone calls to the people who were staying there."

"Hasn't that been done too?" Paul asked.

"Yes, but when I looked over it this morning, not all the people have been marked off as having been called."

"I thought they had been," Dave said in surprise, "before we even went to New York. The list of names and the CCTV footage were all we had to go on so we covered it extensively. What went wrong?"

"A software error," the captain said and wouldn't divulge further. Which meant, in other words, either a breakdown in communication or someone hadn't followed through with instructions. And with the numerous people working on it, it was impossible to tell who had screwed up.

Paul and Dave looked at each other, deciding what to do. "It's your call, partner," Dave said.

"Might be a waste of time, but I'm willing to try anything. Where did you send Krista and Cathy?"

"A DV call came in a couple of hours ago. Not long after that it became a homicide."

Paul pulled a face at the mention of a domestic violence case. This was how this whole mess had begun, he recalled. The two little kids who had watched their mother getting beaten nearly to death by their own father. He couldn't help recalling how the scene reminded him so much of his own childhood. The poor little girl who had been sexually abused, as his own sister had been so many times. He also recalled feeling grateful that he had pulled himself away from all that and had felt confident that he'd never see his father ever again. And not long afterwards, as if that whole event had been a harbinger of doom, his father had shown up at his front door.

He forced his thoughts back to the here and now. "If they're tied up, we'll head out to the motel. You want to drive, Dave, see how your shoulder bears up?"

"I tried it from our house to the grocery store last night and it wasn't too bad. I did bring Cathy with me, just in case I made it there but couldn't make it back. As I told you yesterday, it's nearly healed and by this time next week it will be completely. I'd appreciate the practice so, because I'll have you with me this time, it should be fine. Come on, let's get going."

The drive from the precinct to the Blue Moon motel usually took about thirty minutes, depending on how much traffic there was getting across town. It wasn't exactly a direct route to the motel but once they crossed the bridge that took them to the west side, there was a relatively straight thoroughfare for a couple of miles and then just a couple of turns to the motel.

Approaching the six-lane toll bridge, Dave dug in the cup holder for the appropriate toll and joined the small line of cars waiting to pay the fare to cross the bridge. He was behind a white Buick Enclave and in front of a beat-up green Ford van, taking little notice of either vehicle. He deposited his token in the basket and revved up again but the driver of the Enclave obviously didn't know there was such a thing as a speed limit as it crawled out of the token lane at twenty miles an hour. Dave was forced to keep his speed down until the lane to his left cleared of traffic and he was able to pass the almost stationary Enclave.

He got up to fifty five miles an hour and stayed in the middle lane until he neared his exit. Behind him, the green van had mirrored his every move and, finally noticing it, Dave reckoned it was driving just a little bit too close for his liking. He picked up speed and when the van did the same, he frowned in suspicion.

Paul, who was looking over the list of names of the people who had stayed at the motel, hadn't noticed either the lane change or the increased speed. "The guy from the Yukon, Dave, hasn't it struck anyone as strange that if he were in a Winnebago, what was he doing staying in a motel? Maybe it would be a good idea to check out the campsites in the area, see if they were full, or even if they were open that late in the season. It's a long shot, but we have to try. Don't you think?" Getting no reply, he turned to look at his friend and saw his eyes were alternately fixed on his rearview mirror, then on his side view mirror and on the road ahead. "Did you hear me there, Dave?"

"Later, Paul," Dave said after a moment's pause. He had a really bad feeling about the green van. He had inched his speed up another five miles and it had too. He didn't think it wanted to pass; there was ample space between the flow of cars in the left-hand lane and they'd had plenty of opportunity to pull into it so they could get around him.

The rigidness of Dave's body, his death-grip on the steering wheel, the intermittent increase of speed and the hyper-vigilance in his eyes told Paul immediately there was something wrong.

"What gives?" he asked.

"Maybe nothing, but I think we've got company. Check out the green van in your side mirror."

From this angle, Paul could see the van clearly, including the blue and yellow license plate with the words Empire State on it. Although New York state license plates were far from unusual in Massachusetts, Paul somehow knew, as Dave did, this vehicle was trouble.

"He's right up your ass, Dave."

"Tell me something I don't know." Luckily the traffic had thinned considerably and, knowing there was an exit about a quarter mile ahead, Dave turned the wheel to ease himself toward the right-hand lane, floored the gas pedal and sped towards it at eighty miles an hour.

Unfortunately, the van did the same thing and, without warning, just as Dave had to decelerate as he merged onto the exit ramp, it rammed into the back of Dave's car, smashing the taillights and denting the bumper. Luckily the airbags didn't deploy but the unexpected impact sent Paul and Dave flying towards the window. Paul cracked his head on the windshield but wasn't harmed but Dave felt white hot pain radiate from his damaged collarbone down to his right hand.

He knew instantly he was in trouble but he also knew this assault wasn't over and he pushed the pain away to concentrate on keeping the car on the road.

# CHAPTER FORTY-SIX

"Sonofabitch!" Paul gasped. "You okay?"

The pain in his collarbone burned like fire but Dave nodded grimly. "Just peachy. Hope I can say the same for my car." They were nearing the end of the exit and he checked traffic coming from his left to see if they would be able to merge onto the road. Mercifully, there was no traffic in sight, but even as he thanked his lucky stars, the van rear-ended him again, this time with enough force to jerk the steering violently to the left. The pain came again, much worse this time and how he managed to straighten the car as it hit the road, he would never know. "Oh sweet Jesus," he hissed under his breath.

Paul took one look at Dave's trembling hand as he tried to hold the steering wheel straight and swiftly assessed their situation. "Blow this for a bad trip," he announced and snatched up the radio mike. "Control One, this is Bravo One, we're on highway 73 southbound just past exit 23, about a mile from the toll bridge. We are being slammed by a green Ford van, with New York plates CCI 2843, repeat, New York plates Charlie Charlie India, 2 8 4 3. It has rear ended us twice and is still in pursuit. Control One, send back up, repeat, send back up." He hung up and then, seeing how much pain Dave was in and still trying to keep control of the car, he cursed loudly. Making sure his gun was fully loaded, he twisted around, opened the passenger window and took aim at the windshield of the van. His finger stayed on the trigger until the clip was spent and, although his aim was true, thanks to their swerving and that of the van, not one bullet did any damage. He was about to put a second clip in and go for the tires when Dave yelled at him.

"Paul, I can handle the steering wheel but I can't handle the gear shift too. I need you to change gears for me in case I lose the grip in my right arm."

"It's really that bad?"

"Yes. Least of my worries. I'm taking the next right, it's quiet along there, might even be somewhere I can pull in. At least I can protect the other motorists if I can get off the highway. I can still do the gear shift right now. Can you check to see what ammo we have? I think there are spare clips in the glove box as well as under your seat. I'm pretty sure I have about half a clip in my gun."

"Think you'll be able to shoot?"

"I'll use my left hand if needed." Dave checked his rearview mirror and saw the van was still behind him, hot on his tail. He had gotten back up to fifty miles an hour but the car was shuddering badly and pulling to the right, making it difficult hold the wheel. He was in absolute agony but he had no choice but to do what he could to keep them from further harm.

Ahead about a hundred yards was an industrial park. A lot of the businesses were closed due to the pandemic and at the very end of the park, there was a temporarily abandoned construction site. Dave only knew about it because he had gone to one of the other businesses to get a part for his car, when 2021 was only a few days old.

"You going to the industrial park?" Paul asked.

"Good a place as any." Dave asked him to get his gun out of his holster and, with the safety off, placed it between his legs. Paul set a spare clip on the consul, if needed.

"Excellent choice, partner. Say when for the gear change."

As he pictured in his mind the layout of the industrial park, Dave deliberately floored the accelerator again. The car shimmied and protested but he kept his foot down and managed to put some distance between them and the van. He knew if he turned in to the park, then took an immediate right, he would be behind a building in a matter of seconds. He hoped the van wouldn't see his turn.

There was a dirt lane that took them back out to the main drag and, if the van saw him take the first right, then he could get back to the main road and head for the construction site. He had no way of knowing if the area had been cleared of machinery, equipment or building materials, or even if there would be gates across the entrance to prevent unauthorized entry or vandalism. They would find out soon enough.

The van had caught up enough to follow Dave behind the building so, speeding up as much as he could, he headed for the construction site. There was only a single barrier across the entrance. It wouldn't have done a thing to keep human traffic out but it meant he would have to ram it to keep going and hopefully get out of sight of the green van. Knowing Paul would realize he was going to have to ram it, they braced themselves as best they could. The barrier, which was thankfully made from wood and not metal, shattered on impact.

By the time it took for the van to get to the construction site, Paul and Dave had already abandoned ship and taken up separate concealed look out posts about forty feet from one another. The van screeched to a halt behind Dave's car and they watched expectantly to see how many people would get out. It was impossible to tell the number of occupants in the front because the windows were tinted black.

A full minute passed, a minute that drove Dave crazy waiting for something to happen. He knew better than to go near the van but he also knew the occupants were probably scoping the area, trying to see where Paul and Dave were hiding.

He saw Paul behind a stack of huge backhoe tires and figured he had sufficient cover. He was behind a pile of steel girders and, giving Paul a thumbs up, they turned their attention back to the van. Sooner or later, whoever was inside was going to have to make an appearance and why the lengthy delay, Dave couldn't imagine.

Another minute passed before there was any movement from the van. From their vantage points, Paul and Dave could see the driver and passenger doors, as well as the back doors. The back doors remained closed but the two front doors simultaneously opened and out stepped two black men. They kept behind the security of the bullet proof doors as they continued their surveillance.

It struck Paul and Dave at the same time that they were looking at two men who were almost an exact replica of one another. Twins, not quite identical but certainly close enough. They easily stood six foot eight, dressed the same in emerald green T-shirts, black jeans and heavy leather bomber jackets and between them carried over five hundred pounds of compact steel-hard muscle.

They didn't move away from the van and Dave and Paul saw they each carried fully automatic rifles with 30 round banana clips. The one who had been the driver looked at his brother and nodded. The brother gave a return nod and, with that, the driver shouldered his gun and started walking in Paul's direction. He let loose with a salvo that forced Paul to keep his head down.

The other thug came walking towards Dave, his gun firing in smooth, short bursts of three shots each. The sudden attack forced Dave to stay low. But now they understood the brothers had stayed in the van long enough to look for any slight movement, or shadow, or a small puff of dust rising, or a flash of sunlight glinting off a watch or a ring, or even footprints in the dirt that would lead them to their prey. Whatever it was that had given Paul and Dave away didn't matter anymore. What did matter was they were seconds from being discovered.

Dave was probably the one who had the least cover. He had nowhere to go if the hired killer made it all the way up to him. Paul was mere inches from a partly demolished wall but was high enough and had the remains of a roof over it. He could easily climb a pile of crates and hide up there if needed.

Dave looked over his shoulder and saw all he had was a pile of broken bricks and chunks of concrete to run to. He estimated the gunman was only about twenty feet away, which didn't give him much time to make a decision. He had to move, and move now.

He hurriedly checked to see what Paul was doing, saw he seemed to have plans of his own as he ran in a crouch to the wall and quickly and agilely climbed to the roof. He was still out of sight and the gunman firing in his direction hadn't seen him as he continued firing off to Dave's right.

There were gaps in the pile of girders that had let a few bullets through, narrowly missing Dave. He waited until the gunman was within ten feet and then, dashing towards the bricks, he landed behind them in a rolling motion, just as the gunman fired directly at him. His shoulder screamed in agony when he landed on a piece of concrete but at least he hadn't been shot.

Paul, from his vantage point, needed only a second to sum up Dave's situation and saw he'd have to help him. The gunman coming after him was now close enough that Paul could easily take him. The only problem was, he had seen Dave drop, just as his gunman opened fire on him and Paul automatically assumed Dave had been hit.

Outraged, he stood up and as soon as he knew his pursuer had seen him, and was turning towards him, Paul pulled the trigger on his Glock and fired repeatedly until the gunman fell. Paul had no way of knowing if he was wearing protective gear and he jumped to the ground and crouched low to run to where the gunman was lying. Paul kicked the AK-47 out of the way but knew without having to check the man was dead. A bullet had caught him in the throat, severing his spinal cord, his aorta and pulverizing the base of his brain. He was staring sightlessly up at the gray-blue sky, his final vision.

All this happened in less than ten seconds and Paul was doing everything by sheer reflex. He couldn't see Dave's gunman so he figured now would be a good time to check on Dave.

When he got to him, he let out a moan of despair. Dave was lying on the ground, on his stomach, his head turned to one side. His eyes were open and he was looking in Paul's direction but there was no light in them, they were flat and dull. He didn't appear to be breathing.

Facing one of his worst nightmares, Paul choked down a cry of panic but, before he had a second to check on the whereabouts of the other gunman, he heard a recognizable click behind him. He turned slowly, to stare into the face of death in the form of a huge black man holding a submachine gun aimed right at him.

# CHAPTER FORTY-SEVEN

The tension in Captain Hamilton's office was palpable. The least of his worries at the moment was that it was getting late and he hadn't had time to call Cora to tell her he might not be home for supper. Ever since he received the phone call, he hadn't had time to do anything except make arrangements, so God only knew when he would get out of here.

He got up from behind his desk and went over to the window to see what was happening in the outside world. It was a bitterly cold, snowy afternoon and darkness was starting to close in. He instinctively shivered, a shiver fueled by rage, fatigue and tension.

He looked back at his desk when his phone rang and he hurriedly grabbed it. "Captain Hamilton."

"Detective Andrews, please," came a request spoken in a heavy Brooklyn accent. "Or if he's not available, Detective Cameron."

The captain knew intuitively this was what he had been waiting for. "Who's calling?"

"The Bathville Post. We're following up on a tip that two detectives from the seventh precinct were found dead over on the west side and I would just like to confirm it for the morning edition."

"What names were you given?"

"Uh...we weren't given any names. Just that two detectives from the seventh precinct were found dead. My contact advised me to ask for Detective Andrews or Detective Cameron to get information."

"Who's your contact?"

The caller pressed his lips tightly together. He clearly hadn't expected to get asked so many questions. "I'm not at liberty to say. Can I ask to whom I'm speaking?"

"This is Captain Bob Hamilton."

"Then you have the authority to give me the names of the detectives killed earlier today. Or can you put me through to either Detective Andrews or Cameron?"

"I might have the authority but I can't give out information like that, particularly over the phone. You didn't even give me your name."

"I understand, sir. I should have introduced myself right away. My name is Dominic Delaney."

"Okay, before I tell you anything, who gave you the tip?"

"As you have already said, I can't give out information like that – I have to protect my sources."

The captain let the silence play out nice and slowly. "Then this phone call is over."

"Wait...I...uh...well, I just got this job a couple of weeks ago, it would be a huge favor if you could give me a scoop like this. I have been out of work since February last year, thanks to the virus, and as this would be my first real assignment. A little cooperation would be very important to me. I'm trying to impress the editor, but if you help me, I promise I won't quote your name."

The captain let the silence draw out again. "What's your name again?"

"Dominic Delaney, sir."

"And the name of your editor?"

"Clinton Helford."

The name of the editor at the Bathville Post was Jesse Duncan. The captain knew him personally. "Very well, Mr Delaney. The officers you asked for, Detective Andrews and Detective Cameron, were the ones who were killed in the line of duty today, around two thirty in the old Green Lake Industrial

Park on the west side of the city. Their killers are still at large."

"I see. How were they killed?"

"No more questions. Thank you." Captain Hamilton disconnected the call and looked solemnly over at the two other people who were in the office with him. "Well, boys, think that covers your ass?"

Paul looked expectantly at Dave and nodded. "I think so. And if Pedowski is correct, every single one of the Romanos will be rounded up by this time tomorrow, which should keep them away from us for good. I knew the bastards would be seeking retribution for me killing one of them and I'm glad we were able to outsmart them. Thanks for the idea, Captain, letting them believe we had been eliminated."

"From what you've told me, you very nearly were. Good for you, Cam, you got to pull your trigger first."

"Reflex action, I had no other choice. It was him or me. I got his brother first, they split up to go after us individually. When they started ramming Dave's car, I saw the New York Plates on it and called for backup. Have they been identified yet?"

"The plates on the van have been traced to DeShon Yates of Brooklyn, New York. The IDs on the bodies belonged to twin brothers, DeShon and Clarence Yates."

Paul recalled the moment he had stared down the barrel of the machine gun, the eyes of the man holding it cold and murderous. Paul didn't know which twin he had shot first but eliminating the second shooter had been nothing short of miraculous. One more nanosecond and he would have been dead.

"How did the authorities manage to get the Romanos?" Captain Hamilton asked.

"Stroke of genius, coupled with sheer luck, if you ask me," Paul said. "The containership that the housemaid, Consuela Espanoza, caught sight of on the paperwork she was going through, was supposedly coming in around January fourth. Apparently, it's been on the Coastguard's radar for a while. A raid was done jointly by the DEA and the FBI as soon as it docked, drugs amounting to a street value of over twenty million were seized, one of the crew squealed and that was all that was needed. Once the Brooklyn PD knew the raid had gone public, they were relieved it was the Feds making the arrests. It's only happening now because the crew member who gave the information didn't want to talk and it's taken ten days for him to finally confess what he knew about the Romanos. So that's the end of them and not a day too soon. Oh, and the crew member who spilled the beans is in a safe house until he can get anonymous passage back to his homeland of Estonia. His name won't be released so the Romanos will never know who to retaliate against."

The captain shook his head ruefully. "I just wish the Brooklyn PD hadn't been so pussy about not making any arrests sooner. It goes against everything I, as a cop, believe in, as I'm sure it does with you, too. But I understand that if the threats against the cops and the cops' families were real, why they wouldn't want to tempt providence."

"Although I understand the Brooklyn PD wanting to preserve the lives of their officers and their families, that doesn't mean I agreed with it," Paul said solemnly. "It was no secret the Romanos called all the shots and made the whole Brooklyn police department look lame. However, the Romanos didn't have anyone in their payroll within either the DEA or the FBI. I could understand the FBI not being involved but if I had been the Romanos, I would have had the Drug Enforcement Agency under my thumb in no time. That was to their detriment. At least they're off the streets, Bob, and I don't think any amount of blackmailing and threatening the authorities this time is going to get them out anytime soon. It's all thanks to Consuelo Espanoza. She tipped us off about the container coming in. It's unfortunate she was collateral damage and my heart still breaks for her son. I hope the Brooklyn PD sets up a college scholarship for him. I know the Romanos gave the sister a large sum of money to help provide for the boy but I still hope the Brooklyn PD does the right thing."

The captain nodded thoughtfully. There was more to this story but he had the essentials and that was all he needed for now. "What about your car, Dave?"

"The insurance company called for a tow truck and it's at a garage now waiting for the adjuster. The chassis is shot to hell, I've a feeling I'll be looking for a new car soon."

The captain cocked his head to one side and looked at his detective in concern. "You feeling okay, Dave? You don't look too good."

Dave absently wiped a trickle of sweat from his jawline. For the past hour and a half, while talking with the insurance company and then waiting for Paul to speak with Harry Pedowski to feed information to the Romanos that he and Paul and been killed, his right shoulder had been in the worst agony of his life. He knew the collarbone was either dislocated again, or broken and he had hidden the pain as best he could. Only the thin film of perspiration on his face was solid proof of the strain of trying to hide the pain.

"You're very pale, Big D," Paul commented. "You sure you're okay?"

Dave nodded briefly and arose to go to the water cooler. He felt light-headed and bordering on nausea and he hastily downed a couple of cups of water to see if they would make him feel better. They didn't, so to divert his mind off his dilemma, he tried to think of something to say. "Where's Cathy, captain?"

"Huh? You asked me the same question just before that pseudo reporter phoned and I told you she should be back within the hour. You *sure* you're okay?"

Dave turned slowly to look at the captain. He was dimly aware Paul was looking at him in bewilderment and, realizing he had just asked the same question twice in less than five minutes, he tried to laugh it off. "Mustn't have been listening, Cap. Sorry, won't let it happen again."

Paul went over to him. Without thinking what he was doing, he tugged lightly on Dave's right arm. "You'd better come and sit down before you fall down, partner. You look as if you're about to keel over."

Which was exactly what Dave did. Paul's innocent pulling on his arm had brought the pain alive all over again and the slight touch nearly sent him into orbit. He could feel what little strength he had left slowly drain away.

He had managed to keep the pain hidden from Paul ever since Paul killed the second gunman. He had been in a daze when he'd heard a gun go off in proximity of where he was lying on the ground and he hadn't even been fully aware Paul had saved his life. He had managed to act as normal as possible when Paul helped him to his feet but the pain had been horrendous and didn't show signs of abating.

Dave wiped absently at his jawline when another trickle of sweat run slowly down his face but the movement caused another flare of pain. At that moment he knew he could hide it no longer and, although he tried to remain standing, he lost that particular fight. Feeling as if he was spiraling slowly down a chute, he lost the power of his legs and collapsed slowly to his knees.

The jarring motion as he hit the floor caused the pain to sprint up his right side and center on his collarbone. His mind was still alert, he knew what was happening and for some crazy reason, he felt he owed Paul and the captain some sort of explanation about his antics.

He was swaying slightly, trying to stop the world from spinning out of control, and he knew they were looking at him in alarm. "I sort of forgot to mention that when I ran from those girders to the pile of bricks, I skidded on something on the ground and ended up falling really hard. It wasn't a controlled fall, the way we've been taught, ya know? Clumsy horse's ass that I am. Something happened...something..." He trailed off, knowing he was losing what little bit of lucidity he had left.

Paul had already crouched down beside him, if only to prevent him from falling face forward. "What happened, Dave.

Did you fall on something sharp or bang your head?"

Dave chuckled and it sounded distant, unnatural; he sounded like he was on the brink of hysteria. His eyes focused briefly on Paul's face. The shadowy figure looming behind Paul had to be the captain. Or maybe it was the Angel of Death because right now, even death would be a welcome respite. "No, nothing like that. Hard head, remember?" He paused and gasped, his face pinching up in agony. "It happened again, Paul," he said and even to his own ears his voice sounded abnormal, like it was coming from far, far away. "Uh...my collarbone. Worse than before. Some big drag, huh?" And with that, he slumped against Paul's chest and passed out cold.

"Terrific," Paul snapped, "just terrific. Bob, call an ambulance. I'd rather medics try to move him in case I do more harm than good. I'm happy to hold him like this and I hope it keeps him comfortable." Paul steadied himself and held Dave against him, carefully turning his right side away from any possible contact. "How the hell did he keep this quiet anyway? He started having problems during the car chase but he swore when we were waiting for the squad car to come pick us up that he was fine. His stubbornness comes shining through once again and I'm going to kill him for keeping this quiet."

"The ambulance is on its way," the captain said, hanging up the phone. "I'll get a hold of Cathy. By the time it takes for her to get across town, he'll already be at the hospital."

Dave was in the process of being attended to when Cathy and Krista rushed into the Emergency Department of Bathville Memorial Hospital. Paul was in the waiting room and stood up as soon as he saw them.

"I'm sorry, Cathy," he said, giving her a hug.

She stiffened in his arms, pulling her head back so she could look him in the eye. She wanted an explanation, not his apology. "What the hell happened?"

"It's kind of a long story. Sorry, but I can't talk about it here. And you know what I mean by that."

She nodded reluctantly. He wanted them to be away

from eavesdroppers, unintentional or otherwise. "Can I at least see him?"

"In a little while. Only one person, Covid restrictions."

She nodded again, her chin trembling as she fought off tears. There had been too many hospital admissions, too many injuries and too many uncertainties about Dave's recovery over the last sixteen months. Every hospital stay brought the memories of his coma and the trauma he had gone through flooding back. Every time she heard he'd been injured, her first worry was if it had been a head injury. Being his clavicle again didn't make it any easier to accept. He was hurt and she didn't like it. She didn't know how much more abuse his body could take. He was as strong as an ox but even he had a breaking point and she had to be mindful of that. Problem was, she had no control over what happened to him, she couldn't stop the danger or the injuries any more than she could turn the tides. She could only hope, for the future, he would be less inclined to jump right into a potentially harmful situation.

There were only three other people in the waiting area and they looked like they were getting ready to leave. When they did, she gestured to Paul and Krista toward a quiet corner and she looked at him expectantly. "There's no one else around, Paul. Please just tell me what happened."

Knowing she wouldn't let this one go, he sighed in defeat. Catching a warning look from Krista, he took hold of Cathy's hand. "We were on our way to the Blue Moon motel and we picked up a tail. We were rear ended a couple of times on the highway..." He gave her and Krista the précised version but he didn't leave any major points out. He didn't hesitate in telling them how close he and Dave had come to getting shot and killed. And then, unable to hide his satisfaction, he told them about the call from Pedowski about the Romanos were going to be arrested thanks to the drug shipment being seized. "*Some* good came out of this mess, huh?"

"Some," Krista agreed. "But poor Dave. How on earth could he have kept his injury quiet? He must have been in so much pain and yet he didn't say a word?"

"I'm sick of this!" Cathy exclaimed. "I'm sick of him getting hurt. He's had enough to deal with over the last three weeks to last him a lifetime and I'm just so sick and tired of it."

"Hopefully this will be a cooling off period for him," Paul soothed. "He's going to be out of action for at least a month. In that time he might learn to enjoy life in the slow lane."

Cathy raised a skeptical eyebrow. "And I might suddenly grow another six inches."

"I get your point." He stroked her gently under the chin. "Extra height - it wouldn't look good on you, little dude."

"Neither would Dave sitting on his arse getting flabby on me. You think I love him for him? I love him for his body."

He silently praised her for trying to be upbeat and smiled gently. "For a million bucks, I'll promise not to tell him you said that."

"Wait until my in-laws croak it, then I'll take you up on that." She caught movement down the corridor and turned towards it but there was no one coming towards her and her eyes clouded over. "I wonder how he's doing? How long has he been away, Paul?"

"Half an hour, give or take."

"I wish someone would come and tell me how he is."

"Soon, Cathy," Krista consoled. "Don't worry."

A doctor who looked as if he was barely out of puberty came along five minutes later, but despite his diminutive stature and baby face, he projected an air of authority. After establishing who Cathy was, he started to lead her down the corridor but she hung back, looking hesitantly at Paul.

"You go, sweetie," he obliged. "We'll be right here if you need us."

"Thank you. I'll try not to be too long because I know you want to see him too." She gave a shrug of uncertainty. "If they'll allow another visitor, that is." She hurried after the doctor, who remained frustratingly tight-lipped about Dave's condition. All he was willing to divulge was that Dave was being kept under observation in a quiet room, where they were going to now.

Before they entered the room, another doctor came out. He was older and taller and looked tired but he offered Cathy a sympathetic smile as he took off his glasses to talk to her. He told her that Dave had had to be put under a general anesthetic to enable successful relocation of his clavicle. He informed her the anesthesia had been in Dave's best interests because he was in so much pain. They couldn't put him through the torture and trauma of relocating it while he was awake.

Cathy listened carefully when he went on to say that Dave would have a tough recuperation ahead of him. He would have to wear a sling at all times, attend physical therapy, again, for the soft tissue and muscle trauma and, above all, rest and do whatever exercises he was given by the therapist. If he could refrain from anything strenuous for at least a month he should have a complete recovery.

And then, at last, she was allowed to see him. She walked towards his bed and the nearer she got to him, the more she was able to see the bruising and swelling at the base of his neck. It extended over his shoulder towards his back and down the front towards his chest. He looked like he was just sleeping, albeit in a very deep sleep, and she looked for guidance at the nurse who had been smoothing his bedclothes.

"Will he be like this for much longer?"

"He's already started to wake up so it won't be too long now. Talk to him, if you want, he should be able to hear you and respond. I'll be back in a few minutes to see how he's doing." She checked one more time to make certain the blood pressure cuff was attached properly to the monitor and the saline drip was flowing properly. Satisfied all was as it should be, she turned away to give them privacy.

Left alone, Cathy didn't know what to say to him, so she lifted his hand and stroked it gently. "Hey, Dave," she whispered into his ear after a minute or two had passed. His eyelids had fluttered open once or twice but they hadn't remained open for long. "Can you hear me, sweetheart?" His answer was to feebly squeeze her hand and she smiled. "Paul and Krista are right outside, they will hopefully be allowed to see you in a little while. I'm not sure how long you'll have to stay here for, but hopefully they'll let you home this evening." She leaned over and kissed him gently on the forehead. "Don't try to move, honey, just stay the way you are."

Dave came out of the anesthetic an hour or so later but, although lucid enough to answer questions and tell them how he felt, he was still groggy. He expressed a desire to get home, he definitely didn't want to stay in the hospital overnight and, because he hadn't come in with head trauma, the doctors were happy to release him. These days, hospitals needed all the empty beds they could get to cope with the number of patients being admitted with Covid. Although in the past it would have been prudent for Dave to stay at least overnight, because he was showing no signs of shock or trauma, and was responding appropriately to conversation and other interactions, they were happy to release him. Understandably, they requested that if he showed any signs of shock or reaction to the anesthesia, that he promised he would come back in immediately. Knowing Dave wouldn't promise to such a thing, Cathy promised for him.

His pain was being controlled by strong painkillers but he couldn't move his arm without assistance. Once home, Paul helped Cathy undress him and get him into bed. It wasn't easy but they managed it together.

He was propped up on a lot of pillows and a glass of water with a straw and some painkillers to ensure a restful night were beside him on the bedside table.

It was hoped he would sleep through the night and for once, he was happy to oblige.

# CHAPTER FORTY-EIGHT

By mid-February 2021, Covid was still dictating the pace of everyday living around the world. Courthouses were as much affected as anywhere else, with trials being pushed back as the justice system frantically tried to clear the long waiting lists that had accumulated over the pandemic riddled months.

Paul's indictment should have taken place a month before but because of the waiting lists, it wasn't until February sixteenth when he learned a grand jury had forwarded his case to the Superior court.

As per Ted Reynold's constant warnings, he had expected that. Nikoli Ardolino had busted his balls to ensure the twenty-three members of the public who made up the grand jury would unanimously cast their vote for the case to go to Superior court.

When Paul came out of the indictment, he felt deflated. To give him his dues, Ardolino had presented the grand jury with sufficient evidence to leave no doubt the trial should go ahead.

Paul had met with Ted prior to the indictment and then again afterwards and he couldn't understand why Ted seemed so upbeat. Ted tried his best to explain why Paul should remain upbeat too. Paul, usually an upbeat kind of person, couldn't feel it.

"Ardolino is building his case based mainly on Gabriella Rossini's statement. The longer this drags out, the more her recollection of events is going to fade. When I get the printout of her next statement, I'm going to check it for consistency. I have a paralegal who is excellent at proofing and he will see if she's changed anything. If it remains exactly the same, it will hint at her being coached."

"All *we're* working on is a pair of ripped jeans and accounts from people who were at the motel who claim they didn't see anything."

"Did Captain Hamilton get that sorted? There was something about people having been recorded as giving statements when actually not as many people had, or they were incomplete?"

"Yeah, it was a mess but we got it sorted eventually. We did follow up phone calls even on the ones whose statements we already had, and they matched, but some people didn't seem to remember seeing anything that day. We can't get a hold of a couple of people but we'll keep trying. Otherwise, what else do we really have, Ted? Our trip to New York over Christmas was a complete waste of time, resulting only in Dave getting seriously hurt. We know without a doubt the twin gunmen who rammed us on the highway then opened fire on us at a disused building site before trying to kill us were on the Romanos' payroll but we can't question the twins because they're dead. The only hope we'll have is when the Brooklyn PD or the FBI seize the records on the Romanos' employees, but I have a feeling there are a lot of off-the-books employees who don't appear on those records and any records they do have will have been well and truly laundered. The Romanos, despite being behind bars, are no doubt relishing the thought that we won't find anything to incriminate them, even though *we* have no doubt it was his thugs who killed my dad. We just won't be able to prove it and that's the hardest pill to swallow."

"Have you checked any traffic cams around the motel for pictures of the green van the gunmen were in?"

"Yes, but although there were plenty of green vans on the road, some of them being driven by a black guy with a black passenger, some of the license plates or partial plates were obscured so we can't track them down. There were a couple of partial plates but they were a dead end when we followed up on them but we couldn't tie any of them in with the Yates' van plates. Brooklyn PD was able to inform us that the green van belonging to those guys was caught using the EZ Pass heading north, the day before they arrived here. State police have clocked them on the I-95 North after leaving New York, then into Connecticut and Massachusetts. We're still trying to figure out how they managed to find us but I suppose the Romanos knew we're cops so it was just a matter of them waiting for us to come out of the precinct."

"Any evidence found in the van?"

"It's been stripped and thoroughly searched. Apart from a damaged bumper when it hit Dave's car repeatedly, it was pristine. We found nothing that would tie them in with having been with my dad. Then again, it's been three months since my dad's murder so we can only assume on the day of the murder the van was thoroughly washed to clean away anything they might have tracked in from either my dad or the motel room. They didn't put my dad's body in the van so there was no need to use Luminol to check for blood and there wasn't any trace of his DNA. We didn't even find traces of blood on the front floor mats or the gas or brake pedals."

Ted nodded grimly, his good spirits momentarily eclipsed by the cloud of uncertainty Paul had been living under. There had been nothing but dead ends and bad luck so far and, knowing how used Paul was to achieving a result to help a case, Ted could appreciate how frustrating this all had to be. "I always believe we will find that one piece of evidence we need. It has always happened, in any case I've ever worked on. This one isn't going to be any different."

"When do you think I'll have to give my deposition?"

"Anywhere from thirty days to six months. All depends on Covid."

Paul looked away sadly. He had just had a flash-back to the day the twin gunmen had followed him and Dave. Although the events of that day had been bad enough, it was how Dave had suffered afterwards that still bothered him. Dave's shoulder had been more damaged this time than the first time in New York and now, five weeks on, he was only just beginning to respond to physical therapy.

Paul would never forget the pain on Dave's face when he collapsed in the captain's office. He had hidden it so well but even he hadn't been able to fight it any longer. All Paul could hope for was that the physical therapy would continue to improve Dave's chances of a full recovery.

"At least we've all been given our vaccinations. One good thing about police officers being considered first responders."

"That's good. Hopefully when the rest of the world has had the shots we can return to some form of normality. If it's a new normal, maybe it will strongly resemble the old normal."

"Indeed." Paul glanced at his watch. He wanted to get home to Krista and he knew he would find Dave and Cathy there too, all anxiously awaiting his return so they could hear how the indictment had gone.

They hadn't been expecting a miracle that told the trial had been canceled and they were somber as they listened to Paul tell them what had happened. Krista tried to hide her dismay, they all did, but now they were one step closer to the trial with no positive news to turn their prospects around.

They were sitting in the living room and Paul watched as Dave got up and went into the kitchen. At first he thought his friend was going for a drink or a snack and he got up to follow him to see if he needed a hand.

He found Dave supporting his bad arm with his other arm and grimacing in pain. He was staring out the window, his face pinched but he tried to act normal when he realized Paul had come in behind him.

"Hey, Paul, was just going to get myself a glass of water."

"You can have a beer if you like. Not that you have to ask."

"I know. Don't feel like one but I'll definitely take a rain check." Dave looked down at the sling and pulled an expression of distaste. "Can't wait to get this stupid thing off."

"I'm sure. Any idea when?"

"The therapist today said maybe next week. He gave me new exercises that will help strengthen the muscles and ligaments around the injured area."

Paul relaxed a little bit on hearing that. If Dave was at a PT session today, it would explain why he was in pain again. The treatment always seemed to aggravate him but by tomorrow it should have calmed down. "You spoke with Captain Hamilton recently?"

"I was at the precinct today. Cathy drove me. I'm still waiting on new wheels – not that I could drive yet anyway. That's another thing the therapist said should be back by next week. I spoke with the captain and asked him to look into me coming back to work...even on desk duties. Anything. I'm going crazy at home."

"And is he going to?"

"He told me he would after he hears how I get on next week."

"That's fair enough. I've missed you in the precinct, it's not the same."

Dave gave a slight smile. "With Krista and Cathy there, you're out-numbered. Too much estrogen, not enough testosterone."

Paul would have smiled at that, but he was still subdued after the meeting with Ted. "Sure you don't want a beer?"

"Thanks, but no. Ted give you any indication when your deposition is going to be?"

"Next thirty to sixty days" Then, after an awkward pause, he added, "Or up to six months. It all hinges on Covid. And after that, who knows when the trial is going to happen. Maybe by this time next year I'll either be a free man, able to get on with my life... or maybe I won't."

Dave turned to look moodily out the window. "This

can't all have been for nothing," he said. "All we've done, all we've been through, the leads that went nowhere, the phone calls, the hassle, the having to deal with the likes of Nikoli Ardolino, my car getting totaled, your sister and another innocent woman getting murdered, this all has to mean something."

"Hey, look at it this way: At least I got to meet up at last with the family who was my surrogate family when I was growing up. You got to see two very kind, lovely people who were almost like surrogate parents to *you*. You also got to show us how a rich life can be quite nice sometimes – I mean, Christmas on Park Avenue, anyone? – and, I have to admit, very easy to get used to. And as for that ride in the Ferrari...man, that was *fine*."

Dave shot a glance at his friend, a smile hovering on his lips. "Look at you being all positive."

"Have to be, partner. Most of all, I got to find out just how deep your loyalty is. I couldn't have done any of this without you. You've kept me from giving up, from throwing in the towel, you've made sure Krista is always being looked after when I'm not around. That alone helps me accept what might be my fate. I won't have to worry about her when I'm in prison. I'm not always positive, but it helps me feel better when I am."

Dave shifted his sore arm and pressed his lips together in pain. "If you're convicted, we won't stop trying to clear your name, you know that, right? It won't be the end. That's a promise."

Paul nodded slowly. "Thanks, partner, you just gave me the warm and fuzzies."

Dave chuckled. "I have that effect on people. We going to order some food or are you going to let a brother starve?"

"We're going to order some food. Let's see what the ladies want, we'll tell them what we want and then we'll get what they want anyway."

\*\*\*

Dave didn't get back to work until ten days later. He was still attending physical therapy but his sessions had been reduced to twice a week, instead of three times and he could feel the improvement and benefits of the therapy. He was able to go longer and longer without wearing the sling but he was still barred from driving because he couldn't use his right hand properly to change gears. The physical therapist suggested he consider a car with an automatic transmission and Dave had to tell him no, absolutely not. The only way he would drive a car was with a manual shift, claiming he had more control over the vehicle. The therapist merely rolled his eyes in semi-amusement.

He put getting a new car on hold so he could do proper test drives and was, for now, content to have Cathy, Paul or Krista take him wherever he needed to be.

When he arrived at the precinct, he was greeted fondly by Jim and Mark but he couldn't fail to notice there were a couple of colleagues who were deliberately ignoring him. Not knowing what he had done, especially since he hadn't been in the precinct much since the new year, he didn't particularly care to find out and sat down at his desk. It felt good to be back and when Jim and Mark came over after a few minutes for a chat, life began to feel familiar and normal.

"What's biting the guys this time?" he asked Jim.

"Holden decided to stir things up again when he heard you were coming back today. You know, about your rich father and the money you were able to get just by lifting the phone?"

"What? He's still hung up on that? What the hell is his problem?" Dave looked in Holden's direction and saw the older detective shooting the evil eye at him. He shook his head in faint amusement. "God help him if he has nothing better to do with his life."

Mark glanced in Holden's direction and curled his lip. "He's a jackass. If he bothers you, or says something, do us all a favor and report him to HR."

"It will be my pleasure. You guys got any outstanding paperwork you need help getting done? I promised the captain I would do light duty for the first week or so. It was the only way he was going to let me come back." Out of the corner of his eye, Dave caught movement and turned towards it, only to shake his head when he saw who it was. "Yes, Holden?"

Detective Holden looked Dave up and down in nothing short of contempt. "You look none the worse for wear, Andrews. You get daddy to pay your hospital bills?"

"Used my insurance, same way you would have." Dave reached over and pressed the button to turn on his computer. He didn't want to get into anything with Holden, or anyone, right now. When it came time to enter his username and password, he realized Holden was still there. He also noticed Jim and Mark were eyeing Holden in deep suspicion. He glanced heavenwards, as if praying for patience. "Is there anything in particular you want, Holden?"

"Not any of your money, if that's what you're hinting at."

"That's good because you wouldn't have gotten any of it anyway." Dave refused to let himself be drawn into Holden's sorry little mind game. "Jim, Mark, I meant it about doing any of your backed up paperwork. Just let me clear my emails and internal messages and I'll be glad to do whatever you need me to do."

"I was talking to you," Holden interrupted.

"Actually, you were annoying me," Dave countered. "Get gone, I have work to do and I'm sure you do too."

"Is that work going to include how you're going to keep your partner from being put behind bars for the rest of his life?"

There was a long moment of silence. Jim and Mark each stole a look at Dave and saw a glint appear in the deep blue of his eyes. They knew him well enough to know it spelled a warning. "That is a work in progress, Holden," Dave finally said in something that resembled a calm tone. "Everyone in the department is doing what they can to help him. Everyone, that is, except you, from what I've heard."

"I'm all for helping Cameron, I just haven't had the time. I'm working on what I can do to clear up the mess you caused for him."

Genuine curiosity caused Dave to lift his gaze from his computer and look towards Holden for an explanation. "Mess? What mess?"

Jim and Mark knew this conversation was heading south fast and they came to stand on either side of Dave's desk. The atmosphere was thick and they could tell Dave's infamous temper was starting to simmer.

"As Detective Andrews said, Holden," Jim said, "Get lost."

Dave emitted a chuckle. "Oh no, Jim, wait a minute, let Holden explain himself. I have no clue what mess he's talking about, a mess, apparently, I have created so please, give him a chance to explain himself." Dave pushed himself backwards against his chair and laid his clasped hands on his stomach. "Okay, Holden, you've got the floor. Start talking."

Holden looked nervously from Jim to Mark and then to Dave. He had never liked Dave and the news about his fortune had only solidified his dislike. "I, well, it's like this... You sold your own partner up the river."

Dave knew instantly what Holden was referring to but he kept his expression blank and waited expectantly for Holden to continue. When Holden seemed reticent, he placed an encouraging smile on his face. "I did? And you think you can clear it up for me?"

Holden nodded. "No, but I'm going to at least try. Everybody has been so busy trying to clear Cameron's name, no one has actually sat down to consider why you went to the motel the day before and warned his father to stay away. How do we know you didn't go back after Cameron had been and did what you threatened to do?"

"Because I was at the hospital with Krista and Cathy at

the time of his father's murder. Check the records, moron."

"Oh, I have. And I'll continue to check them until I find a discrepancy. I'd rather see the real murderer get thrown behind bars than an innocent man."

"At least that's something we can agree on," Dave said smoothly. "But for the record, you're wasting your time barking up this particular tree. My alibi is squeaky clean and I wouldn't have gone back to finish a job if it was going to end up in murder. I uphold the law, I don't break it, that's my job. Now, if you'll excuse me..." He reached over to his desk phone. "Er, either of you guys know the extension for HR off the top of your head? I need to report Detective Holden and want to make sure I get the right person to talk to."

"You're bluffing," Holden said.

"I'm really not." Dave knew the number perfectly well but he wanted Holden to be aware of what he intended to do. "Any rookie cop would know it wasn't my intention to go to the motel to do anything other than warn Paul's father off. If I'd known what was going to happen the very next day, going to the motel would have been the very last thing on my mind. I don't have to explain this, or anything, to the likes of you, so if you back off now Holden, I won't call HR to report you. It's up to you."

"I'd take the offer," Mark said smugly. "Your idea of Dave selling Paul down the river is ludicrous but if you want to save face, you'll leave and go about your work like a good little cop. Otherwise, Dave will be calling Human Resources. I know he's a man of his word."

Holden took them all in with a sweeping glare of hatred. Knowing he was outnumbered, he turned to walk away but noticed Paul, Cathy and Krista standing in the doorway. He had no idea how long they had been there but judging by the look on their faces, he reckoned long enough to hear what he'd accused Dave of. "Sooner I get transferred out of this shit hole, the happier I'll be," he said.

"No happier than we will be," Krista interjected icily.

She stepped back to let Holden by and as soon as he disappeared down the corridor, she turned to Dave. "You do know that he's the only one out of the whole department who feels like this, right?"

Paul came into the office and sat down heavily at his desk. He hadn't missed much time out of the precinct since his return from New York several weeks ago and, although he'd picked up on Holden's hatred toward Dave a while ago, he had hoped Holden had changed his outlook by now. He hated the fact that Dave was being accused of something he hadn't done, and the irony of the situation wasn't lost on him. But it wasn't fair on Dave, who had done nothing but try and help.

Paul watched Dave return his attention to his computer and knew Dave was already over the episode with Holden. Aside from that, he thought Dave looked reasonably well. His face no longer bore even a hint of the pain he'd been in for weeks and he seemed to be moving around freely. Paul was pleased his friend felt good enough to return to work and knew it had been a good idea for him to do light duties until he was ready for anything more physical.

Cathy smiled at her husband as he glanced toward her over the top of his monitor. "Glad to see you back, my love," she said. "One of our aircraft was missing for too long. But please, don't - "

" – overdo it," he interrupted and grinned over at Paul. "That's ten bucks you owe me, I told you she wouldn't last two minutes without feeling the need to comment on my well-being."

Paul shot Cathy a pretend filthy look as he dug in his back pocket for his wallet. "Thanks, little dude, you just cost me ten bucks. I gave you five whole minutes."

Cathy chuckled and Krista joined in, and the tension created by Holden lifted.

As they settled in to their work, across town, in the district attorney's office, Nikoli Ardolino sat back in his leather chair and tried not to show his impatience with the young woman sitting in front of him. He knew her history of living with an abusive husband and didn't want to scare her off.

Gabriella Rossini eyed him meekly. "I'm sorry, Mr Ardolino, I keep forgetting what it is you want me to say."

"Just the truth, Ms Rossini. You want to put a murderer behind bars, don't you?"

"I do, but I didn't actually *see* Detective Cameron kill his father. I just *heard* the fight."

Ardolino inwardly groaned. The last thing he wanted was for the jury to be left with one single element of doubt. "It's okay, we've got time, we can go over this again. And again." *Until we get this right, you stupid bitch.* "Now, take it from when you heard the first hint of a physical fight..."

And as he listened to the only eye witness he had butcher what he had so carefully written out for her, he knew he had his work cut out for him. He had no doubt he could coach her to say the right words. He had worked too hard for her to throw this case just because of her incompetency. All he had to do was be patient. And when he couldn't be patient, he would force himself to show Gabriella he could be understanding. He would also show her he could be trusted to be on her side, that not all men were violent wife beaters.

He knew she had been conditioned to believe what men told her, that if she screwed up, she would suffer the consequences. He had to get her to trust that he wasn't going to hurt her. That she wouldn't suffer if she didn't deliver in the way he wanted her to.

But by God, she just wasn't getting it. He couldn't simplify his instructions any further. Assuming it was nerves on her part, he would count to ten each time she got it wrong, and go over it with her again. And again.

Detective Paul Cameron was going to prison. There was no way he was going to let Cameron walk away a free man. Not with a murder charge. And when he heard the "Guilty" verdict he, Nikoli Ardolino, was going to get the acclaim he deserved for making it happen. And the satisfaction of knowing one of

his nemeses was going to jail for the rest of his miserable life.
THE END

# ACKNOWLEDGEMENT

As always, a huge thank you to my editor, Daniel Diehl. I take on board everything you teach me and I know my stories would not be anywhere near as accurate, or believable, without your input.

To my sister, Shirley. Just because.

To Ernest Stone, Massachusetts Attorney for Criminal Law, without whose input and guidance I would not have been able to write this story, or it's sequel. You taught me a lot and I appreciate the time (and patience) you took to ensure I had the facts right.

To my friends, Stacey, Emma F, Valerie, Mandy, Bernie, Sarah, Ann H, Elissa, Paula, for your continued support. A special thanks to Diane L for the reviews and input – more appreciated than I could ever tell you.

To Stephen and Lucy. So glad you like my stories! Thank you for the glowing reviews, they mean the world to me. Hope I have not disappointed with this one. Love you both.

To fellow authors, Amanda Sheridan and Jacqui Jay Grafton, thank you for your support!

Last, but never least, my wonderful husband, Mark. You never cease to amaze me with your ideas and your dedication to promote my books. Your ability to provide a book cover with just a hint of a storyline to go on is nothing short of miraculous. Your tireless work and constant support are something I can never repay. I know I have said it before but I couldn't do this without you. I would not want to. Thank you, always.

# ABOUT THE AUTHOR

## Carol Kravetz

I was born and raised in Northern Ireland, near Belfast. I emigrated to Canada in my mid 20's and while there, started writing. My daytime job was a medical secretary to various health care professionals, but my  spare time was dedicated to my writing. I lived in Canada for 12 years and during that time had almost completed a series of 7 novels. After living at home for a year, I moved to the United States and continued my career as a medical secretary. My writing was shelved for just a little bit while during my time in the States, but since returning to Northern Ireland upon my husband's retirement 9 years ago, I have been able to resume my writing. I currently live in Newtownards and work fulltime within the Education Authority and dedicate as much time as possible to my family and my writing.

# BATHVILLE BOOKS SERIES

Detectives Dave and Paul work in the fictitious Bathville, Massachusetts Police Department. They are joined by Cathy and Krista who arrive in the States from Northern Ireland. This series follows their adventures, deep friendships, and romance as they deal with the challenges they encounter.

## Murder Is Just The Beginning

Dave and Paul work in the 7th precinct of the Bathville, Massachusetts Police Department. Cathy and Krista arrive in the States from Northern Ireland as a part of a special police program. This book lays the foundations for the detectives' working relations as well as allowing for strong romance and deep friendships to blossom and grow.

## The Revenge

Six months after solving their first case together, a former arrest in Detective Paul Cameron's previous police life in Brooklyn, NY has, after 5 years, caught up to him. The ex-con has plotted his revenge against Paul and his loved ones.

## The Consequences

A serial killer is still on the loose after 4 policemowen from several precincts all over Massachusetts have been brutally murdered. There are no obvious connections between the victims, other than their chosen profession, and never any clues at the crime scene to follow.

## The Obsession

Krista discovers she has a secret admirer at the preceinct. Once he realises she has learned of his identity, he does everything in his power to take her away from Paul

## The Return

A chance to return to their home country to work on a top-security case is a chance Cathy and Krista can't pass up. But shortly after arriving in Northern Ireland, they are thrown back into the seedier side of the country's long, tumultuous history. The PSNI police officers are being murdered simply because of their religion, by a paramilitary organization. It is the leaders the detectives must find and put an end to their reign of terror.

## The Injustice

A Domestic Violence case stirs up memories. A string of bad luck foretells that worse is yet to come. An untimely, unwanted visit from a person Paul Cameron detests and wishes was dead. What else could possibly go wrong? Paul's easy going life is shattered when a face from his past shows up and changes his world forever.

# AUTHOR'S NOTE

Thank you for buying and taking the time to read my book. I hope you enjoyed reading it as much as I enjoyed writing it. If you love my characters and the storylines, please take a moment and write a review. Reviews are very important to authors as they show the world whether a book is worth reading or not. It only takes a few minutes. Your time is greatly appreciated, and your feedback is invaluable.

Please feel free to visit and follow me on:

https://belfastlady.wixsite.com/mysite
or
https://bathville-books.com
or
https://www.facebook.com/BathvilleBooks

Printed in Great Britain
by Amazon

64324443R00235